Dead on the Dock

A Shagball and Tangles Adventure

A. C. Brooks

This book is a work of fiction. If you think its not, you're wrong. Any person, place, or thing that bears any resemblance to someone you know, or somewhere you've been, or some thing you've seen or done, is purely coincidental. That's right; it's just a big, fat, coincidence.

So quit reading this and start reading the book. You'll laugh, you'll cry (possibly, if you're a girl), and if you like it enough, you'll buy my next book, which is tentatively titled; *It's no Coincidence.*

ISBN: 1466387955
ISBN 13: 9781466387959
Library of Congress Control Number: 2011918002
CreateSpace, North Charleston, SC

Acknowledgements

First and foremost I would like to thank my wife Penny for her support, guidance, and help with "brainstorming" ideas for storylines. I have found that using only one brain produces mere passing showers and nothing less than a flat-out gully washer is acceptable. Hopefully, *Dead on the Dock*, will leave you soaked from head to toe.

I would also like to thank my family and friends for their help in promoting my work and giving me ideas on ways to reach my target audience through the use of different social media platforms.

Last but by no means least, I would like to thank Kristine Sullivan at The Old Key Lime House, along with owner Wayne Cordero, for promoting my first novel; *Foul Hooked.* Without the help of book-signings and sales generated through the OKLH gift shop, you probably wouldn't be reading this.

Prologue

My name is Kit Jansen, also known as Shagball. A few months ago I was about to have my show, *Fishing on the Edge with Shagball*, canceled, due to nonperformance. Namely, I couldn't catch a fish. My producer gave me an ultimatum that if we didn't catch something on our next trip, he was pulling the plug. As luck would have it, I managed to foul-hook a vertically challenged Elvis impersonator who jumped off a cruise ship in a fit of drunken despair.

Turns out he grew up on a shrimp boat in Biloxi and he was a freakishly gifted mate. His name was Langostino Dupree, but after my producer was dumbstruck witnessing him untangle an incredible cluster of fishing line in record time, he dubbed him Tangles and the name stuck. When questioned about his stature (or lack thereof), he said he was neither a midget, nor a dwarf, nor the hybrid "dwidget," that I suspected might explain his perfect proportions. A childhood surgery resulted in most of his pituitary gland being removed and he hadn't grown an inch since. At thirty-five years old, he was a little over four feet tall and about a hundred and twenty-five pounds. He was also hell on wheels.

In another strange twist, it turned out his mother used to date Rudy, a confirmed bachelor and longtime bartender at The Old Key Lime House; a local waterfront restaurant and bar in my hometown of Lantana, Florida. Circumstances led me to believe he might be the true father of Tangles, but solid proof had yet to be established.

Soon thereafter, my new friend Tangles saved me and my buddy Hambone from certain death at the hands of a hired killer. The end result was one sinking boat, two dead mobsters, and three freaked-out guys wondering what the hell we got into.

What started out as a slightly nefarious plan to help an old lady and her niece from having to sell their marina, turned into something much more. It appeared it wasn't just the neighboring restaurant owner who coveted the marina property, but the Mob too. Why? *Good question.* What *wasn't* in question was the mobsters we killed in self-defense, not to mention the boat, were going to be missed by somebody, and *that* somebody I was *very* worried about.

Chapter 1

Crunch! The bow of the forty-six-foot Grand Banks hit the piling a *little* harder than the captain intended. He let out a mumbled curse and nudged the glistening trawler up to the fuel dock at the Water's Edge Marina in Boynton Beach. His lone passenger heard him mutter another Italian expletive under his breath before barking out orders in broken English.

"Grabba-da-line, grabba-da-line!"

He grabbed the closest rope on the deck, but the captain started yelling at him again.

"Noa, noa! Notta dat one…*dat* one!" He cried, pointing to another rope in the opposite corner of the cockpit, closest to the dock. "Throwa-da-line, tooa-da-man, onna-da-dock! How many time I tell you? "

After spending nearly three weeks with the insufferable captain on the trip down from Jersey City, Carlos, aka "The Colombian," had had enough. Luckily for the captain though, Carlos was so happy to be at their final destination that he decided not to kill him right then and there. That would have to wait for another day. Giving the captain a little taste of his own medicine, though, was the least he could do. So he started doing what came naturally, he began mocking him as he tossed the line to the guy who came walking down the dock.

"Howwa many times? Howwa many times you gotta-tella-mea? As many times as I fuckin' want. I told you before, you little stuffed sausage, boats ain't my thing. You see me wearing a red long-sleeve shirt and a floppy white hat? No. *Why?* Because my name ain't Gilligan, this ain't the SS *Minnow*, and as of now, you're the skipper no more. Comprendo? This is the end of the line, Giuseppe. Your services are no longer required. So why don't you hop the next flight to Newark before I turn your face into a pile of rigatoni."

"Whatsa matta you? Whatta youa talkin' about? Whatsa Gilligan?"

Before Carlos could respond, the guy on the dock finished tying up the boat, and interrupted.

"You guys fueling up?"

Carlos looked up at him, thankful to be able to speak to someone who knew English.

"No, we should be good, we just fueled up a couple hours ago. Is this where we check in though? We got a reservation for a boat slip here."

Robo (the dockmaster), was looking at the stern and the letters *JC* emblazoned across it. Suddenly it clicked and he did a double take, looking from the guy who tossed him the line, back toward the stern.

"Oh yeah, now I remember. I was expecting you last week, but didn't hear anything. I thought you might be a no-show. You don't sound the same as you did on the phone."

Carlos chuckled. "I don't look the same either."

"What?"

"It wasn't me who made the reservation, it was the owner. We just brought the boat down for him."

"Oh, OK. Well, I'm Robo, the dockmaster, and I got you staying over in slip number seventeen, in between the Luhrs and the Viking." Then he pointed to the north canal.

"Robo, huh? Like the cop?"

"Yeah, I get that a lot."

"Name's Carlos, and like I was telling Captain Eggplant here, boats ain't my specialty, so exactly which slip is it?"

"No problem, it's easy; sixth one down on this side of the canal, the dock number's on the seawall. Like I told the gentleman who made the reservation, he's lucky. We're normally full, but we had a boat leave unexpectedly."

"Yeah, that's what he said...*very* unexpectedly."

Before Robo could respond, the captain came storming out of the cabin carrying a suitcase and a bottle of limoncino.

"You showa no respect for the cap-e-tan! Three-a-week on a da water, and you still can no a worka-da lines! No respecta!" The captain brushed by Carlos, stepped up on the gunnel, and threw his suitcase on the dock.

"Cool your donkeys, Geppeto. You're going nowhere before you dock us in the slip."

Ignoring him, the elderly captain leapt up to the dock with surprising agility, and turned back to face Carlos.

"I tella you before. You no showa respect, I no drive a da boat." Then he mumbled another indistinguishable expletive that sounded something like, "Too-fun-goo," and walked away.

Carlos was debating whether to chase after him, when a fishing boat came idling up to the dock behind the *JC.* The guy driving pointed at the fuel pump, and Robo spoke up.

"Looks like we got someone who needs gas, you're gonna have to move the boat."

"You serious? I've never driven one of these things in my life. How 'bout if you dock it for me? I'll make it worth your while."

Robo lived for tips, and was thinking of finding someone to cover for him, when another boat came looking for fuel too. *Shit.*

"I can't do it right now, let me think, maybe we can—"

"I can do it."

Robo and Carlos both turned to see one of the local dock rats, Skeeter, approach from the side of the ship's store.

"I worked on a Grand Banks last winter for two months and did a little driving when the captain needed a break. I can do it, no problem."

Carlos didn't notice Robo giving Skeeter the stink-eye, and waved him aboard.

"OK, kid, you're hired." He pointed to the north canal. "Take us over to number seventeen."

Skeeter stepped aboard, grinning at Robo.

"You got it, Chief."

Robo was none too pleased about getting beaten out of a nice tip, but managed to hide it.

"After you get situated, come on over to the ship's store and I'll give you your paperwork. If you have any questions, feel free to stop by. We're open from seven to five, seven days a week, except for when we're not. How long are you staying again?"

"Good question..." The dark-skinned stranger pondered it as he slowly gazed around the marina, thinking of the nice payday that lay in store. Finally he nodded to himself, and flashed a toothy smile.

"As long as it takes, my friend, as long as it takes."

Chapter 2

Sometimes, when the other shoe *doesn't* drop, it's because the foot in said shoe is so high that it takes a longtime to drop, and when it finally *does* drop, it drops right on your fucking head and knocks the living shit out of you. That's what I was worried about. All was quiet on the western front...too quiet.

A full month had gone by and nobody showed up at the marina asking questions about the missing boat named *The Job*, and its murderous occupants. The Boynton Beach police did a perfunctory investigation into Ratdog's disappearance after his roommate, Skeeter, reported him missing, but nothing came of it. Skeeter insisted to the cops (and everyone else), that Ratdog wouldn't just leave without telling him, but the cops knew that's *exactly* what dock rats are prone to do. Since everyone knew Ratdog was working for the guys on *The Job*, it was logical to assume he left with them. Due to the fact that nobody reported *The Job*, or those on board missing, the case was all but closed. Closed for the cops that is, but certainly not for the boat's owner and whoever the guys that we killed worked for, which was likely one and the same.

That wasn't all I had on my plate either. My new girlfriend, Holly, was a wreck. We had just buried her aunt Millie, the one who owned the C-Love Marina, the property that people were willing to kill over. Millie was like a mother to Holly, having raised her after her parents' untimely deaths when she was just fifteen. Naturally, she was taking it hard. Of course, a lot of people were grieving, me included. Millie was beloved by nearly everyone in the community, but especially the slip holders in the marina.

As we were leaving the cemetery, Millie's attorney, Bob Boone, pulled me aside, and said that Tangles and I should attend the reading of the will, along with Holly, her stepsister Sarah, and a few of Millie's long-time employees.

So that's where I was headed, with Holly on one side and my new sidekick and fishing show mate, Tangles, on the other. As we entered the attorney's office, I couldn't stop wondering when the other shoe was gonna drop and whether it was gonna splatter us on the sidewalk when it did.

Chapter 3

Robo watched Skeeter steer the Grand Banks down the north canal as he handed the fuel hose to his next customer. The new slip holder had said a couple of strange things that him scratching his head. When he told the guy that he was lucky to get the slip because someone left unexpectedly, the guy said, "Yeah, *very* unexpectedly." *What the hell did he mean by that?* Did the new guy on the *JC* know the creepy guys who left without notice on *The Job*? And what was that, "staying as long as it takes" crap, all about? As long as *what* takes?

Robo had been around the block enough times to know when trouble was coming his way, and he just got a big whiff of it. There was something odd about the new guy that he couldn't quite put his finger on. He was dark skinned and in good shape for a middle-aged guy, probably forty-five to fifty years old. He also had a disarming smile that showed off his gleaming white teeth beneath his Frito Bandito mustache. When he spoke though, he spoke with a slight New York accent, and not with a Latino, or some other foreign accent, like you would expect. Maybe that was it; maybe it was just another case of judging the old book by its cover. Maybe that's what had him suspicious. *Who could blame him?* There had been some strange things happening on the docks the last couple months, and too many coincidences equaled funny business in Robo's book. He took his job as dockmaster seriously and vowed to keep a close eye on the new guy, Carlos, Crest smile or not.

***

As Skeeter eased the boat into the slip, it was not lost on him it was the same slip the previous boat (*The Job*), had unexpectedly departed from. It also happened at the same time his roommate, Ratdog, went missing. He confirmed to the cops that Ratdog was paid generously by the guy named Gino (who captained *The Job*), but insisted Ratdog wouldn't leave without mentioning it. It occurred to him that maybe Ratdog *had* left with Gino, but perhaps not willingly. There was definitely something shady going on, just like he overheard Robo mention on the dock.

Now this foreign-looking guy, Carlos, shows up, a guy who's never run a boat in his life, and he says a couple things that make it seem like he might know something. *Coincidental?* Not likely. He spent a lot of time thinking about all the scenarios that might have befallen his roommate and none of them had a happy ending. One way or another, he was determined to find out what really happened to his missing pal. He didn't want to go missing himself, though, so he decided to play things close to the vest.

"Hey kid, what did you say your name was?" asked Carlos.

"I didn't."

"So what is it, a state secret or something?"

"Not hardly, everybody calls me Skeeter." Skeeter slipped past him and began tying off the dock lines.

"Skeeter, huh? Well, that was a pretty good job the way you backed us in just now. In fact, I think you could run circles around that Milanese munchkin who brought us down here. You feel like making a little do-re-me?"

"I think I *already* made some."

"Hah! Good point. You wanna make some more?"

"As long as it doesn't make me sweat too much, I'm game."

"Nah, nothing too strenuous, mostly just some information is all. When the owner comes down, though, he might need somebody to take him out for a spin. Think you can handle that?"

"Sure, but I'm not a licensed captain."

"So what does it matter?"

"If the owner doesn't mind, neither do I."

"Good, good."

"So what kind of information are you talking about?"

"The kind that goes from your lips, to my ear, and nowhere else. The owner, he don't like guys who talk too much, and he—"

Skeeter finished tying off the last dock line with his back to Carlos, and being the smartass that he was, interrupted him.

"Didn't stop him from sending *you* down, though."

Before Skeeter could turn around, he felt a large hand squeezing his neck in some sort of Vulcan nerve pinch. It took his breath away and his legs started to go all wobbly as Carlos whispered menacingly in his ear. "Like I was saying, he don't like guys who talk too much, and he don't like wise-asses… neither do I."

He began slowly releasing his grip while twisting him around so the frightened dock rat faced him. "I'm gonna write this off to us not being fully acquainted, but now that we're getting to know each other, it's all good…right?"

He released his grip and Skeeter immediately began massaging his neck while trying to stop his legs from shaking. Gone was the easy smile as he looked up into Carlos's face. In fact, it hardly looked like the same face at all. His lips were drawn back a little, and his white teeth looked sharp and threatening, like a wolf's.

"I said *right?*"

"Sh-sure...it's uh, it's all good."

Like flipping a switch, the pleasant smile was back on Carlos's face as he reached into his pocket and pulled out a wad of bills.

"Excellent, so here's a little something I'm gonna call a retainer." He peeled off five hundred-dollar bills, and stuffed them into Skeeter's shirt pocket as he continued. "You help me find out what I need to know, and I'll stuff you full of so many bills you can change your name to Benjamin, Benjamin…ummm… Benjamin…*Grant?*"

He was looking at Skeeter for some kind of confirmation, but no way was the frightened dock rat going to correct him. He pulled the wad of bills back out of his pocket and looked closely at the face of one of the hundreds.

"Franklin! That's it. You can change your name to Benjamin Franklin, you'll be so flush. Go figure, you fly a kite and you end up on the hundred. But you lead a revolution, become first president of the US of A, and they put you on the measly one-dollar bill. *Why?* 'Cause you chopped down a fuckin' *cherry tree?* Doesn't seem right, does it?"

Skeeter's fear started to give way to disbelief. *The guy just stuffed five hundred bucks in my pocket! Holy shit!* So what if the guy scared him a little, he was gonna ride him all the way to the bank.

"I uh, never looked at it that way, but uh, yeah, yeah that's not right at all. Washington shoulda got the twenty just for having to wear one of those goofy white wigs, but all he got was a bunch of high schools named after him."

Carlos slapped him on the back as he laughed in earnest.

"That's funny, kid, that was good, real good. I think I'm gonna like you. I think maybe we can help each other out, my friend."

"Me too, so what is it you need to know?"

The Colombian glanced around at the neighboring boats.

"Let's step inside."

Skeeter followed him in and was motioned to sit on the fine leather couch in the nicely appointed salon. The Colombian sat opposite in a club chair, and leaned forward before speaking.

"What I need to know is where did the last boat that stayed in this slip go, and where are the guys that were on it? I'm sure you know which one I'm talking about; it was called *The Job.*"

Skeeter briefly thought about his plan to keep things close to the vest and immediately discarded it.

First and foremost he had dock rat DNA in his blood. He was trying to find out what happened anyway, and now he had a chance to get paid handsomely if he did.

"Yeah, I know the boat, in fact, I'm trying to figure out what happened myself. My roommate, Ratdog, disappeared the same time the boat did."

This was new information to Carlos, and he took a moment to digest it. He had been told that Gino had a local guy on the payroll, but he didn't know his name. Maybe now he did.

"What makes you think your roommate going AWOL had anything to do with the boat?"

"'Cause he was working for one of the guys on it, the guy named Gino."

"OK, OK that could be helpful." *Probably not though.* His employer told him about getting a call from Gino saying he was fourteen miles offshore and that he had "solved the problem." He said Gino made it sound like the work was done and he was just "tidying a few things up." Obviously, he had spoken a bit prematurely, because neither Gino, nor Marco, nor Ratdog, nor the boat, had been seen since. It stood to reason that if Skeeter's roommate was working for Gino, he was probably on board that night too. He thought about it a moment more, debating whether to tell the skinny dock rat what he knew. He didn't like having to play his cards so early, but he needed someone on the dock who could get information without attracting too much attention.

"You know about those diesel tanks that got found just before the marina was supposed to be sold?"

"Hell yeah, it's been a big pain in the ass for everyone, what with the cleanup going on and all."

"Well, I need you to keep your ears peeled on the dock for information about who might have dug them up."

"What? Nobody dug up those tanks, it was some kind of sinkhole. We had a bunch of rain and it just opened up."

"Yeah, that's what everybody thinks, but I know better. They were dug up by some slip holders in order to stop the sale of the marina. We find out who those guys were and we find out what happened to the missing boat and whoever was on it."

"How the hell do you know this?"

"I'm asking the questions here, my friend, don't forget it."

"Sure, OK, but if you know the tanks were dug up, and it has to do with a boatload of missing people, why don't you just go to the police?"

"'Cause this ain't a police matter, and it's gonna stay that way."

He didn't like how the kid was so quick to cry "police," and decided to make sure he *really* understood what the stakes were.

"Lean forward, kid."

"What?"

"You heard me, lean forward and look in my eyes."

Skeeter hesitated for a moment, wondering what the hell he was doing, then leaned forward and looked into his eyes. Carlos smiled at him, looked down, rubbed his eyes, and then slowly leveled his gaze at Skeeter. The smile was gone, and he was again looking at the drawn back lips and sharp teeth that spooked him a few minutes earlier. But the eyes, *Holy Lord in heaven, the eyes*, began morphing from light gray to jet black. The color started changing above the pupil, and then slowly worked its way down, like someone drawing a blind. In less than fifteen seconds he was looking into the blackest eyes he had ever seen. He had seen his fair share of sharks up close, but *these eyes* made a shark's eye's look like Homer Simpson's. He felt short of breath and gasped, thinking he might shit his pants. Carlos could practically taste the fear oozing out of Skeeter's pores, and licked his lips.

"Now listen up. If one word of what I just told you leaves this boat, I will do things to you that will make you wish your mother had never been born. In fact, I may make your mother wish *you* had never been born too. Got it?"

Skeeter was so petrified he could only manage to nod.

"That's good, that's real good."

Carlos was worried he might give the kid a heart attack if he kept up the black-eye trick any longer, and looked down at the floor again. After blinking a couple of times, his eyes slowly returned to their normal color. Then he looked up, sporting his famous smile, and helped the poor kid to his feet. "Don't sweat it, kid, you got nothing to worry about if you do what I say. You help me find out who dug up those tanks and keep your mouth shut, you're gonna make a lot of money. Now get moving and make it happen."

Chapter 4

As we took a seat at the large conference table for the reading of the will, I glanced around, noting the others in attendance. There was the captain of the *C-Love* (Bart), his girlfriend, Regina (who worked in the marina office), Millie's longtime accountant (Barb), Holly's stepsister (Sarah), and some skeevy-looking guy I didn't know, sitting next to her. Along with Holly, Tangles, and me, that was it. There was a little small talk going on while we waited for Millie's attorney, Bob Boone. Everybody was checking each other out, particularly the guy sitting next to Sarah. After a few slightly uncomfortable minutes, Bob Boone entered the room with a "good morning," and began doing a head count. When he got to the guy sitting next to Sarah, he pointed at him.

"Ah, excuse me, but who are *you*?"

Grease boy smiled, flashing his meth teeth.

"Name's Ricky, but everybody calls me Rick-E."

"That's nice, Rick-E, but I'm going to have to ask you to leave-e. This is a will reading, and if your name's not on this document I'm holding in my hand, which it isn't, you shouldn't be here."

"It's OK," piped in Sarah, "he's with me."

The lawyer looked at her, undeterred.

"I'm sorry, Sarah, but this isn't the place to bring a friend, or boyfriend, or whatev—"

"He's my fiancé, and I want him here with me. That's OK, isn't it?"

Before he could reply, Holly beat him to it.

"Your *fiancé*? Since when?"

"Since, oh, I don't know, about a week, week and a half ago. It was *sooo* sweet, Rick-E got down on one—"

"Oh my God…you're *serious*?" Holly looked at the lawyer and then me, but I just shrugged. Rick-E saw an opening and jumped back in the conversation.

"You bet she's serious, go ahead, show 'em the ring, babe."

Sarah drew her hand up from her lap and flashed a gaudy looking diamond ring surrounded by colored stones. There was no doubt in my mind it was either stolen, fake, or both. Holly put her hand to her forehead and closed her eyes as the lawyer interjected.

"Well, in that case, unless anybody objects, why don't we get down to the reading of the will. Does anybody have any questions before we proceed?" Nobody said anything except Holly, who was now shaking her head a little.

"No, please, I-I'd like to get this over with."

Bob Boone sat at the head of the conference table with a bunch of papers stacked before him, and began.

"Agreed, OK then, let's get to it. In case any of you are wondering why you're here, Milfred updated the will shortly before her death." He glanced at me and Tangles, then recited some legalese, confirming Milfred was of sound mind and body when the will was updated. Then he held up the signing page to show it was notarized and witnessed, and looked around the table.

"I'm going to start with Milfred's charitable donation, then friends and longtime employees, and then family."

He cleared his throat and began reading Millie's words.

"To the American Cancer Society I leave one hundred thousand dollars. Everybody should know by now that I died from skin cancer. Please, please do not underestimate the importance of wearing a good sunscreen. It may save your life one day, and trust me, it's not a pleasant way to go."

Everybody nodded in agreement.

"To my new friend Tangles; I have always been a sucker for the underdog, and that title certainly befits you. How such a big heart ended up in such a little body is a mystery to me. What isn't a mystery, is you bringing a smile to my face and helping me and Holly out in our time of need. I do hereby leave you twenty-five thousand dollars. I hope it helps you get back on your feet. I expect big things out of you, little man, God bless."

Tangles' mouth started to move, but no words came out. He looked at Holly with tears in his eyes, and she just smiled.

"To my friend and faithful employee of over fifteen years, Regina, I do hereby leave the sum of seventy-five thousand dollars."

Regina's mouth dropped open and she put her hand to her heart as her eyes began welling up.

"To Bart, a good friend, great captain, and loyal employee for nearly twenty years, I hereby leave the sum of one hundred thousand dollars."

Bart had his arm around his longtime girlfriend Regina, and let out a "Holy cow," under his breath.

"To my accountant of over thirty years, Barb, I can't begin to fathom how much money you saved me, but I *can* show my eternal appreciation. I hereby leave you the sum of one hundred and fifty thousand dollars."

Barb gasped and gripped the arms of her chair as if she were on a Disney ride.

"To my good friend and confidant, Kit; you are one of the few real estate brokers whose worth their salt, as far as I'm concerned. You helped me out with the slip leases at the marina for years, but never asked for a dime. Your advice has always been rock solid, and that was never more apparent than with issues at the marina that you recently helped me and Holly through. If I ever had a son, I wish it would have been you. Although, technically, that would be a little incestuous, with you dating Holly and all, so I'm glad you're not. You two make a fine couple and I hope you make it work. I do hereby leave you the sum of one hundred and fifty thousand dollars."

I couldn't believe it; I never inherited anything from one of my *own* relatives except for an occasional surly disposition and unquenchable thirst. I was completely floored, and looked at Holly, who was still blushing from the incestuous dating comment. She managed a smile and squeezed my arm as I began choking up.

"To my stepniece Sarah; I tried for years to get you involved in the family business at the marina, but you preferred to work for that low-life Slade at Three Jacks instead. If I hadn't made a promise to your mother to look after you, I wouldn't leave you anything but a swift kick in the rear. Fortunately for you, though, I keep my word. Therefore, I am leaving you one million dollars."

Sarah let out a "wooo" and she high-fived Ricky, who looked directly across the table at me and smirked, mouthing the word "yes" in the process. Their demeanor, however, suddenly took a turn south, as the lawyer finished reading Millie's words.

"Knowing that you would likely blow the money if you got your hands on it all at once, I have set it up as an annuity. It will be paid out in monthly installments of twenty-five hundred dollars, beginning on your thirtieth birthday."

Sarah said, "Huh? But I'm, but I'm only…twenty-five."

Ricky stood up, all pissed off.

"*Thirty?* When she's *thirty?* What kinda crap *is this?*"

The attorney smiled to himself before admonishing the sleazeball in front of him.

"It's the kind that sticks in your craw, the way Millie wanted, but it's not yours anyway, Ricky, it's Sarah's, so sit down and keep quiet while I finish reading the will."

"This is bullshit…and it's Rick-E, like I told you before."

"Sorry, guess I forgot-e…now sit down."

Tangles nudged me in the side and we both chuckled as Ricky sat down and sneered at us. I was really starting to like the attorney, which was a rarity. Bob Boone looked back down at his paperwork and continued.

"Finally, to my dear niece Holly, the daughter I never had; you are smart, beautiful, loving, and independent. You put your life on hold to take care of me these last several months, which I know was difficult for you. Per my wishes, you have agreed to give up a successful career in order to run the marina that has been my lifeblood for so many years. Holly, you know I love you with all my heart, and I am so proud of you for the woman you have become."

There wasn't a dry eye in the room except for Sarah and Ricky. Holly leaned on my shoulder and sobbed while I comforted her. Bob Boone had to clear his throat again, before continuing.

"Therefore, I leave you the *C-Love*, the C-Love Marina, my house on Sabal Island, all of my personal effects and property, and the remainder of my estate."

Ricky said, "Shit."

Sarah said, "The remainder of her estate? What's that?"

"Everything that's left."

I was liking the attorney more and more.

"Like what?"

"That would be the rest of her cash, her stock portfolio, and the gold."

This time Ricky chimed in with Sarah, and in unison, they said,

"Gold?"

Bob Boone looked at Holly, who was sitting up now.

"Holly, it's up to you, if you like, I can ask everybody to leave while we go over the amounts."

She looked at me for guidance, and I whispered, "How much more can there be?"

She whispered back, "Heck if I know." Then she looked at the attorney and spoke in her normal voice.

"Bob, did Millie leave any specific instructions as to this part? Did she *suggest* it be done in private?"

"No, it's up to you."

She thought about it for a moment, and decided if it was something that Millie thought should be done privately, she would have instructed her attorney to do so.

"OK, we don't need to have any secrets here, we're all friends…for the most part." She stole a quick look at Ricky and then said, "Go ahead."

"Very well then, after setting aside the annuity for Sarah, and paying the heirs at this table, as well as the American Cancer Society, you are left with approximately three million dollars in cash, two million in stocks and bonds, and…based on yesterday's closing price, almost five million dollars in gold coins and bullion."

Everybody was stunned. Milfred Lutes was obviously *way richer* than anybody ever guessed. I looked at Tangles and his eyes were bugging out of his head.

Holly said, "Oh-my-God…you're, you're kidding me…right?"

"Not a single troy ounce, your aunt was a very shrewd investor."

Then Sarah stood up and cried, "No! No, it's not fair. How could she *do* this to me? Holly gets *all that?* And what about Kit? He's not even family and he gets *a hundred and fifty thousand dollars?* That should be mine!"

Ricky popped out of his chair too, and pointed at Tangles. "Even the *midget* got twenty-five grand? Are you kidding me?"

In a nanosecond Tangles leapt on top of his chair and pointed back at Ricky, staring him down eye-to-eye.

"Watch your mouth, ass-wipe, or I'll cross this table and kick those meth teeth in faster than Larry King says 'I do!'"

I had a hand on Tangles' leg just in case he tried to make good on his threat, but I had to admit I was thinking, *this could be classic.*

Ricky then swung his pointed finger at the attorney and continued.

"This is total *bullshit!* You rigged this!"

Bob Boone had had enough and raised both his hands in the air.

"Whoa, whoa, whoa…Everybody just *calm down.* Sorry, *Rick-E,* you too, Sarah, the fact of the matter is the will was signed, sealed, and now it's been delivered. I hereby declare the reading over. In accordance with Milfred's wishes, I have prepared cashier's checks for the appropriate parties, and you may pick them up on the way out. Holly, we'll need to set up an appointment to arrange for the transfer of funds, etc…please set a time with my secretary. To the rest of you, I wish you continued good luck, and if you should need any legal services, I'd be glad to help."

Ricky grabbed Sarah's arm and they stormed out of the building as the rest of us picked up our checks. Holly made an appointment the following day to meet with the attorney again, and I noticed her legs go a little wobbly as we walked out into the bright sunlight. I held her left arm and Tangles held her right as we walked across the street to the marina. Halfway across, Holly was the first to speak.

"I-I can't, I just can't believe this. I need a drink."

"Me too," said Tangles.

I couldn't believe it either. I had a check for a hundred and fifty K in my pocket and my girlfriend just inherited crazy big money, not to mention a marina and a house on the water. I guided us to the waterfront bar and restaurant called the Habana Boat. It was on the south side of the C-Love Marina canal where it joins the Intracoastal. Needing a drink might have been the understatement of the millennia, and I voiced my consent.

"Me three."

I had momentarily forgotten about the Jolly Green Giant-sized shoe I was certain was ready to drop, but not for long.

Chapter 5

As soon as the kid named Skeeter left the boat, Carlos pulled out his cell phone. He called Rachelle's, the upscale strip club in West Palm Beach that was owned by his current employer. After punching in a special code, the call was routed through a used car dealer in Macon, and then on to a small delicatessen over a thousand miles away in Jersey City, named The Rye Smile. As the phone was picked up on the other end, he pictured the enormous man who resembled an even fatter and uglier version of the detective Cannon, from the seventies cop show of the same name. Per usual, the man on the other end of the line didn't say a word, instead waiting for the other party to identify themselves first.

Carlos knew the drill and obliged.

"You there, Mr. Nutz?"

Donatello DeNutzio, aka Donny Nutz, head of the Carpoza crime family's east coast region, confirmed in his trademark Grim Reaper voice.

"Yeah, it's me, whatta ya got?"

Carlos had no doubt it was indeed Donny Nutz on the other end of the line. He sounded like he gargled with Drano and spoke through a tracheotomy.

"Just wanted to give you a heads up that we made it to the marina and that I already got a kid working the docks for information."

Donny Nutz thought about it for a moment.

"You sure that's a good idea? My guys that went missing had a kid on the payroll and it's looking like it didn't work out so well for them."

"This kid I hired, his roommate was the one working for them and he went missing at the same time. He was already sniffing around trying to find out what happened, so I just gave him the proper motivation to succeed; greed and fear…especially fear."

"I unnerstand you know a lot about that, that's why I hired you."

"Yeah, I'm sorta like the Einstein of pain, only my theories ain't relative, they're excruciatingly demonstrative."

"Pretty fancy words."

"What can I say, I went to NYU."

"That's nice, but if you really want to impress me, just get me some answers. I wanna know what the fuck happened to my boat and my guys. Somebody's gonna pay, in more ways than one."

"Don't worry, by the time I'm finished I'll have more answers than a *Jeopardy* marathon."

"Good, lemme know as soon as you find out anything…*before* you start carvin' people up, or whatever your sort does nowadays. There's liable to be some substantial…how shall I say this…some substantial *repatriation* involved, and I wanna get paid *before* the heads start rollin'."

"Repatriation, huh? Pretty fancy word." *Technically, the wrong word, but fancy, nonetheless,* he thought.

"Don't sound so surprised, I learned the hard way at DFU, where you don't get second chances."

"DFU?"

"Yeah, *don't fuck up.*" Click.

Carlos folded up his cell phone and smiled. He loved how all the mobsters thought of him as a Colombian. Hell, he even heard they nicknamed him; *The Colombian.* Fact of the matter was, he was born and raised in the Bronx and had only been to Colombia twice in his life. He considered himself as American as apple pie and was a full-fledged racist to boot, hating all ethnicities equally. You name it; Guineas, Jews, Ragheads, Chinks, Nips, Moolies, Wetbacks, etc... He was also a sociopath, plain and simple...he hated all socio's in his path. He wasn't bullshitting Donny Nutz either; he did go to NYU for a couple semesters, taking classes in TV and film. He was a product of the seventies and grew up watching all the great cop shows, sitcoms, and variety shows of the era. It was a habit he never kicked, even after finding his true calling as a freelance killer. He was normally hired strictly as an assassin but Donny Nutz paid handsomely to have him help bring his boat down, something he now swore he would never do again. Donny also assured him he would get a chance to ply his trade once he found out who fucked things up for him and was reimbursed for his losses.

It had been a long trip down, way too long, and he needed some rest before checking out the surroundings. He stepped down from the salon into the hallway of the Grand Banks, and headed to the main stateroom for a little shut-eye. Donny Nutz made it clear before they left Jersey City that he didn't want anyone sleeping in his bed, and up till now, no one had. Now that Captain Capicolla was gone, though, all bets were off. As he stretched out on the king-sized bed, he chuckled to himself, knowing how pissed old Donny would be. *Well too fuckin' bad, you Cannon wannabe,* Carlos is calling the shots for now and Carlos sleeps where he wants. Within moments of his head hitting the pillow, he drifted off into one of his recurring dreams. *Policewoman* star Angie Dickinson was frisking him like an overzealous TSA screener, checking out his package, and his package was harder than Chinese calculus.

Chapter 6

After storming out of the will reading, Ricky and his new fiancée Sarah commiserated on the way to her apartment. Initially elated at the prospect of inheriting a million dollars, they were both seriously bummed she wouldn't be getting a penny for five years, while Holly was getting the mother lode immediately. Seriously bummed wasn't actually the right term for Ricky, he was freaked. There was no way he was going to stay engaged for five years without getting paid. Hell, it was the only reason he proposed to her in the first place. As soon as Millie took her final turn for the worse, he made his move and proposed. He hadn't known she was *that* loaded; in fact, it seemed nobody did, but he reckoned Sarah would be getting a nice chunk of change along with some ownership of the marina and/or the house. He had been wrong though, *seriously wrong*. He couldn't believe it, and left Sarah at her apartment on the premise of heading to work.

To the outside world, he was a self-employed exterminator, operating his business out of a run-down, self-storage center, called San Castle Storage. It was only a few miles north of the marina, just west of US1 and the train tracks. While it was true he *did* do a little exterminating, to the inside world (to the world of the storage rats, of which he was one), he was a thief. Basically, storage rats are low-lifes who run businesses out of old mom-and-pop storage centers as a cover for their real occupations. Namely; drug dealing and/or thieving and/or worse. Some, like Ricky, call themselves exterminators. Others might call themselves mechanics or welders or canvass repair guys or window tinters or car stereo installers, but most are involved in some type of criminal activity on a regular basis. The corporations that run the new storage centers seen from the interstate got wise to the program early on, and virtually all prohibit the operation of *any* type of business out of a storage unit. To further discourage the undesirables, they also have security cameras and set hours of operation.

In the older storage centers, however, it's like the Wild West, and anything and everything goes. In fact, many storage rats even *live* out of their units. It provides a perfect setting for dealing in stolen goods, narcotics, and anything criminal. It's hard to believe but storage rats are considered one step *below* dock rats. Dock rats usually commit only crimes of opportunity, like stealing fishing gear out of a truck or boat that somebody left unattended. Storage rats, on the other hand, live day-to-day actively looking for stuff to rip off. When the opportunity doesn't readily present itself, they *make* one. Another problem with old storage centers that allow people to work out of them is it puts a bunch of storage rats together all the time. Unlike putting the long-tailed variety together, the ones that just breed lots of little rats, when you put storage rats together, they breed ideas, lots and lots of *really bad ideas.*

As Ricky pulled up to his storage unit in the dilapidated San Castle Storage Center, in his equally dilapidated 1992 Tacoma pickup, his best friend, Hanky, was unloading a stolen flat-screen TV into his neighboring unit. Ricky hopped out of his truck and helped him carry it inside, for which he was rewarded a can of Keystone Light. As they shared a beer, Ricky began to tell him what happened at the will reading, and another *really bad idea* was about to be born.

Chapter 7

Me, Tangles, and Holly settled into our seats at the outside bar of the Habana Boat and began liberating assorted beverages from their restrictive containers with gusto. It was only eleven in the morning, and although we had the bar mostly to ourselves, we spoke quietly in consideration of the enormous size of Millie's estate. I was the first to speak after eyeballing the scant remains of my first beer and looked at Holly inquisitively.

"You really had *no idea* your aunt was that rich?"

Holly set her lite beer down, spilling some, and looked at me like I was crazier than bat shit. I noticed her hands were shaking as she tried to mop the spillage up with one of those useless mini-cocktail napkins.

"Are you kidding me? Do I look like I knew? I can't even hold a beer steady."

She was right, of course, she was shaking like a leaf.

"You're right, it's incredible. She must have been sitting on something like nine or ten million dollars. Even so, I don't feel right about what she left me."

I thought about what I just said, wondering if I may have stumbled onto a great country song title...*It ain't right what she left me.*

Holly glanced around to make sure nobody was in earshot before responding.

"Forget about it, Kit; the contract to remove the diesel tanks and clean up the contamination came in at $250,000. That's $150,000 less than the deposit we kept from Slade. Millie told me she was leaving you the difference; after all, without you, the marina would be in Slade's hands."

"Maybe so, but I sure didn't do it myself. I should spread some of this around to make it right. Hambone and company deserve a share too."

"Well, that's your call. The money's yours, do whatever you want with it."

"Good point. First I'm gonna buy us another round." I signaled to the shapely bartender, who set us up with fresh ones. After she walked away, Tangles spoke.

"I don't feel right either, Holly, she left me *twenty-five grand.* That's more money than I've ever had at one time in my whole life."

I couldn't resist, and interjected, "Don't you mean half-life?"

Holly punched me in the arm as Tangles delivered his comeback.

"That's very funny, considering until I showed up, the only thing you were catching was sunburn."

"Sorry, bud, you can't set me up for a cheap shot like that and expect me not to take it. It's a DNA thing."

Holly chimed in. "C'mon, guys, enough already. Millie wanted both of you to have some money. It's done and it's yours...end of story. I'm sure you'll figure out what to do with it."

"What about you?" I asked.

She put her hand to her forehead and began massaging her temple.

"Me? I have no idea how to handle everything she left me. I mean, the marina and the house, sure, I can figure that out, but the rest? I just don't know much about stocks and bonds and...did I hear Millie's lawyer correctly? Didn't he say she left me five million dollars worth of gold coins and bullion? What do I do with that?"

Holly looked at me questioningly.

I shrugged and looked at Tangles, who offered up this gem; "Make some extremely rich soup?"

Holly and I groaned at the lame joke before she pressed me for an answer. "Seriously, what should I do?"

"You're meeting with the lawyer tomorrow, right?"

"Yes, at ten in the morning."

"Well, Millie must have the gold in a safe place, like a safety deposit box or something. If that's the case, just leave it there. It's not like you need to liquidate it for cash, she left you plenty of that. I self-manage my own IRA and watch the financial markets pretty carefully. All the so-called 'experts' are saying that the price of gold and other precious metals will keep rising as long as governments all over the world continue to print paper money like it's going out of style, which, ironically, it is. I happen to agree with them. Unfortunately (or fortunately), if you own gold, it doesn't look like there's any end in sight. You should be able to find out when you meet with the attorney, but my guess is Millie never intended for such a large portion of her estate to be in gold. She probably acquired it back when the price was much cheaper. Right now, it's eighteen-hundred dollars an ounce and rising, hence the five million dollars worth you now own. I say leave it be…for now at least. The bigger problem you face is people coming to you for handouts and investment schemes once word gets out how much you inherited."

"I hadn't thought about that, but you're right. Damn! Why didn't I have the attorney tell me in private? He offered, but I said no, I thought I was doing the right thing."

"You probably were, if not for Sarah and her lovely fiancé. I'm pretty sure everybody else, like me and Tangles, are ecstatic to be left anything at all. We know to keep quiet about who got what, out of respect for you and Millie. *That* delightful duo, however, are pissed, because they believe they were snubbed. No doubt they'll be blabbing to everyone about how you got everything and they got nothing…friggin' ingrates."

"I can't believe Sarah's engaged to that sleazoid."

"Believe it," added Tangles. "I've seen him at Three Jacks schmoozing all over her since Millie took her final turn for the worse, the guys a class-A dirtbag. Sleazoid doesn't do him justice."

"Where'd he come from?" I asked. "He's not a dock rat, or I would have recognized him."

"I heard he works out of that storage center up the road, the one that looks like it belongs on the cover of *Nothing Good Happens Here* magazine."

"Shit, are you talking about San Castle Storage, the place next to the tracks?"

"Yep, that's the one; she's a real beauty, huh?"

"Yeah...not so much. That place is like Grand Central Station for storage rats."

Holly raised her hand and waved it in front of my face.

"Helloooo? *Storage rats?* What are you talking about? What's a storage rat?"

"Think one step below a dock rat."

"I didn't know there *was* a step below."

"Well there is, and you just met one, good old Rick-to-the-E."

"Great."

Just then the *C-Love* drift boat came chugging down the Intracoastal, followed by Hambone in his "well-weathered" charter boat, the *Ham it Up*. I was first to notice and pointed them out.

"Here comes Hambone, I should get to the bank and hit him with some of this inheritance money; he earned it."

"I need to do a few things at the marina office," added Holly. "Plus, I want to see how the morning catch was."

I paid the bar tab and the three of us walked across the parking lot to the C-Love Marina office. Holly turned to me as we reached the office door and gave me a nice kiss on the lips.

"Are you coming over for dinner tonight?"

"As long as your kiss is on the menu, my reservation is assured."

She grimaced at my feeble attempt at suavedom, but managed a laugh after I pulled her back for another kiss.

Tangles, however, had seen enough. "Oh, for God's sake, you two, you're mushier than overcooked peas...c'mon!"

Tangles and I left Holly at the marina office and headed over to my car, which was parked in front of my boat, a thirty-eight foot Viking named the *Lucky Dog.* As I fired up my red Beemer (a 1994, 325 convertible), it occurred to me again that I was indeed a lucky dog. My fishing show had been saved; I had a new girlfriend (now a very rich one), and I also just unexpectedly inherited a considerable chunk of change. Things were going good, *incredibly good,* and then Tangles broke the spell.

"Looks like we got a new neighbor."

"Huh? What?"

"Man, you're so googly-eyed over Holly you can't even see straight."

I had backed out of the parking space, and was just pulling away, when I braked to see what Tangles was pointing at. It was a big Grand Banks trawler docked in the slip next to the *Lucky Dog.*

"Googly-eyed, my *ass,* when did *that* get here?"

"Must have come in this morning. It wasn't here yesterday."

I noted the name emblazoned across the stern in big gold letters…*JC.*

"JC, JC…why does that name ring a bell somewhere?"

"Cause it's not ringing one here?"

"Cute. Let's get the scoop from Robo when we get back. I don't like surprises."

"Not even when someone drops a hundred and fifty grand in your lap?"

"Shut up, I'm thinking."

I let my foot off the brake and we headed out the parking lot to go to the bank. Along the way I kept thinking I had heard the name before…JC…but I couldn't remember where. I also started thinking about that big-ass shoe that I was certain was going to drop, and my gut was telling me the laces were loose.

Chapter 8

In the wake of the terrorist attacks on the World Trade Center, the manner in which agencies of the United States government shared intelligence information received a much needed overhaul. It came to light there was a slew of data on some of the terrorists; had it been investigated and disseminated, it may have prevented the attacks. Until the twin towers came down, the one-upmanship attitude and lack of cooperation among the FBI, CIA, NSA, DEA and others was tolerated. Afterward…not so much.

The end result was the creation of the Department of Homeland Security and the TSA (Transportation Security Administration). The TSA was created to ensure airline and passenger safety. Anybody that's ever flown on a commercial airliner since September 11, 2001, is familiar with the TSA, and if you've refused a body scanner in lieu of a pat down, you may even be *intimately* familiar with them. The entire world knows about homeland security and their public face, the TSA, but only a handful of people know about the *other* department created shortly thereafter.

After the investigation into the terrorist attacks revealed an incredible lack of intelligence sharing, the heads of the main security and law enforcement agencies were forced to meet and come up with a solution to prevent a similar attack from ever occurring. Over a long weekend at Camp David, the heads of the FBI, CIA, DEA, NSA, homeland security, and the Defense Department, attempted a brainstorming session. They all agreed that intelligence information needed to be better shared and more easily accessed but they couldn't agree which department should be responsible. They *all* wanted to be in charge of deciding who got what information. At an impasse, the president was called in, and he was none too happy. With his short fuse and Texas twang, he laid into them.

"What the hell do you mean, y'all can't agree?" he said, looking around the conference table. "We are at *war* here, gentleman! And when we are at *war*, this great country comes together for the common good, namely, getting that son of a bitch Saddam Hussein and all his Al-Qaida friends!"

He slammed his fist on the table, and the secretary of defense raised his hand and interjected.

"Mr. President, with all due respect, we haven't been able to establish any definitive ties between Saddam and Al-Qaida *or* bin Laden, for that matter."

The president squinted his famous squint, undeterred. "Do you think I care? Do you think the American people care? They're all the same, for crying out loud! Iraq, Iran, Pakistan, Afghanistan… any damn country that ends in 'stan'…they're all terrorists! They look like the Village People in robes, they smell like wet ass, and they get up every morning with one thing in mind and that's to kill Americans!

Well guess what? Now I get up every morning wanting to *kill terrorists* and if a few goat herders get caught in the crossfire, that's tough nuts! So the next time I hear you mention bin Laden, it better be to tell me he bin killed.

Now here's what were gonna do. I want each of you to pick one of your top people, and we're gonna assign them to a new department that we create *today*. This new department is going to be responsible for analyzing intelligence information and making sure it gets to the right agency, from the CIA, all the way down to the Punxsutawney Police Department. Terrorists are the number one priority, but any information pertaining to serious criminal activity, particularly of the international sort, will be the focus. These elite agents will be given carte branch in their line of duty. Their main purpose is to gather and distributate information vital to this great nation's security, but they will also be licensed to kill, maim, or use whatever means necessary in pursuit of justice. They will report to a person that I will appoint, and that person will report directly to me."

Somewhat stunned, the agency heads fidgeted, and the CIA director spoke. "Mr. President, the CIA is already under intense scrutiny for our interrogation techniques, some of which are strictly prohibited by the Geneva Convention. It seems you are suggesting a certain amount of, shall I say, *disregard* in this area?"

The president shook his head in disbelief. "You're *damn right* I am! The Geneva Convention…shewt, you kidding me? What did the Swiss ever get right? Chocolate, that's what, that's about it, hell, their cheese even has holes in it. They should stick to making chocolate and not telling me how to fight a damn war!"

"Mr. President," spoke the head of the NSA (National Security Agency). "How do you propose a handful of agents monitor the astronomical quantities of information generated by just the agencies at this table?"

"Computers, we got lots of 'em, next question."

"Mr. President," inquired the secretary of defense. "I can barely convince Congress to budget me enough money to fight a few wars here and there…How would we pay for this?"

"Do you really have to ask? OK then, I'll spell it out for you; we have this little place called the U.S. Mint. I'll just tell my buddy Greenspan to print more greenbacks. I don't understand why everybody gets their knickers in a twist over budgets anyways. Why even *have* one when you can just print more money? Doesn't make sense, does it? Besides, you think terrorists have budgets? Hell no, the only thing they know how to balance is an AK-47 on a camel's hump. This is w*ar*, God dammit! We're gonna fight fire with *hellfire*! Budgets be damned! Y'all can thank me down at the ranch at my next barbecue when we're serving trucker-sized portions of terrorist kabob…Extra-frickin'-crispy."

"Mr. President," voiced the head of the FBI. "Are you sure it's a good idea to allow even a *handful* of our own guys to have access to all this information?"

"Course not, that's why it's gotta be supersecret, in case it backfires. So do me a favor, when you come up with a name, don't use numbers, like 'area fifty-one.' I don't wanna be watching a show about it on the History Channel next week. If so much as *one word* of this leaks out I will personally plug it with each and every ass in this room, then I'll deny knowledge of it the way an A-rab denies the existence of soap. Nobody but nobody can know *dick* about this. Are we clear?"

The president looked around the room, and one by one, reluctant heads nodded. "Good, one more thing, then. The person I appoint to head this group needs to be a rocket-scientist-computer-whiz-genius type. I want each of you to recommend someone, but not from within your agency, no playing favorites. I don't care if it's a civilian either, as long as they fit the bill. So that's it. I'll be back in an hour. By then I want the names of the agents you're assigning to this group, your recommendations on who should lead it, and a name for it...a supersecret name...one that nobody's ever gonna know *dick* about. See you in an hour."

An hour later the president walked back in the room. Each agency head passed forward a sheet of paper containing the name of an agent selected to be in the newly created department, as well as a recommendation for the department head.

The president read aloud their choices. "Special Agent Thomas Cushing, FBI. What can you tell me about him?" He looked up at the FBI chief.

"He's one of our best investigators; good with weapons, good with computers, and good at keeping his mouth shut."

"Good...Sounds like he's got all the goods. What about Special Agent Joe Davis, NSA?"

The NSA head didn't hesitate. "He came to us from the FBI, sir. He too is a top investigator, well trained in weaponry and advanced engineering systems, earned a PhD from MIT."

"Wow! A letterman, impressive, I like athaletes... good. OK, so I see we have a Mr. Raphael Angel-Herrera, from the DEA. Hot damn! He's got two last names, what a mouthful. Just saying it gets your tongue working like ladies night at Hillary's. So watcha got for me?" The president looked up at the head of the DEA, who stopped chuckling under his breath.

"Yes sir, uh, Mr. Herrera has a black belt in Tae-Kwan-Jujitsu and advanced degrees in both marine engineering and hydrodynamic propulsion. He's also a master of disguise."

"Maybe so, but I can see he's an excellent choice. We'll take all the master's degrees we can get when we're hunting those scarf-loving bastards. Well done. Next is Wilson Smith, CIA."

"It's not his real name, Mr. President," answered the CIA director. "But Mr. Smith specializes in encryption detection and deconstruction, as well as advanced interrogation techniques. He should fit in well with your vision."

"Excellent, my vision likes what it sees...Now, what about this Judy Larson, from homeland security?" The president glanced over to the homeland security chief, who cleared his throat before speaking.

"Yes, of course sir, Miss Larson is our head of information technology; a computer and mathematical genius. She's a winner of both the prestigious Fields Medal as well as the Cole Prize in algebra and number theory. She's done extensive work on SuperCollider magnocellular receptivity and quantum statistical analysis. You're going to need someone to keep the vast collection of data flowing and that's her."

"I agree, we must never, *ever,* let the data get backed up...excellent choice. Moving right along, lastly, I have—"

"Excuse me, Mr. President?" The homeland chief interrupted.

"Yes?"

"I'm not sure how relevant this is, but since this is such a small group we're talking about, I think I should let everybody know...my choice is gay."

The president threw his hands in the air in exasperation.

"Are you kidding me? First the lead singer of Judas Priest, and now *you?* My director of homeland security? You sure picked a hell of a time to come out of the closet, next you're gonna tell me you're dating Boy George!"

"WHAT? No! No, not me, my choice...My choice, Miss Larson, she's gay."

The president chuckled and let out a deep breath, then put his hand to his forehead.

"Whew! You really had me there for a sec, I can handle *that.* So we got a lesbian number cruncher, no big deal, just don't say it down in Texas or they'll throw you in the pokey for talking dirty. Heh. Hell, I even *like* lesbians; they accommodate my stance on abortion."

"How's that sir?"

"They rarely have 'em."

The president picked up the last slip of paper and held it up.

"All right, here we are, the final selection to our team is a Lt. Col. James K. Callahan, courtesy of the Defense Department."

The secretary of defense sat up, and proudly spoke of the colonel. "He would have made general if he wasn't so adept at killing people. He's a former Green Beret with excellent survival skills, naturally. Expert in hand-to-hand combat as well as automatic weaponry. Former liaison to the American attaché to the French embassy, speaks twelve languages at last count, including Farsi and Urdu. I think he'll be useful."

"You hear that, boys?" The president beamed. "We got ourselves a Farsi and Urdu-speaking, good ol' American badass. How 'bout *them* biscuits? His middle initial probably stands for Kickin' Ass! Man, I sure would like to see the looks on their terrorist faces when he suckers 'em in with that A-rab talk and then whoops the livin' shit out of 'em. Gentleman, this is a great start. Now, let's see who y'all think should run this show."

He picked up the slips of paper with their recommendations and let out a low whistle. "Well how do you like that, looks like three of you picked the same guy. Who the hell is Franklin Post?"

The CIA director looked around the table.

"Who else picked him?"

"I did," responded the FBI chief.

The DEA head also raised his hand.

"Either of you care to fill him in?"

Neither did and instead deferred to the CIA director to brief the president.

"OK then, you've heard about this new company called Gaggle? The one that has the incredible search engine?"

"Sure I have," replied the president. "My kids use it to help them with their homework. So tell me about this incredible engine, what's it run on, nuclear?"

The CIA director watched as the FBI chief rolled his eyes but he managed to keep his composure.

"Uh, no, sir, it's not really an engine, it's computers, it's all computers. It's just that it's so powerful, accesses so many databases, it's referred to as a search engine."

"That's a good thing; running an engine on computers could get expensive…go on."

"Anyways, Franklin Post is the brains behind Gaggle. By all accounts he is the world's foremost expert and leader in cybertechnology, nanotechnology and transdermal techno-integration systems."

"Huh, bet he's a good speller too."

"If anyone has the ability to analyze, process, and disseminate the astronomical volumes of intelligence information we're talking about here, he's the man."

"He already has the same security level clearance as everybody in this room but you, Mr. President," added the FBI chief. "He's done consulting work for all of us, trying to help us bring our systems up to speed."

"Hmm…Sounds like he's our man."

"One thing though, like most otherworldly geniuses, he's a bit eccentric."

"Concentric? What, he talks in circles?"

"No, no, *eccentric*, he's got some strange habits, particularly concerning astronomy. He lives in a ten-thousand-square-foot dome-shaped house on the Puget Sound and the entire ceiling is an exact recreation of our solar system. Rumor has it he has a full-time painter who keeps adding stars and planets as they're discovered."

"You call it concentric, I call it star struck. Either way, who cares as long as he can do the job."

"Problem is, Mr. President, he obviously doesn't need the money. You'll have to convince him why he should start working for the government when he's a self-made billionaire. There is one thing working in our favor though."

"What's that?"

"His only his sister went down with Flight 93. You would think it would motivate him to come on board."

"Son of a bitch, how could he say no?"

"Like I said, he's eccentric, you never know."

"I don't have the time *or* the patience to go round and round with these concentric types. If I ask him to help and he doesn't agree, why…that would be unpatriotic, in direct violation of the Patriot Act. I'll threaten to throw his ass in jail and paint a black hole on his ceiling, that oughta do it. Don't worry, I'll get Stargazer on board. OK then, it's settled, looks like we have our group together."

"Wait, what about the other candidates?" queried the head of the NSA.

"Forget about it, it's a mute point, I just eighty-sixed 'em…Stargazer's our man."

"But—"

"But nothing, don't you know what a *mute point* means? When someone says it's a *mute point,* they don't want to *hear* about it anymore, they want it *muted.*"

The president shook his head, amazed that the head of the NSA didn't know what a mute point meant. He made a mental note to start searching for his replacement. The note said: FIRE DUMBASS. "All right, now that we're clear on that, what name for the organization did y'all come up with?"

Not happy about having his candidate so casually dismissed, the secretary of defense decided to beat the others to it, and cleared his throat.

"Mr. President? We took our cue from you; you provided the inspiration for the name of the new department."

"Is that right? Well, don't just sit there, *lay it on me*, we got terrorists to kill!"

"Mr. President, by unanimous consent, we think it should be called the Department of International Criminal Knowledge, the D-I-C-K, or DICK, for short... No pun intended. You said it yourself, you don't want anybody to know *dick* about it, well, nobody's gonna know dick about DICK."

While the president leaned back in his chair and began rubbing his chin, the secretary wondered if he was moments away from having to turn in the letter of resignation he always kept in his pocket. Being a highly educated four-star general with a cushy retirement waiting, he could only take so much. But a few seconds later, the president leaned forward and commented on the name.

"DICK...yeah...DICK...that's good, that's *real* good...I like DICK...I like it a lot, I'm all for DICK." He sat forward in his chair and looked around the table grinning.

The director of the CIA wasn't about to let the moment pass and he kicked the FBI chief under the table as he reinforced the notion.

"Mr. President, if I may, I've been in this business a long time, and I can tell you it's the perfect clandestine name. Think about it, even if—"

"Hold your horses there, pardner; my geology's a little sketchy. Where the hell is Clandestine? Next to Palestine?"

The DEA chief kicked the FBI chief, who kicked the NSA chief, who kicked the homeland security chief, who kicked the secretary of defense, who inadvertently kicked the president.

"Ow! What the—?" The president turned to the secretary of defense who quickly apologized.

"Sorry sir, I, uh, I had a leg cramp."

"Yeah? Well give it to somebody else next time." The president rubbed his leg and added, "Maybe you should get checked out for post-traumatic kick the president in the shin syndrome. Pay attention, General, you probably don't know where Clandestine is either."

"Uh, no, what I meant, sir," continued the CIA director, "is that clandestine is a word, not a place, it means 'secret.' DICK is the perfect secret name, is what I meant."

"Very clever, now I get it. It's a secret word that means secret. That's why nobody knows what it means…brilliant…go on."

"Yes sir, as I was saying, even if somebody stumbles on to us, they'll never believe there's a government agency named DICK. They'd think it's a joke, it's the perfect cover, the perfect name…DICK."

"It's a real beaut, that's for sure, Cheney's gonna love it."

"You can't tell him sir, remember?" The head of the NSA put a finger to his temple and added, "believe me, it'll be tough for everyone here, but nobody can know about DICK."

"Dammit! You're right...We got the ultimate top-secret name in DICK and nobody's gonna know dick about it. Heh. If that ain't ironic, I don't know what is. Oh well, it's a small price to pay for helping to keep this country great, and terrorist free, of course. All right then—"

The secretary of defense couldn't take it anymore. His resignation letter was burning a hole in his pocket. He had to correct the president's incorrect use of the word "ironic."

"Mr. President, excuse me, but never being able to reveal the name of a top-secret agency because it would no longer be top secret, isn't ironic, it's more of a conundrum, or a catch—"

The president furrowed his brow and held his hand out like he was stopping traffic.

"Ixnay on the jibber-jabbay. General, that's another mute point. Now y'all get those agents you picked in here for a briefing, post haste. I'll handle Stargazer, we gotta talk strategery. I hereby declare this meeting sojourned." He rose to his feet and clapped his hands together.

"Gentleman, let's get the DICK rolling! And remember, DICK is our little clandestine."

Chapter 9

Federal Agent Thomas Cushing was going on ten years working for DICK, and loved it. *Why?* That was easy. He worked for a department that was so top secret, so guarded, that outside the agents themselves, only a handful of people on the planet knew it existed. In a radical effort to keep it that way, it was structured with no headquarters and no field offices. That meant no day-to-day boss or supervisor. He was given badges to every federal agency of the United States government and access to all the weapons and gadgets used by any of them—including the Pentagon.

It was like working for the CIA but without all the oversight and layers of bureaucracy. Although assigned to a geographical region, all agents were mobile and worked out of their apartments or homes. The formula proved to be successful. Thanks to information provided by DICK, numerous terrorist plots against the United States had been uncovered and prevented. Even Osama bin Laden, along with several top terrorist leaders, had finally been tracked down and killed. With the war on terror taking a favorable turn, DICK began focusing more attention on high-profile domestic and international crimes. Agents like Cushing still had a little paperwork to do, but for the most part they could prioritize as they saw fit. The pay was excellent, as were the perks. Cushing was staring at his computer screen, working his way through his quarterly expense report, when his DICK phone rang.

"Cush here."

As with all DICK phones, the call wasn't patched through until his voice print was verified. As soon as it was, the line was secured and his response transmitted.

"I bet it is, you lucky bastard, better than being up here in bumfuck North Carolina."

Recognizing the voice of his former roommate Joe Davis (also an original DICK agent), from their training days with the FBI, Cush returned the greeting in kind.

"C'mon, Joe, bumfuck's not so bad. Just put a pinch between your cheek and gum, toss on your number "3" T-shirt, and watch your idols make left-hand turns on TV all day while you pound Budweisers."

"My idols? *Shit,* I like NASCAR about as much as I like the WNBA."

They both shared a laugh and vowed to get together when their schedules put them in the same vicinity, and then Cush inquired as to the real nature of the call.

"So what's up, Joe?"

"The coast guard off Nag's Head towed in a semi-submerged boat that some fisherman found in international waters. The only part sticking out of the water was the radar arch and some electronics on the bridge. When they got it to shore they discovered bullet holes in the cockpit floor and traces of blood. That's when they called the FBI and we picked it up."

"And this affects me *how?*"

"Well, if you let me finish, I'll tell you. The boat was named, *The Job*, and it was registered to a Florida corporation with a West Palm address. Care to take a guess where?"

"No, I haven't even finished my first cup of coffee, just tell me."

"My favorite gentleman's club whenever I get to south Florida, none other than Rachelle's."

"Rachelle's? No shit."

"Yep. The same corporate entity that owns the boat, owns Rachelle's."

"Son of a bitch, Donny Nutz."

"Bingo."

"So what else you got?"

"Well, here's where it gets interesting. Coast guard says that if the boat came up the Gulf Stream from south Florida, it may have been in the water a good month or so, but nobody reported it stolen. Nor are there any missing person's reports that tie in with it."

"Not so fast, Joe."

"What? You got something?"

"Well, for about the last six months or so, I've been gathering intel on Nutz involving Rachelle's. The FBI's got an informant on the inside and there's all kinds of shit going on—loan sharking, money laundering, drug dealing, prostitution…naturally, and possibly some international arms trafficking, which is what got the boss interested. That's just what we know of. About six weeks ago the informant told his handler one of the managers didn't show up for work, and hasn't been seen since. Same for his right-hand man, one of the bouncers. These guys are prone to move around a lot, so I didn't think much of it—until now."

"Interesting."

"It certainly is now, anything else?"

"Well, there wasn't much to be found on the boat because it had been submerged, but they managed to pull a print off the chart plotter. There's some data from it that might be useful. I'm gonna e-mail it down to you."

"Good, what about the print?"

"There was a hit from the FDLE database; it came back to one Connor Jansen. I'll forward his last known address along with the data from the chart plotter."

"What's on his sheet?"

"Nothing, he's pretty much clean as a whistle. The only reason FDLE has his prints is because he submitted them in order to become a state-licensed real estate broker."

"You said he's pretty much clean. What's the *pretty much* part?"

"You're gonna love this, Cush. Only thing that comes up is he got popped on New Year's Eve, 1999, for banging a chick in a Palm Beach lifeguard stand."

"Sounds like he's not the only one who got popped...but since when's that a crime?"

"It's not, unless the chick is the nineteen-year-old daughter of the chief of police, and you were caught sharing a post coitus joint in the buff."

The old roommates busted out laughing together and laughed even harder when Cush added, "So the only reason he's not clean as a whistle is because he was cleaning his whistle."

After the laughter died down, Joe added, "It was only a first-degree misdemeanor. I'm surprised it even made the file. Somebody must have put it in for the entertainment value."

"Yeah, it's priceless."

"Maybe there's a MasterCard commercial in there somewhere."

"Maybe, guy's ballsy."

"That's what she said."

After laughing some more, Cushing again looked at the unfinished expense report on his computer and decided it was time to get back to it.

"OK, Joe, e-mail me the stuff, by the time I get through with it the FBI should be done talking to this Jansen guy. It'll be interesting to see what, if anything, shakes out. On the surface it doesn't seem like it's something he'd be involved with. You never know though, thanks for the heads up. Either way, we need to nail Nutz. The boss is getting antsy and I can't blame him. He thinks Nutz is involved in some arms trafficking through Port Everglades and some of the weapons are ending up in terrorist hands."

"That's what I heard."

"Good talking to you, bud."

"Ditto here, Cush, let me know how it goes."

"You got it, talk at you later." Click.

Chapter 10

Hanky was not an atypical storage rat. At thirty-five years old, he had already spent several years in the South Bay Correctional Facility on a variety of charges. They included DUI, driving on a suspended license, resisting arrest, possession of a controlled substance, firearms possession, and most recently, grand larceny. His cover at the storage center was running a pressure cleaning business, but if you looked around the cluttered unit, what you mostly saw were stolen goods: bicycles, electronics, yard equipment, a motor scooter, a couple of generators, some fishing rods and reels… the usual suspects.

On his last stint in the slammer, he had plenty of time to reflect on the risk/reward ratio of the botched theft that put him there. He had busted into a nearby lawn mower sales and repair shop on Dixie Highway and loaded up his pickup full of yard equipment. Although the shop was only two miles from his storage unit, he ran out of gas on the way back. It ended up costing him nearly two years in the can, and he vowed not to smoke any more crack before doing his next job. He also realized that at the rate he was going, he was never gonna be able to upgrade to a bigger storage unit; every storage rat's dream. So when his greasy protégé, Ricky, took another hit off the crack pipe, and finished telling him about the will reading, Hanky's fried brain was in overdrive. He heard some crazy shit come out of Ricky's mouth before, but nothing like this.

"You gotta be shittin' me, did you say *five million in gold?"* He asked.

"Yeah, and lots of cash and stocks and stuff, not to mention the marina and house."

Ricky passed the pipe to Hanky, who took a large hit and whistled as he exhaled. As the superheated cocaine wrapped its insidious tendrils around his cerebellum, he spoke without thinking (a common occurrence).

"It could all be yours."

Ricky was wasted and missed his tone; all he could think about was how he somehow got screwed again.

"I got screwed, we got screwed, I mean uh…Sarah got screwed. Fuck, we're *all* screwed."

"Or… *are we?*"

"Well, I don't know about you, but didn't you hear what I said? Sarah's not getting anything until—"

"I heard what *you said,* but you didn't hear what *I said.*"

"Huh?"

"It could *all be yours.*"

Hanky pulled out two more cans of Keystone Light from his stolen mini-fridge and handed one to the perplexed Ricky. Although he was confused and whacked out of his gourd, Hanky had his full attention. Ricky was all aboard the "Me-Train."

"How, ah, how do you figure?"

"You said that Holly and Sarah are the only surviving relatives?"

"Yeah, yeah, that's right."

"And Holly, the one who got all the loot, you said she's divorced?"

"Yeah, yeah that's what Sarah told me. She's got a boyfriend though, the dickhead who got a hundred and fifty grand."

"But they're not married, that's the point."

"Not yet at least, but I know I'd be popping the question if I was in his shoes. He'd be set for life."

"Exactly, which is why we need to make sure he's not."

"What do you mean?"

Hanky took a big gulp of beer, wiping the corners of his sore-chapped lips with his sleeve. He was pretty certain how Ricky would react, but wanted to make sure they were on the same page.

"We been friends a long time, right? We help each other out when we need to…we got each other's back…right?"

"Sure we do, bro, that's the way it's always gonna be."

"So if I were to help you out and in the process make you more money than you ever imagined, you'd split it with me…*right?*"

"Sure, sixty for you, forty for me— even up, like always. What gives?"

"What do you suppose would happen to all that gold and money if something happened to Holly?"

"You mean like…an *accident?*"

"Yeah, say she's killed in a car accident or something before she gets married."

"Huh, I hadn't thought about that. I suppose it would go to...um...charity or whatever, whatever's in her will...I guess."

"She just inherited all this stuff, you think she already has a will? I doubt it, and if she's not married, then everything would go to the next of kin, who would be..."

"Sarah...of course...It would *all* go to Sarah!"

"Don't you mean you're *soon-to-be wife,* Sarah?"

"Hell yeah!"

The two storage rats high-fived each other and scraped half-empty cans of beer together. Then Hanky laid it on thick.

"You'd be set for life."

"No, *we'd* be set for life."

"So let's make it happen, dude, no more of this closet-sized living, we could have a big warehouse!"

Ricky though about how nice it would be to be in a seedy old industrial park, in a giant warehouse full of stolen goods, with his best friend Hanky, livin' the life.

"That would be great, but what are the odds something happens to her?"

Hanky got out of his chair and walked to the front of the dark, windowless, storage unit. The garage door was half opened to let some light and air in. He lifted it up over his head and peered outside to make sure no one was in earshot. As the stale smoke wafted out, he turned around and closed the door so it was only knee-high from the ground.

"I think there's a 100 percent chance...that's what I think...if we *want it* to happen. But you really gotta *want it,* Rick-E...so what do you say?"

Ricky thought about the way the guy named Shagball and his twerpy little friend smirked at him at the will reading. Then he thought about all the money they were getting and he wasn't. Then he thought about how Sarah's stepsister Holly acted *so surprised* at everything, when he *knew* she aced his clueless fiancée out of her inheritance. He crushed the empty beer can in his hand and threw it toward a giant trash can in the corner, missing, as usual.

"Fuck those assholes!" he spat out.

"That's right, fuck 'em. So what do you say?"

"I say I need another beer."

"And?"

"And the *bitch* has gotta go."

Although they had been friends for years, Hanky had never seen the strange expression that engrossed Ricky's face in the dim light, and it gave him goose bumps. Ricky was having a moment, his moment, having mentally crossed the threshold that he knew one day would come. That day, that moment, was now. He was ready to make the leap from small time crook, to killer. He *wanted it.* He wanted it *bad.*

Chapter 11

After we concluded our bank business and headed back to the parking lot, I placed the small bag containing twenty-five thousand dollars in neatly wrapped hundreds into the trunk of the Beemer. I never had that much cash in my hands before and I needed to deliver it quickly before I changed my mind.

It was all I could do to not jump on I-95 and head up to the Black Bart store on Blue Heron Boulevard. As a fishing show host I got plenty of free stuff, but not the cherished Black Bart lures that I had developed an addiction to. They were the one sponsor we hadn't yet landed, and it was killing me. Whenever I had cause to be on the north side of town, I was inexorably drawn to the store like a junkie looking for a fix. I never once left without spending at least a hundred bucks, which would get me two rigged lures, if I was lucky. Not only are they incredibly effective at raising and catching fish, but they're works of art.

On more than one rainy day I've sat in my apartment and pulled out my prized collection of Black Bart's, displaying them on the kitchen counter where I can easily handle them, admire them, and even talk to them. I see nothing wrong with assuring such beauties with names like Pelagic Breakfast or San Sal Candy, that the rain will eventually stop and we will not be denied our big bull dolphin or giant wahoo. It was a ritual that cost me a couple of girlfriends over the years. It always came down to, "So you'd rather sit here and play with your stupid lures than go to the mall with me?"

I was smart enough not to answer, but my facial expression would always give me away. It's like the look on Charlie Sheen's face when he says, "Duh, winning!"

Tangles poked me in the arm as we drove down US 1.

"What's with the weird look on your face?"

"Huh? Oh, I was just thinking how much damage I could do with twenty-five grand at the Black Bart store. Do yourself a favor, don't ever go in there. It's like how you can't eat just one Lay's potato chip, you can't buy just one Black Bart lure. Buy one and you're done. You'll develop restless wallet syndrome whenever you get in the vicinity."

"Sounds like my kinda place; let's go check it out."

"Did you *not* hear a word I just said? No, absolutely not, I'm meeting Hambone back at the dock; besides, it's about lunchtime."

We pulled into the marina and found Hambone leaning against his old pickup, talking on his cell. It was a weekday, out of season, and like most other charter guys, he was looking for a customer. I parked next to him and pulled the sack of cash out of the trunk.

Hambone concluded his conversation and offered his trademark rapid-fire query. "Whaddup, Whaddup, Whaddup?"

As he bumped fists with Tangles, I let him know.

"I got something for you, Hambone, here, let me show you."

I set the bag in the back of his pickup and opened it up, exposing the stacks of hundred dollar bills. Hambone had his hands on the side of the truck as he peered down, squinting. Realizing it was a pile of money, his head immediately popped up and swiveled from side to side, making sure nobody else was looking.

"Wa-wa, where did you get that? And, uh, why, uh, why are you giving it to me?"

"Millie left me some money, more than I deserve. There's twenty-five grand in there, I want you to give five grand each to Eight-Toe and Kodak, you keep the rest."

"HOLY SHIT!"

"Not so loud, this needs to be on the down-low. Be sure to remind the guys to keep their traps shut about the sinkhole."

"Are you kidding me? With this kind of money they'll probably disappear down to the Keys for a couple months. Don't worry, they won't be a problem. Me, on the other hand..."

Hambone let out a low whistle and suddenly grabbed me in a bear hug, lifting me off the ground and spinning me around. I could barely breathe while he started going, "Wooooooooo, woooooooo...all aboard the Hambone Express! Next stop...Fat City!"

Tangles was laughing his ass off as Hambone finally set me down and I needed to grab the side of the truck to steady myself. Luckily, I hadn't eaten yet, or I probably would have been puking in the pickup.

It was a fresh reminder of how incredibly powerful he was. *Wow.*

Hambone continued, excited about his windfall. "I love you, man; seriously, you have no idea how much this is gonna help. Business is slow, I mean *really, really* slow."

Then he looked down at Tangles questioningly.

"What about little big man?"

"He lucked out, Millie left him something too."

"Hey, guys? I'm right *fucking* here; quit talking like I'm not. I *hate it* when you do that!" Tangles had his arms crossed and looked miffed. It was the perfect time to strike.

"You know what he's talking about, Ham? I got no idea."

"Me neither, must be that microchip on his shoulder he carries around all the time. Gonna get him in trouble someday."

Tangles put his hands on his hips and looked up at Hambone. "Oh, that's real cute, a *microchip?* Nice… friggin' bastard."

We shared a good laugh and then I remembered wanting to talk to Robo about the new slip holder next to the *Lucky Dog*.

"I gotta roll, Ham, I need to see Robo. Stay out of trouble."

He zipped up the bag of cash and then turned and gave me another hug, this time not so bone crushing. "I really appreciate this Kit. I know the other guys will too. I won't forget it. Thanks, buddy."

"Hey, everybody earned it as far as I'm concerned, enough said. Tangles, you coming?"

"Fast and furious, boss, like always."

We headed across the parking lot to the tiny ship's store at the fuel dock and found Robo soaking up the air conditioning inside. He looked up from his paperwork and greeted us.

"Hey, guys, how's it going?"

"Good, real good, but it looks like it's a little dead on the dock." I replied.

Tangles saluted Robo and announced,

"I need to make a call."

As Tangles walked down the fuel dock, Robo asked where our next fishing show segment was being shot.

"Right here, the next thing we have scheduled is the Lantana Fishing Derby."

"Hope the fishin' picks up by then. It's been slow lately. I'm sure you don't need to be told."

"Yeah, I heard the ocean temperature is up to eighty-five degrees. When it gets that hot the fishing bites, but not in a good way."

"It's the dog days of summer, Shag, I think it's gonna be a long one."

Trying to sound as nonchalant as possible, I began my probe. "Speaking of dogs, the *Lucky Dog*, that is, I noticed we have a new neighbor."

"Oh, yeah, they came in this morning."

"They?"

"Well, there *were* two guys, but they had some kind of argument and the captain bailed. Nice vessel though."

I began to feel a little relieved, thinking that maybe the boat was just docked until the owner found a new captain.

"So what's the scoop? Is he looking for another captain so he can be on his way?"

"No, no, I think he's gonna be here for a little while. The owner rented the slip for at least a month, booked it three or four weeks ago. Can't wait to see what the guy looks like, he sounded like Darth Vader with tonsillitis."

My temporary ease had evaporated. *Poof,* gone.

"So who's the guy on the boat?"

"I think he said his name was Carlos. From what I gathered he was hired to bring the boat down, seems kind of odd, though."

"Who, this Carlos guy?"

"No, well…maybe, what I meant was, it seems odd to hire a guy to bring a boat down when he doesn't know a thing about boats."

"What?"

"You heard me right. Guy couldn't even move the boat from the fuel dock to the slip, Skeeter did it for him."

Now my inner, shit-hitting-the-fan-radar, was on high alert. I mumbled, "Jesus Christ."

"You think? Nah, I doubt it, it probably stands for the city."

"What? What are you talking about?"

"The name of the boat; aren't you trying to figure out what JC stands for? I think it probably stands for the place where the boat is registered."

"Which is *where?*"

At sixty-seven years old, Robo's prostate wasn't the only thing bothering him, he was also having more and more "senior moments," like the one he was currently having.

"Dammit! I should be able to remember, here, here's the file right here, let me see…"

As Robo was skimming through the paperwork with his index finger, I kept trying to think where I had heard the word "JC" before. Was it in the context of a place? Then it hit me. When we were being held at gunpoint on the missing boat, *The Job*, the big goon named Marco said something about doing stand-up in JC.

"Bingo! Here it is, Shag, the boat is registered to a corporation in Jersey City, New Jersey. I bet that's what the JC stands for, Jersey City. What do you think?"

Not only had my temporary ease vanished, but it had been replaced by a knot of apprehension in my gut, complete with a tiny ribbon of fear. *Here comes the shoe.*

Chapter 12

I stood there letting it all sink in. Robo had to be right, the JC on the back of the Grand Banks stood for Jersey City, had to. *Oh, Shit.*

"Something the matter, Kit?"

"Huh? No, uh, no I was just thinking you're probably right."

"Yeah, that's gotta be it, kinda weird for a snowbird to be coming down here this time of year though."

I suddenly had the urge to leave and turned to see Tangles out on the end of the dock, still talking on the phone.

"I gotta get moving, Robo, talk to you later."

"OK, see you soon."

As I walked toward Tangles, I was thinking, *not very likely*. Tangles must have heard me walking up behind him and when he turned, I waved for him to follow me. I glanced back as we crossed the parking lot and saw him pumping his tiny legs trying to keep up.

By the time I reached the Beemer, he was only a few steps behind and I heard him say, "Me too, can't wait to see you, Mom," click. He snapped his phone shut and gave me a questioning look. "What's the big hurry?"

From the driver's seat, I pointed at the big Grand Banks parked next to the *Lucky Dog*. "See the name on the new boat parked next to us?"

He craned his neck a little. "*JC?* Yeah, I see it, so what?"

"When me and Hambone were kidnapped, the big guy holding the gun on us said something about doing stand-up in JC. I forgot about it, until now. Until Robo just told me that that boat parked next to us, the *JC,* is registered out of Jersey City."

"Could be a coincidence."

"Really? *That's* what you take away from it? Could be a *coincidence?*"

I backed the Beemer up and started pulling out of the parking lot when he not so convincingly added, "Could be."

"Yeah, and maybe you could be point guard for the Miami Heat next season."

"Why do you always have to throw in a dig about my height? How would you like it if I kept bringing up the fact that you're so pussy-whipped you can't think straight?"

"Pussy-whipped, my ass."

"Yes, she has."

"Very funny."

I stopped the car in front of the C-Love Marina office and hopped out to see if Holly wanted to join us for lunch. I said, "Be right back."

He smirked at me and tilted his head to the side. "See what I mean?"

I smiled and flipped him the bird. Two minutes later I was back in the car and as we pulled out of the marina, Tangles asked,

"What, no Holly?"

"No, she's trying to get caught up on some paperwork. I told her about the *JC* though, told her to keep an eye peeled. We need to lay low, *real low.*" I shot Tangles a glance, "Should be easy enough for you."

"What's *with you,* dude? Did Hallmark name this national cut-down-a-short-guy day? Give it a rest."

He was right; of course, I have a nearly uncontrollable habit of taking cheap shots…the cheaper the better.

"Sorry man, you know I'm kidding. By the way, that was pretty funny, national cut-down-a-short-guy day. Pun intended?"

"No, and besides, it's not a pun."

"Sorry, didn't realize you were with the pun police."

"I'm just saying, it's not a pun, all right? Don't you know what a pun is?"

"Of course I do. You want a pun? How 'bout: Once a pun a time I cut down a short guy."

He looked away, rolling his eyes and shaking his head. "Shagball?"

"Yeah?"

"That's the worst joke I ever heard in my life."

"It wasn't a joke, it was a pun."

I started laughing when he stuck his head out the window and yelled,

"Help! Help me!" He pulled his head back in and begged, "Please, for the love of all things holy, no more puns…So, where we headed for lunch, The Ole House?"

"Nope…The Old Key Lime House."

"What? Where's that?"

"Same place, new owner, different name. It's a real mouthful though; I think I'll just keep calling it The Ole House."

"Why not just call it The Old House…you know, for short."

"Same thing, Ole House, Old House, it just has that English touch, you know, like, 'I request thine young maiden accompany thee to Ye Ole House for happy hour.'"

"Shag?"

"Yeah?"

"Your Shakespeare sucks."

"OK, fine, call it The Old House if you want, but it's always gonna be The Ole House to me."

"Didn't you tell me it was the oldest waterfront bar and restaurant in Florida?"

"Yeah, 1886, I think, a good year for Grover Cleveland."

"Well, hellooo…why not call it The *Oldest* House?"

"Tangles?"

"Yeah?"

"Shut up…Anyways, I guess it changed hands a week or so ago, and they've already repainted the place—wait till you see it."

Recalling the end of the conversation I overheard Tangles having on his phone, I asked, "did I hear you talking to your *mom* a few minutes ago?"

"Yeah, I'm flying her down here for a visit with the money I got from Millie. I haven't seen her in a few years and she's having marital troubles with hubby number two. I was gonna ask you if she can stay on the boat with me, it'll only be for a week or so."

"Sure, no problem, but we gotta move the boat. We need to put some distance between the *Lucky Dog* and the *JC*."

"Where you thinking of taking it?"

"I'm not sure, but we gotta find someplace fast. I got a real bad feeling about the *JC* and the guy staying on it."

"Why?"

"Robo said the owner had the guy bring the boat down from Jersey City with a captain who went AWOL as soon as they hit the dock. Problem is, the guy doesn't know spit about boats, he had to have Skeeter dock it."

"That does sound a little strange."

"Yeah, if boats aren't his thing, what is? What's he here for?"

"Shit."

"That's what I said. He's gotta be here to find out what happened to the missing boat."

"You're right; we gotta get the *Lucky Dog* out of there."

As we pulled in to the parking lot of the newly renamed, The Old Key Lime House, Tangles let out a whistle in reference to the fresh coat of ultra-bright neon green paint adorning its exterior.

"Holy shit is that green! I bet you can see this place from Outer Space."

"No kidding. I haven't met the new owner yet, but I'm guessing he might be an extrovert."

I maneuvered the Beemer to the side lot and parked in front of the chickee-hut, a thatch-covered bar overlooking the Intracoastal Waterway. We walked in, sat at the bar, and ordered a couple of beers while we looked at the menu.

Tangles tilted up his 1980s vintage, Porsche Carrera sunglasses, (the same ones he won at the pool table a few months earlier), to admire the derriere of the cute bartender serving us. I don't think he intended for it to be heard, but he let out a clearly audible groan of approval, culminating in a sigh.

The bartender heard it too and as she turned to set a couple of XX Dos Equis in front of us, she looked at Tangles with one eyebrow raised. "You all right, honey?"

Oops, *busted.* I started to chuckle as Tangles flicked his shades back down and nervously tried to feign an injury. "Huh? Oh, uh, yeah. Yeah I'm fine, thanks, just, uh, just tweaked my lower back a little." He leaned forward on the barstool, reached his hand over his shoulder, and started rubbing it around.

With her hands on her shapely hips, she dropped her voice an octave and shot Tangles a disbelieving look. "I thought you said you tweaked your *lower* back."

"Baby" he replied, raising his sunglasses again, "With me? It's *all* lower."

He winked at her and flicked his shades back down as the bartender and I busted out laughing. I even started gagging as some beer went up my nose. What a piece of work. He hated being teased about his height, but had no problem making short jokes himself if he thought it might go over well with the ladies.

Amazingly, it had. The curvaceous bartender with a name tag that read "Kat," rolled her eyes and smiled as she reached her hand across the bar to introduce herself. "Name's Kat. You two must be the guys Rudy told me about."

Tangles slowly shook her hand and replied, "Depends what he told you. I'm Tangles and this is Shagball."

She looked at me intently as she let go of Tangles' hand to shake mine. "I know I've seen *you* here before, but I don't think we've properly met. *Shagball*, is it?"

"You can call me Kit if you want, I'm not picky."

Tangles cut in as she gave me a friendly smile. "Don't call him at all, he's practically married. Me, on the other hand, well, I just so happen to be available. So what did Rudy tell you?"

"He said you guys were on a fishing show and that you were hard to miss." Then she pointed at Tangles. "Unless you weren't on a bar stool, then you were hard to see."

I started laughing again and Tangles got a little miffed. "He really said that? Shit, I thought he was a nice guy."

"I'm just kidding. He calls you guys Squanto and the Lone Ranger—has nothing but good things to say. Hey, here comes the new owner, let me introduce you."

She glanced around the bar to make sure everybody was taken care of as a guy in a lime green golf shirt, navy blue visor, and sunglasses, walked up. Both the shirt and the visor had The Old Key Lime House embroidered on them.

"Hey, Kat, how's it going?" he asked.

"Great, what can I get you?"

Scratching his chin and looking uncertain, he glanced down at the bottles of XX Dos Equis sitting in front of me and Tangles.

"You know? I think I'll have what *these* gentleman are having." He stuck his thumb out sideways at us.

Kat jokingly said, “Gentleman? You must not have met them yet. Let me do the honors.” She held an open hand in front of the owner and then held the other hand open in front of Tangles and then me.

“Layne? This is Tangles and this is Shagball. They’re on a fishing show. Guys, this is Layne, the new owner.”

We shook hands and as Kat bent over to grab a beer out of the cooler, Layne raised his sunglasses a little and mouthed the word “mommy.” I wasn’t sure what kind of relationship he had with his mother, so I did what I always do upon meeting someone I’m liable to have ongoing contact with; I profiled him. He was in good shape for a guy I pegged as being about sixty. He was trim, about six feet tall, with a deep golfer’s tan, and what looked to be a set of gleaming new chompers in his mouth. When Kat set a beer down in front of him, I signaled that we needed another round too and Layne stepped up to the plate.

“Put those on mine, sweetheart.” As she bent back over, he sighed and shuddered almost imperceptibly. Profile update: *potential Viagra abuser.*

With fresh beers, we thanked him and he held his up for a toast. With a dead-on, Latin-lover accent, he quipped, “I don’t always drink Dos Equis, but when I do, I prefer talking like Fernando Llamas….stay horny my friends.”

We clinked bottles and laughed. Tangles and I complimented him on his impression of *The Most Interesting Man in the World*, which was perfect. We shared some stories, gleaning a little background information on each other, and he seemed particularly interested in the fishing show.

“So where do you keep your boat?” he inquired.

"Down at the Water's Edge Marina, in Boynton... for now at least."

"What do you mean, *for now?*"

"I'm looking for a new slip, at least temporarily."

He looked out at the water and said nothing for about thirty seconds; he just nodded his head a little. I looked at Tangles and he shrugged. I looked at my watch while picking up the menu and looked at Tangles.

"C'mon dude, let's get something ordered, we gotta get going."

"You guys haven't eaten yet?" Layne asked. "Me neither, how 'bout some crab cakes? I guarantee you'll like them, I brought my grandmother's recipe down from Maryland...they're *crabulous.*"

"I like crab cakes," stated Tangles.

Then Layne looked at me.

"How 'bout you, Shagball?"

"Sure, who doesn't like crab cakes?"

After chitchatting some more and devouring the crab cakes, Layne said,

"Shagball? I have a proposition for you: how 'bout I let you dock your boat here for free, and in return, you give me some advertising on the fishing show. It'd be a win-win."

I couldn't believe it, it was exactly what I needed, free dockage, even closer to my apartment. "That would be great, but I thought all the slips were taken."

"They were, until after I closed on the restaurant. I guess the reason the last owners sold me the place was the same reason the boats are leaving; the Intracoastal bridge is being demolished and it'll be a couple years before the new one is open. The restaurant owners got scared about revenues falling off a cliff and so did some charter captains. I think it's all overblown though. I've had my eye on this place for a long time. Hell, it's the oldest waterfront restaurant in the state of Florida. Sure, business will suffer a little for a couple of years, but once the new bridge goes up, this place will be busier than ever. So what do you say? You can have either of those slips right there, take your pick." He pointed at two empty slips where the parking lot met the water. I looked at the slips and couldn't help but smile.

"Layne?"

"Yeah?"

"You got yourself a deal."

As we shook hands, he said,"You know, standing here, looking out across the water, is not unlike the last scene in Casablanca, where two unforgettable characters cement a friendship with that great line; 'This could be the beginning of a beautiful friendship'."

"You said it, Layne. I sure am glad you're the one who bought this place, I have a good feeling about it."

I paid Kat for the first couple beers we had, making sure to tip her hard. As we left the bar, I waved back at Layne.

"Thanks again for the crabs and the beer, see you soon."

He pointed his finger at me and smiled, flashing his uber-white chompers. "That's what she said…ciao."

Chapter 13

Eight-Toe Earl was feeling no pain. In fact, he was feeling about as good as possible, having just been given five thousand dollars in cash and a reminder to keep quiet about the digging-up-the-diesel-tanks caper. *No problem.* As he knocked back his third Schlitz malt liquor, he looked around his run-down 1950s-era block house in the Cherry Hill section of Boynton Beach and let out a loud burp. It was something he had been doing a lot of in the few weeks since his wife split to go back to Clewiston and live with her mother. He could hardly blame her; his commercial shark fishing business was in the shitter and the neighborhood had gone from bad, to worse, to God-fucking-awful. Despite its fancy name, Cherry Hill in Boynton was like Overtown in Miami, or like 99 percent of Riviera Beach, it was practically a war zone. Gangs dominated the area, which was so rife with crack dealers and hookers that hearing gunshots was commonplace. The sound rarely brought the attention of the police unless someone lay dying. Even then it could take a while. All the CRA plans to revitalize the blighted area went up in smoke with the economy and the only change occurring was more and more crime, if that was possible— which it was. Despite his linebacker's build, if any of his neighbors knew he had five grand sitting on the kitchen table his life expectancy would be down to a matter of minutes.

Five grand...*wowwwww.* He still couldn't believe it. He stuffed most of it into a Tupperware container and then put it in the freezer next to a box of Omaha steaks. Most of it, that is, because he owed a few people some money, a few people some drinks, and some both. He locked the front door, jumped in his battered, fifteen-year-old Dodge pickup, and headed to the local watering hole, Three Jacks. Once there, he promptly plopped a hundred dollar bill on the bar and the drinks started flying.

***

Skeeter was still a little shaken from the sit-down with his new benefactor, Carlos. The guy had a serious psycho switch. The look he gave him when his eyes turned black and his gums receded, displaying his wolfish teeth, had him in the Three Jacks restroom doing some BVD clean-up. Money was money though, and he needed it like everyone else. The guy said if he came through with some good information, the Benjamin's would be flowing. He wanted to find out what happened to his roommate Ratdog anyway, so why not do a little poking around?

The docks looked dead, so he decided to head into the bar and check things out, even though it was still fifteen minutes before happy hour started. He wasn't two steps in before Eight-Toe stood up from his barstool and bellowed, "Who wants to join me for a shot of tequila?"

The bar only had about ten people sitting around it, and five raised their hands.

Looking at the barmaid now, Eight-Toe continued. "Linda? It is Linda, isn't it?" He squinted at her name tag to try to read it, even though she had been there for the better part of ten years. The name tag read "Lindsey" but she couldn't care less; she saw he had a pile of cash for once and aimed to end up with a chunk of it.

"You want me to set everybody up, big guy?"

"Damn straight, sweetheart. Shots for everybody!"

Skeeter grabbed a seat a few down from Eight-Toe and casually asked one of the busboys what the celebration was all about.

"Don't know what he's so happy about but word is the old lady who owned the C-Love Marina, the one who just died, was really loaded. They just read her will and there's a lot of happy people around. Supposedly her stepniece, who works here, got stiffed, but her other niece inherited nearly everything and some friends and employees were well taken care of."

"Eight-Toe inherited money from old Milfred?"

"Hell if I know—why don't you just ask him? He sure seems like he's in a good mood, been in here buying drinks for everyone for the last hour. He's getting *all* assed up."

Skeeter wasn't exactly friends with Eight-Toe, but he wasn't exactly enemies either, at least not yet. *What the hell,* he decided, *might be worth a drink.* He got up from his stool and walked over to Eight-Toe, patting him on the back.

"Congrats, man, must be nice."

Eight-Toe was in the middle of his third Jack and Coke, and looked down at the diminutive Skeeter with confusion. "Whadda you, whadda you mean, congrats?"

"Congrats on the inheritance. Didn't you get left some money from old lady Lutes?"

Eight-Toe looked at him sideways, then chugged the rest of his drink before slamming his fist on the bar. He wiped his lips with the shoulder area of his T-shirt and smiled. He was reaching the point of no return.

"Who me? Nah, not exactly. Let's just say what comes aground goes aground."

"What ah, what do you mean by that?"

"Forget it, how 'bout a drink? Bartender!"

Just then Hambone came walking in the bar. It was exactly four o'clock and happy hour had officially started. He walked straight up to Eight-Toe, eyeing Skeeter suspiciously after noting the large pile of cash on the bar.

"What's going on Eight-Toe?"

"Hambone! Commere, bud, lemme buy you a drink, whadda you having?" The bartender came back and looked at Hambone.

"What are you having, Ham, the usual?"

"Yeah, hit me with a Silver Bullet."

As she pulled out a Coors Light from the cooler and set it down in front of Hambone, Eight-Toe leaned forward.

"Hey Lin-Linda, set up those girls at the end of the bar with a drink on me. Literally, set it up right here, on me, right here." He pointed at his groin and let out a big guffaw, slapping Hambone on the back. Then he pulled out a wad of hundreds and laid another on the bar.

"Get this little weasel a drink too," he added, pointing at Skeeter. Then he started singing: "There's a Skeeter on my peter whack it off, whack it off. There's another on my brother—"

Hambone cut him short and walked him to the edge of the bar, by the water. "What the fuck are you doing, man?" he whispered.

Skeeter strained his ears to listen in, casually inching his way closer as the bar began filling up.

"Wha-What?"

Hambone looked around quickly and began talking in a loud whisper.

"I told you to keep a low profile, but here you are buying drinks and flashing money around like you just won the lotto! What's the matter with you?"

Eight-Toe's smile disappeared. "I uh, I'm sorry, man, I just wanted to-to have a little fun. Marge, Marge left me. She left me, man, went back to-to Clewston. Can you believe it? She left me, aw shit...whaddem I gonna do, Ham?"

Eight-Toe, the big shark fisherman, started to break down on Hambone's shoulder. Hambone, embarrassed, led him back to the bar.

"C'mon, dude, I'm gonna take you home, it's gonna be all right."

Skeeter watched as Hambone stuffed the remaining money in Eight-Toe's pocket, save for a couple twenties.

"Whadda? Whaddabout my-my truck?"

"Don't worry about your truck. It's not going anywhere."

"Can't leave my truck, man, c'mon, I can, I can drive, where's my, where's my keys?"

Hambone snatched his keys off the bar and noticed Skeeter looking at him. "You wanna make twenty bucks?"

"Depends, what do you want me to do?"

"I'm gonna drive Eight-Toe home, he lives right around the corner, just follow me in his truck— I'll bring you back."

"Sure."

Hambone left a twenty on the bar and handed Skeeter the other twenty and Eight-Toe's keys.

On the way back, riding in Hambone's F-150, Skeeter tried probing for information. "Wow, he was really wasted. Guess that's what can happen when you come into a bunch of money."

Hambone looked at him out of the corner of his eye. "He told you that?"

"Didn't have to, I saw that wad of hundreds he was sporting, everybody did."

"He's in a cash business; it's not that unusual for him to be carrying a bunch of money."

Now Skeeter was looking at Hambone out of the corner of *his* eye. He *knew* what a tough time the commercial guys were having.

"Maybe, but if he has all this money, why'd his wife leave him?"

Hambone pulled up to the bar entrance and stopped for Skeeter to get out. As he opened the door, Hambone grabbed his arm and looked him straight in the eye.

"Why are you so interested about how much money Eight-Toe has? It's none of your business, so keep it that way." He let go of his arm and Skeeter stepped out, looking back through the open window.

"I'm *not* interested, I was just talking…sorry for helping." He slammed the door and watched as Hambone drove off. *Hmmm.*

One thing was for sure, Hambone was worried about what Eight-Toe might have said…*why?* And what was it he *had* said? "What comes aground goes aground?" Clearly, they were hiding something. Carlos told him the whole diesel tank mess was no accident, that somebody in the marina dug them up. Was it Hambone and Eight-Toe? Were there others involved? He looked across the marina at the big Grand Banks and began walking toward it, rubbing his palms together in anticipation of the payday this new information should provide.

Chapter 14

Holly sat in the marina office trying to focus on the financial report she asked for, but couldn't concentrate. Millie's immense wealth had caught her and everybody but Millie's attorney off guard. Things were happening fast, way too fast. She couldn't believe how quickly her life had changed in the few short months since divorcing her husband and moving back to be with her dying aunt. Their desperate plan to stop the marina sale had worked, but they didn't know a third party was involved, and was willing to kill for it. Now it was just a matter of time before somebody showed up seeking answers, and it had her jumpy. She always thought that being financially secure would have a calming effect but her sudden windfall hadn't sunk in yet, and she was worried. She looked down at the profit and loss statement and put it back in the file. It would have to wait.

As she put the file away, Barb asked, "Done already?"

"I wish, I just can't deal with it right now, I'm a little overwhelmed."

"You got a lot on your plate now, honey, why don't you go home and get some rest?"

She looked at Millie's longtime accountant and nodded in agreement.

"That's a great idea, Barb, I'm gonna do just that."

After making the short drive to her aunt Millie's house (now hers), in Ocean Ridge, she had mixed feelings. The bustling home of her childhood was now eerily quiet. No more Millie, no more nurses, no nothing, just quiet. It was empty, and it *felt* that way. She walked through the kitchen and out onto the deck, looking at the Intracoastal. Letting out a big breath, she said to herself, *now what.*

She missed her aunt Millie terribly and couldn't fathom not having her to talk to anymore. Stepping back inside, she opened the fridge for a bottle of water and the doorbell rang. *Who could that be?* she thought, heading toward the front door. Looking through the open plantation shutters, she had her answer. It was her stepsister Sarah with her shady boyfr—scratch that— fiancé, Ricky. *Hmmm.*

She opened the door, and Sarah said, "Sorry to just pop in, but Rick-E and me were wondering if you had a minute?"

Although she was tempted to blow them off in favor of a nap, her gracious manners took over. "Sure, come on in." She held out the bottle of water for display and walked toward the kitchen, following with, "Would either of you like a bottle of water? It's all that's in the fridge."

"I'm good, thanks, how 'bout you, babe?" Sarah glanced at Ricky, who was curiously looking around the front entrance.

"Huh? Nah, not unless you got any beer."

Holly mentally shook her head, still not believing her stepsister was going to marry him.

"Sorry, it's water or nothing…let's go outside and we can talk."

This should be good, she thought, leading them out to the deck and motioning for them to take a seat on the sofa. The unlikely lovebirds sat down and Holly did the same, in Millie's favorite seat. After a couple of seconds of awkward silence and sideways glances between the couple, Ricky looked at her and spoke.

"I, uh, I just want to apologize for what I said in the lawyer's office. I was, uh, I, uh, shouldn't have said what I did…I'm sorry."

Holly was practically amazed, even if she thought Sarah probably put him up to the apology. The incredulous look on her face gave her away, and Sarah cut in.

"I know what you're thinking, you're thinking I dragged him over here but I didn't, *he* called *me,* he means it. He asked me to bring him over so he could say he was sorry." Sarah smiled and kissed Ricky on the cheek, adding, "You'll see, once you get to know him like I do, you'll see he's a really good person."

Holly was even *more* dumbfounded and wasn't quite sure what to say.

"I, um, OK, sure, apology accepted, but to be clear, I had no idea how wealthy Millie was, or what was in her will, I'm as shocked as anybody. It still hasn't sunk in." She only lied a little, she *did* know she was getting the C-Love Marina, but that was it.

"I know that now. I shouldn't have accused you otherwise, sorry about that," said Ricky. Then, he added, "Can I, uh, can I use your bathroom?"

"Sure, it's just past the kitchen on your right." Holly pointed the way and watched as Ricky disappeared into the house. Wanting to change the uncomfortable subject of the inheritance, she asked with feigned interest,

"So, have you set the big date yet?"

***

Ricky walked through the kitchen and stopped where the room opened up to a TV room on the right, with a bathroom in a little alcove. He noted the bathroom window was small and high and the TV room had two sets of French doors leading outside and a non-opening bay window on the back wall. *No good.* He glanced back at the women who appeared to be yakking it up and proceeded straight through the living room and down the hall. He quickly peered to his left, noting a small bedroom at the front of the house, and as he stepped to the right, opened the door to another bedroom, with a bathroom between the two. He proceeded down the hall where he found the master bedroom and bath, which was also accessible by the hallway. He quickly crossed the bedroom to the sliding doors facing the water and looked for an alarm mechanism, like Hanky told him. Finding none, he checked the windows, which were also devoid of any devices. He picked up an overnight bag on a chair, and looking inside, found a pair of cut-off jeans, a couple of tank tops, and some lacy underwear. Smiling, he removed a pair of panties and held them up to his greasy nose so he could take a big whiff. *Mmmmm,* he thought, *what I'd do to that.*

Remembering it wasn't part of the plan and he was taking too much time, he stuffed the panties in his pocket and quickly retraced his steps. He checked the other bedroom windows for alarms and recalled what Hanky told him. "First check for an alarm panel by the front door, then figure out where she's sleeping and unlock a window as far away as possible, one that we can access without being seen.'

He looked back down the hall to the kitchen and could see the women were still talking outside. He stepped back into the front bedroom and looked out at the drive, noting the large tree in the middle of the turnaround and all the dense bushes on either side of the drive. He looked out the side window, and there was a big hedge shielding the neighbors' view. *This is it.* He opened the plantation shutter and unlocked the side window, then closed the shutter. As he stepped back into the hall, he saw Holly about to open the kitchen door, with Sarah behind her. *Shit!*

He stepped into the Jack and Jill bathroom and shut the door, turning on the faucet. He flushed the toilet, splashed some water on his face, and opened the door to find the women standing there.

"You all right?" asked Sarah.

"Yeah, must have been something I ate, sorry." He patted his stomach like it was upset. "I'll be OK."

"Is there something wrong with the bathroom off the kitchen, the one I told you to use?" asked Holly. She was disconcerted to find him on the other side of the house and it was evident.

"Huh? Oh, there's a bathroom back there too? I thought you meant straight down the hall to the right, I must have walked right past it. Sorry, I'm not used to big houses like this. Must be nice having all these bathrooms to pick from."

Sarah could tell Holly was a little miffed, and grabbed Ricky by the arm. "C'mon, babe, we've taken up enough of her time, let's go." She escorted her fiancé to the front door, with Holly following. "Sorry again for dropping in, but Rick-E really wanted to apologize and clear the air. I did too; I said a few things I shouldn't have. I'm sorry."

She squeezed his arm and he added, "Yeah, like I said before, I'm really sorry about blowing up at the lawyer's office; I'm not usually like that. We're all good, right?"

Wanting nothing more than to be rid of both of them and take a nap, she replied, "Sure, no problem, all's forgiven, but next time, please call first."

The couple stepped outside, and Sarah said, "You'll let me know about that thing we were discussing?"

"Yes, I need to get some rest and think about it. I'll need to consult an attorney too, to see if it's even possible, but I'll let you know."

"Oh, I almost forgot," Sarah said. I don't have your cell number."

Holly thought, *be careful what you ask for*...damn. She really didn't want them to have her number, but saw no way out. After she gave Sarah her number and they left, Holly walked back inside and went in the bathroom Ricky used. She sniffed and looked around, wincing with apprehension, but didn't smell or notice anything unusual. She saw that one of the spare bedroom doors was half-open, peered inside, then closed it.

Wasn't it usually shut, like the other one? She walked down the hall to the master bedroom that she had been using and opened the dresser drawer where she had some jewelry. Relieved that it was all there, she suddenly felt guilty for having such suspicious thoughts about Ricky. Still, she couldn't help but wonder if he had been poking around.

Chapter 15

As soon as Tangles and I left the bar I called my buddy Tooda and he picked up on the second ring.

"Shag, what's up?"

"Hey, Cap, I'm wondering if I could trouble you for a favor."

"Depends, whatta you got?"

"I need you to come down to the marina, pick up the Beemer, and drop it off up at the chickee-hut at The Ole House, which is now called The Old Key Lime House, by the way."

"Yeah, I heard. Well, you're in luck, the admiral's here with me at the VFW. I can probably talk him into helping before he goes home. How soon are we talking?"

"Right now, if you can. Tangles and I are moving the *Lucky Dog* to a slip up there, and I need my ride when we're done."

"What are you moving your boat up there for?"

"I got an offer I couldn't refuse and I want to jump on it before anybody changes their mind. I'll tell you about it later. So, you'll do it?"

"Sure, I'm on my way; if the admiral can't help I'll find someone else."

"Thanks, I owe you one. I'll leave the keys under the driver's mat. Do the same when you leave it for me."

"You got it, Shag, catch you later."

"Thanks, Cap." Click.

"Not wasting any time, are you?" commented Tangles from the passenger seat.

"Hell no, not with that Grand Banks called the *JC* suddenly docked next to us. We need to be out of there pronto, for a while at least, and the price is right."

"You're probably right…Damn, I'm gonna miss those Habana Boat waitresses."

"Don't worry, The Ole House has plenty of talent and way more action."

"That's good, 'cause I could really use some."

"You ain't kidding, little buddy."

"What the hell does that mean?"

"It's an endearing term…little buddy…you know, me Skipper, you Gilligan."

"That's not what I mean, asshole."

"I'm just kidding, bro, c'mon let's get the *LD* out of here."

We pulled through the marina parking lot and parked in front of the *Lucky Dog*. I was relieved to see no activity next to us on the *JC*, but you could never be sure with a boat that size. We quickly got on board and after unlocking the cabin, I turned to Tangles.

"Let's make this quick. You get the lines and I'll get the engines started."

"What about the stuff in the dock box?"

"Let's worry about that later."

Tangles scrambled up to the bow and started untying lines while I went up to the bridge and fired the engines up. Two minutes later we were chugging down the canal.

Robo came out to the end of the dock and put his hands up to his mouth like a bullhorn. "Goin fishing?" he hollered, as we turned north toward the inlet.

I turned, nodded, and gave him a thumbs-up. He waved as Tangles climbed the ladder to join me on the bridge.

"We're goin fishing?" he asked.

"I wish, no, no we need to get situated over at The Ole House. I'll call Robo tomorrow and tell him we're going to the Bahamas or something, that we won't be back for a couple weeks."

"The Bahamas would be nice...why *don't* we go there?"

"What?"

"If you want to lay low, well, the Bahamas might be as good a place as any." I thought about it for a second. *Little shit has a point.*

"That's not a bad idea—let me think about it."

As we chugged north I glanced over at Sabal Island and spotted Millie's house on the point. Thinking of Holly, I dialed her cell, but was kicked to voice mail. I hung up rather than trying to leave a message over the sound of the engine. I scrolled through my contact list and dialed my producer's number.

Jamie answered, "El Shagito! I was just about to give you a call."

"Then you owe me one...I wanted to remind you we're signed up for the Lantana Fishing Derby. Bring plenty of film."

"Don't worry, I haven't forgotten. We need some footage *bad*, dude, ever since Tangles joined up with us the ratings are off the hook. In fact, that's why I was calling you; I think we should shoot another segment before the Derby."

I looked down at Tangles in his Kid Rock T-shirt and vintage 1980s Porsche Carrera sunglasses and had to chuckle. He looked up at me and shrugged.

"What about the Bahamas?" I asked.

"The Bahamas? Man, that would be great. What are you thinking? You wanna run over to Bimini?"

"Nah, everybody fishes there, I was thinking Cat Cay, or Rum Cay or somewhere a little more exotic." I knew this wouldn't thrill Jamie because it meant chartering a plane. Despite being six feet nine inches tall, his pockets were a little deeper than his arms were long.

"Hmmm. You know my wife has a friend who recently bought a place over in...Eleuthera...I think... supposedly right on the beach. Let me see what the deal is, maybe I can work something out with them. What's your schedule like?"

I thought about all the money I just put in the bank and how slow the commercial real estate business was. It didn't take long to answer.

"I think I can safely speak for Tangles when I say we're flexible right now."

"Great, I'll make some calls and get back to you."

"All right, talk to you later." Click

"Did I hear you say Bahamas?" asked Tangles.

"Jamie's gonna look into it, we'll see."

"Cool." Tangles reached into his pocket, pulled out his phone, and stared intently at it, shielding the sun with one hand. "Well, that was quick," he announced.

"What's up?"

"My mom just texted me. She's flying in to Palm Beach International tomorrow at three."

"You're right, that *was* quick, where did you say she lives?"

"Houston."

"Can't blame her, that place is like hell…with humidity."

With the Ocean Avenue Bridge in Lantana rapidly approaching, I eased us out of the channel toward The Ole House. Tangles scrambled down to the cockpit and in minutes we were all tied up and plugged in at our new slip. A big burly black man suddenly popped out of the cabin of a forty-six Hatteras next to us.

"I was gonna ask if you two needed a hand, but by the time I got done fixing a drink, you were all tied up." He stepped up onto the dock and we did the same. He extended his huge hand out to introduce himself and I shook it.

"I'm Captain Ferber, but everybody calls me Ferby. Welcome to The Old Key Lime House Marina, where if the fish don't bite, the women might."

"Good to meet you. I'm Shagball and this is Tangles." I let go and the names dawned on him as he shook Tangles hand.

"Wait a second, I *know* you guys, I've seen your show…*Fishing on the Edge with Shagball*…right?"

"That's us," I confirmed.

"You guys are friends of Layne's too?"

Tangles cleared his throat and cut in. "Uh, actually, the name of the show is; *Fishing on the Edge with Shagball* and *Tangles*."

"Huh?"

"I'm just saying, you know, that's what the name is."

I looked down at Tangles with an expression that said, *really?*

He turned up his little palms and shrugged.

"What? Look at the TV guide."

Captain Ferber laughed, then glanced at his watch. "Guess what, gentleman, happy hour's started. How 'bout a cold one?"

Not wanting to be unsociable, especially with a TV show to promote, I readily accepted.

"Sounds great, Captain, after you."

As we trailed Captain Ferber across the parking lot to the chickee- hut, I saw the Beemer waiting, thanks to Tooda. Then I kneed Tangles in his side just hard enough to make him stumble a little. He regained his balance and ran up to me, puffing his little chest out.

"What the hell did you do that for?"

"Don't act like you don't know. 'Uh, excuse me; the name of the show is Shagball *and* Tangles.' You came off like a douche."

"Well, that *is* the name of it."

"I know what the name is, it's my show! *Remember?* Jesus..."

"All right, all right, my bad."

We found three stools at the bar and Rudy walked up with his famous Rudy grin in place. He set a rum and Coke down in front of Ferby and gave him a fist bump.

"Here you go, Bubba."

He looked at me and Tangles and nodded toward Ferby. "When you guys came across the parking lot it looked like Fat Albert in the *Wizard of Oz*. What are we drinking today, boys?"

As we drank a couple of beers and shot the shit with our new friend Ferby, I kept thinking about the Tangles and Rudy situation. So much had happened in the month since nearly being murdered at sea that I hadn't had a chance to ask Tangles about their budding bromance. I had seen Rudy out on the *C-Love* chatting it up with him and knew they'd had lunch together a couple times. Did Tangles suspect Rudy was his biological father? I wasn't sure. Was Rudy thinking the same thing? He had to be, *didn't he?* I watched Rudy as he picked up a tip from a customer across the bar, fist-bumped him, and delivered his trademark line: "Thanks for the justice, Bubba."

I remembered that Tangles' mom was flying in the next day and quietly asked Tangles, "So are you gonna tell Rudy your mom's coming for a visit?"

He lifted his shades slightly and his eyebrow arched a little. "Nope."

"Hmmm. What about your mom, did you tell her you know Rudy? That he lives here?"

"That would be no again." He smiled at no one in particular, and added, "I want it to be a surprise…for both of them."

Chapter 16

After waking from his power nap in the master berth of the *JC*, Carlos made a few calls and arranged for a rental car to be delivered to the slip. It was nothing fancy—a dark blue, four-door Chevy. After providing his fake identification and signing the requisite paperwork, he took a spin and picked up a few things at a nearby convenience store. He had just finished putting some stuff in the refrigerator, when there was a rap on the cabin door. He turned to see the dock rat Skeeter standing there and let him in.

"Good to see you, my friend, I was a little worried you may have had a change of heart after our conversation. I take it you have some information. Please...sit down." Carlos gestured to the leather sofa and Skeeter took a seat.

Although he scared the piss out of him earlier, Skeeter was determined not to let it show. "Yeah, I got some info. I take it you have more cash?"

"Ah, good, direct and to the point. Well, I guess that depends on what you tell me."

Skeeter proceeded to tell him about the gossip concerning the big inheritance that the old lady who owned the marina left behind. He also told him about

Eight-Toe's big wad of cash and drink buying at the bar, and then Hambone's effort to squash it.

"So? Maybe he got left some money. That doesn't mean anything. What else you got?"

"Hang on a sec, I assumed he got left some money too, but when I congratulated him, he denied it. Thing is, everybody knows how bad the commercial fishing has been. In fact, his wife recently left him because of money troubles. Not anymore though, somehow he came into some money, it *has* to be connected to the inheritance everyone's talking about. The other odd thing is that after I helped drive him home cause he was so hammered, his buddy Hambone told me to mind my own business about why Eight-Toe is suddenly cash rich."

"Interesting, so you think maybe they had something to do with digging up the diesel tanks?"

"Could be, guys like Eight-Toe don't have money for no reason, they get paid to do jobs. Same with Hambone, but digging up those tanks looks like more than a two-man job to me, there had to be others involved too. Plus, if they *were* involved, somebody else put them up to it, somebody with some money."

"Or, somebody *about* to come into some money, no? Somebody who would benefit when the deal to sell the marina fell through. Hmmm, let me think about this."

Skeeter watched as Carlos closed his eyes and leaned back in the chair he was sitting in. With eyes still closed, he asked, "You said you drove this man Eight-Toe to his home, and his wife has left him?"

"Yeah, that's right, he's probably passed out—he was hammered."

"Any kids, any pets?"

"No, he lives alone, why?"

Carlos opened his eyes, leaned forward, and looked straight at Skeeter. "I ask the questions here, remember?"

"Yeah, OK, sorry." Skeeter started feeling a little nervous; he didn't want a repeat of the black-eye stare-down, that was for sure. Carlos sensed it and reached into his pocket, pulling out a pair of hundred dollar bills and handing them to Skeeter.

"This is exactly the kind of information I was looking for, good job." He pulled out another hundred and handed Skeeter a pen and note pad that was sitting next to him.

"One more thing, does this man live somewhere not too far away?"

"Yeah, maybe five minutes or so."

"Good, I want you to write me directions to his house. I need to find out who's responsible for digging up the tanks."

Skeeter jotted down the directions and handed them to Carlos, who handed him another hundred in return. He couldn't believe he just made *another* three-hundred bucks on top of the five-hundred the scary stranger gave him earlier in the day. *What a bonanza!* He was gonna find out what happened to his roommate Ratdog *and* get rich in the process. He rose from the couch and stepped toward the cabin door, suddenly feeling a hand on his shoulder.

"There's one more thing," Carlos said, turning him around. "If anybody asks, you never told me anything, never gave me directions, and never did anything but dock the boat for me, right? You don't talk to nobody."

Skeeter patted the hundred dollar bills stuffed in the pocket of his T-shirt and smiled. "Mister, for this kind of money, I won't even talk to myself."

"Good, once I get to the bottom of this, I assure you, you'll *really* be taken care of."

Chapter 17

Skeeter left the boat with visions of swimming in money like Scrooge McDuck. Carlos could tell the greasy dock rat saw nothing but dollar signs, oblivious to what he meant by *really* taking care of him. Oh well, he would know soon enough. He quickly put together a small carry bag containing tools of the trade: a large flat-head screwdriver, a small flashlight, a Taser gun, a garrote, a switchblade, a modified pry bar, and a 9 mm Glock fitted with a silencer.

He needed a couple of other items and remembered the nearby ACE Hardware store he saw earlier. He drove his rental around the corner to Boynton Beach Boulevard and noticed a small pizzeria nearby. Realizing he was hungry, he stopped in and ordered a large pepperoni, then headed across the street to ACE. He picked up a roll of waterproof duct tape, some box cutters, and a pair of latex gloves. Then he did a quick drive-by of the location Skeeter provided directions to. It was a seedy area, for sure, so he scoped out a good parking spot only a half block from the target house.

He drove back to the pizzeria, scarfed down two slices, and took the rest to go. It was just getting dark as he eased the rental car up to the curb, a hundred yards or so from the house. He pulled out the gloves and slipped them on. Then he tucked the Taser in his waistband under his shirt, slipped the switchblade in his pocket, grabbed the small carry bag and the pizza, and left the vehicle. He positioned the carry bag under the large pizza box so it wasn't visible and walked up on the front porch of the derelict wood-frame house. There was a faded yellow bug light emitting a weak glow but other than that he didn't see any lights on in the house. He glanced around but nobody was paying attention. In areas like these, he knew that neighbors tended to keep their heads down and mind their own business. It was how you kept from getting shot. He set the carry bag down next to the door and knocked, then pulled out the Taser and held it under the pizza box.

Eight-Toe *had* passed out on the couch and he was flitting on the edge of consciousness when someone began knocking on his door. His eyes slowly opened and he felt his large stomach rumble as the knocking persisted. Still half drunk, he staggered to the door barefoot and peered out the window to see a guy holding a pizza. Now, he was *really* hungry. *Must be my lucky day*, he thought, as he opened the door.

The pizza guy asked, "Large pepperoni?"

"The large, the larger the better," he belched out. "I was jus, I was jus dreaming about pizza, this's, this's mazing. How? How much?" Eight- Toe started reaching in his pocket for some money.

"Nothing, pal, this one's on me."

Carlos pulled the trigger on the Taser, hitting Eight-Toe in his midsection. Eight-Toe stumbled backward and his knees buckled a little, but he didn't go down. Surprised by his size, Carlos stepped through the doorway and Tasered him again. This time the large man fell backward on the couch, twitching, his eyes rolling back in his head. Carlos quickly stepped outside and retrieved his carry bag. Then he stepped back inside, shut the door, pulled out the Glock, and smashed the butt into the side of Eight-Toe's head.

Eight-Toe woke up to someone splashing water on his face and quickly realized his mouth was taped shut. As his eyes regained focus he saw the dark-skinned pizza guy standing in front of him. Aside from confusion, his next feeling was rage, and he attempted to lunge at the man. Suddenly he felt himself teetering and the man reached out a hand to steady him.

"Take it easy," he said. "You're not going anywhere and you're too fucking big to pick up if you tip over."

It was then he realized he was sitting on one of his kitchen chairs in the middle of the living room, his arms duct taped behind him and his legs duct taped to the chair. *What the fuck?*

"I know, I know, you look a little confused. Well, let me clear things up for you. I think you and some of your friends might have been involved in digging up those old diesel tanks at the marina. You know the one's I'm talking about, no?"

Eight-Toe's eyes got a little wider, but he shook his head no.

"You sure? 'Cause I thought I just detected a little confirmation in your eyes. That's not good, cause that means you're lying to me, and I don't take kindly to liars."

Carlos suddenly noticed the big man's dirty bare feet and let out a whistle. The pinky toe and the one next to it on his right foot were missing, as well as the tip of the middle toe.

"Now I see why they call you Eight-Toe, Seven and a Half-Toe just doesn't have the same ring. Wow, that must of hurt…shark get you?"

Eight- Toe nodded yes.

"I imagine you have some balance issues, you know, missing practically half the toes on your foot."

Eight-Toe didn't nod yes *or* no; he just tilted his head a little, looking confused again.

"You know, I think I can help you with that. Let me see what you got laying around here."

Carlos walked in the kitchen and started opening drawers. "Oops, forgot about the pizza, let me keep it warm while we get better acquainted, maybe we'll have a slice in a bit."

He turned the stove on and then grabbed the pizza box, putting it in the oven. Then he went back to going through drawers. Not finding anything suitable he opened a door that led to a converted one-car garage. Hanging on a hook on the wall was a small pair of garden shears. He put them in his back pocket and covered them with his shirt, then stepped back in the house. He walked in front of Eight-Toe, slipping his hand in his pocket as he knelt in front of him.

"All right, so where were we? Oh yeah, I was just telling you how I don't take kindly to liars. So I'm gonna ask you one more time. Did you dig up those tanks or know who did?"

Eight-Toe was sobering up fast, but he still wasn't thinking clearly. If he had been, he might have nodded yes and told the stranger whatever he wanted to hear.

But he wasn't thinking clearly, he was still half-drunk and in denial, so he shook his head no.

With lightning speed, Carlos pulled the switchblade from his pocket. In one fluid motion he flicked the blade open to its six-inch length and impaled Eight-Toe's left foot to the hardwood floor. With bulging eyes and muffled screams emanating from behind his duct taped mouth, Eight-Toe watched in horror as the stranger withdrew a pair of garden shears (*his?*), and snipped off the two littlest piggies on his left foot. As blood spurted everywhere, the stranger repositioned the shears and snipped off the tip of the middle toe too. He stood up, and proudly said,

"There you go, my friend, now you're feet match, that should help with your balance."

The muffled screams continued as Eight-Toe tried in vain to rip his foot from the floor. Carlos laughed as he walked into the kitchen, and Eight-Toe vaguely heard him opening drawers again as excruciating pain wracked his immobilized body. The stranger returned with some tongs and picked the bloody toes off the floor, dropping them into a Ziploc baggie. He held them inches from Eight-Toe's contorted face.

"I think by now you know I'm serious, so I'm gonna give you one more chance to tell me the truth. If you don't, I'm gonna snip my way up to a more sensitive area. So, one more time, do you know who dug up the tanks?"

The time for heroics was long past for Eight-Toe, and with tears falling from the corners of his eyes, he feverishly nodded yes.

"Good, good, I thought you might come around."

Carlos pulled the box cutters out of the bag and continued his nonchalant spiel. "So, here's what I'm gonna do. I'm gonna cut a slit in the tape so you can answer me. If you scream or do something stupid, well, a few missing toes will be the least of your problems, understand?"

Eight-Toe closed his eyes and nodded yes.

Carlos sliced open the tape covering his mouth and Eight-Toe started desperately sucking in the air. Then he made loud panting noises and spat out a muffled, "Jesus Christ! Jesus Christ! You cut off my fucking toes, man! What the fuck's the matter with—"

That was all he managed before Carlos backhanded him so hard it knocked a couple teeth loose.

"Tell me something I don't know, asshole, and keep it down. So you *did* dig up the tanks?"

Eight-Toe nodded his head and looked down at his bleeding foot.

"Please, man, please put a towel on it or something, you gotta stop the bleeding."

"First some answers."

"Yeah, yeah I did it. Oh, sweet Jesus!"

"Who else was in on it? This Hambone guy?"

"Huh? Who?"

"Don't play dumb with me!"

"Yeah, yeah, it was me and Hambone, we dug up the tanks. Please, please do something!"

"Who else, who put you up to it?"

Eight-toe hesitated just long enough for Carlos to know that whatever came out of his mouth was gonna be bullshit, which it was.

"Aggh! Jesus, it hurts man!"

"Answer the question, asshole, whose idea was it?"

"Uh, Hambone's…as far as I know."

"Now you're lying to me again. That was very foolish."

Carlos knelt down again and picked up the duct tape, looking none too happy.

"Wait! Wait! Maybe it was—"

Carlos slapped some tape across his mouth, picked up the shears, and with considerable effort, snipped off a big toe. Eight-toe felt the crunching of bone and watched in shock and disbelief as another fountain of blood spurted from the tattered nub. Immense pain engulfed him as his eyes rolled back in his head and he passed out again.

When he woke up, there was a terrible smell in the room and he saw the stranger standing over the stove using one of his frying pans.

He looked down and was thankful to see a blood soaked towel wrapped around his foot. Carlos sensed movement and turned to see Eight-Toe looking over at him with pain and fear in his eyes. It reminded him of how much he loved his profession. Being handsomely paid to be grotesquely psychotic was the gift that kept on giving, and he was about to take it to a new level. He turned the stove off and walked back over in front of Eight-Toe.

"You ready to talk straight with me, big guy?"

Eight-Toe had had enough, he wanted nothing more than for his misery to end and he nodded yes.

"Good, that's what I thought. Just answer me truthfully and I promise, no more toe-snipping. In fact, I'll even give you a slice of pizza, smells good, no?"

Eight-Toe was semi-delirious, but not so much that he couldn't tell the house reeked. If it was the pizza, he wanted none of it, and shook his head no.

"No? Suit yourself, more for me. OK, you know the drill, here we go." Carlos pulled out the box cutters and sliced another slit in the tape over Eight-Toe's mouth. This time he didn't say anything, he just breathed deeply.

"You know? I think you learned your lesson, I'm gonna give you a little more breathing room."

Carlos reached up and tore the tape off his mouth, noting the faraway look in his eyes.

"Good for you, not screaming like a little girl… So…you were about to tell me who put you up to digging up those tanks. Don't use the word maybe, though, you say maybe and the shears *definitely* come back out. Got it?"

In a barely audible voice, he responded, "Yeah."

"So, who was the ringleader?"

"Sh-Shagball."

"This Shagball ran the show?"

Eight-Toe nodded yes.

"It was a big job digging up those tanks, who else helped?"

"T-Tangles and…and Kodak."

"Shagball and Tangles and Kodak? You gotta be kidding me, what's with you guys and your names? Isn't anybody named Joe or Frank? Who else?"

He closed his eyes, not wanting to look at the psychopath, and not wanting to give up Holly. Carlos sensed it.

"There *was* one more, wasn't there? Spit it out or they're gonna be calling you No-Toe-No-Dick."

Eight-Toe was done, and he gave her up.

"H-Holly…Shagball's girlfriend."

"Finally… a normal name, but why'd he drag his girlfriend into it?"

"Her aunt, her, her aunt owns, I mean, owned, the marina...Its hers now."

Carlos let out a whistle.

"Finally, it's starting to make sense. Is that it? Is that everybody?"

"Yeah, now please, please just go."

"One more question, what happened to the boat?"

"Wha, what boat?"

"The boat called *The Job*, it was docked in the marina for about a month, then it disappeared. There were a couple guys on it."

"I-I dunno, I dunno anything about it."

"You're lying to me again!"

"No, no, I swear...on my mother's grave! Please, I only helped dig up the tanks, I dunno 'bout any boat. That's all, I swear to God! Don't cut off any more toes...Please! Please don't cut me any more."

"You know what? I actually believe you, so as a reward, I'll give you a slice of pie. You can enjoy it while I tell you a story."

"No, no thanks." The awful smell continued to permeate the small house.

"Lost your appetite, huh? Well, maybe my little story will change your mind. I have a cousin, Felipe, who's about ten years older than me. He was a great rugby player for the Uruguayan national team. Back in October of 1972, the team was on a chartered flight heading to Santiago, Chile, for a match. They never made it. Pilot error caused the plane to crash into the Andes, somewhere along the border of Chile and Argentina. Maybe you heard about it?"

As his foot throbbed relentlessly, Eight-Toe shook his head no, wondering what in the fuck the psycho was talking about.

"No? Well, unaware the pilot deviated from the flight plan, Chilean search and rescue couldn't find the plane. They searched the desolate snowy mountains for ten days before it was called off. All forty-five people aboard were presumed dead, but in reality, thirty-two survived the crash. They huddled in the shell of the fuselage and what little food and water they had was gone in days. By the time search and rescue was called off, eight more had died from their injuries.

"A couple of weeks later they were buried in an avalanche, killing another eight. The remaining survivors considered it Divine Providence that their friends were sacrificed to continue to provide sustenance for them. Convinced they would eventually die of starvation before anyone found them, the two strongest members of the group decided to try to hike their way out. One was my cousin, Felipe. Seventeen days later, after hiking out of the rugged snow-covered mountains, they were found by a rancher. No one could believe that the scraggly hikers were from the missing plane because it had gone down *seventy-two days earlier.* It took two days to relocate the site of the crash, which was nearly forty miles away.

"Again, their story was questioned. How could they possibly have made it forty miles through the unforgiving mountains without any climbing gear or experience? It is a feat that has grown even more incredible nearly half a century later. Of the original thirty-two who survived the crash, sixteen managed to make it out alive. The international press—in fact, the entire world, was stunned to learn they survived by eating the bodies of those who died. Their will to live necessitated they resort to consuming human organs, body parts, and flesh. My cousin Felipe used to tease me that I was soft, that I wouldn't have made it. He said I should be thankful to not know what it's like to have the taste of another human being in your mouth. Well, Felipe passed away a few months ago, God rest his soul, and I never did get to say good-bye properly."

Carlos walked in the kitchen, pulled the pizza out of the oven, and then shoveled the contents of the frying pan on top of it.

"So this is my tribute to Felipe. I wanted to try them raw, but after seeing their condition, I changed my mind. I washed them, pared them, and sautéd them up with a little garlic and butter. Sure smells like shit, but I think I can choke down a slice in his honor."

Carlos walked back over to Eight-Toe and removed the bloody towel from his foot. Then he slapped another piece of tape across his mouth and yanked the switchblade free. Eight-Toe let out a muffled scream as blood poured from the top of his foot. Carlos held the knife in front of him and licked the blood off the blade as Eight-Toe's eyes went wide. He walked back over to the kitchen, cut himself a slice of pizza, and then walked back in front of Eight-Toe. He held the slice up toward the ceiling as Eight-Toe struggled to free himself from the tape.

"To you, Felipe, I know they're not raw, but they'll have to do, Dios los bendiga."

He brought the slice down to his mouth and took a big bite, making sure to get some toe in the process. Eight-Toe strained back in revulsion as a gooey toe-chunk dropped in his lap, and promptly threw up. With nowhere to go, the vomit filled his mouth and esophagus and some of it forced out his nasal cavity. Carlos stepped back and looked on in amusement as Eight-Toe began choking and convulsing. He took another bite, wiped some cheese from his mustache, and commented,

"You know, it's really not too bad, sorta tastes like llama."

Eight-Toe's entire body heaved as it gasped for oxygen, and he tipped the chair over on its side, desperately trying to squirm free. Carlos calmly reached into his carry bag and pulled out the silenced Glock. After chambering a round, he squatted down in front of the writhing, purple-faced, Eight-Toe.

"I swear on my mother's bible I'll cut my own toes off if they ever get that fucking dirty. Don't think I don't have a heart though, I won't let you choke to death on your own vomit; that would be disgusting." He smiled, and added, "I know what you're thinking, really, don't mention it."

Then he shot him point blank in the forehead.

***

The first thing Carlos did after getting back to the boat was to call Donny Nutz and let him know that he found out who the players were. He filled him in about the ringleader named Shagball and his girlfriend, Holly, who just received a large inheritance from her aunt— an inheritance that included the marina. He neglected to inform him that he obtained the information by systematically torturing and killing one of the participants. Nutz's instructions had been very clear; keep a close eye on the girl and a low profile until he got there. Nutz knew from word on the street that he had a capacity for spilling lots of blood and reiterated his earlier directive not to carve anybody up until he got paid. *Oops.*

Chapter 18

It was the next morning, and despite everything going on, I still had a job in commercial real estate that I needed to show up for once in a while. Fresh from a shower, I donned my Palm Beach work clothes: a nice pair of khakis, a custom short-sleeve Brooks Brothers shirt, a crocodile-skin belt, and a pair of fine Italian loafers, minus the socks. I was having a quick glass of juice before making the twenty-minute drive from my Lantana apartment to the office, when there was a knock at the door. I set the empty glass down and headed to the door, briefly wondering if it was my ex-girlfriend Melody about to make another reconciliation attempt. When I looked out the peephole, however, I saw two guys in suits—cheap suits. *Huh?* Practically nobody wears a suit in south Florida in the summertime. Certainly not by choice, which meant they *had* to. *Hmmm.*

Reluctantly, I opened the door and the shorter of the two asked, "Are you Connor Jansen?"

Not good, definitely not good. They didn't look like the kind of guys who would just walk away if I said no, so I didn't try to deny it. I went for levity.

"Yeah, that's me, you guys sweepstakes' representatives? A check for ten million from Publisher's Clearinghouse would come in handy right now. Show me the money and I'll buy you each a decent suit."

The short guy with the crew cut looked at the taller guy with the crew cut. Neither one of them smiled. The taller guy pulled out a badge. "I'm Special Agent Fred Hill, FBI." He nodded at the guy next to him. "And this is Special Agent George McIlroy, we'd like to speak with you in private. Can we come in?"

Oh, shit. I didn't know what to expect to hear from the two guys standing at my door, but it sure wasn't that they were with the FBI. Maybe somebody was pulling a stunt on me?

"The FBI? You're kidding me? C'mon, this is a prank…right?"

"No, sir, here's my card, feel free to call headquarters to confirm our identity."

He showed me a badge and then handed me a card that had U.S. government and the FBI embossed all over it. They both looked official. *Gulp.*

"Uh, what the, what's this all about? There must be some sort of misunderstanding here."

"Yeah, we get that a lot. Can we talk inside?"

I looked around and noticed a couple of my neighbors hanging on our every word.

"Uh, yeah, sure…c'mon in."

I had a one-bedroom apartment, which left little leeway for options as to who would sit where. I took the recliner and they took the couch. The smaller one, George, spoke first.

"Mr. Jansen, what can you tell us about a forty-two foot Cruiser's Express, called, *The Job*?"

My mind was racing, and all I could think to do was stall. So I muttered to myself,

"The job, the job, hmmm, let me think." Problem was, the only thing I could think of was how much shit I was in. I didn't know what to say. The taller agent, Fred, rescued me.

"Maybe I can refresh your memory, it was recently docked at the Water's Edge Marina in Boynton Beach. In fact, it was right next to your boat, the *Lucky Dog*. Ring any bells?"

I wanted to say, 'You have no fucking idea,' what I said was, "Oh, yeah…yeah, *The Job*…Funny name. Yeah, that's right; it *was* parked next to me. What about it?"

"Did you spend any time on it?"

"Huh? Me? No, no I didn't even know those guys."

The two agents looked at each other and the short one took over.

"You didn't know *what* guys?"

Shit.

"Uh, the uh, there were two guys staying on it…I think."

"So there were two guys staying on it, but you never met them?"

"No."

The two agents shot each other a look that said, *This guy is full of shit.* The taller guy continued the questioning. "How long was their boat docked there?"

I felt like I was digging myself a hole…a deep, deep hole. "I don't know, three weeks, a month maybe?"

"I'm trying to work this out in my head, Mr. Jansen. This boat shows up with a couple guys on it, docks next to you for a month, and you never once had a conversation with either of them?"

"Nope."

"So you have no idea who they were, where they came from, what they did, where they were going?"

"None at all."

"You were never on their boat?"

"Never."

I was starting to feel a little better about my situation. I learned in high school that when somebody tries to implicate you in something by going on a fishing expedition, don't give them any line.

"You sure about that, Mr. Jansen?"

"Sure I'm sure, what's this about?"

The agents shot each other knowing glances, and the short guy took over again. They definitely had the short cop/ tall cop routine down pat.

"Mr. Jansen, three days ago, the boat in reference; *The Job*, was found off Nag's Head, North Carolina, by a couple of fisherman. The only part not submerged was the radar arch and some electronics on the bridge. The coast guard towed it in and an inspection turned up a number of bullet holes in the cockpit floor. There were also some blood stains and a 9 mm slug that was pulled from cabin ceiling."

I figured they couldn't detect my ass puckering, but wasn't so sure how good I was at not looking scared shitless. The only thing I could spit out was, "Wow."

"Yeah, wow. So what me and my partner are trying to figure out is; if you never met these guys, or never set foot on their boat, then how come your fingerprint was on the chart plotter? In fact, it was the *only* identifiable print salvaged from the entire boat; the techs said it was wiped clean. Except, like I said, for yours. Maybe you can help us with that. Maybe you can help a couple of cheap-suited FBI agents figure out what happened here."

The other shoe was dropping and I was looking for cover. I looked from the short guy, to the taller guy, and back, trying to determine if they were bluffing. *Shit.* I reasoned they weren't bluffing, because how else would they know to show up at my door? I would have heard if they were snooping around the marina, asking about *The Job*. It was time to start digging myself out of the hole I was in and avoid getting a face full of shoe.

"Oh yeah, *that's* right, the chart plotter, *now* I remember."

"Remember *what?*" asked the taller guy.

"I forgot, one evening I was getting on my boat and this guy asks if I know anything about chart plotters. I told him I only know about mine, a Raytheon unit. He says he has a Raytheon too, but he's having problems using it and asks if I can show him a couple things."

The two agents both started nodding their heads a little.

"So I showed him."

The taller agent looked doubtful. The shorter agent looked doubtful. I probably looked doubtful too.

"So now you're telling us that you *did*, in fact, board *The Job*? That you *did*, in fact, meet one of the people on board, and that you *also* handled their chart plotter?"

A few moments earlier I was the mayor of Doubtville, but the way the agent described it sounded completely plausible and I started to believe it myself.

"For maybe five minutes, yeah." "Convenient... this guy have a name?"

"I'm sure he did, but I don't remember."

"You seem to be having some memory issues. That happen a lot?"

"In direct proportion to how long I've been at the bar. I told you, this was in the evening, it was after happy hour. I was probably a little tuned up, that's why I forgot."

The shorter agent, George, cut in.

"My partner asked you, 'This guy have a name?' And you said, 'I'm sure he did.' Any particular reason you used the past tense?"

"Any particular reason you're giving English lessons?"

"OK, smartass," said the other agent. "Let me tell you what *we* know, and *then* maybe you'll come to your senses and level with us. *The Job* is registered to a corporation controlled by one Donatello DeNutzio, aka Double D, aka Donny Nutz. He's one of the most notorious and ruthless mobsters in recent memory. He controls most of the East Coast; everything from Jersey south, including Florida and parts of the Caribbean. We've been after him for years but somehow he's always managed to stay one step ahead. Nutz is pretty reclusive, if he's not at home, he's at his delicatessen headquarters in Jersey City. Once in a blue moon, he might take his yacht piddling down the Hudson.

"Same thing when he's down here for a few months in the winter. He rarely leaves his condo except for an occasional boat ride. He used to be a hands-on guy, but now he uses freelancers to do his dirty work. It could be because he got too big to do the job himself, he weighs north of four hundred pounds. Nutz also controls a local strip joint down here called Rachelle's, maybe you've been there. Anyways, about five or six weeks ago, around the same time *The Job* went missing, guess what, so did one of his bouncers and a manager from Rachelle's. Do the names, Marco DaVita, or Gino Tortetta, ring a bell?"

I shook my head no, but with a queasy, unsettling feeling, growing in my stomach.

"No? You should hope not, because it turns out Mr. Tortetta is a suspect in at least eight unsolved gangland hits in the Jersey area alone. He's a real bad apple. Guess what his specialty is."

"Uh, I take it it's not northern Italian cuisine?"

"Funny guy, but no, it's wet work."

"Wet work?"

"Yeah, Mr. Tortetta specializes in one-way boat trips. Kinda like a Roach Motel on the water."

"Huh."

"Yeah, huh. So what we're thinking is; maybe old Gino and Marco were taking someone out to swim with the fishes, only this time it didn't turn out so well for them. What it's all about we have no idea, but that's what it looks like."

"Sounds like maybe they got what they deserved."

The tall agent, Fred, shot a sideways glance at his partner, who took over.

"No doubt about it, we certainly won't lose any sleep over it, so what if a couple more mobsters got whacked, happens all the time."

"Sounds like it's no big deal, then. Well, thanks for the interesting story, but like I said, I don't know anything about it." I looked at my watch and it was almost nine. "Look, guys, I have to be getting to work, so if that's it..."

The agents stood from the couch, and the taller one, Fred, paid tribute to the late Peter Falk, *Columbo* style.

"Well, there is *one* more thing."

"What's that?"

"Donny Nutz has been known to hold a grudge. In fact, you could say he holds a grudge the way a skydiver holds a ripcord...He doesn't *ever* let go. We just got word that early this morning he was seen getting into his armor-plated Escalade with his driver and bodyguard. Nothing newsworthy in itself, but when you add in the fact that they were seen loading suitcases in it, well, it got us thinking. Where's he going?"

I didn't say anything, I *knew* where he was headed, and I knew that they knew too.

"What's the matter, no quick comeback? Well, our last update said he was heading south on I-95, in North Carolina. Our guess is he's coming right here, to Boynton Beach, to the Water's Edge Marina, where he has his boat called the *JC* docked. You've probably seen it, a big Grand Banks, parked right next to your boat, just like *The Job* was. Some coincidence, huh?"

"I'm not docked there anymore."

"Since when?"

"Since yesterday."

"So why'd you feel you needed to move your boat, if you don't know anything about this?"

"I found a better place to keep it, closer to my apartment."

"Lucky you. Thing is, even if you *weren't* involved, even if you *don't* know anything, if Donny Nutz has the slightest inkling otherwise, well, maybe you're not so lucky after all. So think about this; if you *were* involved with what happened on *The Job*, hypothetically speaking of course, we could probably provide some sort of immunity from prosecution and/or protection from Donny Nutz. The only thing we would require from you is your cooperation."

"Hypothetically speaking; what kind of cooperation are you talking about?"

"The kind that starts with you telling us how a real estate broker with no criminal background got on the wrong side of the Mob and ends with you helping us nail Nutz to the wall, where he belongs."

I let out a deep breath and considered my options. I didn't see any I liked, and I needed to think. I had to consult with Hambone and Tangles before making any decisions. I had to talk to Holly too, *shit.*

"OK, let me ask around, I need to talk to some people, I'll let you know."

I ushered them out the door, and the short guy, George handed me his card.

"You got our cards, call anytime, day or night."

They turned and started walking to the parking lot, and I said,

"Don't hold your breath."

The taller agent, Fred, turned around and stepped back in front of the open doorway.

"Mr. Jansen? If Donny Nutz gets a hold of *you,* before *you* get a hold of us, *you're* the one whose gonna be needing to hold his breath, *forever*. Got it? He's on his way, so don't fuck around too long. I'd sure hate to see my favorite fishing show go off the air. Have a good one."

Chapter 19

Carlos woke up feeling refreshed. Torturing and killing people had the same effect on him that a day at the spa had on others. That was, as long as his hunger was satisfied and he had a good night's sleep under his belt. He was sitting in the salon of the Grand Banks, drinking a bottle of Zephyrhills, when he saw Skeeter making a beeline across the parking lot. It was a good sign. It meant that Eight-Toe's body hadn't yet been discovered, because if it had, and Skeeter got wind, no way would he be coming to visit him. More than likely it would be a swarm of cops. Carlos was hoping the body wouldn't be discovered for at least a day or two. To increase the odds of that happening, he moved Eight-Toe's pickup out of his driveway and left it a few blocks away, with the keys in the ignition. It was such a blighted and crime-ridden area that chances were the truck had already been swiped. Anybody coming to check on Eight-Toe would notice his truck was gone and his blinds were drawn, and assume he wasn't home. That was the plan at least. Skeeter didn't know it, but how long he lived depended on how long it took the body to get discovered, or when Carlos was through with him, whichever came first.

He opened the cabin door as Skeeter stepped from the sidewalk to the wooden finger dock, which extended out into the water alongside the boat.

"Permission to board?" the skinny dock rat asked.

"By all means, please, my friend." Carlos smiled and waved him aboard and they settled in the salon. Skeeter wasted no time in telling Carlos what he learned the previous night.

"So last night I'm over at Three Jacks and there's this buzz going around. One of the waitresses is the stepniece of the old lady who owned the marina. Word is she didn't inherit anything but a trust fund that doesn't kick in until she's thirty. She and her fiancé are all pissed because the other niece, Holly, got left the marina, the house, the cash, the stocks and bonds, and…wait for it…five million dollars…*in gold*."

"Five million? In *gold?* Aye chimunga, that's a lotta enchiladas. You sure about that?"

"That's what I heard…in actual gold bars, or coins, or whatever it comes in."

Carlos let out a little whistle. "Interesting, and the only reason she got left the marina was because the deal to sell it fell through. And it fell through because someone dug up those tanks. What do you think? You think she was in on it?"

"Probably, her boyfriend is good friends with Hambone and Hambone's good friends with Eight-Toe. Did Eight-Toe tell you anything?"

"No, nobody was there. The blinds were drawn and there wasn't a vehicle in the driveway."

"Really? Man, I can't believe he went out again, that dude was lit up like the fourth of July. He'll be lucky if he didn't get a DUI."

"You're right, some people just don't know when to say when. So what can you tell me about this Holly girl?"

"Not much, other than she's smokin' hot and stinkin' rich."

"Where does she live?"

"I heard she's living in her aunt's house, which is now hers. It's on a point lot over on Sabal Island."

"Where's that?"

Skeeter pointed at the Ocean Avenue Bridge.

"If you go over the bridge to A1A and take a left, about a mile on your left you'll see a sign that says Sabal Island. It's the last house on the point, can't miss it."

Skeeter knew better than to ask if he was going to pay her a visit. Carlos made it abundantly clear who asked the questions and paid well for the answers.

"What about her boyfriend, this Shagball guy?"

"Shagball? That lucky bastard has his own fishing show and now he's got a hot, rich, sugar mamma. It just ain't fair."

"No kidding, so where's *he* live?"

"I don't know, exactly, somewhere in Lantana, just a ways up Dixie Highway. Heard he spends a lot of time at The Ole House, it's a waterfront bar and restaurant up there. If you want to talk to him though, just hang around here. His boat is docked right next to you, right—" Skeeter turned around to point at the thirty-eight-foot Viking called the *Lucky Dog,* but it was gone. "Huh, the boat's gone, he's probably fishing. Anyways, like I was saying, he keeps his boat right here, it's called the *Lucky Dog.* He's got a friend of his living on it, a midget named Tangles. He's part of the fishing show too."

"A real midget? No shit."

"Yeah, I guess he's a wizard in the cockpit, he really knows how to fish and handle a boat."

"Tangles, huh? So chalk one up for the short people. What about Kodak?"

"Kodak? He's a friend of Eight-Toe's, a lobster fisherman, how do you…you think he's involved?" Skeeter caught himself. He was about to ask how he knew about Kodak. *How did he?* Skeeter had never mentioned him and Carlos had only been there a little over a day.

"Just a hunch, I figure it took at least three or four guys to dig up those tanks. Is he a pretty big guy too?"

"Kodak? Nah, he's normal size, nothing like Eight-Toe."

Carlos stood up, stepped to the galley, and grabbed a Tupperware container sitting next to a small carry bag on the counter. He sat back down and smiled at Skeeter.

"My friend, you've provided me a wealth of information. I'm way ahead of schedule thanks to you. I said I'd really take care of you, and I'm a man of my word." He tilted the container toward Skeeter and opened the lid. Skeeter's eyes went wide when he saw it was stuffed full of hundred-dollar bills. Carlos pulled out a wad, not even bothering to count how much was in it, and handed it to Skeeter. Skeeter tried to play it cool, but his hands trembled with excitement as he tried to guess how much was there. A thousand bucks maybe? *Holy shit.*

"Mister? I uh, I really like working for you. Just name it if there's anything else I can help you with, anything at all." He shoved the bills deep in the front pocket of his shorts

"Well, now that you mention it, one of the toilets up front doesn't seem to be getting any water to it. You mind taking a look?"

"Hell no, I don't mind. I'm not much of a plumber, but if I can't fix it, I know somebody who can. Which bathroom?"

"All the way down on the right."

"OK, let me check it out."

As Skeeter walked down the passageway, he couldn't help but wonder about Carlos asking if Kodak was a big guy too. He obviously meant in reference to Eight-Toe, but he said Eight-Toe wasn't home when he went to see him, so how would he know what Eight-Toe looked like? And how did he even know about Kodak in the first place? Something didn't add up, Carlos already seemed to know some stuff. So why'd he pay him all that money? He opened the door to the bathroom, thinking how rich he was gonna be by the time he finally figured it out.

The Colombian watched Skeeter head down the hall. He realized he slipped up by mentioning Kodak, and noticed Skeeter caught it too. Fortunately, he had all the information he needed, and he needed to take care of the dock rat sooner or later anyway. He looked out the cabin window at the concrete dock and parking lot, which appeared to shimmer in the oppressive heat. Everybody, it seemed, had wisely sought refuge from the blistering sun. It was midmorning, in midsummer, in south Florida, and it was absolutely dead on the dock. He turned to the galley counter, reached in his carry bag, and pulled out the garrote. He loved the simplicity of the strangling device and the quiet intimacy it created between killer and victim. *Oh well,* s*o much for keeping the body count down.* He glanced back out the cabin window one more time and not a soul could be seen. Licking his lips in eager anticipation of the futile life-and-death struggle about to ensue, he quietly stepped down the passageway. *It really is dead on the dock,* he thought, *and it's about to get deader.*

Chapter 20

It was hotter than hell in Hanky's cramped storage unit. He had a big industrial fan blowing in a back corner but it just seemed to recirculate the stifling air, providing little relief. He had the overhead door open halfway, trying unsuccessfully to create a little breeze. Hanky wiped the sweat off his face with a dirty rag and leaned forward on the milk crate he was sitting on.

"OK, one more time, walk me through it and tell me exactly what you saw."

"C'mon, man," replied Ricky. "I already told you; besides, it's too fuckin' hot in here, I feel like I'm baking."

Hanky stood and turned around to a cluttered workbench, then pulled something out of a toolbox. With his back turned to Ricky he placed a small piece of crack cocaine in a pipe, turned, and handed it to him.

"Here you go; now you're *really* gonna feel like your baking. Maybe it'll help you remember a detail that'll help."

Ricky took the pipe and put a lighter to it, inhaling deeply. He felt the powerful sensations rushing to his brain, then held the burning smoke in his lungs as long as possible before exhaling.

"Whewwwwww, that hit the spot. Thanks, bro." He handed the pipe back to Hanky, who smoked what little was left and then sat back down on the milk crate.

"C'mon, Rick-E, from the top, what did you notice?"

"Like I said, there was no alarm pad by the front door and none of the windows or doors had any devices on them."

"Good, did you notice any pet bowls in the kitchen or anywhere else?"

"No, I'm pretty sure there aren't any pets."

"Pretty sure? I still got a chunk of ass missing from a place I broke into that I was 'pretty sure,' didn't have any pets. You better be *damn* sure."

"Yeah, I'm sure, a little old lady lived there for the last forty or fifty years, maybe there could be a cat lurking around but I didn't see one."

Ricky proceeded to give a description of the layout of the house, the driveway, the dock, and the adjacent neighbors' houses.

"Wait a sec," interrupted Hanky. "You said the neighbor's house on the canal side had a 'For Sale' sign in the yard?"

"Yeah."

"Do you have any idea if it's vacant?"

"I'm pretty sure it is. The yard looked scraggly and it also said 'Bank Owned' on the sign."

"You see, this is why I had you go over everything again, this is exactly the kind of thing that can make or break us."

"What is?"

"Man? You gotta lot to learn. It sounds like a perfect setup. If the house next door is vacant we can tie up on their dock. That's how we'll get in and out. I got a small inflatable with an electric trolling motor I acquired awhile back. We can drop in on this side of the Intracoastal, pretty much directly across from her house. It's only maybe a quarter mile to cross."

"Why don't we just park in the driveway of the vacant house?"

"Seriously, dude? No more crack for you until the job's done. Ocean Ridge is an island, and Sabal Island is an island within the island. There's only one way in and out. It would only take one nosy neighbor to call the cops on us and we'd be dead ducks. We come by boat and we have a lot more options if something goes wrong."

"OK, so we go by boat, how we gonna do her when we get there?"

"I've been thinking about that. If we can creep up on her while she's sleeping, I say we just bash her in the head and drop her in the water. Maybe the cops will think she fell on the dock and hit the seawall with her head or something. Maybe they'll call it an accidental drowning. That would be best."

"What do we bash her with?"

Hanky pointed to an aluminum billy club propped up against the wall. It looked like a miniature bat, maybe two feet long.

"We use that."

"What if she hears us? What if she puts up a fight?"

"Then I'll introduce her to my little friend."

This wasn't what Ricky expected to hear at all and he perked up.

"Sweet! You're gonna rape her? Man, I'd like to hit that too, but what about the DNA?"

"What the *fuck* are you talking about?"

"Uh, what uh, what are *you* talking about?"

"This, dumbass." Hanky reached into a five-gallon bucket sitting on the floor and pulled out a shiny handgun. "She puts up a fight and I'll cap her ass. *That's* what I'm talking about. We'll cap her and then trash the place, make it look like a burglary gone bad."

"Damn."

"What."

"I was just thinking how much I'd like to rape that hoity-toity bitch."

"Forget it Rick-E, this is strictly business. Once we get our hands on some of that money you can bang all the bitches you want."

Ricky leaned forward and fist-bumped his coconspirator.

"You ain't kidding, bro, I'll be lead conductor of the Ho train— I can't wait."

"Me neither, so here's what we do. We take a little a drive by her house today and make sure the neighbor's place is empty. If it is, we go *tonight,* no sense putting it off."

"Wait, if we have to use the gun, somebody's gonna hear us for sure. Like you said, the cops will be there in no time flat."

"You think this is my first go around? You think I haven't already thought this through?"

"Sorry, dude, I shoulda known better. Obviously, you got a silencer, right?"

"A silencer? Hell no, I don't have a silencer. Those things are hard to come by and expensive as shit. I'll just use a potato; it's the oldest trick in the book."

"Huh? A potato?"

"Yeah, you stick a potato on the end of the barrel and it works just like a silencer."

"Really? You've done that before?"

"Well, not *personally*, but I, uh, I saw it in a Steven Seagal movie. Works like a charm."

"Cool."

"No, *very cool*, and there's a side benefit too."

"What's that?"

"Hash browns."

When they got done laughing, Hanky put another rock in the pipe and fired it up. After taking a big hit he passed it to Ricky and exhaled.

"Wowwwww...This shit is the rock in Rock and Roll. Enjoy it, bro, 'cause this is all we're smoking until we tuck that bitch in a bed of barnacles. Now I'm gonna ask you one more time, are you sure you're up to it? This ain't the same as swiping Schwinns, dude, this is the big leagues."

Ricky set the pipe down and picked up the aluminum billy club. He hefted it in one hand, tapping the meat end of the club in the open palm of his other hand. Then he looked at Hanky, stone-faced.

"Put me in, coach, I'm ready to play. I'm going deep tonight, you can bank on it."

Hanky smiled as Ricky set the billy club back down and took a monster hit from the crack pipe.

That's my boy, thought Hanky.

Ricky held the hit as long as he could without passing out, then slowly exhaled. He watched with fascination as the smoke got sucked out under the garage door, aided by the powerful fan in the corner. It was here one second and gone the next, just like Holly was gonna be. *Poof.*

Chapter 21

I shut the door after the FBI agents left and my mind was racing. I was in deep shit, to put it mildly. If I believed what they were telling me, which I did, there was a ruthless Mob boss on his way down to fuck my world. I had no reason to doubt it, especially after the agents told me the *JC* was owned by a ruthless mobster named Donny Nutz. I didn't know what to do, but I knew what *not* to do, which was go to work. I pulled out my cell and called the office. As usual, my longtime secretary, Jan, answered.

"Well, hello there, running a little late, are we?"

Clearly, the caller ID had tipped her off.

"No, I'm running a lot late, something came up and I can't make it in today."

"Is everything all right?"

"Yeah, well, I hope so. We got anything pressing that has to get done today?"

"That would be a big-fat-*No.* You sure you're OK? You sound a little stressed. I hope it's not problems with your new flame, I really like her."

I knew she was expressing sincere concern, but that would never stop her from digging for a little information.

"No, everything's fine between me and Holly. If you need me call me on my cell, OK?"

"Yes, sir."

"Thanks, Jan." Click.

I did a quick change, jumped in the Beemer, and headed over to the *Lucky Dog* to talk to Tangles. Two minutes later I pulled into The Ole House parking lot and was able to park in front of the boat. Tangles was in the cockpit, cleaning the cabin door, and turned around when he heard me pull up.

"Hey, boss, what's goin on? I thought you were working today."

"Change of plans, let's go inside and I'll explain."

I followed him into the cabin and he plopped down on the sofa.

"So what's up?" he asked.

"What's up is the fucking FBI just showed up at my door."

"*What?*"

"You heard right, a pair of agents just grilled me as to what I know about *The Job.* It was found off North Carolina and they pulled my fingerprint off the chart plotter. Naturally, they had a few questions concerning bullet holes and blood stains."

"Holy crap! What did you tell them?"

"As little as possible, naturally, but they knew I was holding back. Shit! Can you believe it? I woulda bet good money that thing was gonna sink. But that's not the worst part. Get this, the boat is owned by some bigwig mobster named Donny Nutz and he's on his way down here right now. He also happens to own that Grand Banks called the *JC* that docked next to us yesterday morning. From what the agents said, he has a tendency to hold a grudge. We are in some serious shit."

"We? I thought you said they found *your* fingerprint."

"Nice try, you little shit, you're in this up to your eyeballs too…just like Hambone. Don't worry though, if it all comes out, I'll make sure everybody's covered."

"Whadda you, whadda you mean?"

"They offered me some sort of deal. Apparently, they really want this Nutz guy. They said if I tell them what happened on the boat and cooperate in taking him down, they'll likely grant me immunity from prosecution and protection from Nutz."

"What did you tell them?"

"I told them I needed to talk to some people, which is what I'm doing, so c'mon, we have to go find Hambone."

"Why don't you call him?"

"It's the FBI, dude. They might have my phone tapped…I can't fucking believe this."

We jumped in the Beemer and headed down to the Water's Edge Marina to see if Hambone was there. Halfway there, Tangles asked,

"Do the FBI guys have any idea who left the blood stains?"

"Oh, I forgot to mention, more good news. They said Nutz owns Rachelle's, and roughly six weeks ago one of his managers and a bouncer went missing. They figured it's about the same amount of time it might take for the boat to drift up there, so yeah, they know. They also said Gino specialized in one-way cruises, and he's a suspect in at least eight unsolved gangland hits. They correctly theorized that he and Marco were taking someone offshore to get whacked and the tables got turned. What's got them puzzled is how someone with no criminal background like me got involved and didn't end up dead. The Mob obviously had an interest in Slade acquiring the marina. Maybe they were silent partners with him? Shit, I don't know. What do you think?"

"If you take the deal, what does that mean? How do they expect *you* to help nail Nutz? Are you gonna end up in a witness protection program?"

"How the hell do I know? They just sprung it on me. But I can't go into any witness protection program; I'm a fishing show host, for Christ's sake."

Tangles cleared his throat as we pulled into the marina.

"Well, you know, I could always take over the show, until, uh, until you come out of hiding."

I looked over at him and he was grinning.

"You know? You're a pretty funny guy for a munchkin, but go *fuck* yourself."

"Dude, I was just kidding."

"Do I look like I'm in a kidding mood? *Do I?*" I pulled off to the side of the road in front of the C-Love Marina office, hoping to find Holly inside. Tangles waited in the car while I went inside. Holly was in the back office doing paperwork.

"Can you break free? We need to talk."

She looked up from what she was doing. "Wow, this doesn't sound good. No, 'Hi, how you doing, I missed you last night.' What's going on, Kit? Please don't tell me you're leaving town with your inheritance money so you can 'find yourself.'"

I bent over her desk and kissed her on the lips.

"Don't be silly. This is serious—can we go to your house?"

"Now?"

"Yeah, right now. Trust me, it's important."

"Sure, of course, let's go."

She grabbed her purse and told Regina that she'd let her know if she was coming back. Tangles saw us coming out the door and he got into the backseat. We headed farther down the dock and spotted Hambone selling fish out of the back of his truck. I pulled up next to him and rolled down the window.

"Hambone, can you come over to Holly's house right now? We need to talk."

He looked at his watch and then leaned down to see Holly and Tangles piled in the Beemer.

"What, uh, what's going on?"

"Nothing good, and we can't talk here, it's important."

"OK, let me finish up with this customer and I'll be right there."

"Can Tangles ride with you? He can fill you in on some stuff on the way."

"Sure, no prob."

Tangles got out and I drove around the Three Jacks valet circle, past the north canal where I normally kept the *Lucky Dog*. I was looking at the Grand Banks called the *JC* and stopped the car when I saw someone exit the cabin. I pointed at the dark-skinned man as he stepped from the cockpit up to the dock.

"Take a good look at that guy, he arrived yesterday on that Grand Banks called the *JC*. It's owned by the same person who owned the boat that those goons tried to kill us on, *The Job*. Well, guess what? I just found out for sure that the owner is a big-time Mafia boss from Jersey and he's on his way here right now."

"*What?* Wait, where's *your* boat?"

"I moved it up to The Old Key Lime House Marina. I called you yesterday afternoon but you didn't answer."

"I fell asleep and didn't wake up til late. Sorry about dinner."

The dark-skinned guy got into a blue Chevy and took off.

"No worries there, but did you get a good look at him?" I asked.

"Yeah, he looks foreign... with Tom Selleck's mustache. Now tell me about this Mafia guy."

As we drove over to her house I told her about the visit from the FBI guys and she just about had a conniption. I wasn't too thrilled myself.

She said, "You absolutely have to call the FBI guys back and take the deal. This is way over our heads, this is crazy!"

"I'm not sure what to do, that's why I want to talk it over with Hambone and Tangles, they're involved too."

"But Kit, they have *your* fingerprint. Do you think this Mafia guy knows you were involved too?"

"I don't know. I sure hope not. He doesn't sound like the forgive-and-forget type."

Chapter 22

A few minutes after Holly and I got to her newly inherited house on Sabal Island, Hambone and Tangles arrived.

The first thing out of Hambone's mouth when he came through the door was, "The FBI and the Mob? Dude, you sure know how to pick a fight."

"Me? Really? Me? All right, I admit I talked you guys into this scheme, but c'mon, we're all involved here. That's why I wanted to think this through with you."

Hambone looked at Tangles, who nodded back at him before he resumed talking.

"Yeah, about that, on the ride over, Tangles said the FBI came up with your fingerprint, and your print only, *right?*"

"Well, yeah, but—"

"But nothing; we figure we take care of you, we take care of the problem."

Tangles added, "Yeah, no more Shagball, no more problem."

They both stepped toward me, looking serious. Alarmed now, Holly stuck her arm out in front of me.

"Wait!"

Immediately the guys busted out laughing and I had to laugh too.

"You should know by now to never take these assholes seriously," I said.

She looked semi-pissed and gave Hambone a punch in the shoulder.

"I can't believe you guys are joking about this. We're talking about the FBI and the Mob. Kit, you have to take the deal, I don't care what these jokers say, you have to take it."

I looked at the guys.

"So what do you think? What would *you* do?"

Hambone answered, "It's your call, Kit. I suppose if they offer immunity you should take it. I'd want to know more about what they expect in return though, setting up a Mob boss is dicey. Something goes wrong and you're a dead man."

"That's what I'm thinking too. What about you, Tangles?"

"I'm with Hambone, it's your call."

"Shit. If I rollover to the feds I have to tell them about digging up the tanks and queering the marina sale, which started this whole mess. If *that* gets out, well, I can certainly kiss my broker's license good-bye, but that's the least of my worries. Holly could be forced to sell the marina to Slade and she and I would be facing potentially huge civil and criminal penalties. I'd have to make sure *everybody* got immunity and I don't know if they'd go for that. Speaking of everybody, Hambone, you reminded Eight-Toe and Kodak to keep extra-hush about everything, right?"

"Uh, yeah, I did, but, uh, we had a little problem with Eight-Toe last night."

"How little?"

"He was in Three Jacks buying everybody drinks and flashing a wad of cash. He got so hammered we had to give him a ride home."

"Super. So basically he did the exact opposite of what he was supposed to do. So…you and Tangles took him home?"

"Uh, no, Tangles wasn't around. Eight-Toe rode with me and Skeeter followed in Eight-Toe's truck. On the way back to the bar, Skeeter was getting nosy about where Eight-Toe got all the money. It's my fault, I knew his wife recently left him and he's having a hard time with it. I should've figured he'd want to blow off some steam and taken him somewhere discreet. I think I'll go check on him when we're finished here."

"That's probably a good idea. Also, Tangles told you about the Grand Banks named the *JC* that came in yesterday?"

Tangles cut in. "Yeah, I was just telling him in the marina parking lot when we saw a guy getting off it. He was dark skinned, sorta wiry, maybe fiftyish… with a brostache."

"We checked him out too. I don't know what he's doing but I'm thinking whatever it is, it's no good. And Robo said the guy doesn't know anything about boats; Skeeter had to dock it for him. The fact that Skeeter was asking questions about Eight-Toe's sudden windfall makes me think he might be doing some recon for the guy."

"Could be," said Hambone. "But everybody on the dock knows how much Skeeter's been digging for info on Ratdog. He was his roommate and he filed a missing person's report. He's the only one who's convinced that Ratdog disappeared with the guys on *The Job,* and he's right. Maybe he's working both sides; maybe he's trying to dig up something from the new guy on the Grand Banks."

"Well, he sure as shit better be careful about it if he doesn't want to end up like Ratdog," added Tangles.

"This is crazy, guys," said Holly. "Kit, I want you to call those FBI guys right now and make a deal. I don't care if it costs me the marina. I don't want to be responsible for anybody else being killed, especially you three."

She was probably right; I probably should have called the FBI. But I probably should have done a lot of things in life that I didn't. If I'd done what my mom wanted me to do, I'd probably be some schmuck lawyer working for Bendham, Dickem, and Goode. *Not in this lifetime.* If I did what my dad wanted me to, I'd probably have an engineering degree, working in a fifty-year-old coal-fired power plant on the Ohio River...probably battling depression and lung disease. *No thanks.* Thing is, I'm just not good at being told what to do. *Who is?* I seem to have some sort of ingrained response built in. Tell me to do this, and I'll do that. Tell me I can't do something, and I'll definitely give it a go. Maybe I was being a bit selfish but if I were to call the FBI, my life, as I knew it, would be over. No more fishing show, no more commercial real estate, no more freedom, no more fun. As far as I was concerned, calling the FBI was an absolute last resort. It would still be another day before Donny Nutz was in town, so I figured I had a little time before a decision needed to be made.

"The FBI said that Nutz was in North Carolina. Even *if* he drives straight through, he won't be here till tomorrow morning. We don't know exactly what he wants anyways. Let's wait and see what happens when he gets here. There's no sense in panicking...yet."

Holly didn't like my response.

"Are you crazy? You said it before; he's going to want payback. He's going to want compensation for the boat and the guys and who knows what else? If it was just money, I could give it to him, but you said the FBI guys told you he's known to hold a grudge."

"Did I say that?"

"Quit trying to be funny. Yes, that's exactly what you said. Even if I pay him off, there's no guarantee he won't seek revenge just to maintain his reputation."

"True, but he's probably not going to whack anybody until he gets paid, wouldn't make sense."

"Oh, that's just great. He's 'probably not going to whack anybody until he gets paid.' Are you listening to yourself? Are you willing to bet your life, or mine, or anybody else's, on *probably?*"

"Maybe...probably...at least until tomorrow. Remember, the FBI only *suspects* me. They don't know anything about anyone else at this point and Donny Nutz doesn't know anything at all, as far as we know."

Tangles came to my defense. "He's right, Holly. Maybe we should just play it by ear, no sense getting all worked up about it."

Somehow I knew that wasn't going to sit well with her, and I was right.

"Oh-my-God...You're like his mini-me. I should start calling you Shagsmall! What's the matter with you two? Did you forget about the dark-skinned guy on the Grand Banks? He's been here since *yesterday* and maybe Skeeter's helped him find something out. Maybe he already knows *everything*. Maybe that's why this Mafia boss is coming down. Didn't you two brainiacs think about that?"

Actually, she was right. But what I was really thinking about was how damn sexy she looked when she got all worked up. Me taking advantage was looking less and less likely though. Especially after I put my foot in my mouth by saying,

"That's a lot of maybes."

If looks could kill, I would've been dead before I hit the floor. *Oh, shit.*

"That's it! Get out of here, all three of you. I don't want to see anybody until you've called the FBI, I'm not kidding. And don't wait too long or I'll call them myself, got it?"

Hambone started to say something, but she cut him off with the grace of a machete-wielding yard monkey. Hambone was first out the door with Tangles on his tail. I probably should have followed, but once again my stubbornness was in charge.

"All right, just calm down now, let's talk this—"

"The time for talking is done, Kit. It's time to act. Either call the FBI, or get out."

I took a step toward her with my hands open, semi-pleading. "Can't we just—"

She slipped one of her sandals off and raised her arm like she was going to throw it at me.

"I swear I'll throw it and the next thing I bean you with will hurt a lot more. So what's it gonna be, Kit, the FBI, or the door?"

"C'mon, sweetie, you're not gonna—"

"Throw it?" she said, as she whizzed the sandal at my head. I ducked and it knocked a table lamp over by the door. *Crap.* I turned toward the door and fled as she launched her other sandal, which smacked the door behind me.

Hambone and Tangles were standing at the edge of the driveway and apparently heard every word through one of the screen windows.

"You're a real charmer, bro," said Tangles. "I'll never know how you hooked up with her in the first place."

"You got a lot to learn about women, Kit," chimed in Hambone. "The only time they take their shoes off is to bathe, sleep, or get a pedicure. You see those puppies coming off in an argument, head for cover."

"Damn, she's really upset."

"And she's gonna stay that way until you call the FBI. So, are you gonna do it?"

"Probably…she was right about the guy on the Grand Banks…and Skeeter. Maybe they know more than we think. Why don't you track down Skeeter and feel him out about what they know. I didn't think Skeeter was helping him, but at this point I'm not so sure. Who knows? This is *all* assed up and now I got Holly pissed at me too. Shit."

"All right, I'll have a little chat with Skeeter and then I'll check up on Eight-Toe to make sure we don't have a repeat performance of last night."

Hambone got in his truck and split, and Tangles and I did the same. As we left Sabal Island and pulled up to A1A, I instinctively turned north, toward Lantana.

"Where we headed?" asked Tangles.

"Good question…After the will reading I thought we were headed down Smelling Like a Rose Boulevard but now it looks like we're on Fuck Street and we need to find an exit fast."

Chapter 23

With everything going on, I forgot all about Tangles' mother flying in. So after we had a late lunch I drove him to the airport to pick her up. I would have preferred to loan him the Beemer but without some sort of contraption attached to the gas and brake pedals, no way could his tiny legs reach them. We sat in the cell phone parking lot at PBIA waiting for her to call and discussed our plight.

I pointed out to Tangles that we still didn't know exactly why the Mob got involved in the first place. It seemed unlikely that the owner of Three Jacks (Slade), would partner with them to buy the marina. We had to be missing something.

"You're right," agreed Tangles. "It's understandable that Sonny might have got in a bind and needed to borrow some money without going to daddy, but once he paid them off, that would be the end of it. The Mob would only care about getting their money back, not whether the marina deal closed or not."

"I know, I just can't figure it out, I wonder if the FBI has any idea."

"Who knows? Bottom line is we destroyed a Mob boss's boat and killed his help. It really doesn't make a difference at this point."

"Yeah, but it might give us an edge if we knew what the deal was."

Tangles' phone started playing a Kid Rock song and he answered it. "OK, Momma, we'll be right there." He closed the phone and looked at me. "Continental baggage claim."

We pulled through the terminal until Tangles pointed at a slender lady standing by the curb with two large suitcases.

"That's her."

I eased the Beemer to a stop and Tangles popped out of the car.

"Tino!" she cried. "My little Tino!" She rushed forward and knelt down to give him hugs and kisses. *Tino?* I thought. *Of course,* it had to be short for Langostino, his real name.

"I missed you too, Momma, but please don't call me little Tino. You know I never liked that name." He was smiling, though, and I could tell he was happy to see her.

Noting the large suitcases, I put the top down so we had somewhere to put them. Tangles managed to cram one of the suitcases in the small trunk and I got out of the car to hoist the other in the backseat.

"Baby? Aren't you gonna introduce me to this nice-looking gentleman who was kind enough to pick me up?"

I smiled and took a good look at her. She was about five foot seven and maybe a hundred and twenty pounds. Her hair was auburn colored and she resembled the actress Sela Ward, but a little rougher around the edges.

"Momma, this is Shagball. Shagball, this is my momma, Marie Dupree."

I shook her hand. "Pleased to finally meet you, Marie, Tangles has told me a lot about you, and yes, it's all been good."

Marie slid into the passenger seat and Tangles climbed in the back, next to one of her suitcases.

"Tangles, you say?" She raised an eyebrow over the top of her sunglasses.

"I told you on the phone, Momma, it's my new name, it's the one we use on our fishing show…*Fishing on the Edge with Shagball and Tangles.*"

"Ah, yes, the infamous *Shagball*, so *you're* the one who made my little Tino a star. I always knew there'd be big things in store for him. You can't keep a good man down, even a little one like my Tino."

"Momma I'm right here, please quit talking like I'm not. I hate that almost as much as I hate being called Tino. From now on, can you please just call me Tangles? Please?"

"Baby, I'm so glad to be here I'll call you Mr. Bo Jangles if you want. This trip couldn't come at a better time for me; business back in Biloxi has been slow to recover. You know, between rebuilding after Katrina and the economy and all."

"Biloxi? What are you talking about Biloxi? What happened to Houston?"

"Oh, yeah…I guess I forgot to mention, I moved back to Biloxi about a year ago.

"What?"

"Yes, siree. I'm back dealing blackjack and I'm single again."

"WHAT?"

Marie held her left hand up.

"You don't see a ring, do you, honey?"

"Why…why didn't you…why didn't you tell me?"

"I didn't want you to worry about your momma while you were doing so well on the cruise ships. You should know by now I can take care of myself. I'm like a cat; I always land on my feet."

"Sure you do, Momma, but sometimes you land in the kitty litter."

Marie and I both laughed.

"Well, if you're talking about my choice of husbands, no argument here. Live and learn, baby, that's all a girl can do. Oh, honey, I'm so happy to see you!" She twisted around in her seat and pulled Tangles toward her by the back of his neck so she could plant a barrage of kisses across his face.

Tangles struggled to pull back and protested, but he was smiling. "Stop it momma! You're getting lipstick all over me."

As we passed through Lake Worth on Federal Highway, Tangles had me pull into a Chase branch so he could get some money. When he disappeared into the bank, Marie turned to me.

"Thank you so much for helping out Tino. He had a tough home life growing up, not to mention all the teasing he got at school because of his size. From what he told me on the phone and seeing him now, it looks like he's happier than he's been in a long time."

"No thanks are necessary. He's probably the finest deck hand I've ever seen and the fishing show has really taken off since he came on board. Still, if he wasn't good people, he wouldn't be on the show. You did a fine job raising him. You should be proud."

"I am. I only wish I could spend more time with him, he's all I've got…Has, has he been seeing anybody?"

"Well, I know he had a girlfriend on the cruise ship he was working on but it didn't work out. He's dated a few local gals but I don't think anyone he would classify as a girlfriend. I'd say he's definitely single at the moment. I wouldn't worry about his love life though; he seems to do just fine. Especially when he starts singing, watch out."

Marie started laughing. "Tino always had a beautiful singing voice, it's a shame he gets treated as a novelty act because of his size. What about you, though? I don't see a ring on your finger either. I take it there's no Mrs. Shagball?"

Now it was my turn to laugh. "No, but I do have a girlfriend and I'm sure you'll get a chance to meet her. She's also a big fan of your son. Speak of the devil, here he comes."

Tangles came bounding up to the Beemer and dropped an envelope in his mom's lap before launching himself into the backseat.

His mom opened the envelope and started fingering through the bills inside. "Oh, my! Honey, the ticket was only six hundred dollars, like I told you. There's three times as much in here."

"Momma, I told you I was paying for the trip and that includes a little spending money. Besides, I just got an unexpected windfall, so don't worry about it. There's a great bar next to the boat we're staying on and we're almost there. If it makes you feel better you can pick up the tab."

She turned to face Tangles and reached her hand toward him.

"Come here, sweetie."

"Aw, not again, Momma…*really*?"

Tangles leaned forward despite his feigned reluctance and his mom gave him a big fat smooch on his cheek.

"You know you didn't have to do that, honey, but thanks…and yes, the drinks are on me."

A couple of minutes later I announced our arrival. "Here we are."

We pulled into The Ole House parking lot and stopped in front of the *Lucky Dog*. I grabbed the suitcase out of the backseat and Tangles got the one in the trunk. We started schlepping Marie's luggage toward the boat and she asked, "This is the boat?"

"Yep," replied Tangles. "She's a beauty, huh? You can't imagine all the fish we caught on it, but don't worry, you don't have to, 'cause we got it on tape."

We put her luggage in the cabin and Marie said she wanted to freshen up.

Tangles said, "Momma, if you need to use the head, let's go next door and you can use one of the ladies' rooms. We try to keep the holding tank as empty as possible."

We walked across the lot and I suggested to Tangles that he take his mom around to the ladies' room inside the front entrance, theorizing it was likely to be cleaner than the one by the chickee-bar. As they looped around the front of the building, I peeled into the chickee-bar. The bar was in full swing and Rudy was working his magic. I found two empty barstools and sat on one of them. Moments later, Rudy approached.

"What'll it be, Bubba? Bud Light?"

"Sounds good to me."

He set one on the bar and cocked an eyebrow.

"So where's your littler half?"

"He's here; he'll be by in a minute. Set him up with a beer too, I'll save him a seat."

"You got it, Bubba."

Rudy set another Bud Light down in front of the stool next to mine and went about serving the other customers. I couldn't wait to see what would happen when Tangles' mom walked up. A few minutes later, it happened. Rudy was facing the parking lot, talking to one of the locals, and Tangles and his mom approached from inside the restaurant. I slid off my chair and offered it to his mom, who thanked me and took my seat.

Tangles took the empty barstool next to her and pointed at the Bud Light. "Is this mine?"

"Yeah, but I didn't know what to get your mom."

"Momma? You still drinking those whiskey sours?"

Tangles' mom had her purse on the bar and was using a little makeup mirror to recheck her face.

"You know it, honey," she answered, while peering into the tiny mirror. "Double whiskey sour, hold the cherries."

Tangles saw that Rudy was bullshitting with one of the locals and called out to him. "How 'bout a little help, partner."

Just as Rudy turned around, Tangles' mom went to put the mirror in her purse and it slipped out of her hand, falling to her feet. She bent down to reach for it and Rudy fist-bumped Tangles.

"Hey, Bubba, you need a shot to go with that beer?"

"No, I need a double whiskey sour, hold the cherries."

Rudy did a double take.

"Bubba, there's only one person I know who drinks that and that's—"

"Marie Dupree?" said Tangles.

Then he held his hand out for his mom to hang on to as she sat back up on the stool clutching her makeup mirror. It was like two deer looking at each other in the headlights. They were both frozen in time, completely speechless. The spell was temporarily broken when Tangles' mom dropped her mirror for the second time, this time on the bar.

"Marie? My God, Marie? Is it *you*? Sweet mother of Moses," mumbled Rudy.

"R-Rudy? My, my Rudy…Tutti? Oh, Lord, oh dear Lord. I think, I think I'm gonna faint." She started to tilt to one side, so I stepped behind her and grabbed her shoulders.

Tangles cried, "Don't just stand there, Rudy, get her that drink!"

Rudy snapped out of it and whipped up a whiskey sour in record time. He set the drink down in front of Marie and her hand was trembling so badly that a good amount spilled on the bar before it reached her mouth. She winced at the first big gulp and looked wide-eyed at Rudy.

He confessed, "I took the liberty of making it a triple."

"So, I guess it's true, then; you two really do know each other," commented Tangles. His mother took another large gulp and set her drink down, her hand still trembling.

"You *know* him?" she asked. "You, you know him, and know he works here? And you…you didn't tell me?"

"I thought it would be a nice surprise, for both of you."

She grabbed her drink and knocked back the rest of it in one final gulp.

"Flowers are a nice surprise, honey, Jesus H. Christ; I almost had a heart attack."

Rudy reached down below the bar and quickly made her another drink.

"It's just a double this time. I can't *believe* it's you, Marie, you look fantastic…you always did." He reached his hand across the bar and put it on top of hers. She put her free hand on top of his and smiled.

"I-I can't believe it's you either, you haven't changed at all. My God, it seems like it's been forever."

One of the waitresses yelled for Rudy and he gave her a hand signal.

"Don't you *dare* leave this bar, Marie Dupree, I'll be back as soon as I get caught up."

Rudy went back to serving drinks at a record pace. He had a bounce in his step I had never seen before. Tangles' mom said, "So…so you know about me and Rudy?"

"Yeah, small world, huh?"

"What, uh, what exactly did he tell you?"

"That he used to run around with you back in Biloxi, when you were working at the casino. He really had a thing for you and by the looks of it, I'd say he still does. I've gotten to know him pretty well, he's a nice guy. In fact, he's a helluva lot nicer than *Dad* ever was. How come it didn't work out?"

I was standing behind them looking around the bar, pretending not to listen. In reality, I was glued to every word. According to Rudy, Tangles' dad was impotent, but Tangles didn't know it. Rudy thought Marie must have divorced and remarried in order to have kids. It had to have occurred to him that he might be Tangles' real father, but he couldn't know for sure. The only one who knew was drinking double whiskey sours and she looked mighty flustered.

She said, "Honey, I need to use the bathroom."

"Go straight back by the pool table, on your right." Tangles pointed the way and his mom headed off. I noticed Rudy watching out of the corner of his eye. Tangles flagged Rudy down for a couple more beers and then swiveled his stool around toward me.

"Man, that was classic! Did you see the looks on their faces? I bet Rudy shit his pants. Seriously, dude, I bet he heads to the restroom at any minute to lose his drawers."

"You definitely pulled one over on them, that's for sure."

Rudy set us up with a couple of beers and quickly checked everybody's drink at the bar. I saw him talk to one of the waitresses who nodded and ducked under the bar. Rudy set his bar towel down and headed toward the restroom. Tangles saw it too and laughed.

"See, there he goes. Bet if I go in there next I'll find a pair of crapped up Jockeys in the trash can. He'll be working the rest of his shift commando style."

Tangles swiveled back around just before his mother came out of the ladies' room. I watched as

Rudy walked up to her and put his hands on her shoulders. Then he led her toward the corner of the inside bar. Tangles was hitting on the waitress that was covering for Rudy and didn't notice. I kept stealing glances toward Rudy and his mom, who were now very animated in their conversation. At one point, Rudy pointed directly at Tangles. Marie nodded and said something, and then Rudy put one hand on his forehead and the other on the corner of the inside bar. It looked like he was trying to steady himself. Marie put her arm around him and said something in his ear. Rudy covered his face with both hands and then lowered them as he and Marie shared a tender kiss and embraced. Tangles was focused on the assets of Rudy's stand-in bartender and missed the whole thing. *Holy moley,* I thought. *There's Shaq-sized shoes dropping all over the place.*

Chapter 24

Carlos was exhilarated. Two kills within twenty-four hours had him all amped up. He was also starving; having eaten only two slices of pizza the night before and a couple of semi-disgusting bites of a toe-laden third slice. He drove his rented Chevy south on Federal Highway, looking for a fast-food place. He spotted a McDonald's and stopped in for a cup of coffee and a breakfast platter. With his stomach no longer growling, he decided to check out Sabal Island. Skeeter told him the girl that inherited the marina was living in a house there. He crossed over to A1A and headed north a mile or so before seeing the entrance sign on the Intracoastal side of the road. He crossed over a small bridge, noting the waterfront homes on either side of the canal. The road ran in a loop, with waterfront homes on the outside of the loop and interior homes in the middle. He could go clockwise, or counterclockwise, and chose to head straight, which put him on the counterclockwise path.

As he rounded the first turn, a beat-up old Tacoma pickup heading in the opposite direction almost clipped him. He swerved just in time and saw the wide eyes of a couple of greaseballs staring at him through a dirty windshield. He muttered a Spanish expletive and watched in his rearview mirror as the pickup disappeared around the bend. He slowed the car to a near crawl, remembering that Skeeter said Holly's house was at the end on the point. As he crept along, he saw a couple of "For Sale" signs on both sides of the road. He got to the end of the island where the road looped back toward the entrance and he could just barely see a house tucked away amid dense foliage.

As he followed the road leading away from the house on the point, he saw a "For Sale" sign by the mailbox of the adjacent house. It said "Bank Owned" on it and listed a phone number. He backed the car up a little and pulled into the driveway of the property, positioning the Chevy behind a hedge that kept it out of view from the road. He saw that the front door had a black box on the doorknob and he had an idea. He pulled back out to the street and looped around the little island again, writing down the names of a couple of real estate companies that had "For Sale" signs up. He pulled back in to the bank-owned house adjacent to the home on the point lot and again parked the Chevy behind the privacy hedge. He pulled out his cell and dialed the number on sign. A few moments later a female voice answered.

"Good morning, this is Realty Liquidators, how may I help you."

Carlos had his little cheat sheet sitting on his lap with the names of the other real estate companies he jotted down. He picked one and began his spiel.

"Yes, this is Ronaldo Samuels with Illustrious Properties. I am with a client who would like to see your property at 25 Sabal Island Drive, in Ocean Ridge."

"Please hold one moment while I connect you with the listing agent."

A minute or so later the listing agent got on the phone and Carlos repeated his spiel to him. The listing agent asked, "You say you're with Illustrious Properties?"

"Yes, I just showed several properties on Sabal Island to my clients and we are in front of your listing right now."

"I'm afraid I'm tied up at the moment, but you can show the property yourself. The house is vacant and it's on a lockbox. The code is two, four, six, eight. If you would, please leave your business card on the kitchen counter when you're done."

"Of course, thank you, my friend." Click.

Carlos smiled as he exited the vehicle and then stepped up to the front door. He punched in the code on the antiquated metal black box and quickly removed the key. Moments later he was milling through the waterfront home. He looked out the back toward the canal and the boat dock, and then closed the blinds on the sliding glass door. He systematically went through the entire house, making sure to close all the shutters and blinds. He worked his way upstairs to the south side of the house and found a bedroom with a window facing the neighbor on the point. He looked out the window and it had an excellent view of the back and side of the house next door. He nodded and went back downstairs through the kitchen to the garage. He opened the door to the garage and flicked a light switch on, illuminating the space. It was empty, and big enough for two cars. It had a workbench along one side and a large freezer on the other side. He walked over and lifted the top of the freezer, noting it was only about a quarter filled with packages. He reached in and pulled one out, seeing that it contained some type of frozen fish labeled "Ballyhoo." He dropped it back in and closed the lid, relishing the feel of the icy air swooshing out on his skin.

He walked across the garage and opened a door leading to the side yard from the garage. There was a big hedge separating the property from the house on the point next door. He walked along it and found a break in the hedge where there was some pool pump equipment and an air conditioning unit. There was a chain-link fence about four feet high that ran along the backside of the hedge, from the street, all the way to the water. He stepped back through the side garage door and locked it up. Noting a large button next to the light switch, he pushed it and the garage door began opening. He quickly pushed it again and it closed. There was a remote controlled garage door opener hanging on a hook next to the big button. He lifted it off the hook and pressed it, and the garage door opened again. He pressed it again and the door closed. Satisfied, he slipped the garage door opener in his pocket and walked back to the front door. He shut the door behind him, locked it, and put the key in his pocket. He relocked the empty lockbox and drove away, pleased with his progress. Donny Nutz told him to keep a close eye on the girl, and he couldn't get much closer than watching from the next door neighbor's. He was looking forward to nightfall and getting a good look at the girl next door. Donny Nutz was paying him well, but five million dollars in gold changed *everything*. Somehow, someway, he was going to get his hands on it, and God help anyone that got in his way.

Chapter 25

Holly was still flustered as she walked into attorney Bob Boone's office. She couldn't believe Kit didn't call the FBI and seek immunity and protection. The fact that she was so upset she hurled her shoes at him told her something else too. Something she wasn't prepared to admit after only a couple of months into their relationship. Namely, that she was falling in love with him.

She stepped into a waiting area and the receptionist picked up a phone to contact Bob Boone and announce her arrival. A minute or two later the stately attorney came walking down the short hallway and greeted her.

"Miss Lutes, please, come this way." He shook her hand and she followed him into his richly appointed office. He took a seat behind a large oak desk and signaled for her to use one of two leather chairs in front of it. After she settled in, he smiled.

"So, how does it feel to be a very wealthy woman?"

"It hasn't really sunk in yet."

"Well, perhaps it will after we get this paperwork done and Millie's accounts are transferred over to yours. So let's get to it."

Holly handed the attorney some documents with her personal bank and brokerage account information. There was a lot of paperwork filled out and she signed her name numerous times. After about twenty minutes of signing and paper shuffling, Bob Boone leaned back in his high-back leather chair and sighed.

"I think that just about does it."

"Great, thanks for all your help; I'm sure I'll have more work for you in the future." She rose from her chair and extended her hand toward him. He made no move to shake it; rather, he held his hand out palm first, indicating for her to stop.

"Not so fast, young lady. You're forgetting one very important matter."

"What's that?"

"The gold."

"Oh, oh of course, is there a safety deposit box or something?"

"Actually, I have no idea."

"*What?*"

"Please, Miss Lutes, have a seat."

She sat back down and said, "It's Holly, please, so what are you saying, there really *isn't* any gold?"

"Oh there's gold all right, a lot of it. I just don't have any idea where she has it."

"Then how do you know she even had any? She just *told* you she had gold?"

"No, I bought a lot for her."

"What?"

"Over a twenty-year period, starting around nineteen ninety, I personally acquired over a hundred and sixty pounds of gold for her. She started out buying ten-ounce bars when the price was around three hundred and fifty dollars an ounce. She even bought some two-pound kilobars when the price dipped below three hundred. Once the price rose to over five-hundred an ounce, she started buying Krugerrands, and stopped buying altogether when the price hit eight hundred an ounce. I guess she figured she had enough. Naturally, I thought she was crazy when she started, and tried to talk her out of it. Shows what I know, the price of gold today is floating around eighteen hundred an ounce, which is how I came up with the five million dollar number."

"And you have no idea what she did with it?"

"Oh, I have a few ideas, but I don't know for sure. I urged her to put the gold somewhere safe, like in a bank vault, but I don't know if she did."

"Well, where did she take delivery of the gold, at the house?"

"Hell, no. It was delivered by courier right here to my office where it went straight into the safe. She came and picked it up."

"So how am I supposed to find it?"

"Well, we know your aunt wasn't stupid, that's pretty clear. I'm guessing the location of the gold is spelled out in here." He pulled a large, sealed envelope out of his desk and handed it to her. On the cover, in Millie's handwriting, it read, 'For Holly's eyes only, to be opened in private, upon my death.'

"If the location of the gold isn't in there, call me, and I'll give you my best guess. I don't think it'll come to that though. So that's it, unless you have any other questions."

Holly was staring at the handwriting on the envelope and started to choke up a little.

"No, no you're probably right. I'm sure it's in here too, thanks for your help, Mr. Boone, and thanks for seeing me on a Saturday."

"No problem. And please, call me Bob, just like your aunt did."

Holly was walking across the street to the C-Love Marina office when her cell rang. She didn't recognize the number, but saw that it was local and answered.

"Hello?"

"Is this Holly?"

"Yes."

"This is Marianne, from Hot Headz, you had a three-thirty appointment?"

Holly suddenly remembered the appointment she made to get her hair done, and looked at her watch. It was three thirty-five.

"Oh, damn! I forgot all about it, is it too late to come now?"

"Let me check with Jasmine, hang on."

Holly was put on hold, and a few seconds later she heard the line being connected.

"Holly?"

"Yes, I'm here."

"Jasmine says if you can make it in the next fifteen minutes, she'll take you, otherwise, you'll have to reschedule."

Holly reached the door of C-Love Marina office and looked down at the envelope she was holding. Then she looked up and saw her reflection in the glass and made a decision. *Her hair was a mess.*

"Tell Jasmine I'm on my way." Click.

Holly was a little surprised to see that no one was in the office. She let herself in and went straight to the wall safe. She unlocked it, put the envelope in the safe, closed it, and spun the dial. As she was leaving, Regina came walking in, looking a little flustered.

"Sorry I'm a little late, it took forever to get my hair done."

"Were you at Hot Headz?"

"Yeah, how'd you know?"

"I had the same problem last time, but right now it's me who's late for a three-thirty appointment. I have to scoot. Just so you know, I have some important papers in an envelope in the safe. I'll be back to get them when I'm done."

"No problem, I won't even be going in there until after the night trip leaves the dock."

"See you later, then." As Holly hurried to her car, she couldn't help but wonder what was "for her eyes only." She had no idea that it would change her life forever.

Chapter 26

After leaving the meeting at Holly's house, Hambone went back to the marina to sell the rest of his fish and keep an eye peeled for Skeeter. Once the big cooler in the bed of his pickup was empty, he strolled down to the fuel dock and found Robo finishing up with a customer.

"Robo, how's it going?"

"Not too bad, Ham, how 'bout you, going out today?"

"Nah, no sponsors, it's been slow. Hey, have you seen Skeeter around?"

"Skeeter? Nah, not today, but you might want to take a look over by that Grand Banks that came in the other day."

"I already did, I didn't see anybody there. Do me a favor and give me a call if you see him."

"What's up? You have some work for him?"

"Uh, yeah…maybe…we'll see."

"OK then, I'm closing up in about a half hour, I'll buzz you if I see him lurking."

"Thanks, Robo."

Hambone walked across the parking lot and got in his white pickup with its "Ham it Up Charters" logo and phone number on the sides. As he was pulling out, a dark blue Chevy pulled in, passing right by his driver side window. Hambone's head instinctively turned to look at the driver as he passed by and the driver of the blue Chevy did the same. Despite the driver wearing sunglasses just like he was, Hambone noticed the mustachioed man gave him a menacing look. Realizing it was the guy from the Grand Banks, Hambone took his foot off the gas. As he coasted toward Ocean Avenue, he saw the Chevy's brake lights light up. Never one to walk away from a fight, Hambone briefly considered throwing his pickup into reverse and confronting the stranger. Then he thought about what Shagball told him earlier. The Grand Banks was owned by a Mob boss who was on his way down from Jersey and the guy on board was up to no good. As he watched the Chevy start to turn around in his rearview mirror, Hambone made a decision. He needed to check on Eight-Toe and find out what he could from Skeeter before doing anything rash. He punched the gas pedal and turned west on Ocean, and then made a hard right through the old Bank of America parking lot. He caught the light at Boynton Beach Boulevard just as it went yellow and blew through it heading west. As soon as he crossed the train tracks he took the next right into an industrial area. He checked his rearview mirror again to confirm the Chevy wasn't on his tail, *just in case.*

Hambone knew the industrial area well; he owned an old triplex on the edge of it he inherited from his father. It also happened to be a back way to Eight-Toe's house, which was only about a half mile away. As he drove the access road along the tracks, he was wondering whether he was being a bit paranoid. He let out a nervous chuckle and began weaving his way through the back streets toward Eight-Toe's. About three blocks away, he made another turn and passed a pickup on the side of the road that was missing all four tires. Suddenly, he slammed on the brakes and pulled to the side of the road. He jumped out and trotted over to the abandoned vehicle; quickly realizing it was indeed Eight-Toe's. The large cooler in the bed of the pickup was gone and a quick glance in the stripped out cab confirmed it was empty. *What the fuck?* He jumped back in his pickup and sped the last couple of blocks to Eight-Toe's, pulling straight into the empty driveway. Hambone hopped up on the front stoop and banged on the front door, noting all the blinds were drawn.

"Eight-Toe! You there, buddy?" he yelled. He knocked a few more times calling out his friend's name, but got no response. As he walked around to the side entrance by the kitchen, he pulled out his cell and dialed Eight-Toe's number. He saw that the blinds on the side windows were also drawn as he held the cell tight to his ear. He heard the sound of ringing from his phone and then faintly heard it coming from inside the house. He held the phone down at his side and pressed his ear to one of the side windows. Eight-Toe's phone was definitely ringing inside. *What the hell's going on?*

He yelled, "IS ANYBODY HOME?" But again, got no response.

Sensing something was wrong he ran around to the back shed where he knew Eight-Toe stashed a spare key. He retrieved the key and ran back to the front of the house, taking a deep breath as he slipped it into the dead-bolt and opened the door.

Chapter 27

Four blocks away, veteran officer Vinnie Lorenz and his rookie partner, John Castle, were on routine patrol. They were cruising the industrial zone bordering the rough, Cherry Hill neighborhood. As they turned a corner, Vinnie saw a stripped down pickup on the side of the road, missing all four tires.

"Check it out, partner," he said, pointing as he casually pulled to the side of the road. Despite its abandoned appearance, the officers approached the vehicle warily. Each had a hand resting on the butt of his service weapon as they peered in on both sides. While Vinnie pulled the keys out of the ignition, Officer Castle walked to the rear of the truck and ran the license plate. Within seconds he found it was registered to an Earl Parsons, whose address was only a few blocks away.

"Hey, Vin," he announced, "the owner of the truck lives around the corner; let's go break the good news to him."

***

Hambone pushed open the door and immediately recoiled from the horrific smell. He stepped back on the front stoop, took a deep breath, and lifted his T-shirt up over his nose as he went back inside. His eyes went wide as he took in the blood-soaked floor and the lifeless body of his good friend Eight-Toe Earl. Hambone stood there with the front door half-open, shell- shocked at what he saw. Eight-Toe was bound to a kitchen chair, lying on his side. His mouth was duct-taped and there appeared to be vomit caked in his nostrils and around his face on the floor. There was also a large pool of blood, possibly coming from a bullet hole between his eyes, or from his left foot, which was missing several toes. Hambone started to gag and rushed to the kitchen sink where he promptly threw up. He turned on the faucet and swished some water around in his mouth before spitting it out. Then he splashed water on his face while talking to himself.

"Oh my God. Oh my frickin' God." He slowly stood up and as he wiped his face with a dish towel, he noticed an open pizza box on the stove top. Something didn't look right about the half-eaten pizza and he winced at the funky smell as he bent over to look closely. *Holy Christ! Is that the tip of a toe on top of that pepperoni?*

Realizing it was, he started to gag again and bent back over the sink.

***

Vinnie parked on the street in front of the Parsons residence and he and his partner walked to the front door. They both noted the white pickup in the drive, with the "Ham it Up Charters" logo on the side. As they reached the front stoop, Vinnie noticed the front door was ajar and there was a key in the lock. He held his hand up, signaling his partner to stop, and then put his finger up to his mouth to signal "quiet." Cautiously, they stepped up to the front door, each with a hand resting on his weapon. Vinnie reached the door first and gently pushed it open.

"Mr. Parsons? Hello? Is anybody—?"

"HOLY SHIT!" Screamed his partner, who drew his weapon with one hand and pointed at the body on the floor with the other. Vinnie's eyes quickly darted from the body to Hambone, who stepped toward them, saying, "Thank God. I was just about to—"

"FREEZE, MOTHERFUCKER!" Yelled Vinnie, as he drew his weapon and pointed it at the middle of Hambone's chest.

Hambone stopped and held his palms out. "Officer, I swear, I was just about to call—"

"PUT YOUR HANDS IN THE AIR, NOW!"

Hambone complied and started to talk again but Vinnie was having none of it.

"SHUT THE FUCK UP AND GET DOWN ON THE FLOOR!"

"Right here? There's *blood* all over the place."

"No shit, asshole. Back it up and lie down on the kitchen floor. Keep your hands where I can see 'em… NOW!"

As Hambone protested while lying prone on the floor, Vinnie's partner stomped his foot in the middle of his back and cuffed him.

"Not one fucking word unless we ask you something, got it?" he advised.

"Yeah."

The rookie stood hovering over Hambone as Vinnie walked over to the body and stooped down to look at it, careful not to step in any blood.

"Wow. Hey, Johnnie, come here and take a look, you don't see *this* every day. Somebody really worked this poor bastard over. Looks like they cut off some toes before capping him right between the eyes. I ain't seen this kinda job since I worked the south side of Philly. It's a helluva way to get some answers, that's for sure."

The rookie had only a year on the force but he knew it was a violation of protocol to not immediately call homicide and secure the scene. Plus, he had a weak stomach and the place stank like hell. He wanted some fresh air, badly.

"C'mon, Vin, you know the drill, we need to call homicide, pronto."

"Yeah, yeah, yeah…I know the drill. Wait a second, what's this? Looks like there's a piece of…what the hell *is this?*" He pulled out a small knife from his pocket and opened the blade. Then he turned a little chunk of something over on the floor. "I'll be a son of a bitch, look at this. It's part of one of his toes, all covered in… in…" He stuck his nose up to it, took a big whiff, and nodded. "Commercial grade, low-fat, mozzarella."

"Vinnie! C'mon, man, call it in already."

"All right, all right, I'm just trying to show you the ropes, kid. You'll never learn nothing if you stick strictly to the book. Haul the perp up on one of those chairs while I make the call, then we'll see what he knows."

Vinnie radioed headquarters and then turned toward his younger partner. He was standing next to

Hambone, who now had his hands handcuffed behind him through the arms of a kitchen chair.

Vinnie took two steps into the kitchen and looked down at the open pizza box on the stove. He took his knife and flicked a couple things around. Then he shook his head and laughed.

"Never question my nose, Johnny, looks like someone has a taste for deep dish peppertoni… sick fuckin' bastard. Check the corners of the perp's mouth, he has any cheese or sauce there, then he's our man…case closed."

Hambone had seen and heard enough.

"*You're* the sick bastard. Eight-Toe Earl is a friend, or, *was*…a friend of mine. I came here to check on him just before you got here."

The rookie officer couldn't stop his curiosity and bent over the pizza box, peering closely at the topping.

"A friend, huh, *that's* what you are? A real, honest to goodness, *friend*? Well, where I come from, friends don't turn friends into condiments."

"Are you nuts? I had nothing to do with this. I even gave him a ride home last night 'cause he was too drunk to drive. When I saw what happened here, I puked in the sink."

Suddenly the rookie cop stepped over to the sink and tossed his cookies all over it.

"Just like that," Hambone added.

Vinnie glanced at his rookie partner bent over the sink, making God-awful noises, and shook his head .

"You said his name's Eight-Toe Earl?"

"Yeah, he's a…*was*…a shark fisherman. He lost a couple toes on the job."

"Maybe he was 'Eight-Toe' last night, but today he's more like 'Four-Toe,' and only one of them's big. He's like a poor man's Tom Dempsey."

The sound of sirens could be heard approaching, so Vinnie grabbed Hambone by the arm, hoisted him out of the chair, and began marching him toward the front door. The rookie cop finished hurling and began wiping his face with the same towel Hambone had used minutes before.

"Let's move it, Johnnie," barked Vinnie. "Start taping off the house, you know what pricks those homicide Dicks can be."

Chapter 28

Pleased with her freshly cut and styled hairdo, Holly walked back into the office just as the *C-Love* departed with a good-sized group of anglers. Regina complemented her on it and then looked at her watch.

"Seven o'clock? Please don't tell me it took *that* long."

"No, it wasn't bad at all this time. I decided to get my nails done afterward."

"Good for you, honey, it's important to take care of yourself, especially during these trying times."

"That's what I keep telling myself, thanks."

Holly crossed the room, dialed the combination to the safe, and withdrew the envelope. Then she went into her private office and closed the door. She took a deep breath and used a pair of scissors to snip open the seal on the envelope. As she slid the contents out, she thought; *OK, Millie, what else did you have up your sleeve?"*

Holly placed the small stack of papers on the desk. On top of the papers was a handwritten letter that was rubber banded to them. She lifted the stack and slid the rubber band off. As she separated the letter from the papers, an old black and white photograph dropped to the desk. She picked it up and peered closely at the scene. In the picture, a very young (and beautiful) Aunt Millie was smiling from ear to ear. She appeared to be maybe seventeen or eighteen years old. A handsome young black man had his arm around her and was also beaming. They were standing between two coconut palms that rose apart in the shape of a V. The picture was taken at some elevation and she could see rolling terrain and a small island in the water behind them. Holly instinctively knew that it was a picture of two people very much in love. *What in the heck?* She thought. *Who was the young man and where was the photo taken?*

Millie had always been evasive about her love life. Whenever Holly inquired about it, Millie always changed the subject back to her. But when the topic of sex or relationships came up, Millie never shied away from dispensing advice. Her caveat was, "I was a young lady once, too," and she left it at that. Holly set the photo down and shook the papers, hoping more photographs might spill out, but none did. Her curiosity now piqued, she began reading the lengthy letter.

Dearest Holly, if you are reading this, then I am in a better place. The last few months of my life would have been unbearable if not for your love and companionship and for that I am eternally grateful. I know I don't need to remind you, but I will anyways. Don't forget the sunscreen! You are a beautiful young lady and I want you to stay that way. You are also a very wealthy young lady. I am sure my dear friend and attorney Bob Boone has told you about the gold I accumulated over the years and that he has no idea where I left it. That is, of course, precisely the way I intended it.

While he has been a good friend of mine for many years, he is still an attorney. Once the price of gold skyrocketed I became fearful that the temptation to read this letter before you did would be too much for him. This is why its location is not spelled out per se. You, and only you, will know where to look once you have finished this letter.

Bob, if you are reading this, your fired.

Holly, I know what you're thinking; "Enough about the gold, what about the picture?"

Holly laughed out loud; it was exactly what she was thinking. She shook her head in wonder and continued reading;

Ah, yes, the picture. You have no idea how many times I've held that picture in my hands, wondering what might have been.

The year was 1948, and I was fresh out of high school. A friend of my dad's named Kilroy had just returned from a trip to the Caribbean. He was on the dock raving about what an adventure he had sailing through the islands. He went on and on about the beautiful waters, beaches, and friendly people he met on his journey. He said he met a French girl in St. Maarten that he was head over heels about and he was going to make her his wife. How exciting! He also told us about one island in particular that held his fancy, the island of St. Croix. He explained how it was sparsely inhabited by descendants of the Dutch and that it was an underdeveloped, tropical paradise. He moored his sloop at a small marina in a natural cove on the north side of the island. He said the sea was teeming with life and told incredible fishing tales that had Father and me riveted. According to Kilroy, the steady trade winds provided for excellent sailing too. He also told of learning how to dive underwater for prolonged periods using a new device invented by the great Jacques Cousteau, called the Aqua-Lung. An enterprising charter boat captain who managed to acquire a pair of them took him diving off of a "great ledge" that dropped from sixty feet below the sea's surface, to as far down as the eye could see. Kilroy was hooked on this new sport called "scuba diving" and went into great detail about the astonishing array of sea life it allowed a diver to interact with. It all sounded fantastical, but the gleam in his eye had us convinced it was true.

The best part, he added, was that the small marina he stayed at was for sale. He asked Father to go back with him to check it out, and if a fair deal could be struck, he was going to buy it and move there. He even offered Father an ownership stake if he wanted to invest. Father said he was interested, but was reluctant to leave his own marina for any length of time.

"What if I pay to fly us down?" asked Kilroy. "We can be there and back in a week."

None of us had ever flown in an airplane at that time, and naturally, I strongly encouraged Father to take him up on the offer.

"Just think what an adventure it would be!" I exclaimed.

Kilroy saw my enthusiasm and must have sensed how to get Father to agree.

He said, "C'mon, I'll even pay for a ticket for Millie if you say yes."

Well, needless to say, that was that.

We arrived in St. Croix the first week of June, 1948, and it was all Kilroy made it out to be—an unspoiled, tropical, paradise. The gentleman who owned the marina that Kilroy looked to purchase let us stay in a small house he owned on the hillside overlooking the cove. Unlike Father's marina in Boynton, it was in great need of repairs, but it was considerably larger and Father thought it had potential.

On one particularly beautiful day, Kilroy arranged for us to go on a fishing charter. It was with the same captain who took him scuba diving after acquiring the Aqua-Lung. The captain also owned the boat, a well-maintained Bertram, and his son was the mate. We caught more fish than any of us ever dreamt of; Father caught a large blue marlin, I caught several wahoo, and Kilroy landed a mammoth, mahi-mahi. It was a spectacular outing and I became quite taken with the captain's son, Joseph. He was the same age as me, and strikingly handsome.

When we got back to the marina, Kilroy and Father invited the captain to join them at the bar for some rum. I stayed on the dock to watch Joseph clean the fish, and time flew as we shared stories about our upbringings, which were surprisingly not so different. We were both raised on the water and shared a mutual love of the ocean. Joseph invited me to go snorkeling the next day and I readily accepted, pending Father's approval, of course. Fortunately, Father was in such a good mood due to the rum and having caught his first blue marlin, that he granted me permission to go.

Joseph picked me up the next morning in a small skiff of his own, and we zipped eastward along the shoreline as Joseph shouted out landmarks along the way. We rounded a corner and he pointed out the town of Christiansted, with its large Fort Christiansvaern, looming over the harbor. Joseph explained that it was built by the Danish military in 1749, to protect the islanders from pirates and other marauders. I was captivated, imagining the cannons that once protruded from its massive walls. Joseph pointed to a small island, farther east in the distance, which he said was our snorkeling site. With each passing minute the small island grew larger, until we were right on top of it. Joseph tilted up the small engine on the skiff and landed it on the most beautiful beach I have ever seen. He announced that we had arrived at Buck Island, and it had one of the finest beaches in the Caribbean, with an equally amazing reef for snorkeling. He was right on both counts.

We spent the rest of the morning snorkeling over the most stunning reef I've ever witnessed. Even better than any I had been to in the Florida Keys. We saw starfish, parrotfish, leopard rays, snapper, grouper, and the most glorious coral formations imaginable. I was a little concerned about sharks, but Joseph assured me they stayed in deeper water on the other side of the reef that surrounded the island.

After a while we went back to the skiff and Joseph retrieved a picnic lunch he packed. Under the shade of some coconut palms we ate some smoked fish, rice and beans, and plantains. I was getting my first real taste of island food and loved it as much as the company. The water was an incredible, aquamarine blue, and it was truly like being in paradise.

We decided to take a swim, and we laughed and splashed each other in the warm, crystal clear water. I jumped on Joseph's back and he rolled me over on the sandy shore as gentle waves caressed our glistening bodies. I don't know what came over me (well, I do now, but I didn't then). I reached up and pulled Josephs head down, kissing him madly. Joseph pulled away, much to my dismay, but only for a moment. The next thing I knew, we were rolling around in the sand in a passionate embrace, like Burt Lancaster and Deborah Kerr in From Here to Eternity. *I had kissed a few boys before but this was something else entirely. I never wanted it to end and could tell Joseph felt the same. The color of his dark skin mattered no more to me than the man on the moon.*

Back at the marina was a different story, however. I agreed with Joseph that we should keep our budding romance under wraps. If Father knew I was becoming even remotely intimate with a black boy, we would have been on the next plane out, never to return. In 1948, it was altogether taboo for such a thing to occur, and I was fearful what might happen to Joseph if we were found out.

***

Suddenly, there was a knock on the door to Holly's office and she heard Regina's voice.

"Holly?"

Holly had one hand over her mouth and the other clutching Millie's letter. She was so wrapped up in the words coming off the pages that she lost track of time. She dropped the letter on her desk and invited Regina in.

"C'mon in, Regina."

Regina stuck her head through the open door and Holly continued.

"I was just, uh, just finishing up reading these documents Millie's attorney left me."

"Oh, OK, I wanted to let you know I'm heading home. I finished up tallying the receipts for the night trip and everything's in the safe. FYI, Bart called and they're slaying the yellowtails."

Holly looked at her watch. It was almost eight o'clock and getting dark out.

"You know what, Regina? I'm heading home too—give me a second and we'll leave together."

"OK, I'm ready whenever you are." Regina went back to her desk and started straightening a few things up while she waited for Holly.

Holly picked up the letter and saw that she was about halfway through it. She put it back on top of the other documents and secured it with the rubber band, placing the old photograph on top. As she slid the stack back into the big envelope, she shook her head in amazement. *What other secrets do you have, Millie?* Holly grasped the envelope with one hand and grabbed her purse with the other as she headed toward the door.

Chapter 29

Rudy was stunned on two fronts. First, was the sudden appearance of his long lost love, Marie Dupree. Second, was Marie's confession to him that he was Tangles' biological father. Her rationale for not telling him and breaking off the relationship was simple. Her husband would have killed them all. From the stories that Marie had told him in the past, he was hard pressed to argue otherwise. Still, it didn't make it a whole lot easier to digest, and they weren't sure how or when to break the news to Tangles. Rudy called in a favor and asked another bartender to come in on her night off to cover for him. As soon as she showed up, Rudy came out from behind the bar and suggested the four of us go somewhere together.

"Where are you thinking?" asked Tangles.

"Let me think…" Rudy scratched his chin and looked at Tangles' mom.

"You still like to place a wager once in a while, Miss Dupree?"

"Once in a while? Sure, why not?"

"Great, then why don't we head up to the Palm Bitch Kennel Club? We can watch the dogs run and maybe play a little poker. What do you say, guys? You up for a little action?"

I thought about how pissed Holly was at me and shrugged.

"Sure, I'm game. Tangles, you in?"

"Hell yeah, I'm in like Flynn, let's do it."

We took separate cars. Tangles and I rode in the Beemer and Marie rode with Rudy in his Corolla. Along the way, we again discussed whether I should call the FBI and try to make a deal. I decided that I would call in the morning before Holly preempted me. I didn't want to drag her any further into it than necessary.

Fifteen minutes later, we were up against the rail of the track, watching the dogs being led to the starting gates.

"I don't know a damn thing about dog racing," I confessed.

"Me neither," said Tangles. "But look at the number six dog; he's trying to hump his handler. He must be all backed up, probably has a lot of energy to burn. I'm betting on him."

"Save your money, Bubba," said Rudy. "He's gonna finish in the back of the pack. See how he's sniffing at the dog in front of him now? That's just where he wants to be, running in the back, sniffing all that *dog ass*, figuring out which one he wants to hump after the race."

Marie and I both laughed and Tangles looked up at him.

"You really know that for sure?"

"Sure as Casey Anthony's never gonna be on the cover of *Redbook*. Number six may not finish last, but I guarantee he won't finish first. Think about it, if he gets in front there's no ass to sniff."

"Can't argue with that logic," I commented. "What about number two? He just took a dump by the inside rail. He's got to be a little lighter and feeling better, right? Should we bet on him?"

"I don't think so," said Marie. "He's probably number two for a reason. Maybe he's got digestive issues and that's all he does is poop everywhere. Plus, he's probably got some chafing as a result. You can't run fast if you're all chafed up."

"So who the heck are we gonna bet on?" asked Tangles.

"I'm betting on number seven to win."

"Better listen to your mother, Bubba. She always had a knack for picking winners. Why do you like number seven, Marie? He's going off at twelve to one."

"You mean *she,* is."

Rudy looked down at his program and nodded. "I stand corrected, so why do you like her?"

"Simple, she's the best looking dog of the bunch. See how finely she's groomed? See the way she carries herself? Trust me, that girl didn't get that way by getting a bunch of dirt kicked up in her face. Look, she's even leading the pack to the starting gate. C'mon, let's get our bets down before it's too late."

We hurried to the betting window and Marie bet twenty dollars on number seven to win. Rudy bet twenty across the board, to win, place, and show. I looked at Tangles.

"What are you gonna do?"

"I'm sticking with Momma, twenty to win."

"What the hell, hope she still has the knack." I plopped down twenty on the number seven dog, named, Fly Baby Fly. As we were heading back to the track to watch the race, I caught a breaking news alert on one of the overhead monitors. A reporter was standing in front of a house, talking to the camera, and a caption scrawled across the bottom of the screen; *Boynton man killed in apparent home invasion.* Unfortunately, that kind of thing happens on a fairly regular basis in south Florida, so I didn't think twice about it.

The four of us huddled by the finish line and heard the announcer's voice over the loudspeaker. "Here comessssssssss... Sparky!" A fake rabbit attached to the top of the inside rail came zooming past the starting gate and the dogs went wild as a bell rang and the gates opened.

"AND THEY'RE OFF!" cried the announcer.

The dogs stampeded past us and it was nearly impossible to tell which dog was where. As they rounded the first turn, the announcer began giving out their positions. Fly Baby Fly was on the outside, in the middle of the pack.

"Our girl better start picking up the pace," I said.

"I told you she didn't like dirt in her face," responded Marie. "That's why she's on the outside. Don't worry; she's in a good spot to make her move. C'mon baby, show Momma what you got!"

Rudy got in the act too.

"C'mon darling, pump those sexy legs…Gimme some Tina Turner!"

The dogs were on the backstretch and about to make the final turn toward the finish. Suddenly, the announcer said, "Here comes Fly Baby Fly, on the outside!"

Tangles started jumping up and down, trying to get a better look. I was watching on the large screen monitor at the far side of the track and pointed it out to Tangles.

"Look, here she comes! Baby's got some wheels!"

Tangles started yelling, "Fly Baby Fly! Fly Baby Fly!"

We all started screaming "FLY BABY FLY!" as the dogs rounded the final turn. The announcer called the action.

"It's Hard Money on the inside, followed by Pistol Whipped and Daddy's Money. Here comes Fly Baby Fly closing fast on the outside!"

We were going crazy, screaming like idiots and waving our betting stubs in the air.

"Look at 'em go! It's Hard Money leading Daddy's Money with Fly Baby Fly on the outside! Now it's Hard Money with Fly Baby Fly on the outside, followed by Pistol Whipped as Daddy's Money fades! It's Hard Money and Fly Baby Fly separating from the field. Here they come! It's Fly Baby Fly and Hard Money neck and neck! Holy Cow! It's......Fly Baby Fly at the finish! What a performance by Fly Baby Fly!"

We were high-fiving and hugging and laughing all the way back to the cashier's window.

"You still got it, darling, after all these years, you still got the touch." Rudy gave Marie a big kiss on the cheek and she reached a hand down to ruff up Tangles' hair.

"You're not too bad yourself; did you see where number six finished?"

"Just like I thought, dead last, but you picked the winner. Hot damn! What a way to start, we make a helluva team, Marie...always did."

"Anybody see where the number two dog finished?" I asked.

"Middle of the pack," answered Marie, as the cashier counted out her two-hundred-and-forty-dollar payday. Tangles and I collected the same, but Rudy made three hundred and sixty big ones. Being at the dog track was just the sort of diversion I needed to take my mind off the gigantic mess of trouble I was in. I resigned myself to the fact that I would call the FBI guys in the morning. Holly was right; with Donny Nutz's appearance imminent, we were *way* over our heads

Race after race, Marie and Rudy hashed out the best prospects for us to bet on. As far as I could tell, their handicapping had little to do with past performance. Marie based her decisions strictly on appearance and whether a dog used the track to relieve itself. Rudy went with ass sniffing and perceived horniness. Incredibly, it worked. By the end of the night, Tangles and I each pocketed over five hundred dollars. Marie won more than we did, but Rudy was the biggest bettor and won over a grand. He was one happy camper and insisted that he treat everybody to some food and drink.

We went up to the clubhouse level and got seated at a table. It took forever for the waitress to bring us a round of drinks and after we ordered some food, Rudy pointed it out. "Man, the service here sucks. Next time I'll take everybody down to Seminole Casino, where I get the VIP treatment."

"You're gambling *that* much?" asked Marie, with a hint of concern in her voice.

"No, not really, not like the old days. I go down maybe two or three times a year."

"Then how do you get the VIP treatment?" asked Tangles.

"I'm a native, and we take care of our own."

"Huh? You're saying they give special treatment to *all* Florida natives? How can they afford to do that?"

Rudy laughed.

"No, no, I'm a native In—"

I felt Marie's leg brush mine as she kicked Rudy under the table and he stopped talking midsentence. He looked at Marie, who was staring wide-eyed at him. Tangles was taking a swig of his beer but didn't miss it. He slowly lowered his beer to the table and looked at his mother first, then Rudy.

"Say what? You're a native In…Indian? You're an *Indian*?"

Rudy was in a pickle and started to squirm as he answered. His eyes darted from Marie to Tangles and back.

"Uh, um, well, actually, uh, owww!" Tangles' mom kicked Rudy again, this time a little harder.

"Momma, what's going on here? Wait a second!" He pointed at Rudy. "*You're* the Indian my dad used to cuss up and down about? *You're* the one? You're the no-good skirt-chasing Injun my dad swore he'd tear to pieces if he ever got his hands on?"

"Actually, I'm only, uh, part, uh, part…Indian."

"I bet, probably the lying, cheating, good-for-nothing part."

"Now Tino, don't get mad at Rudy; it's not his fault, he didn't know."

"Didn't know what? Didn't know he was an *Indian*? Bullshit! Dammit, Momma, quit sticking up for him, and quit calling me Tino!"

Some of the other clubhouse customers were looking at our table as Tangles got louder.

Marie looked at Rudy and then back at Tangles. "I'm sorry, honey, we were trying to figure out the best way to tell you. I didn't want it to be like this…in public. I just told Rudy today, he never knew."

"Never knew *what*? What the hell's going on here?"

Rudy took a big gulp of his drink and Marie let out a deep breath before answering.

"Honey, the truth is…Rudy's your real father."

Tangles looked at me and laughed.

"You in on this too? Did you put them up to this?"

I shook my head no and didn't laugh. He looked back at his mother, and then at Rudy, who said, "It's true, but we should probably get a DNA test to make certain."

Tangles was no longer laughing. "Momma? Tell me this is some kind of joke."

"I'm afraid not, sweetie, and a DNA test isn't necessary. I wasn't with anybody else but Rudy at the time, and your father, or who you *thought* was your father, was impotent. He said if I ever told *anybody*, especially Rudy, that the baby wasn't his, he'd kill us all. You know what he was like, you know he would have. Still, he was always good to you, except when he got drunk."

"He was always drunk! That's when he'd call me a little bastard and start mumbling about me having Injun blood. I never understood it; I didn't know what the hell he was talking about. He practically tortured me on that Goddamned shrimp boat, Momma. You don't know the half of it."

"I'm sorry, baby; the bottle got the best of him. I think it tore him up when he found out he was impotent. He wanted to kill me when I told him I was pregnant, but he wanted a child so bad, he didn't. I should have told you about this after he passed away, but you were working on the cruise ships and we barely saw each other anymore. I thought it best to just leave it alone. Besides, I had no idea where Rudy was. You'd probably be searching for the father you never knew for the rest of your life. It would have turned your whole world upside down. The fact that you somehow became acquainted without knowing your relation to each other is practically a miracle. Rudy and I were in love, honey. I thought about telling him I was pregnant and asking him to run away with me, but I was too scared. We would have always been looking over our shoulder."

Rudy reached his hand across the table and put it on top of Marie's. "You should have, Marie, you know how I felt about you. How I *still* feel about you. I would have found a safe place for us to live."

"Like where?" asked Tangles…"In a teepee on the reservation?"

Rudy gave Tangles a look that said, *seriously?*

And his mother said, "Enough with the Indian jokes, honey, he's your father and that makes *you* part Indian too."

Tangles shook his head.

"I-I can't *believe* this. I don't know what to say."

The waitress showed up with a plate of nachos and some spring rolls and put them in the middle of the table. Rudy ordered us another round and I glanced at one of the many televisions on the wall as I shoveled some nachos on a small plate. The same reporter I saw earlier was back on, and the scrawl at the bottom read; Update…man questioned in deadly home invasion released. The reporter was chasing after the man with a microphone. When he reached him, the man turned to the camera and pushed the microphone away. I did a double take and blinked my eyes, but there was no question about his identity…it was Hambone. I dropped a loaded nacho on my lap when my mouth went slack.

"Holy shit! It's Hambone!" I pointed at the TV on the wall. Everybody turned to look, but the picture was back on the reporter's face as he talked to the camera.

"What? Where?" asked Tangles.

"He was just on TV! It said something about him being questioned about a deadly home invasion. What the hell's going on?" I quickly pulled out my cell and dialed his number but it went straight to voice mail. I wiped the nacho off my lap and stood up.

"Rudy, thanks for treating. I'm sorry, but I've gotta run. Thanks for the hot tips, Marie. I'm sure I'll see you soon."

Tangles started to get up, but his mom put her hand on his shoulder.

"You're not leaving too…*are you?* Please, honey, I think we need to talk about this some more."

"Sorry, Momma, if Hambone's in some kind of trouble, I need to go with Kit. We can talk in the morning or on the boat later if it's not too late when I get back."

"Are you sure?" I said. "I think maybe your mom's right. I'll fill you in when I find out anything; just keep your cell on."

"Wow, what is this? Everybody be a dad to Tangles night? Thanks, but I'll pass on the suggestions. I mate for Hambone and he's a friend. If you're going, I'm going too, end of story."

His mom pulled him close and gave him a big kiss on the cheek.

"Be careful, honey, we can talk later, I hope you understand why I did what I did."

Rudy stood up and extended his hand to Tangles. Tangles looked at it, hesitated, then shook it. Rudy pulled him forward and put his other arm around his shoulder.

"If there's anything I can help you with, just let me know. I'll give your mother my cell number."

Tangles pulled away and looked him square in the eye. "I'll be fine, but thanks for asking."

Like somebody turning on a faucet, Rudy's eyes immediately welled up with tears. Tangles followed me out of the clubhouse and not a word was said until we were in the Beemer. I kept glancing at him as we left the parking lot.

"What?" he said.

"You just found out that Rudy's your dad and you have nothing to say about it?"

He turned to me and smiled.

"Well, there's one thing."

"What's that?"

"Who knew Tonto was such a softie?"

Chapter 30

As Holly exited the parking garage she decided she needed to clear her head a little. She was already upset about the fight with Kit and now her mind was reeling from Millie's letter. Somehow she resisted the temptation to call Kit. She was going to stick to her guns and not give him the time of day until he called the FBI and told them what happened. Not ready to go back to an empty house and lose herself in the letter, she headed west on Boynton Beach Boulevard and ended up at Marshall's by the mall. After picking up a couple of pairs of shorts and a pair of sandals, she stopped in at Jason's Deli to hit their wonderful salad bar. Her diet and exercise regimen had suffered over the last month of her Aunt Millie's life and she was determined to turn it around.

After getting a little something in her stomach, she headed over to the mall. She didn't really need anything, but she had a Starbucks craving and caved. She had a weakness for their Venti sized, vanilla-nonfat-no-foam-latte. Within ten minutes of window shopping, stores started closing. She looked at her watch and it was nearly nine o'clock.

By nine fifteen she was back at home on Sabal Island. Darkness was settling in and as she walked out onto the deck overlooking the Intracoastal she heard splashing and crashing along the seawall. The telltale sounds of predatory fish activity.

Quickly she dashed into the garage and retrieved her favorite spinning rod. It was rigged with a white bucktail jig and a yellow worm. She trotted across the grass out to the point, where a soft light hung over the edge of the seawall. Standing back a few feet from the edge, she could see shadows darting around the perimeter of illuminated water. She opened the bail of the reel, pinched the line against the rod, and flung the jig out into the darkness. As she cranked the handle to retrieve the line, she dipped the rod tip with a rhythmic cadence. Just as the lure reached the edge of illuminated water by the point, she felt a big tug. As quickly as the fish struck, it was gone.

Slightly miffed, she cast again, this time parallel to the seawall, toward the open Intracoastal. She retrieved the lure with the same motion, keeping it a few feet out from the wall. Ten feet before reaching the point light, her jig got slammed. The twelve-pound test line began peeling off the reel as the fish headed for deeper water. She tightened the drag a touch, and the fish slowed a little. She ran along the seawall toward the Intracoastal, reeling as she followed the fish. It tried to run under the neighbor's dock, but she managed to turn it around. After a couple more runs, she had the fish under the point light. It was a decent-sized snook. She grabbed a net that hung on a coconut palm and kneeled down by the seawall. With the rod in one hand and the net in the other, she maneuvered the fish closely enough to get it in the net.

"Yes!" she congratulated herself as she hoisted the eight-pound snook onto the ground. Although they were an excellent tasting fish she knew they were out of season and deftly removed the hook from its toothless mouth.

"It's your lucky night, Snooky, back you go."

She kneeled back down and leaned over the seawall so she could gently let the fish slide into the water. As it swam away, she wiped her hands on the grass and briefly thought about its relatively simple existence. Snook are ambush predators that lay in wait in the mangroves or underneath docks or along seawalls or under boats or anywhere else that might have smaller baitfish swimming by. Where there was one snook, there were usually several more nearby. When a small fish swims by, a snook will dart out and suck its victim in through its large, toothless mouth. They were kind of lazy, preferring their food to come to them rather than the other way around.

As she thought about it some more, she laughed. "Let's see…you're lazy, you hang out with your friends, you have a big mouth, and you're slimy…very slimy. Hey, Snooky, come back! You'd be perfect on a reality TV show."

Not caring that her neighbors might see her talking to a fish, she waved toward the water.

"See you next time, Snooky."

Pleased with herself over landing a nice snook, Holly put the rod away and washed her hands in the kitchen sink. Between Starbucks and the excitement of catching a fish, Holly realized she still had energy to burn. Honoring her pledge to start taking better care of herself, she decided to go for a short run. She normally didn't run at night because of safety issues, but in Ocean Ridge the sidewalk was set well back from A1A. Getting run over was unlikely, but getting bug-bit was not. After donning her jogging shorts and running shoes with their reflective strips on the sides, she liberally applied some bug spray.

She ran at a good clip and less than ten minutes later she was standing on the Boynton Inlet Bridge. She stopped to look at the fishing boats floating over the reef with their lights on. She could make out the silhouette of the *C-LOVE* and wondered how they were doing. Looking at her watch, she saw that it was after ten o'clock. The *C-LOVE* and other charter boats would be heading in soon. As a little girl, she used to love watching boats come through the inlet. She still did. A mosquito buzzed her face, undaunted by the repellant. She swatted the air and dismissed the thought of waiting another twenty minutes to watch the boats come in. She turned around and jogged her way to the Boynton Oceanfront Park and then back home.

As she headed down Sabal Island Drive, she noticed an upstairs light flick on and off toward the end of the street. As she proceeded down the street she wondered if her eyes were playing tricks on her. There was only one two-story home at the end of the street, but it was vacant and for sale. She eyed it as she slowed to a walk and headed down her driveway, but it looked as vacant as ever. It was a little before eleven when she entered her house through the kitchen door, breathing heavily from exertion. She grabbed a towel from the bathroom and wiped herself down as she drank a cold glass of water.

Standing in the kitchen, she saw the *C-Love* through the glass door and smiled. It was chugging its way back to the dock after another night of fishing. She downed another water and poured a glass of Pinot Grigio from the fridge. Then she grabbed the envelope with Millie's letter off the kitchen counter and headed to the living room. She set the wine down on a coffee table in front of an old leather sofa, plopped down in it, and then reached across the arm of the sofa to turn on a lamp. Fingering the envelope in her lap, she took a sip of wine, set it back down, then scooched her way into a comfortable position at the end of the couch.

Before pulling out the letter, she excitedly rubbed her hands together. "Now, let's see…*where were we?*"

Chapter 31

Franklin Post (aka Stargazer), sat at the helm of his operations center in a pyramid-shaped glass building connected by a sky-bridge, to his dome-shaped home on Puget Sound. The 125-foot-tall pyramid was made of a newly developed, solar-powered, two-way, LED glass. Each wall gave him a clear view of the outside when not being utilized as a gigantic monitor on the inside. Being a big fan of *Star Trek,* he ran the center from an oversized captain's chair in the middle. It was basically a super pimped-out La-Z-Boy with enough state-of-the-art technology in it to give Stephen Hawking a hard-on. He should know, it certainly gave *him* one. The chair was wirelessly interfaced with the interior walls of the pyramid. He controlled its movements and the wall monitors through an array of joysticks and touch-screen panels on the arms of the chair. Although he designed the chair and pyramid and invented the photovoltaic, two-way, LED glass, he had no idea of the actual cost to build it all, because it was paid for by Uncle Sam. *Five-hundred million? A billion?* He didn't know and he didn't care. He chuckled to himself—*at least it's energy efficient.*

He was about to contact one of his field agents (Thomas Cushing), to fill him in on some new developments in the Donny Nutz case, but took a moment to reminisce about how he became head of the most secret intelligence agency in the world.

It was two days before Christmas, 2001, and he was sitting alone in his dome-shaped home, staring at the ceiling. Although it was a cold and rainy night outside, he had an incredible view of the planetary system because he had an exact replication painted on the ten-thousand-square-foot ceiling. It took an army of painters a legion of time, and cost a fortune, but he didn't regret spending one single penny of it. Looking up at the cosmos helped spark some of his most brilliant ideas. When it was finished, he was told there were over two million stars and planets on it. Whenever a new one was discovered, he had it added on. He was already at the point where his painter was asking for a larger ceiling.

He sat alone because the divorce from his second wife had been finalized only two weeks earlier. He was on his second martini because he was still smarting from it. He couldn't believe he was twice divorced and childless at forty years old. He was also in a three-month-long funk that started on September eleventh. That was the day he lost his only sister to terrorists when they crashed the plane she was on into a farmer's field in western Pennsylvania. Being a relative teetotaler, the alcohol had slowed his thought process down to Mensa level.

He was pondering the immense gap between being genius smart and smart with women, when he noticed that the planet Mars was flashing. It was a security feature he installed to let him know there was someone at the front gate of his quarter-mile-long driveway. He looked at his watch and saw it was after eleven o'clock in the evening. *Who in the hell could it be?* He took another swig of his martini and reluctantly headed to the front door where the video monitor of the gate was located. As he left the comfort of his seat he had another idea. *Wouldn't it be nice if I could do everything from the recliner?*

When he reached the front door he saw there were several vehicles lined up at the gate…all limo's. *Huh?* He pressed the speaker button to talk to whoever was in the lead car.

"Sorry, wrong Christmas party, there's nothing going on here."

He caught a glimpse of a face leaning out the window toward the speaker box.

"We're not here for a party, Mr. Post. The president has an important matter to discuss with you."

"The president? The president of *what*?"

"Of the United States of America, Mr. Post. It's a matter of national security."

"What? Is this a joke? Wait, how'd you know my name?"

The driver held out a badge toward the speaker box.

"Because I'm with the Secret Service, Mr. Post. Just like the gentlemen in the rear vehicle and those riding with the president in the middle one. He's traveled all night to get here and would be most appreciative if he could talk to you for a few minutes."

He knocked back the rest of his martini and let out a laugh. "You gotta be kidding me, did my ex-partner put you up to this? Wow, he really went all out this time. I gotta admit, you're pretty convincing, but the charade's over, pal. Don't worry though, I'll tell him you did a good job. Have a merry Christmas."

As he walked away from the front door shaking his head, his cell phone rang and he pulled it out of his pocket. It was playing the theme from *Star Wars* and the display read, "The Prez. "

Annoyed now, he answered it.

"I don't know how you got my cell number, but I've had—"

"Franklin? Franklin Post?" The voice that came across the line was a dead-on impression of the president with his Texas twang in full force. Slightly less sure of himself now, he responded, "Y-yeah, that's me. Man, you guys are *really* good. I'll recommend you for a bonus when—"

"Look, Stargazer, I got no time for dillydallying when there's terrorists running around crashing planes into buildings and killing American citizens. Now you gonna let me in or do I have to land *Chopper One* right on top of your roof over Uranus?"

"What? How the hell do you know about—?"

"I know everything there is to know about you, Stargazer, except why you're not lettin' me in. Don't you have video on your gate? Don't you know what your president looks like?"

He turned around and quickly stepped back to the video monitor by the door. He had never been more stunned in his life—except for after hearing the proposition he received only minutes later. Standing in the rain, at his front gate, stood two Secret Service agents. They both held umbrellas over the man standing between them who had a cell phone pressed to his ear: the President of the United States of America.

"You there, Stargazer? It's gettin' cold out here."

"Oh-my-God."

"Not till I get promoted, for now I'm just the prez. Heh."

He opened the gate and watched the procession of limos pass through, still not believing his eyes and ears. *The president was coming in the middle of the night to talk to him!* He quickly dashed to the kitchen and splashed some cold water on his face before returning to the front door. When he heard car doors slam, he opened the front door and was frisked by the first Secret Service agent that entered. Several agents came through the door flanking the president, who extended his hand.

As he shook the president's hand, he offered an apology.

"I'm, uh, real sorry about the mix-up, Mr. President. It's just that my ex-partner has been known to go to great lengths to play practical jokes. I uh, still can't believe you're really here."

"Oh, I'm here all right, just like the terrorists."

"What? There's terrorists here? Right here on my property?"

The president squinted at him.

"Could be, the sneaky bastards are everywhere, that's why I need your help."

"*My* help? What, uh, what do you mean? What *kind* of help?"

The president looked around at the dozen or so agents flanking the outside wall of the dome-shaped room and signaled to the nearest one.

"Commere, Blinky." The president called virtually everybody by a nickname. He called his lead agent, Blinky because he never blinked...ever.

Blinky walked up and nodded. "Yes, sir."

"I need to speak with Mr. Post in private for a few minutes. Send the guys somewhere, you too."

"But, sir, you know that—"

"Save it, Blinky, I know you're not supposed to let me out of your sight—but guess what? Terrorists aren't supposed to crash planes into the World Trade Center neither. Now I got some important matters to discuss to insure it doesn't happen again—private matters."

"But—"

"But nothing. I know how to signal you if Mr. Post goes crazy on me. All I have to do is touch the face of my watch to activate the secret alarm, just like we practiced. So gimme a little breathing room, just for a few minutes."

"Yes, sir." The agent shrugged and posted four agents outside the front door, four out the back, and went in the kitchen with the remaining agents.

Once they were alone, the president got straight to the point, as he usually did.

"Mr. Post, the reason—"

"Please, sir, just call me Franklin."

"Franklin? Sure, whatever you want, Franklin's a great name. He was one of our country's finest presidents."

"Roosevelt? I'm surprised you would endorse a Democrat."

"I don't. I endorse checks, big ones. Roosevelt wasn't great. If it wasn't for World War Two he woulda left office with 20 percent unemployment and a failed economic policy. Hitler was to Roosevelt what Simon was to Garfunkel. He *was* the bridge over troubled water. No sir, I'm talking about Benjamin—Benjamin Franklin. One of the greatest thinkers of our time. You know why? 'Cause he invented the kite. Once he started flying that kite he had a lot of time to think. That led to even more inventions...like lightning. Nobody ever knew what to do with it until he flew that kite up in a storm and channeled that lightning right into a telephone pole. I believe he invented that too. He was a great, great man. A real thinker's thinker, much like you, which is what brought me here."

"Uh, OK."

"I don't have to tell you that what I'm about to tell you is top secret and a matter of national security—but I just did. You've heard of the Patriot Act?"

"Of course, it's one of the most contentious pieces of legislation ever enacted by Congress."

"Contentious, yes, controversial too. You know what it does?"

"It dramatically reduces restrictions on US law enforcement agencies' abilities to conduct surveillance on telephone and e-mail communications, medical records, financial records, and so forth, particularly those involving foreign persons and entities. It also grants broad authority to detain and deport immigrants. It's unprecedented in American history."

"*Was* unpresidented, until I *presidented* it. Too bad we didn't have the Patriot Act *before* September eleventh, then maybe I wouldn't have had to sign such a controversial bill."

"Huh?"

"What I'm saying is if our law enforcement agencies were doing a more thorough job communicating what they knew about 7-Eleven owners whose last names had more than two vowels, maybe we wouldn't have a giant crater in the middle of Manhattan."

"I'm not sure I follow you, sir."

"That's neither here or there. Let me spell it out for you: we knew about the impending attacks, but we didn't put it all together. The FBI knew this, the CIA knew that, the NSA knew a little somethin' somethin', but none of them told each other a Goddamn thing! If they had, we coulda stopped Sadaam and the bin Laden boys dead in their dirty tracks. We coulda unraveled them tunic by tunic, exposing them as the no-good, goat humpin' terrorists they are. We shoulda been able to stop 'em, but we couldn't see the forest *or* the trees. That's where you come in."

"*Me?* How? I don't know anything about terrorists."

"But you know about computers, right? My advisers tell me you are the country's leading expert on quantum, uh, quantum trans-am— aw hell, you know what you are. You're the next best thing to Einstein this country's got and it made you a billionaire."

"Sure, I know a lot about things that most people can't pronounce and I've invented some things most people never even dreamt of, but I still don't get why you're here."

"Maybe my Einstein reference was a stretch."

"Maybe, but good luck having a sit-down with *him.*"

The president laughed. "You got a sense of humor, just like me, that's good."

"So humor me, sir; what's this matter of national security you want to talk to me about?"

"You know what the Patriot Act stands for?"

"I thought I just told you."

"No, I mean the letters themselves. The USA PATRIOT Act is a cinnamon. Each letter stands for something. You know what it means?"

"Uh, yes…yes, I do, but, uh, did you mean synonym?"

"Yeah, that's what I said, a cinnamon."

"Actually, an acronym is the—"

"That's a mute point, Stargazer. Please, this is a matter of national security, do you know what it means or not?"

"It stands for 'Uniting and Strengthening America by Providing Appropriate Tools Required to Intercept and Obstruct Terrorism."

"Wow. I take that back about Einstein. You really *are* a whiz. You're the first person I met who knows what it stands for. I knew you were the right man for the job!"

"What job?"

"Franklin, knowing what that stands for tells me you are a true patriot, which is exactly why I want to give *you* all the appropriate tools required to intercept and obstruct terrorism."

"What?"

"Two days ago, I called a meeting at Camp David. In attendance were the heads of the FBI, CIA, DEA, NSA, Homeland Security, and the secretary of defense. I called them out for their failure to communicate with each other about the terrorist threat. We decided the Patriot Act needed a pick-me-up, a little git-go in the giddy-up, if you know what I mean. So we created a new, super-top-secret agency whose purpose is to analyze other security and law enforcement agencies' databases and incoming communications for terrorist and international criminal activity and then direct the findings to the appropriate agency. Their main focus is to apprehend terrorists, of course, but any criminal activity deemed to be a potential threat to the US of A is not to be ignored. I had the head of each agency pick one of their top agents to be appointed to this new group. And by unanimous decision, it was decided that *you* would be the best choice to lead them."

"ME?"

"That's right, *you.* You will be given whatever tools necessary to do the job. You want to build the most sophisticated computer snooping center in the universe right here? Done. Money is no object. You will have the entire faith and credit of the United States Treasury at your disposal."

"You're kidding me, right? How can you do that?"

"Simple, you know who my secretary of the Treasury is?"

"Henry Paulson."

"Right again. I just call up my buddy Hank and say, 'Run the presses.' If he asks what it's for, which he won't, I'll just tell him I'm terrorist hunting. He's like me; the only Allah he likes is ala mode. Of course, it helps that nobody's ever gonna know about it."

"How so?"

"When I say secret, I mean super-duper-zip-your-lips-and-go-down-with-the-ship *secret.* Not like the CIA, everybody knows about them. No sir, this operation is strictly off the books. Nobody but nobody's ever gonna know dick about it. Heh. Not Congress, not the Senate, not the American public, not the conventioners in Geneva, those pussies, and especially not the terrorists—until it's too late, that is. So what do you say, you want free reign to design and run the most ultimate top-secret terrorist-hunting network in the universe? I know you like to think big."

The president pointed up at the star-covered ceiling.

"I don't know, I'm not in a good place right now. I have to think about it."

"Well think fast, 'cause I need an answer before I leave. You'd be doing your country a great service. Think about this too; I understand you've been drinking a little too much on account of your wife leaving, and this would certainly help take your mind off that... and your sister too; my sincere condolences. Franklin, you've got a chance to prevent other Americans from feeling the pain that you and all the other victims' families of the September eleventh attacks have endured."

"Of course, you would know about my sister, Alison, being on flight ninety-three."

"Seat twenty-four B, again, I'm truly sorry."

The president put his hand on his shoulder and Franklin felt that he really meant it. He couldn't believe it, but for all his buffoonery and the way he was depicted in the press, he actually *liked* him.

The president was right too. He *had* been drinking too much from being depressed over losing his sister and then having his wife leave him. Plus, the thought of designing his own intelligence-gathering center and running an elite group of highly trained agents on someone else's dime was too great to pass up. His mind was made up.

"Don't be sorry for me, Mr. President, feel sorry for those sons of bitches who killed my sister, 'cause they're goin down."

The president flashed his famous grin. "That's what I wanted to hear! Revenge is a dish best served with a heapin' portion of terrorist in the middle and a pedophile or two on the side. I hate those bastards too."

"Who do I report to?"

"Nobody but me…You call the shots; I make sure they get fired."

"You got your man, sir, I'm in."

The president beamed as they shook hands. "Great! I'll have Hank send you a check to get started. Besides terrorists, our number one enemy is time. I need you to put your thinking cap on and get moving on this el pronto."

"Mr. President, with all due respect, I never take it off."

"No respect due, Franklin, just spiff it up, then. How much do you need?"

"Honestly, I'm not sure. I have some conceptual ideas for—"

"I like to deal in round numbers, how about a hundred million for starters?"

"A *hundred million*?"

"You're right…go big or go home. I'll have him send you two-hundred. We need to fast-track this. Any more questions before I leave?"

"This top-secret department I'm going to run, does it have a name?"

"You bet, only the best super-top-secret name ever." He winked and whispered, "The Department of International Criminal Knowledge."

The president rose and headed toward the front door, calling out,

"Let's hit the road, Blinky."

Franklin walked behind him.

On cue, the Secret Service agents piled out from the kitchen and in from the back door.

They shook hands once more in the doorway, and the president handed him a business card embossed with the seal of the President of the United States of America.

"Call me anytime, Stargazer, especially if you just nailed a terrorist."

"Yes sir, I look forward to it."

As the president's motorcade disappeared down the driveway, he took a moment to digest what occurred. He agreed to build and run a new top-secret agency, reporting directly to the president, who dubbed him 'Stargazer.' *Sure didn't see that one coming.* He sat down in his recliner and gazed up at the starry ceiling, mulling over the name of the agency he was now heading: the Department of International Criminal Knowledge. He said it out loud to himself and thought about how it would sound.

"Franklin Post, director of the Department of International Criminal Knowledge…Franklin Post… Head of…of…*DICK?*"

Realizing the acronym that the organizational name made, he laughed for the first time in over three months; since his sister Alison went down on flight ninety-three into the Pennsylvania countryside.

Chapter 32

Holly took another sip of wine and then delved back into Millie's letter.

The rest of our week in St. Croix flew by! Joseph and I went hiking through the rainforest one day and I snuck out to go dancing with him one night after Father fell asleep. We were both undeniably smitten with each other and I couldn't bear the thought of leaving. Kilroy told Father that he planned on staying a couple of more weeks, so the day before Father and I were scheduled to fly out, I approached him with an offer; I would help him learn some of the tricks of the marina trade if he would help convince Father to let me stay a bit longer. Kilroy knew that I spent my entire childhood working in Father's marina and readily accepted. Father was a bit reluctant at first, but he saw how much I was enjoying my first real adventure and agreed.

My romance with Joseph went into full swing once father left and I was having the time of my young life. While working on the dock one day I got a sliver in the bottom of my foot. Although I removed it and cleaned the wound, it became infected and I had to go to the hospital. After running some blood tests, the doctor told me my foot would recover, but not my uterus, because I was pregnant!

Holly gasped and blurted out, "WHAT?"

My head was spinning and I didn't know what to do. It was only two days before I was supposed to return to Florida and I was pregnant! Unsure of what to do, I confided in Kilroy. He was a good ten years younger than Father, and we had become friends. Kilroy was shocked, just like I was, and he was fearful that Father would blame him for letting me run around un-chaperoned. He also knew that Father would never invest in the marina with him if I came home pregnant. I begged him to help me, and he agreed—on the condition that I give the baby up for adoption. He said he would help make sure the baby went to a good family. I told him that I would have to discuss it with Joseph and he tried to convince me not to tell him. He said that as soon as Joseph found out I was pregnant; he would never have anything to do with me. He said, "It's just how the islanders are." I knew Joseph well enough to know he would never do that, but I needed Kilroy's help and told him with my fingers crossed that I would keep it a secret.

Kilroy had a meeting with the marina owner, and the next day, Kilroy called Father and told him he struck a deal. He was going to lease the marina with an option to buy. That way, he could see how much business was done in both the off-season and the season before deciding whether to purchase it. The only problem was he desperately needed my help and was willing to pay me handsomely if Father would agree to it. I got on the phone with Father and Mother, and practically begged them to let me stay. They had a difficult time saying no as they raised me to be independent and self-reliant. In the end, they agreed to let me stay after I promised to come home for Christmas. I had my fingers crossed again because I figured by then I would be six months along.

Naturally, the first thing I did was tell Joseph. I must admit I was relieved to see him so excited. He was over the moon! It was agreed that he not let Kilroy know that he knew I was pregnant. We decided that once I began showing we would tell Kilroy of our plan to raise the child ourselves, and deal with the consequences.

The next few months went by in a blur. Joseph and I were very excited about the future and purchased a plot of land on a hillside where we planned to raise our family together. We even had a secret wedding ceremony and Joseph's best friend borrowed a camera and took a photograph for us. It's the one that was attached to this letter, the only picture I have of my beloved Joseph.

The people of St. Croix (called Crucians), were, and I suppose still are, somewhat fanatical about their jewelry. They all wear these silver and gold bracelets with a particular design that identifies them as Crucian. Of course, we had our own bracelets that we exchanged during the ceremony instead of rings. Joseph (like most Crucians), was also a firm believer in the power and value of gold and was adamant we set aside a "baby" fund. Each week we took whatever money we had left over after expenses and went into downtown Christiansted to purchase gold coins from one of the many dealers there. We put the coins in an empty rum bottle that we kept buried on our land. Every time we added coins to the bottle we would sit beneath those beautiful palms in the photograph and dream out loud about our family's future together. Eventually, Joseph put his entire life savings into the bottle and I did too. Believe me, it was no small feat transferring money to a Caribbean island in 1948, especially without having Father find out. I had been working the docks since I was five years old and had amassed a nice sized savings account. It was fattened considerably when I unexpectedly received five hundred dollars from my grandfather when I graduated high school. It was a lot of money back then, heck, it's a lot of money now, if you ask me. Anyways, Joseph and I felt comfortable that we had enough money to build a small house.

I was five months along and showing to the point where I couldn't excuse it solely as too much rice and beans. Joseph wanted to present me to his family at Thanksgiving where he planned to announce our secret marriage and my pregnancy, but first I needed to tell Kilroy that I wouldn't be giving the baby up for adoption. I knew I would have to tell my parents at some point but hoped to convince Kilroy not to spill the beans just because I was going to raise the baby with Joseph instead. I was nervous, but reasonably confident he would still support me. I worked hard for him on the dock and Joseph and I were friends with Kilroy and his fiancée, Genevieve (the girl he met on St. Maarten). She was a strikingly beautiful French girl maybe five years older than me. All the women envied her for her milk chocolate-colored skin and perfect complexion. When we went out together, Kilroy and Joseph usually scuba dived, while Genevieve and I snorkeled and tanned on the beach.

Joseph wanted to accompany me when I told Kilroy, but Kilroy still thought Joseph didn't know about my pregnancy, so I chose to do it alone. Since it was Thanksgiving week it was fairly busy. Joseph was out on a fishing charter with his dad, and Genevieve was in the marina office with Kilroy. There was a lull on the dock when I went in the office and asked to speak with Kilroy in private. Kilroy looked at me funny and said that whatever I needed to say could be said in front of his fiancée. That made me more nervous because I hadn't told Genevieve a thing about being pregnant. I started stammering and finally he said to just spit it out, which I did. I told him that Joseph and I were going to raise the baby ourselves, that I wasn't giving it up for adoption. I said I had just told Joseph and that we were going to break the news to his family on Thanksgiving, which was just a few days away. Genevieve started to say something but Kilroy quieted her and asked her to leave the office. I thought she would hug me or congratulate me or act surprised, but she just walked right past me. At first, Kilroy was very upset. He began telling me what a mistake it was and how my parents would be destroyed and how it would ruin my life. He kept reiterating how there were so many couples who could give the baby a good stable home right away, and that I could always have more kids in the future. I could see he was unhappy with my change of heart, and I felt a little guilty about deceiving him, so I asked him to be the baby's godfather. He seemed oddly put off and said he needed to think things through. Thankfully, a customer walked in and I was able to excuse myself.

I didn't talk to Kilroy or Genevieve the rest of the day and didn't know what to expect the next morning when I came down the dock. When I entered the marina office, Kilroy came out from behind the desk and gave me a big hug. He said he would be proud to be the baby's godfather but thought we should still keep my pregnancy under wraps. I told him that nobody else knew but Joseph, but he couldn't keep it from his family any longer. And besides, I was starting to look pregnant. Kilroy was agitated. I thought it was because of me, but I found out later that morning that Genevieve had cancelled her plans and gone back to St. Maarten. When Joseph got back from another fishing charter I asked him to invite Kilroy to Thanksgiving dinner because Genevieve left. Kilroy accepted Joseph's offer and asked him if he would take him diving on Thanksgiving morning to catch some lobster for the celebration.

Thanksgiving day wasn't picture perfect. In fact, there was some weather moving through and I told Joseph I didn't think they should go diving. He was young and strong though, and wasn't deterred by a little foul weather. He was an excellent diver and almost always returned with a nice bounty of crustaceans. He sold whatever we didn't eat to the local restaurants, which helped pad the "baby fund." Reluctantly, I let him go, but not before we ducked behind the office to sneak a kiss. He was nervously excited about the big announcement he planned to make at Thanksgiving dinner and so was I. It was about nine in the morning when they headed out of the marina in Joseph's skiff. I can still remember him waving back at me and smiling, just like it was yesterday. He was the most handsome young man imaginable and we were going to spend our lives together!

About an hour later it all changed, and my life would never be the same. I was tending to a customer on the dock who was refueling when I heard Kilroy's voice on the boat's marine radio. He was yelling "Mayday, mayday, diver missing…mayday." I jumped onto the customer's boat and called him back to find out exactly where he was. My heart was in my throat and I had trouble talking, but managed to get the location. After alerting the marine patrol, the customer offered to take his boat to the site. I asked one of the locals to watch the marina and within minutes we were speeding across the water. We found Kilroy driving around in circles about a half mile past a famous dive spot called "the wall." He said that he lost sight of Joseph on their first dive and he never resurfaced.

Naturally, I was frantic by this point. We all knew that if Joseph was still under water, he had to have drowned. Our only hope was that he resurfaced and couldn't make it back to the boat for some reason, or that he swam to shore, which was about a half mile away. The marine patrol showed up and soon we had several boats searching for Joseph. I knew that

Joseph was a strong swimmer, so I directed the owner of the boat I was on to run in closer to shore. We went five minutes along the beach heading east and then turned back west after not finding him. The sandy shoreline soon turned to rocky cliffs and after rounding a bend we found one of the marine patrol boats idling dangerously close to an outcropping of rocks. As we slowed our approach I watched in horror as two men leaned over the side and hauled Joseph's lifeless body on to the deck. I tried to climb onto the marine patrol boat but was physically restrained by an officer while another tried in vain to resuscitate Joseph. I could see blood coming from his head and after several minutes of CPR, the officer shook his head and said, "I'm sorry, he's gone."

Chapter 33

As Hanky and Ricky loaded the inflatable Zodiac into the back of Ricky's pickup, Ricky asked, "How come we're taking my truck?"

"'Cause this is *your* night, bro. Besides, my tags are expired."

"Isn't that how the cops nailed you last time?"

"No, that was a broken taillight."

"You sure?"

"Yeah, I'm sure. I spent almost two years in the joint thinking about it."

"Huh, coulda' swore it was expired tags."

"That was the time before. Now shut up and grab the trolling motor."

Hanky pointed to the corner of his storage unit and nervously glanced around as Ricky worked his way through a pile of stolen stuff to get to it.

Ricky unplugged the trolling motor from an extension cord and gingerly worked his way back to the front of the storage unit.

"You sure this things gonna work?"

"Sure I'm sure…checked it yesterday. Quit asking so many questions, all right? This ain't my first rodeo."

Ricky stood under the dim light on the outside wall of the building and gave Hanky a puzzled look.

Hanky asked, "What?"

"You were in the rodeo?"

"No, dumbass, it's just an expression. Now put the motor in the truck and let's do this. You still wanna do it, right?"

"Yeah."

"Yeah? We're about to snuff out you're sister-in-law-to-be and all you got to say is *yeah*? That don't sound too convincing. You wanna pussy out, now's the time. Don't be getting' squirrely on me once we get down to business."

"I ain't pussying out and I ain't getting' squirrely. In fact, I can't wait to beat her hoity-toity brains in. I just don't wanna get caught."

"Me neither, so do what I say and everything should go smooth."

Hanky pulled a tarp over the bed of the truck, then shut the overhead door to his storage unit and locked it. He nodded to Ricky and they climbed in Ricky's truck. As they exited the storage facility, Ricky asked, "What about last time?"

"What a*bout* last time?"

"Last time you got caught."

"That was for grand theft. I never been nailed for offing someone. I'm two for two in that category. So quit questioning everything I say unless you wanna be number three."

"You sure that homemade silencer is gonna work?"

"What did I just say? You wanna find out the hard way? Besides, we're only using it as a last resort. The plan is to club her over the head and dump her in the water to make it look accidental."

The two conspirators headed south on Dixie Highway and when they got to MLK Boulevard, Hanky told Ricky to turn left toward the Intracoastal. Hanky directed Ricky to a dirt road hidden in the mangroves. It ran alongside an abandoned home, courtesy of hurricane Wilma. They parked the truck, off-loaded the Zodiac, and hooked up the trolling motor at the water's edge.

Ricky swatted his hands around his head and muttered, "Fuckin' no-seeums."

Hanky reached into a small duffel bag and produced a can of bug spray. "Use some of this, I put some on back at the unit."

As Ricky sprayed some repellant on, Hanky climbed back in the cab of the truck. When he was done spraying himself, Ricky went around to the driver's side and got in.

"Whatcha doin?" he asked.

"Putting the silencer on, just in case."

Hanky had a small potato in one hand, and a pocket knife in the other. He carved a small hole out of one end, and then jammed it over the barrel of a thirty-eight special. He pointed it out the windshield and nodded his head.

"That should do it…silent but deadly." He looked at Ricky and added, "Just like your farts."

They both laughed and then Hanky put the gun back in the duffel and withdrew a pipe. As he stuffed some crack in it, Ricky said, "I thought you said you weren't gonna smoke any more before doing a job."

"For a simple burglary, no, but for what we're gonna do, we need to be amped up."

He lit the pipe, took a big hit, and passed it to Ricky. Once they were totally fried, Hanky said, "All right, rookie, let's go bag your first kill."

Ricky's brain was in overdrive from the crack and he couldn't think of anything to say except a line from one of his favorite movies, *Talladega Nights.* "Shake and bake, baby, shake and bake!"

They dropped the Zodiac in the water from a run-down dock, and climbed in. Hanky turned on the electric motor and they silently slipped through the narrow, mangrove-lined channel, out to the Intracoastal.

"Damn, it's dark out here," commented Ricky.

"The darker the better, bro. No more talking till we get to where we're going and then keep it to a whisper."

He handed Ricky a black knit cap to put on and did the same.

They crossed the quarter mile or so to Sabal Island, then hugged the shoreline as they headed along the seawall that bordered Holly's property. There was a small light hanging over the point that Holly's grandfather installed to attract fish, and as they approached it, Hanky reached into the duffel bag and pulled out a thick black trash bag. He handed it forward to Ricky.

"Tie this over the light when we pass by."

"What if somebody sees us?"

"They won't be able to once you cover the light; just do it!" he hissed.

The light was fairly dim to begin with, and once Ricky tied the trash bag over it, they were in complete blackness again. Hanky steered the raft around the point to the dock behind the vacant neighbor's house. He tied the raft up to a cleat, and whispered, "I'll hand you the duffel when you get up on the dock, let's go."

They both climbed up the ladder and then crouched down by the large hedge that divided the two properties.

"What time is it?" whispered Ricky.

"What? Who cares? It's killing time, that's what time it is. I already told you, you better not be getting squirrely on me."

"I'm not; I'm ready to do it. I'm just wondering if it's late enough. We should make sure the neighbors are asleep."

"Dude, this house is vacant and the one on the other side was pitch black when we went by. Most of these rich old people go to bed by nine and it's gotta be close to midnight."

"What about that house across the canal, it looks like someone's watching TV inside."

Hanky glanced across the canal and saw what Ricky was talking about. You could see the light in somebody's living room changing illumination from the TV screen.

"Don't worry about it. If they're watching TV, they're not watching us. If it makes you feel better though, I'll keep an eye peeled while you go scope out the situation. I'll wait a couple of minutes to make sure the coast is clear and then I'll join you."

Ricky wasn't thrilled with the idea, but he thought about all the money he was gonna get his greasy hands on by killing his fiancées half sister, and agreed.

"OK, just remember, there's a break in the hedge where the air-conditioning unit is. I'll jump the fence there, then creep up to the front bedroom where I left the window unlocked."

"Got it, now put these on." Hanky pulled two pairs of latex gloves from the duffel and they both slipped them on. Then he pulled out a lead pipe about two feet long with a handle fashioned from duct tape and handed it to him.

"Here's your bitch tamer, but don't even think about getting started until I join you, I wanna see the show."

"I thought I was gonna use that little aluminum bat."

"I almost forgot…they don't sink."

"Good thinking, man."

"That's why I'm here, bro, now get moving."

Ricky slapped the pipe against the palm of his hand a couple times, and Hanky could see the whites of his teeth when he smiled. Without another word he stayed in a crouch and ran along the hedge toward the air-conditioning unit.

***

Upstairs, in one of the second-floor bedrooms of the vacant house, Carlos sat patiently looking out the window. He had been watching Holly for the better part of an hour, contemplating his next move. Suddenly, something caught his peripheral vision and he looked down. The light casting from one of the windows of Holly's house shone through a small gap in the hedge, directly below him where the A/C unit was.

He mumbled, "What the *hell?*"

He couldn't believe his eyes as he watched someone in a black cap carrying what looked to be a pipe, step through the break in the hedge and disappear over the fence.

Chapter 34

"Oh- my-God!"

Holly took a big sip of wine and then set it down along with the letter so she could hurry to the bathroom. When she settled back into the sofa she glanced at her watch and saw it was after eleven-thirty. She was hardly sleepy though, she couldn't believe what she was reading.

I was devastated over Joseph's death and it's no exaggeration to say that I still am. Whoever said time heals all wounds, never lost the love of their life, I can tell you that. Well, you can imagine my plight. I was eighteen and pregnant with a dead man's child. I was lost and didn't know what to do. At Kilroy's urging, I kept hiding my pregnancy by wearing baggy clothes; not that any islanders would notice or care if I put on some weight. The investigation into Joseph's death was cursory and ruled an accidental drowning. The autopsy revealed a large contusion on the back of his head but it was attributed to having occurred when he washed up against the rocks where he was found. Kilroy seemed genuinely upset. He blamed himself for losing sight of his dive partner and friend. I wanted to call Father and go home, regardless of the consequences, but Kilroy convinced me otherwise. He reminded me I was only three months from giving birth and that my pregnancy would remain secret if I gave the baby up for adoption.

With Joseph gone and my dreams crushed, I wasn't thinking clearly and agreed. When Christmas came I told my parents that I had an island bug and was too ill to travel. They were none too happy and I promised them I would be back by April first at the latest. When I was in my eighth month, Kilroy hired a private doctor to examine me and I was prescribed bed rest until I gave birth. Kilroy's fiancée, Genevieve, returned and helped take care of me. She seemed almost as excited as I was and assured me I was doing the right thing by giving the baby up for adoption. She must have sensed I needed assurance because I can tell you I was having second and third thoughts about my decision. Genevieve said she met the couple who were adopting my baby and that they came from a fine family who would make sure the baby never wanted for anything. I asked to meet them and she said she would talk to Kilroy to see if it was possible.

I wasn't due for a few weeks, but the very next day my water broke and I went into labor. I expected Genevieve to rush me to the hospital, but instead she called the doctor who showed up ten minutes later and began barking orders at her. I was giving birth in Kilroy's rented house! So began the four most painful hours of my life. When I finally thought my insides had split open, out popped the most precious little boy ever! The doctor wanted to immediately give me a shot of pain medication, but I wouldn't let him until I held my baby. I counted his fingers and toes and was relieved to find them all there when I noticed he had an unusual birthmark. On his lower right arm he had a dark red stain that resembled a four-leaf clover. I called him "Lucky" and was kissing his face when I felt the sting of a needle in my thigh. That was the last thing I remembered until waking up the next morning.

"Oh, Millie!" Holly dabbed the corner of her eye with a tissue she grabbed from the bathroom. She couldn't believe the terrible heartbreak her aunt suffered at such a young age. And nobody knew about it! She sniffled into the tissue and then picked the letter back up. She was getting near the end.

Kilroy and the doctor were at my bedside when I woke up. It was February 23, 1949, and I had given birth the day before on President's Day. I asked to see my baby and Kilroy said it wasn't possible because the baby was with his new parents and they had left the island. Kilroy had me sign some papers regarding the adoption almost immediately after Joseph's death. According to Kilroy, the adoption agreement ensured the adoptive parents would remain anonymous. I was sick to my stomach because I was so distraught after Joseph's death I barely looked at it before signing. I felt I made a horrible mistake by giving up the baby and was desperately trying to think of a way to undo it. I thought maybe Genevieve might help me persuade Kilroy to try and fix things and asked to talk to her. I couldn't believe it when he told me she was back in St. Maarten. It finally occurred to me that Kilroy had seemingly manipulated my naiveté and trust in him as my father's friend. Within a week I was back home in Florida and shortly thereafter developed a pelvic infection which left me unable to bear anymore children. I felt like God was teaching me a lesson about motherhood and I sunk into a deep depression. I never went back to St. Croix and I would never see my baby "Lucky" again.

"Oh, how awful!" Holly dabbed her eyes again and took another sip of wine before continuing.

I thought about it, but even if I somehow managed to find Lucky, I convinced myself it wouldn't be fair to turn his world upside down. I wanted to believe that Kilroy placed him with a good family and that I should just let it be. So that's what I did. But I deeply regret never being able to tell him about his father and how we planned for our future together. I wanted to tell him how much we loved him and show him the beautiful site where we were going to build our home. The "baby fund" we established to build it should be right where we left it. The deed to the property is in the envelope. I set up an escrow account to pay the taxes on it with an attorney on the island. His card is attached to the deed. I probably should have sold the property years ago but always held out hope that one day Lucky would find out who his real parents were and get what was intended for him.

Maybe now you know why I love you so much, Holly. When your parents were killed in that terrible crash and you were left to be raised by me, you filled the emptiness in my soul from losing Lucky. You were the child I never had and never would have, so I gave you a double dose of love. Of course, you being you made it easy. I'm the one who should be thanking you for saving me from a life of regret. I can't imagine my life without you and I leave this world knowing it will be a better place with you in it. My only advice is: don't wait till tomorrow to tell someone you love them today. The only solace I take from Joseph's death is that our last words to each other were "I love you."

Tears were flowing down Holly's face and she fought a losing battle trying to keep them off the letter as she read the final words.

Oops, I almost forgot. When you get to be my age, dear, you'll find you say those words a lot. I forgot to tell you where the rest of the gold is. As I explained, Joseph was the one who got me started buying gold and I continued doing so up until three or four years ago. Bob Boone thinks I bought all my gold through him but the fact is I started long ago and I'm not even sure how much there is.

At first I kept the gold hidden in the house but later placed it in a few large safety-deposit boxes at the bank. Then the financial crisis of 2008 hit and I moved the gold out. I was a child of the Great Depression and wasn't taking any chances. I wish I could just tell you where it is, but like I said; I was worried somebody might read this letter before you did and steal the gold.

The first time you came home from college we spent the whole day together. We did some shopping and ran some errands in the morning and then we went fishing on the C-Love in the afternoon. I believe you caught a nice wahoo that we ate for dinner.

Holly remembered it well, it was the only time she ever caught a wahoo on the drift boat.

Well, forget about the fishing part, the important thing you need to remember is where we had lunch that day and the place I took you to afterward.

Holly racked her brain. She remembered going to the mall with Millie and then having lunch at a place on Lake Osborne. It was off of Hypoluxo Road just west of I-95. She couldn't remember the name of it but knew exactly where it was.

The name is the key. If you can't remember it, don't worry, the restaurant is still there. After we ate I needed to pick something up for the C-Love and took you somewhere I'd never taken you before.

Holly remembered perfectly. Millie took her to an old storage center where she had a unit stuffed full of dock junk. As she recalled, it was filled with extra buoys, ropes, fishing gear, and all types of accessories and spare engine parts for the *C-Love.* For the life of her she couldn't remember which storage center it was and there were plenty around to pick from.

Well, dear, that's where the gold is. If you can't remember where it is, the answer is in the books. When you go there, think of the restaurant's name and you'll figure it out. I decided to leave all the gold to you because I know you won't squander it. In fact, I expect you'll use most of it to help out the less fortunate; it's just who you are. That's enough about the gold.

So now you know my real story. The main thing I hope you take away from it is to live life to its fullest and without regret. When I think of Joseph, I choose to remember our last moments together. We snuck away for a kiss or two and professed our love for one another. I must tell you, dear, I see the same sort of sparks going off when you and Kit are together. The both of you need to overcome your stubbornness and not let something special slip away; otherwise, you'll have done something stupid like me that haunts you for the rest of your life. Don't feel sorry though, because if you are reading this, then I am finally together with my beloved Joseph again.

Perhaps I'll introduce you to him someday. Until then, just remember that I love you with all my heart.

Aunt Millie

"Jesus Christ," sobbed Holly. She blew her nose into some tissues and wiped her eyes. Her mind was whirling. The letter was incredible. She had to read it again. Then she realized it was almost midnight and she stunk to high heaven from her earlier run. She went to take a shower and remembered Millie had a Jacuzzi-style tub in the master bathroom. *Even better, I'll re-read it in there.* She turned the hot water on in the tub full blast and then lit a couple of candles. She put on her robe, walked back into the kitchen, and refilled her wineglass. Then she put the letter in the pocket of the robe, retrieved her iPod, and headed back to the Jacuzzi.

Chapter 35

As quickly and quietly as he could, Ricky hopped over the chain-link fence separating the two properties. There was some landscape lighting in both the back and the front yards, but the only light that shone on Ricky's side of the house was cast from a hall window. He avoided the patch of light and scrambled behind a small shed to survey the scene. Suddenly, another interior light came on. From his reconnaissance effort he had it pegged as the master bath. As he looked on, Holly passed by the hall window…completely naked! Another light switched on and she disappeared down the hall in a loose-fitting robe. Ricky licked his cracked lips. He *had* to get a better look. Like a cockroach he darted through the patch of light into the darkness on the side of the house.

He crouched low under the master bath window and pressed his ear to the wall. He could hear water running, lots of water running…she was going to take a bath. *Fuckin-A!* He peeked his head up and was pissed that he couldn't see the tub, but as he looked closer; he saw that a mirror on a closet door was angled just right. He took a step to the side of the window and had a direct view of the tub. *Yes!* He nestled in behind a cluster of palm trees and waited with eager anticipation. One by one all the lights in the house were switched off except for the master bath. He watched as Holly pulled some papers out of her pocket and set them down with her wine on a ledge next to the tub. Then she slipped on the headphones of her iPod and fiddled with the player. He could hardly wait for her to take off the robe.

He started saying, "Yes, yes, yes," under his breath as the robe finally slipped from her shoulders. Then it was, "No, no, no," as she hung it over the mirror on the closet door. *Fuck!* His view was almost totally obscured. He craned his neck through the palms and caught a glimpse of a long leg draped over the side of the tub. She was checking the temperature of the water. He craned his neck some more and caught a glimpse of the gentle swell of her bosom. With one hand he was the gripping the pipe and with the other he was playing squeeze the sausage. He was mesmerized and thinking of all the ways he'd like to take *her* temperature.

Out of nowhere a strong hand clamped over his mouth and a sharp knife was pressed to his throat. Then a voice whispered in his ear, "Let go of the pipe and don't make a sound."

Ricky released his grip and raised his left hand up. The guy with the knife jerked Ricky's head back and pressed the blade a little deeper.

"The *other* pipe, you fuckin' pervert."

Ricky dropped the pipe into the mulch.

"I swear to God if your dick's sticking out I'm gonna cut it off." Carlos slowly took his hand off Ricky's mouth.

"It's not, I swear, whatta you, whatta you want?"

Carlos pushed Ricky up against the side of the house, face-first.

"First I want you to keep it down, asshole," he whispered.

"She, she's in the Jacuzzi...with some headphones on. Please, please don't cut me. You're *cutting me,* man. Who, who are you?"

"Shut the fuck up for a second." Carlos shoved Ricky along the wall until he could see into the bathroom and confirm the girl had headphones on. Then he marched him up against the shed. With one hand he held the knife to Ricky's throat and with the other he held one of Ricky's arms behind his back.

"So what are you doing here, Spanky? You don't need a lead pipe to get your rocks off. And keep it down, unless you want me to yank your fuckin' tongue out through your trachea."

Ricky was scared. No doubt about it, he was scared shitless. Not being able to see who it was made it even worse.

"I uh, I uh, I was just uh, just gonna—"

"You were just gonna lie to me, Spanky, that's what you were gonna do. Bad decision, my friend, I hate liars more than I hate perverts."

Ricky started to squirm and plead as Carlos dug the knife into his throat.

From somewhere in the darkness behind Carlos, a voice said,

"Drop the knife, dickhead. Drop it before I blow your fucking head off."

Carlos cursed himself because he had left his gun in the rental car. He hadn't planned on doing anything other than observing the girl and forgot to retrieve it before sneaking up on the kid with the pipe. It hadn't occurred to him that there was a second punk involved. He needed to size up his new adversary before deciding what tactic to take, so he stalled.

"You shoot me and the sound will wake the whole neighborhood. The cops will be here before you know it."

"What do *you* care, you'll be dead. Besides, I got a silencer, I ain't no idiot. Drop the knife now!" Hanky yelled in a loud whisper.

Carlos knew that a silencer greatly reduced the accuracy of a weapon. They were meant for use only at close range. Unfortunately, the guy sounded like he was right behind him, but it still gave him some hope. He reluctantly released Ricky and dropped the knife to the ground. As Ricky breathed a sigh of relief and stepped away from Carlos, Carlos turned to face the mystery voice. He couldn't see the face of the punk with the gun, but he could see the barrel sticking out from the darkness. He couldn't believe it but there was something stuck on the barrel. It wasn't a silencer, *what the hell was it?* It looked like a fucking potato, but there was no hole in the end of the potato for a bullet to cleanly exit. It looked like the idiot had just shoved a potato over the end of the barrel! It was playing out like a bad episode of *The Dukes of Hazzard.* This changed everything.

"Hey *asshole*, who told you to turn around?" The punk with the gun waved it like he wanted him to face the other way. "Face the shed and don't make a sound until I ask you to, got it?" Carlos complied and turned back around.

Hanky turned to Ricky and asked, "What the hell happened?"

Ricky was rubbing his neck where Carlos held the knife. "I think he *cut me,* dude. Seriously, am I bleeding? It fucking hurts."

Hanky pretended to look but he kept his eye peeled on the guy facing the shed. "You're fine, if you *are* cut it's a surface wound."

"Dude, the surface is my *neck.* My hand feels wet, man, I'm bleeding! That fucking knife he's got is *sharp!"*

"You're gonna be fine, man, what the hell happened?"

"I was watching the bitch when this guy came out of nowhere and jumped me from behind."

"He was jerking off." Carlos was getting ready to make his move and wanted to keep them off balance. "He was playing, *Pop goes the Weasel,* watchin' the girl in the bathroom."

"Fuck you, man!" hissed Ricky. "Who the *fuck* are you, anyways?"

"Yeah, answer the question, dickhead."

Carlos slowly turned around to face the two conspirators.

"Better yet, why don't you two punks tell me what *you're* doing here and I might let you live."

Ricky and Hanky looked at each other like the guy was crazy, which he was.

"*I'm* holding the gun, shit-for-brains, so tell me what you're doing here, *now,* we got work to do."

"Why don't you tell me what *kind* of work; that would be a start."

"I got a bad feeling about this," said Ricky. "Just cap him and let's get on with it. The fucker cut me, bro. Cap him before she gets done with her bath."

"I'm calling the shots here! So who the hell *are* you?" Hanky stuck the gun out a little farther toward Carlos and watched in disbelief as the stranger stepped toward it into the light. Then he smiled, displaying a set of wolfish teeth and a hypnotizing stare.

"I'm the guy that lives under your bed and grabs you by the ankles when you get up to piss in the middle of the night. And I say a punk like you doesn't have the balls to pull the trigger."

"Shoot him!" cried Ricky. "Shoot the fucker!"

Hanky didn't need any more encouragement and pulled the trigger. Although Carlos was relatively certain the gun would backfire, he nonetheless dove toward the house. Whatever movie Hanky saw the potato silencer used in, he forgot one key element. That was to make sure there was a hole in the end of the potato for the bullet to travel out of. The gunpowder igniting in the chamber went toward the path of least resistance and exploded in his face. The bullet smashed through the potato, sending home fries everywhere, then thumped the shed. Hanky fell to his knees and cried out in pain. Carlos rolled on the ground and came up in a crouch holding the pipe. Ricky saw Carlos come up with the pipe and took off over the fence without looking back. Hanky managed to hold onto the gun with one hand and with the other he rubbed his singed face.

"Help me...Ricky...wait..." Hanky sensed the stranger coming at him and fired in his direction. This time the bullet flew out the chamber relatively unobstructed, barely missing Carlos as he charged him. It smashed into the stucco on the side of the house, sending concrete chips flying. Hanky tried to stand up and was about to fire again when the pipe caught him flush in the temple. Carlos knew from the sound that he hit him a little higher than he wanted. It sounded like A-Rod hitting a watermelon piñata. The guy went down face-first, like a drunken David Hasselhoff into a plate of spaghetti. Only this time the spaghetti was coming out of his head. *Shit.* He was aiming for the guy's ear, hoping to just knock him out. He wanted to tie him to a chair and get some answers. *What the hell were they about to do?* Rape her? Kill her? Rob her? All of the above? Do they know about the gold? Do they know where the gold is? Is it in the house? *Shit again.* Suddenly another light came on in one of the rooms adjacent to the bathroom. She was out of the tub!

Carlos picked Hanky up off the ground by his armpits and dragged him over to the gap in the hedges by the fence. He went to one knee and slung him over his shoulder, then sprung up and heaved him over the chest-high fence. He scrambled over it and heard a noise coming from the dock. He ran along the hedge toward the dock and crouched down behind a large bush. He peered out at the dock and it was empty. He squinted to try to see better but it still looked empty. Then he heard a distant slapping sound and looked down the canal in the direction it came from. In a faint light cast on the water he saw a small black shape round the point as it headed toward the Intracoastal. *The other punk was getting away on a raft!*

Carlos had even bigger concerns though, namely, did the girl hear something and call the police? He dashed back to Hanky's lifeless body and dragged him over to the side door that led into the garage of the empty house. He kneeled in silence for a few seconds to catch his breath and listen for sirens. He was looking toward Holly's house when the light that suddenly turned on, was turned off. *Did she go back to the bathroom?* He listened hard for the sound of a siren but heard none. Maybe she *didn't* hear anything.

He considered the situation and realized that his knife was still in the dirt by the shed. In fact, the gun and the pipe were laying in the side yard too. *Shit.* He crept back over the fence and sidled around the shed. When he got to where he thought his knife was he went down on all fours and felt around in the dark. He had a pen light in his pocket but didn't dare risk using it. He didn't need to. Moments later he had his cherished switchblade back in his pocket. He crawled over to where he bludgeoned the guy and found his gun nearby. He was searching for the pipe when a shadow crossed the light coming from the bathroom window and he froze. He cautiously looked up toward the window and saw a finger press against it followed by the face of the girl. There was something stuck to the window and she was trying to figure out what it was. He saw it too…*what was it?* Then it hit him. *It was the fucking idiot au gratin…*a potato chunk from the punk's silencer. He knew how difficult it would be to see out into the darkness from inside the lit bathroom, but as soon as the face disappeared from the window, he took off. Moments later he was dragging the body into the neighbor's garage. He shut the door, pulled the pen light out of his pocket, and switched it on. The dead guy's head was lying on a doormat and soaking it with blood. He stepped over to the large chest freezer he spotted earlier and opened the lid. A light mounted on the inside of the lid faintly lit the freezer's interior. Then he bent down and picked the dead guy up, cradling his head with the doormat.

He chuckled and said, "We have to stop meeting like this…feel like chillin' out?"

In one fluid motion he pivoted around to the open freezer and dropped him on top of the frozen bait inside. A couple broken legs later he had him stuffed in tight; he was getting good at it. He was about to shut the lid when he spotted a card sticking out of the guy's shirt pocket. He pulled the card out and read it; Hanky's Pressure Cleaning Service. There was a phone number and an address in Hypoluxo at a place called San Castle Storage. He nodded and slipped the card into his pocket.

There was a bathroom in the laundry room between the garage and kitchen. He stepped inside, closed the door, and turned on the light. As expected, he had blood all over his shirt. He stripped it off and dropped it along with the potato-gun into a small trash can with a plastic liner. He quickly washed his arms and face and then pulled the liner out of the trash can. He went back to the garage and popped open the trunk of his new rental car. He had a duffel bag in it with a change of clothes and he pulled a new shirt out. Then he tied off the trash can liner and put it in the duffel. He flicked on his pen light again and swept it around by the door, checking for blood stains. Seeing none, he quietly opened the side door again and listened for sirens or any sounds coming from next door. He was basking in the silence when he noticed that the bathroom light in the house next door was turned off and another light was turned on. *Was she finally going to bed?* Relieved to be undetected, he stepped inside the garage and locked the door. He shined the penlight on his watch and saw it was twelve thirty. Time to go; he didn't want to push his luck.

He went back upstairs to the room he was watching from earlier and made sure he didn't leave any trace of his presence behind. After he did the same with the bathroom and garage, he climbed behind the wheel and turned the ignition on the convertible Chrysler. After he unsuccessfully tried to tail the guy called Hambone earlier in the day, he thought it prudent to switch rentals. He also got a room at a nearby hotel because he knew that once Eight-Toe's body was found, the police would look for Ratdog, which would lead them to the boat. He felt as good as possible about his situation under the circumstances and pressed the garage door opener. He pulled out of the garage, pressed the opener again, and drove down the street a half a block before switching on the headlights. He needed to get back to his hotel room and get some rest. Donny Nutz would be in town in a matter of hours and he had to deal with him next.

Chapter 36

Holly had been unsuccessfully trying to relax in the Jacuzzi when she realized she didn't have her cell phone nearby. She hoped that listening to a little soft jazz on her iPod would loosen her up enough to properly get her head around Millie's letter. She was wrong. She would have to read it again…in the morning. Like millions of people around the world she had become addicted to having her smart phone within arm's reach at all times. She hoped that as she transitioned from computer consultant to marina operator she might somehow loosen its grip on her. Probably not though; the grip was more likely to get even tighter. She believed (like so many others), that technology equaled freedom. Holly was all about rockin' the techno-freedom. She was a high-tech girl in a high-tech world…and damn proud of it.

She got out of the tub, slipped on her robe, and headed to the bedroom to retrieve her cell from her purse. She touched the screen and it flashed, "No new messages." *Shoot!* She was hoping Kit would call to tell her he was going to the FBI. *God, he was stubborn!* She thought about the words in Millie's letter about not letting stubbornness get in the way. If *he* didn't call them first thing in the morning, *she* would. She really wanted to talk to Kit too, but she swore she wouldn't until he called the FBI. She had to stick to her guns and not call him. Was she being stubborn too?

Oh my God, what am I thinking?

She quickly quashed the comparison of her relationship with Kit to that of Millie and Joseph's. It was *way* too soon to think like that. Way, way too soon. *Wasn't it?* She didn't know *what* to think as she walked back in the bathroom and was even more perplexed as she looked at the bathroom window. There was something plastered to the window. Whatever it was, she was certain it wasn't there when she filled the tub. *Huh.* She walked up to it and put her finger on the glass as if she would be able to feel it. Then she took her headphones off as if she would be able to hear it. Then she finally pressed her nose up to the glass to get a close-up view. *What the heck?* Was it a piece of bird poop? Did a lizard lose its lunch? She sniffed at the glass as if that would help identify it, and she laughed. One thing was for sure, it would remain a mystery if it meant having to taste it. *How weird*...just like everything else lately.

Chapter 37

Within a few minutes of leaving the dog track, Tangles and I were zipping south on I-95 at a respectable eighty miles an hour. I didn't want to push it because it was Saturday night and I figured it was prime time for the state troopers to shine. The last thing I needed was to get pulled over when we needed to talk to Hambone *yesterday*.

"Where we headed, to his house?" asked Tangles.

"Yeah, it's as good a place as any to start. See if you can get him on your cell."

Tangles called but was kicked to voice mail just like I was a few minutes earlier. He shook his head and snapped his phone shut.

"No luck, boss. You said the TV at the track showed him being released after being questioned in a home-invasion homicide?"

"That's what it said, shit, who do you think got killed?"

"I dunno what to think. There's so much shit going on it's hard to keep track."

We exited at Woolbright and headed to Hambone's house, which was in a nice development on the east side of Congress Avenue, just south of Golf Road. As soon as we turned in we saw the street was lit up with news trucks. We crept past Hambone's house and I pulled to the side of the road.

"I don't see his truck," said Tangles.

"I don't see his wife's car either. Let's see if any of these reporters know anything."

We exited the Beemer and I walked up to the first one I came to. He had just finished talking to the camera and his cameraman was starting to break down some equipment. I noticed that there weren't any vehicles in Hambone's driveway at all.

"Excuse me, can you tell me what's going on here?"

A young guy turned to face me. He had an ID tag hanging from a lanyard around his neck that identified him as Gibby Gomez from Televiso Mexicano.

"Jess?" I was looking ahead to the next news vehicle thinking of a knight's scene from an *Indiana Jones* movie…I had picked *poorly*. I took a little Spanish in high school though, so figured why not give it a shot? It was time to flash my linguistic ability.

"Que Pasa?" I asked him.

"Jew speak Spanish?"

"What?"

"Jew, do jew speak Spanish?"

"Oh, oh, I see."

"Si? Jew do speak Spanish?"

"Uh, well, I uh, I actually do speak a *little* Spanish." I gave him the international hand symbol for "a little," made popular by the TV show and movie of the same name, *Get Smart*.

He looked down at Tangles and furrowed his bushy brow. Then he twizzled his shiny mustache and gave me a skeptical look.

"Who are jew two?"

"We are a, we are a…amigos…of a…of el hombre… who lives in la…who lives in la casa." I pointed proudly at the house. *Nailed it.*

His eyes went wide.

"Jew two? Amigos?"

"Si, so que pasa?" I was on a roll.

"Are jew joking me?"

"Huh? No" I shook my head. "No, me no joking."

"Jew two are amigos de la Pescador?"

I was pretty sure that Pescador was Spanish for fish…or…fishing…or fisherman. *Bingo!* Gotta be fisherman.

"Si, si, we are amigos de la Pescador…Que pasa? He's not here, is he?"

He shook his head no.

"Is no a good day for pescadors. Are jew two amigos with dee other pescador?"

"What other pescador?"

"Dee one who got murdered."

"What? There was a fisherman murdered? Who?"

"Dee police no say, but he live in Jerry Hill."

Jerry Hill? *Oh shit.*

"You mean Cherry Hill? The other pescador lives in Cherry Hill?"

"Si, Jerry Hill. Dee police no give detail but I hear dee scene of dee crime was greeeezly."

"Grisly?"

"Si, greeezly. Day say it look like el Tiburon eat el Tiburon pescador."

Now I thought my Spanish was pretty good, but el Tiburon was a new one on me.

"El Tiburon? Que is el Tiburon?"

"El Tiburon? Is dee shark. Dee rumor is dee shark eat dee shark fisherman."

I looked at Tangles and he said what I was thinking.

"Holy shit, it's gotta be Eight-Toe."

The mustachioed Mexican reporter sensed that we knew the victim.

"Jew know him? What did jew call him? Eight-Toe? Octo-Toe? Dees is his name?"

Tangles and I headed to the Beemer and Gibby Gonzalez ran after us with his card.

"Pleez, pleez, senor. Jew find out anyting, jew call me, pleez?" He tossed his card at me before I could close the driver's door and it landed in my lap.

I powered down the window a touch and waved at him as we pulled away.

"No problemo, Gibby. Gracias!"

I looked in the side mirror as we pulled away. He had his index and pinky finger up to the side of his head, signaling for me to call him.

Chapter 38

Franklin Post (aka Stargazer), had enough memories of the seven years spent working for the forty-third president to last a lifetime. He regarded him as hands down the most unintentionally funny man he ever met. When the president's second term was up and the 2008 election was unexpectedly won by a young Democratic newcomer named Obama, it created a problem. Namely, the president was concerned that Obama wouldn't appreciate DICK because he created it without congressional or senatorial knowledge and approval. The other agency heads that met with the president at Camp David back in 2001 agreed as well. If DICK was revealed to the incoming President and he didn't embrace it, the fallout would be enormous. It would create a political and legal firestorm that would undoubtedly cost them their jobs, their pensions, and possibly their freedom. There was just no way to know how the incoming president would react and the risks were too high if he blew the cover off DICK.

It was therefore decided that the new president would be kept out of the loop and Franklin would not report to him. Instead, he would meet once a year with the same group that nominated him to head

DICK in the first place: the heads of the FBI, CIA, DEA, NSA, Homeland Security, and the Secretary of Defense. DICK had been wildly successful and they were more than happy to cover its paltry billion dollar a year operating budget out of their own slush funds. They especially liked that since DICK nailed bin Laden and several other high-profile terrorists, they were able to redirect DICK toward some high-profile criminal cases that nagged them. Each time they met, the group would give Franklin a wish list of cases that they wanted help with. Recently, at the CIA's request, DICK exposed a Russian spy gang led by a voluptuous redhead. At the FBI's request, they found notorious Irish Mob boss “Whitey” Bulger. For Homeland Security they uncovered several terrorist plans to bomb planes and trains in New York City. For the NSA they cracked a worldwide computer hacking ring that was pilfering customer data and classified information from dozens of US-based international companies and government agencies. Of course, the biggest coup for DICK was nailing down Osama bin Laden's whereabouts. The military and Seal Team 6 received all the credit publicly, but privately, Franklin and his team were given the royal treatment. Altogether, Franklin had established an excellent working relationship with the group, and could call on any of them at anytime for backup or support.

Although Franklin met in person once a year with the supervisory group, he *never* met in person with any of his agents. He communicated only by phone, using a nifty voice-altering device he invented. When spoken into it, the device changed his voice to sound like virtually anybody he wanted. He had a handful of favorites that included Sean Connery, Stephen Hawking, John Forsyth, Dr. Smith from *Lost in Space,* and the voice of the car from the seventies' TV show *Knight Rider.* He was always adding new voices to his invention that he called the Oralator…name subject to change. When he needed to call DICK agent Thomas Cushing, he programmed the Oralator to speak in the voice of Higgins, from the eighties' smash-hit detective show, *Magnum P.I.*

He pressed the hyper-speed dial on the arm of his control chair and leaned backward as a helmet apparatus with attached microphone automatically rose from the back of the chair and positioned itself directly over his head. Roughly four thousand miles away, in Delray Beach, Thomas Cushing's DICK phone rang and he answered it.

"Hello, boss."

Once his voiceprint was confirmed, the call was connected, and Franklin Post answered.

"Thomas! So good to hear your voice, old boy!"

Cushing shook his head at the unusual way the leader of the most secret intelligence organization in the world contacted his agents. Like all other DICK agents, he had no idea who his boss was. The only clue was a longtime rumor inside of DICK that his nickname was "Stargazer." The agents thought it was because he always contacted them using famous actors' voices. They figured the boss was some kind of TV and movie buff, which, of course, he was, but they never pegged him to be a world-renowned astronomer, billionaire, and Internet start-up guru, which he also was.

"Higgins again?" he answered.

"You know I can't resist calling you 'Thomas' in my 'Higgins' voice. It just sounds so *right.* Oh, how I wish there were more characters on TV like the incomparable 'Higgins,' but alas, we are awash in mindless reality shows with the likes of 'The Situation,' 'JWoww,' and 'Snooki'."

"Please, sir, don't tell me you watch *Jersey Shore.*"

"Good Lord, *No*! I would rather have feces-tipped needles driven under my fingernails like the Bunga-Bunga did to the Burmese in the Indo-Asiatic war... which reminds me of when General MacArthur asked me to translate for him in negotiations with Papuan tribesman for access through the—"

"You're doing it again, sir."

"What."

"You're not just using Higgins' voice, you're role-playing."

"Damn, I can't seem to stop doing that. Once you start talking like someone, you instinctively start to think like them too. Much like the great silverback ape in the Zambezi rain forest will mimic—"

"Sir?"

"Dammit. I did it again, sorry. Here, let me switch over to a more conducive voice." Stargazer scrolled through a "voices list" on the left arm of his control chair and pressed "Peter Graves."

"How do I sound now?" he asked.

"Serious."

"Good, then I'll get to the reason for my call. You watch the news tonight?"

"As a matter of fact, yeah."

"You see the home invasion story?"

"Which one?"

"The one in Boynton where the guy got killed."

"I caught the tail end of it, what's the deal?"

"The deal is that the guy who got killed is a shark fisherman who fishes out of the C-Love Marina."

"No shit."

"Yeah, the same marina that Donny Nutz's last boat disappeared from before being found half-sunk off Nag's Head. The same marina that his other yacht, the *JC*, is docked at right now."

"I know."

"Well, what you probably don't know, which is why I'm calling, is that the guy who got killed is a known associate of another fisherman named Hambone, who is a known associate of—"

"Let me guess; Kit Jansen, aka Shagball."

"You got it."

"Son of a bitch."

"Aren't we all? Anyways, the FBI is convinced this guy Jansen knows what happened to Donny Nutz's boat. In fact, their working theory is that Jansen was taken offshore to get whacked and somehow turned the tables. They offered him a possible deal if he fills in the blanks and helps bring Nutz down."

"What did he say?"

"He told them not to hold their breath. The FBI thinks that Jansen thinks that Nutz doesn't know who did what, because if he did, he would already be dead."

"Good point. He must not know. This guy Jansen sounds pretty sharp."

"He might be, and he may have been right about Nutz not knowing what happened…until tonight."

"I have a feeling there's some details about the home invasion you left out."

"Your feeling is right. It seems that it wasn't your ordinary home invasion. For one thing, nothing appeared to be stolen. For another thing, he was gagged, duct-taped to a kitchen chair, and tortured. Six of his toes were cut off and it appears the assailant cooked some up and ate them on a pizza."

"Jesus Christ."

"Yeah, I imagine the victim was asking for some divine intervention at one point too. Probably before he choked on his own vomit and took a bullet between the eyes."

"Man, I can see why most of it didn't make the news."

"Right, it's not exactly dinnertime fare, so what do you think?"

"Except for the eating the toes part, I'd say it's classic Donny Nutz. I don't know what to make of that toe-eating shit. Who would do that?"

"Nutz has been known to sub out work. Especially after losing two guys down here, it would make sense. Maybe he hired someone who is a little unorthodox."

"Wow, I guess. One's thing's for sure, though, whatever the shark fisherman knew, Donny Nutz does too."

"Which means he's probably on to Jansen and whoever helped him."

"Which means they're next."

"Which is where *we* come in. When Jansen calls the FBI to make a deal the call will be routed to your phone."

"How do you know he's gonna call? It could be awhile before he gets the details about the home invasion and puts it together."

"Don't worry, he'll be calling, there's one more thing I forgot to mention."

"What's that?"

"His friend Hambone was found at the scene and taken in for questioning. When it became obvious he had nothing to do with it, he was released...ten minutes ago. He saw the crime scene, Thomas, and he's probably made contact with Jansen. They have to figure Nutz is on to them by now, they have to be scared, who wouldn't be?"

"Yeah, he'll call. Unless he's an even *bigger* psycho, he'll call. How do you want me to play him?"

"The usual, find out everything he knows. See if he can be useful, if he can, maybe we can use him to get to Nutz. He's got to be stopped. I've been sifting through some data that seems to link him to arms trafficking through Port Everglades. It's even looking like some of the weapons are ending up in terrorist hands and you know how much I like *those* guys."

"Yeah, let's just say I'm glad my last name isn't El dash something or other."

"You got that right, Thomas. Donny Nutz should be in Palm Beach County by morning. Play Jansen however you want, just nail Nutz with something good. It's time to close this case; we have even bigger fish to fry. Are you clear on your mission?"

"Crystal, sir."

"Any questions before I hang up?"

"Yes, is my phone going to self-destruct in ten seconds?"

"Damn, was I doing it again?"

Chapter 39

Less than ten minutes later we were in the Cherry Hill neighborhood. I had been to Eight-Toe's a couple of years earlier and vaguely remembered where his house was. We pulled up and down a couple of streets and finally found one with police cars and a news van parked in front. It was definitely Eight-Toe's. *Shit.*

"Damn, looks like it's Eight-Toe's. What the hell happened?" I wondered out loud.

"We gotta find Hambone, what about his triplex? He has those rental units right around the corner."

"Good call; let's see if he's there."

We made a few quick turns and found ourselves on the border of the industrial area by the train tracks. Hambone inherited a small house with a triplex behind it and he almost always had one of the units available for rent.

I knew he had the house rented but had no idea which (if any), of the triplex units were vacant. There were cars parked in the driveway, but I didn't see his truck. I parked the Beemer across the street and Tangles and I walked up the drive. As soon as we reached the house a dog started barking and some lights came on. An unfriendly voice came from an open window.

"Who's there?"

"It's Shagball, I'm looking for Hambone. Is he here?"

"No, so hit the road, before I let Queenie out."

"Queenie?"

As soon as I said the name, a deep growl came from the shadows on the other side of the chain-link fence. The guy in the house laughed.

"On the other hand, maybe you should stay, I think she likes you."

"He has that way with the bitches," said Tangles.

"Who said that?"

Another voice came from farther down the drive and it was Hambone.

"It's OK, Jeb, let 'em pass, they're friends of mine."

We started walking up the dark drive while Jeb consoled the dog.

"Sorry, Queenie, no midnight snack tonight."

"Don't wait up on account of us," cracked Tangles.

"Don't count on it, pardner."

On cue, the dog growled again.

Hambone flicked on the outside light of the first triplex unit. He was clad in nothing but a pair of promotional Budweiser boxer shorts and cradled a shotgun above his rock solid beer-belly. It would have been a great snapshot for the cover of *Trailer Park Magazine*. I noticed the bumper of his truck peeking out from behind a trailered boat, and he signaled for us to go inside the apartment.

"Where'd you get the gun?" I asked.

"I always keep one handy for pest control. C'mon in, I don't want to wake the other tenants."

We stepped inside the small studio apartment and he set the shotgun down behind the door. I was a little surprised not to see his wife, Maureen.

"Where's Mo?"

"She wanted to stay with me but I made her go to her sister's until this gets sorted out."

"We tried calling to find out what happened but kept getting kicked to voice mail."

"That's 'cause I had to leave my phone with the cops if I wanted to be released. They're checking my call history to verify my story and whereabouts. I guess I'll get a new phone in the morning."

"So what happened?"

Hambone told the entire story, and at the end, said, "Kit, they tortured him. As tough as he was, he must have spilled the beans, they cut his *toes off*, man. Jesus."

I put a hand on his shoulder and he shook his head. I could tell he was shaken up.

"I'm sorry, Ham, I know you guys were close. So what do the police know?"

"Not much. I told them I was just checking on him from the night before. That I let myself in with his spare key after I found his truck stripped a few blocks away and he didn't answer his cell. The only reason they let me go was I didn't have any blood on me and I had his spare key. Plus, you could tell he had been dead awhile. Their working theory is the killer gained entrance by delivering a pizza last night. If he had the key, he wouldn't have had to use the pizza ruse, and I wouldn't have been able to get in without breaking a window. I didn't tell him about the guy from the Grand Banks that tried to tail me, though—the guy I think might have done it."

"Why not?"

"They killed my buddy and they killed my love of pizza. It's payback time, bro, plain and simple. I wanna get my hands on that son of a bitch."

"Amen to that," added Tangles.

"So what do you wanna do? Go over to the marina and see if he's there?"

"I already did and he's not there. Neither is Skeeter. The cops are trying to find him to back up my story but he's nowhere to be found. "

"Robo said Skeeter's on the guy's payroll; he docked the boat for him."

"Are you shittin' me? That would explain it; Skeeter was asking some pointed questions about Eight-Toe's bankroll on the way home last night. He's probably in cahoots with him."

"Wait a second," said Tangles. "Do you really think Skeeter helped murder Eight-Toe? C'mon, no way. What did the cops say? Do they think there's more than one killer?"

"Well, they didn't exactly say so, but Eight-Toe's a…*was,* a big guy. I don't see how one person could have handled him like that."

"You did say he was all assed up though, right? If he was *that* drunk anything's possible," added Tangles.

"We don't know what happened," I said. "Shit, I don't know what to think."

"Maybe you should take Holly's advice and call the FBI."

I looked at Tangles trying to comprehend what he said and a knot of fear began twisting in my stomach. *Oh shit, Holly.*

"You talked to Holly, didn't you?" asked Hambone.

I pulled out my phone and tapped her name on the touch screen. After a couple of nervous rings she answered.

"Kit?"

"Holly, thank God you're all right."

"What's going on? Why are you calling so late?"

"Did you see the news?"

"No, I just got done taking a long bath and was getting ready for bed, why?"

"Eight-Toe was murdered."

"Oh my God! What happened?"

"I'll tell you when I get there, I'm on my way."

"It has to do with those damn tanks, doesn't it. Oh my God!"

"Listen to me, Holly, make sure all your doors and windows are locked. I'll be over as fast as I can, if anybody but me shows up call nine-one-one."

"You're scaring me, Kit."

"I'll be there in five, honey, lock it down." Click.

Chapter 40

As soon as I hung up the phone, Hambone asked, "Do you guys have any protection?"

Tangles reached in his pocket and pulled out a roll of six condoms.

"Sure, how many you want?"

"No, smartass, I'm talking about *serious* protection." He picked up the shotgun and displayed it. I looked at Tangles and was 99 percent sure the little wannabe horn-dog wasn't packing anything lethal.

"No, but we're going to a gun store first thing tomorrow. C'mon, Tangles, let's go."

We left the apartment and were halfway down the drive when Hambone came jogging after us.

"Hang on a sec."

Tangles was a couple of steps behind me and Hambone reached him first.

"Here, take this." Hambone handed him a small handgun and Tangles switched it from hand to hand.

"Be careful, it's loaded."

"What is it?"

"A five-shot, thirty-eight special...hammerless, fits in your pocket real nice. Hopefully you won't have to use it."

"Thanks, man." Tangles slipped the gun in his pocket and fist-bumped Hambone.

"Glad to see you're prepared," I commented.

"When it rains it pours and when it pours it floods. That's when the rats come out. That's when you turn 'em into ratatouille."

I didn't have time to explain to Hambone that ratatouille was a vegetable dish and had nothing to do with rats except in a movie. We needed to get to Holly's.

"Well said, Ham. Call me when you get your new phone, we're outta here."

***

As we turned off of A1A onto Sabal Island Drive, a convertible Chrysler with the top up was pulling out. Instinctively, I looked at the driver whose face was partially visible thanks to a streetlight. I only had a fleeting glimpse as we headed in opposite directions, but the face looked familiar. It was him! The guy from the Grand Banks! *Wasn't it?*

"Shit! Did you see who was driving that car?"

"No, who was it?"

"It looked like that guy from the Grand Banks." I hit the gas and sped the last quarter mile toward Holly's.

"Seriously?"

"No, I'm joking, wasn't that funny?"

"But I thought he was driving a Chevy."

I thought about what he said and he was right. Were my eyes playing tricks on me? I wasn't so sure.

"Maybe he's got more than one car, how do I know?"

We zipped into Holly's turnaround driveway and pulled up to the front door. I was glad to see the entranceway lit up and could see Holly looking out a window at us. *Thank God.* As soon as we got to the door she swung it open and we went in. She fell into my arms and I hugged her tight.

"Kit, what happened? I-I can't believe Eight-Toe was…was murdered." Her voice cracked a little.

"Believe it. We just left Hambone; he was the one who found him, it's way worse than anybody knows. So…everything's been normal here? You didn't see or hear anything unusual tonight?"

I tried to sound as nonchalant as possible. I didn't want to alarm her any more than she already was. I didn't think it would help the situation to tell her I thought I just saw a suspected killer leaving her neighborhood.

Tangles started walking toward the kitchen and we followed.

"Well, after you called I made sure the doors were locked because usually only the front one is until I go to bed. The windows almost always stay locked this time of year because it's too hot to have them open and the air conditioning is always on. Sure enough, they were all locked, *except* for the side window in the front bedroom."

"Are you kidding me?"

"No, and I could have sworn it was locked. I *always* keep the windows locked. I've seen too many of those *CSI* shows. Would you guys like something to drink? Help yourselves."

Tangles opened the fridge and pulled out a bottle of water. "You want one?" he asked me.

"Yeah, thanks."

We slugged some water down and I turned back to Holly.

"That's a little odd, the bedroom window being unlocked. But that's it? Nothing else unusual?"

"Nothing I can think of."

"Good."

As soon as she said there was nothing else she could think of, she thought about the strange thing stuck to her bathroom window.

"But now that you mention it…no, forget it, I'm sure it's nothing."

"What? What's nothing?"

"Well…when I got out of the bath there was something weird stuck to the window. I can't figure out what it is, it's probably nothing though."

"Show me."

The three of us walked down the hall and turned into the master bath, which was still warm. I briefly thought about Holly in the bath and got distracted. She had a way of doing that to me. As soon as she flicked on the light we could see what she was talking about. There was a whitish, yellowish splotch, about an inch long, stuck to the middle of the window. I thought it was a slug at first, but a close-up inspection ruled that out.

"Looks sorta like a fat inchworm, but I don't see any of those little hairs…nah, that's not it." Tangles shook his head, mystified.

I looked out the window and it was nearly pitch black. It was the east side of the house, the same side where the unlocked bedroom window was. *Coincidence?*

"Why don't I grab my flashlight and we'll take a look outside."

Tangles and Holly followed me out to the car and I pulled my Surefire flashlight out of the glove box. I had it on a lanyard and slung it over my head so it dangled down my chest. It was a compact, but very potent flashlight, throwing off 125 lumens. I clicked the tail-cap and the beam shot out as we walked around the side of the house.

I shined the light on the side of the house by the bathroom window and there was a bunch of stuff splattered on the wall.

"What the hell *is* that?" asked Tangles. He walked up to where I shined the light on a smattering of gunk and scraped some onto a sea grape leaf. Whatever it was, was all over the place. I plucked the piece of gunk off the bathroom window and dropped it on Tangle's leaf.

"Let's go inside and take a look at this stuff."

We started walking back with me leading the way, when Holly went,

"Whoa!"

I turned with the light to see Tangles holding her arm.

"What happened?"

"My foot rolled over something and I lost my balance. I nearly went down. Thanks, Tangles. What is that?"

I shined the light on the ground and then reached down and picked up a length of pipe. It had a handle made of duct tape and the end of it was stained. *Holy crap.*

"It uh, it looks like a piece of pipe, let's look at it inside."

I knew it was more than a piece of pipe, it was a weapon, a *deadly* weapon. What the hell was it doing outside her house and what was all the crap stuck to the wall? A couple of feet away was a large chunk of something mushy. It looked like it might be the same stuff as what was on the wall, so I picked it up and gave it to Tangles.

We marched into the kitchen and I spread a newspaper out on the counter- top before placing the pipe on it. Tangles put the leaf next to the pipe and picked up the largest piece of gunk for closer examination.

"That's not just a piece of pipe, Kit; it has a handle on it." Holly looked at it closer and added "There's dirt stuck to the end too, it looks wet…is that, is that blood?"

"I dunno, maybe. Tangles, what do you make of that stuff that's splattered all over the place?"

He held the piece up to the light and turned it over. It was brown on one side and white on the other.

"If I didn't know better, I'd say it was a russet."

"A russet?"

"Yeah, you know, a potato. Look, isn't that skin on one side?"

He held it out for me and Holly to look at. He was right; it looked like a chunk of potato. He sniffed it and then tasted it as we winced.

"Yeah, yeah that's what it is, just needs salt and a skillet."

"Forget about the potato, guys, the pipe looks like it has *blood* on it. What's it doing on the side of the house?"

There was no easy explanation. Hell, I had no explanation period. Not for the pipe, not for the potato, and not for thinking I saw Eight-Toe's killer drive by only minutes earlier. The gig was up. I could almost convince myself Ratdog got what he deserved, but not Eight-Toe. And now it appeared Holly had been in imminent danger, hell, we probably all were. All because I agreed to help blow up a real estate deal to save a marina from being developed by a sleazy family of restaurateurs. I had been completely ignorant of the fact that the Mob had an interest in it and now a ruthless gangster named Donny Nutz was on the warpath. *Oops, my bad.* Oh yeah, and he was only hours away from paying a visit. Nice.

I shook my head at the pickle I was in. I had a pile of cash in the bank and should be off filming a fishing show at some exotic destination— living the good life. Instead, I was about to rat myself out to the feds. I reached into my pocket, pulled out a business card, and looked at it hard. I had a feeling that things would never be the same once I dialed the number, but I had no choice. If something were to happen to Holly (and it almost just did), or Hambone, or even Tangles, I wouldn't be able to live with myself. I was *already* feeling guilty for what happened to Eight-Toe. Guilty and a little bit scared. I closed my eyes and took a deep breath.

"Kit? What are you doing? Are you all right?" There was concern in Holly's voice.

"We didn't tell you what happened to Eight-Toe. It's bad, honey, it's really bad…and it's gotta stop."

I flicked open the phone and started dialing.

"Are you calling the police?"

"No, the FBI."

Chapter 41

DICK agent Thomas Cushing rolled over in bed and grabbed the ringing cell phone off his nightstand. The display was flashing a name...Kit Jansen. Even after ten years he was still impressed with the technological wizardry of his boss, Stargazer. He not only rerouted Jansen's call to the FBI but programmed his phone so Jansen's name would appear on the display. He swung his feet over the side of the bed and flipped the phone open.

"Mr. Jansen, I knew you'd be calling."

"How did you...is this George McIlroy? With the FBI? You don't sound the same."

"You're right; I don't sound the same because I'm not him. He and his partner have been assigned to another case. Lucky you, you get the cream of the crop, that's me. So, you ready talk?"

"A friend of mine was tortured and killed."

"So I heard."

"Someone's been creeping around my girlfriend's house too. We found a bloody pipe by her bedroom window."

"Is she all right?"

"Yeah, yeah she's fine, but as you can imagine, it's got us a little jumpy."

"Just a little?"

"Maybe a lot. That's why I called."

"Good idea. I'm sure you realize that whatever your buddy knew, Donny Nutz does too, and he should be here shortly."

"Yeah, I know."

"So, you ready to tell me why the Mob's coming after you?"

"If you can guarantee that we won't end up in jail and provide protection for my girlfriend, yeah, I'll tell you everything."

"I can't guarantee anything until I hear what you did, but based on your criminal record, or lack thereof, I'm sure we can work something out."

There was a prolonged silence on the line and he thought he might have lost the connection.

"You still there?"

"Yeah, I was just...*shit,* I can't fucking believe this is happening."

"It could be worse, Mr. Jansen."

"How's that?"

"You and your girlfriend are still breathing."

"You ever think of becoming a motivational speaker?"

"No."

"Good, because you suck."

Cushing smiled; he liked his attitude.

"Thanks for the kind words, where are you?"

"At my girlfriend's."

"I can be there in a half hour."

"How do—"

"How do I know where she lives? Please, give the FBI a little credit."

"At this point? Very little, but hopefully that'll change for the better. Let me check with her."

He smiled again, the guy definitely had an attitude. He could hear a woman's voice in the background and then Jansen came back on.

"OK, c'mon over. But be discreet, it's a quiet neighborhood and it's late."

"Mr. Jansen? Trust me, discretion is my middle name. I'll see you in a half hour." Click.

As soon as he snapped the phone shut, he chuckled and picked up one of the new business cards he made after getting the call from Stargazer. It was virtually indistinguishable from the legitimate FBI ones. Nestled under the embossed seal and intricate design work was his name du jour, Dan D. Kramer. Although he changed his name for every new assignment, he always kept the same middle initial; D. It was a private joke that Jansen had inadvertently touched on. Whenever he was asked what the D stood for, he always gave the same answer: Discretion.

Ten minutes later he pulled out of the garage of his new townhome in the Pineapple Grove district of Delray Beach. He headed east on Atlantic Avenue and was not at all surprised to see that downtown Delray was still hopping at one fifteen in the morning. The vast array of restaurants, bars, live entertainment venues, and shopping, was one of the main reasons he chose to live there. As he waited for the light to change at the corner of A1A and Atlantic, a pretty girl pressed the crosswalk button. He powered the window of his Porsche down, smiled, and waved for her to cross. Halfway across the street, directly in front of him, she smiled and waved back. The light changed but he didn't budge, he couldn't help but admire the view. She really had it going on in back, she was simply *specbackular.* For a moment he wished he had the rest of the night free and then a car behind him honked, jolting him back to reality. *Shit.*

He turned north on A1A and less than fifteen minutes later turned onto Sabal Island Drive. He followed the road counterclockwise and pulled into the circular drive of the house on the point. It was the only house on the street with interior lights on. As he walked up to the front door it swung open, and a very attractive woman stepped out to greet him.

"Thank God you're here; this whole thing has gotten way out of control."

Chapter 42

Less than five miles away, at the Homey Inn, Carlos asked the night clerk if there were any vending machines. The unanticipated adrenaline burst left him hungry.

"Sure, there's one around the corner by the ice machine but it only takes singles."

Carlos reached into his pocket and pulled out a twenty.

"Can you break this for me?"

As the night clerk counted out twenty dollars he eyed the guest suspiciously—he looked familiar.

"There you go."

"Thanks."

The guest scooped up the cash and headed around the corner. When he turned away from him, the night clerk noticed what appeared to be a blood smear on the back of his neck. The clerk heard the vending machine being activated and then footsteps as the guest headed down the hall. He pressed a button on the monitor below the check-in counter and rewound the security tape. He played it again and paused the tape so he could study the guest's face.

Reaching into a drawer, he pulled out a three-ring binder that the hotel owner put together after the terrorist attacks on September 11, 2001. The management and staff had been horrified to learn that three of the terrorists who crashed one of the planes into the World Trade Center had been staying there. Although it seemed highly unlikely that the same hotel would be chosen to house future terrorists, it was management's policy to keep a vigilant lookout for anybody resembling one. The binder held all the newspaper articles about the attacks and a timeline of the terrorists' activities leading up to them. The timeline included a lengthy stay for the three terrorists at Boynton's own Homey Inn. On the very first page of the binder was a picture of them and the clerk compared it to the image of the guest on the monitor. *Son of a bitch!*

Now he knew why the guest looked familiar, he was a dead ringer for one of the terrorists named Diqueed al-Salaami. The guest might have been a little more muscular, but there was no denying the uncanny resemblance. The dark skin, the facial features, the mustache, the piercing black eyes—they were identical. He looked at the phone number for Homeland Security written on the inside cover of the binder and considered it. Resembling a terrorist wasn't a crime but who's to say he wasn't one? He sure looked like one. Then he thought about the smear of blood on the guy's neck and made up his mind. Even if the guy *wasn't* a terrorist, he was probably up to no good. Besides, it was the dead of summer and things were slow, he could use a little excitement. He picked up the phone and dialed.

***

Down the hall, in room fifteen, Carlos finished scarfing down a Snickers bar. He was tired and ready for some shut-eye, but he was due for a progress report. Reluctantly, he pulled out his cell phone and dialed Donny Nutz. The call was routed through several businesses and ended up at his headquarters, The Rye Smile, before being forwarded to his cell phone. Donny Nutz was in the backseat of a big, black, bulletproof Cadillac Escalade, barreling down I-95. He was on the outskirts of Jacksonville when his phone rang and he flipped it open. Per usual, he waited for the other person to identify him or herself before speaking.

"You there, Mr. Nutz? It's me, Carlos."

"Yeah, you on a clean line?"

"Don't worry, it's a throwaway cell."

"I worry about everything; that's why I ain't dead or doin' time. If I was you I wouldn't forget it…so whadda you got?"

There was no mistaking the voice. It sorta sounded like James Earl Jones impersonating Robert De Niro… with emphysema.

"There's a small problem."

"That's for me to decide. Explain."

"I was watching the girl, like you asked. I gained access to her neighbor's house, which is vacant, and was watching when somebody else came into the picture."

"How so?"

"All of a sudden I see this guy with a pipe going over the fence toward her house. I collared him and was about to find out what he was up to when another guy pulls a gun on me from behind."

"Sounds like you're losing your touch."

"The guy who pulled the gun might disagree with you, if he could."

"So what's the problem?"

"While I was dealing with the guy with the gun, the other guy got away."

"So who are they?"

"I don't know. Unfortunately, the guy with the gun wasn't too talkative after he developed a case of pipe-on-the-brain. I do have a lead though. I found an address on a business card in the guy's pocket. I'll check it out in the morning, maybe I can find the one that got away and get some answers."

"You think they were gonna *rob* her?"

"Could be, it's pretty well known that she inherited a big chunk of change. There's also a rumor she got some gold too."

"Gold? How *much* gold?"

He knew the mention of gold would get him interested, but he wasn't about to tell him too much.

"I don't know. I figure if I can find the other guy he might be able to tell me. Maybe he even knows where it is, maybe it's in the house and that's what he and his buddy were going after."

"Maybe, maybe not. Breaking in while she's there gets me thinking they don't know *where* the gold is. Otherwise, they'd go in when the house was empty. And why would they need a pipe? That's for breakin' heads."

"Maybe they were gonna kill her after they got her to tell them where the gold was."

"Why?"

"'Cause it's fun."

"Only a sick fuck like you thinks killing is fun. When I do it it's strictly business. You being able to turn the tables on the guy with the gun makes me think he didn't know what he was doing. Doesn't sound like the cold-blooded killer type. So I ask you again; why would they want to kill her?"

"I don't know."

"Seems to be the common theme here, so what *do* you know?"

What he wanted to say was, *I know I'm gonna double-cross your fat ass.* What he said was, "I know you wouldn't know where to fuckin' start if it weren't for me, so watch it."

"Don't be so touchy; for what I'm paying you I expect results, not a bunch of 'I don't knows.' Capiche? So listen up. I'm stopping at my condo in Stuart for a shower and then I'm heading straight to the boat. Try to find out how much gold this girl who screwed me out of the marina has. It'd be helpful to know before I squeeze her. Of course, if you can find out *where* it is, even better."

"That's the plan."

"Good, then were on the same page. Call me about eight, I should be in Boynton by then." Click.

Donny Nutz turned to his personal bodyguard and enforcer, Eddie "The Ear" Fanatucci. He was an ex-fighter and Vietnam vet who had an ear that looked like a rotten piece of cauliflower. When he spoke *of* him he called him "The Ear" and when he spoke *to* him he called him Tooch (which was short for Fanatucci).

"Tooch, I don't like it. The fuckin' Colombian's holdin' out on me; I can feel it. I think he's thinking about double-crossing me somehow. As soon as I get a handle on who's who and what's what, I want him taken care of. He's a loose cannon and he's too big for his stinkin' britches."

"Whatever you want, boss."

"That's *exactly* what I want. That bean eatin' motherfucker actually told me to 'watch it.' Can you believe that? *He* told *me* to watch it?"

"Maybe he's suicidal."

Tooch looked at Donny Nutz and they both busted out laughing.

"That was a good one, Tooch. That was beautiful. Well, one thing's for sure, he don't know it yet, but Juan Valdez's evil twin has humped his last donkey."

Chapter 43

As soon as Carlos got off the phone with Donny Nutz he remembered about the garbage bag in the trunk of his rental car that had his bloody shirt and the potato gun in it. He spotted a dumpster in back when he pulled in and decided to get rid of the evidence. As badly as he wanted some shut-eye, he didn't want to risk dumping the bag during daylight hours when he might be seen. He stepped out into the deserted hallway and entered the parking lot through the rear entrance. Just as he got to his vehicle he saw two police cars with their lights flashing pull up in front of the hotel entrance. *Shit.* He ducked down behind the car and watched as four officers exited the vehicles and the flashing lights went off. As they entered the hotel he got a better look at the cars and the odd uniforms the officers were wearing. *What the hell? Homeland Security?*

Feeling confused, but marginally relieved, he crept along the side of the building and peered through a window. One of the officers was talking to the night clerk, who was pointing at a TV monitor on the lobby wall. There was a frozen image of a man standing at the front desk. The man was handing a twenty-dollar bill to the clerk…and it was him! *What the fuck?*

The clerk turned to the wall behind him that had a bunch of cubby holes and pulled a plastic key card from the one marked number fifteen. *The fucker gave them a key to his room!*

He dashed back to his car, thankful that his kill bag and spare clothes were inside of it rather than the room. In his line of work he knew to always travel light and leave nothing behind. It had served him well over the years and once again allowed him to leave at a moment's notice. As he pulled onto Federal Highway he had no idea where he was going. He had only one thought—*Homeland Security?* Actually, he had two thoughts. He really wanted to go back to the hotel and carve up the night clerk. *Why in hell did he call Homeland Security on him?* He needed to get some sleep but now he was without a room. He didn't dare go back to the boat or the vacant house though, both were way too risky. *Shit!*

He wanted to put a little distance between himself and the Homey Inn, but not too much. Ten minutes later he saw a vacancy light flashing on a sign for a roadside hotel called the Barefoot Mailman. It looked liked just the kind of place he needed for a few hours' sleep. He pulled in, and ten minutes later he was snoozing in la-la land.

This time, however, he wasn't dreaming of Angie Dickinson giving him a pleasurable pat down. He was lying facedown on a four-poster bed, naked, his hands and feet tied to the posts. His least favorite seventies detective show star, William Conrad (of *Cannon* fame), was directing Cagney and Lacey through a full cavity search while wearing a Homeland Security uniform.

"Dig deeper, girls! I know he's hiding something!" bellowed the enormous Cannon.

Carlos twisted and turned in his sleep as the face morphed from William Conrad to a smirking Donny Nutz.

Chapter 44

Ricky was semi-freaked out but somehow managed to make it across the Intracoastal and through the dark, mangrove-lined channel, to where his truck was parked. After dragging the Zodiac out of the water he quickly let the air out and heaved it into the cargo bed. As soon as he got in the cab he looked at his neck in the mirror and cried, "Shit!"

He found a dirty rag under the seat and wiped the blood off his neck and the top of his T-shirt. Then he peered closely at the wound, which was about four inches long. It was still bleeding. He pressed the rag to his neck and headed for the apartment he shared with Sarah, hoping she was still at work. He didn't know *what* to do about Hanky because he didn't know what *happened* to him. The last thing he heard as he was jumping into the raft was a muffled gunshot. Had he shot the guy? Had the guy somehow shot *him?* Who *was* the guy with the knife? He almost wanted to call the cops but he couldn't very well tell them that he got ambushed trying to kill someone else.

He was relieved to see that Sarah's car wasn't in the parking lot when he pulled in and hurried into the bathroom. His relief turned to panic when he heard the apartment door open only a minute or so later. Sarah called his name.

"Rick-E? You here, honey?"

"Yeah, yeah. I'm here, babe, in the bathroom."

"Why was the door unlocked?"

He heard her voice get louder as she walked toward him down the hall. If he shut the bathroom door he thought she might get suspicious so he launched into his story.

"Oh, I, uh, I was in a hurry. I, uh—"

"Jesus! What did you do to your neck?" Sarah looked on incredulously at the nasty slice that Ricky was trying to clean.

"I, uh, I ran into some fishing line."

"What? Since when do *you* fish? Here, sit down and let me do that."

Ricky sat down on the toilet and winced as Sarah dabbed some peroxide on the cut. "I don't know, looks pretty bad, maybe you should go to the ER."

"No, no I'll be fine, just wrap it up with some gauze or something."

Sarah did as she was told and wrapped his neck with a few layers of gauze before securing it with some first aid tape.

"There you go, mister fisherman, that must have been some kind of line." She was already mildly suspicious when she noticed his cargo jeans were soaked.

"Why are your pants wet?"

"Oh, uh, because, uh, we were fishing. In, uh…in the water."

Sarah crossed her arms and gave him a hard stare.

"Really? You were fishing in the water? What, you were swimming around with the fish trying to talk them onto your line? C'mon Rick-E, quit lying to me! How'd you really cut your neck?"

"I, uh, I swear, we were—"

"Bullshit! You're pants are all muddy too. C'mon, Rick-E, you know I just cleaned the apartment *yesterday*. Take 'em off and I'll put them in the wash while you come up with a better story."

Ricky shrugged, pulled off his cargo jeans, and then he handed them to Sarah along with his shirt and socks. He was left sitting on the toilet in his NASCAR print underwear. Sarah opened the laundry room door and got the washing machine filling with water while she routinely went through Ricky's pants pockets. She pulled out some change and a *Chapstik* from one pocket and then felt something unusual in one of the cargo pockets. She squinched her eyebrows together as she reached in and pulled out a pair of women's panties. She let out a gasp which was followed by the sound of Ricky popping open a beer.

She walked into the kitchen and he was standing in front of the fridge in mid-slurp. Sarah looked at him standing in his stupid race-car underwear with white gauze wrapped around his neck and wondered how he could have a secret lover. What kind of woman could possibly find him attractive? Good God, how did *she* find him attractive? Then she thought about the kind. They were the kind that got picked up on Dixie Highway and they worked for crack, or cash, or both. She thought of the image and shuddered as she held out the panties in front of her. She pinched them between her index finger and thumb, trying to come into as little contact with the material as possible.

"Want to tell me about *these*, mister fisherman?"

Ricky lowered the can of Keystone Light from his mouth and stared at his fiancée holding the panties he lifted from Holly's bedroom. *Gulp.*

"I, uh, I—"

"Don't tell me you caught them fishing, Rick-E! Don't you tell me that!" Sarah's voice was raised and her face was getting red.

"Those are, those aren't mine. Those—"

"I know they're not yours, Ricky! They're some whore's! The question is what are they doing in your pocket? Does this have to do with that cut on your neck? Is that it? We're you playing sickko sex games with some whore?"

She no longer called him Rick-E the way he liked. When she got pissed she called him Ricky, because she knew he hated it.

"What? No! I don't—"

"Don't want what? Don't want me to know about you crawling around on your knees while some crack whore strangles you from behind with fishing line?"

"WHAT?"

"You know what I'm talking about mister fisherman, it's called auto-erotica something or other. We watched a whole show about it on *Jerry Springer.* We were gonna try it for our two-month anniversary until I chickened out, remember?"

"No! I mean, yes, yes, I remember the show, but that's not what happened. I swear! Besides, you're talking about erotic asphyxiation, it's the other kind when you do it to yourself."

"Oh-My-God…you did that to *yourself?* You trying to tell me *you* were wearing these panties? I think I'm gonna throw up."

"No! No, it wasn't like that at all."

"So you *were* with some whore. I knew it!" She threw the panties at Ricky and screamed, "Get out!"

Ricky instinctively moved toward the door as Sarah punched him in the chest and arms. Realizing he was in his underwear he started to protest.

"Wait, babe, can't we—"

"Talk about this? No, you lyin' bastard! I can't believe I was going to marry you."

She tried to punch him in the face and he blocked the blow with his arms. She took advantage of his defensive position by opening the apartment door and pushing him out.

"Baby, I can explain. I—"

Sarah stuck out her hand palm first, like she was stopping traffic.

"Talk to the hand, Ricky, 'cause the face ain't listening. Now get out of here…for good!"

She snatched his truck keys off a hook inside the door, removed the apartment key, and then threw the keychain at his crotch. Ricky managed to catch them before they impaled the smiling face of one of his NASCAR heroes.

"Watch it baby, that's below the belt!"

"Oh, yeah? Watch this!"

Sporting a pair of hell-hath-no-fury eyes that complemented her reddened face and crocodilian jaw-set, she stepped toward him. He backpedaled toward his truck and she followed while ripping the engagement ring off her finger. She winged it as hard as she could and it hit the driver's door as he closed it behind him. The ring ricocheted onto the asphalt and Ricky rolled down his window.

"Don't lose that ring! That cost me a lot of money, it's—"

"It's a fake, Ricky, just like you, I took it to a jeweler!"

Ricky sped off, hoping to God he didn't get pulled over wearing nothing but his Jeff Gordon skivvies.

Chapter 45

After Shagball and Tangles left the dog track, Rudy took Marie back to The Old Key Lime House. It was Saturday night and busy, per usual, even though it was the off season. They listened to the band play their last set while they sat at the newly constructed "sky lounge" that overlooked the chickee-bar and had great views of the Intracoastal.

As the band packed up their gear, a concerned Marie wondered out loud, "I hope everything's all right with Tino."

Rudy smiled, not believing how beautiful she was and that she was sitting next to him, close enough to touch. In what little light there was, she really *did* look like Sela Ward.

"Don't worry, darlin', he's in good hands with Shagball. I've known him since back in the day and he's good people. He's got plenty of friends on both sides of the track and gives everybody a fair shake—just like he did with our boy. And besides, from what I've heard, he's pretty good at mixin' it up if he needs to."

"Is that supposed to make me feel better?"

"I hope so. You need to realize that Tangles isn't a fragile little doll. In fact, he's tough as nails and proud as a peacock, just like you. Not quite as pretty though, thank God."

Rudy grinned and Marie laughed.

"All right, I'll take your word for it. But you know what else would make me feel better?"

"What?"

"You calling him by his real name, Langostino Dupree. It's a beautiful name."

"I agree, but if he wants to go by Tangles, we should respect that. He's building some great name recognition anyway, with the fishing show and all. Those two are like the Tango and Cash of the high seas."

"Oh, please. That stupid movie was his fath— was you know who's favorite."

"Really? So, besides being a wife-beating son of a bitch he had really bad taste in movies."

"Maybe so, but you shouldn't speak of the dead like that. It's bad karma."

Rudy looked at Marie and couldn't figure her out. Back in the day she was in constant fear of her husband and practically wished him dead. Now she was flip-flopping. Something didn't add up.

"Speaking of you know who, when did he pass away? What happened? He have a heart attack or something?"

"Yeah."

"Yeah, *what.*"

"Yeah, he had a something. I don't want to talk about it."

"What? What's the big secret?"

"It's no secret, it was in the papers and everything. He was killed in…in an accident."

"Really? What kind?"

"The kind that leaves you dead. Look, Rudy, I *really* don't want to talk about this."

"Why the tight lips, darlin'? No need to get upset, I was just asking…that's all."

Marie took another sip of her drink and then put her hand on Rudy's.

"I'm sorry, I didn't mean to get testy, it was a bad time for me. He was winching crates of shrimp from the boat onto the dock when he accidentally… when he must of…dropped one on his head. That was what the coroner put on the death certificate; it was an accidental death. It was just a terrible, terrible accident."

Marie fidgeted and didn't make eye contact.

"Marie?"

"Yes?" Now she looked at him.

"Is there something that makes you think it *wasn't* an accident?"

"What? Why would you say that?"

"'Cause the way you just told it makes me think you might have some doubts. Do You?"

"I, uh…no. Well…maybe…dammit, Rudy, why'd you have to bring him up?"

"I didn't, *you* did."

"Yeah? Well, I don't want to talk about him anymore. It's late, why don't you walk me down to the boat. Tino should be back soon."

Rudy pointed down at the *Lucky Dog,* which was gently bobbing in the dark water.

"We can see the boat from here, we'll know when he gets back. So did you tell Tangles you thought maybe it wasn't an accident?"

"Heaven's no, I just told him what the papers reported, even though they had it wrong. They reported he was killed on the boat when a crate of shrimp fell on his head. He was actually found dead on the dock and a crate was floating in the water. I doubt it would have made a difference to Tang—to Tino, if it was an accident or not anyways. They hadn't spoken in years."

The bartender announced it was last call and Rudy could tell Marie was a little uncomfortable.

"Set the lady up with a double whiskey-sour, hold the cherries. Just a water for me."

He nodded to the bartender who went about making her final round of drinks for the night and then he looked back at Marie.

"So, what makes you think it might not have been an accident?"

The bartender set her drink down and Marie took a big sip before exhaling deeply. She looked around at the few customers left at the open-air upstairs bar. No one was paying them any attention but she lowered her voice a notch anyways.

"It's just a feeling I have. And I feel guilty about what happened, accident or not."

"Why?"

"Cause I was happy when the police told me he had been killed, that's why. *OK?* It was like a huge weight had been lifted off my shoulders. I was glad he was gone for good. It's horrible to think that way."

"No, no, it isn't. Not for the guy who inspired the wife-beater T-shirt."

"Stop it!"

"He may as well have, he was a real shit-heel. So what gave you this feeling it wasn't an accident?"

Marie took another sip of her drink and suddenly her cell phone lit up and started ringing. The name "Tino" flashed on the display and Marie answered.

"Baby, where are you? I was starting to get worried."

Chapter 46

DICK agent Thomas Cushing, posing as FBI agent Dan D. Kramer, sat back and let out a long whistle.

"That's one helluva story, Mr. Jansen."

"Could you drop the 'mister'? Nothing good ever happens when somebody calls me mister."

"No problem—you prefer Connor?"

"No, everybody calls me Shagball, 'cause of the show, or Kit."

"Kit?"

"Yeah, like Kit-Kat, minus the Kat."

"I hate cats."

"Me too."

"OK, Kit, that's one helluva story. And you two can back it up?"

He looked at Holly and Tangles who looked at each other and nodded in agreement.

"So let me make sure I got this straight." He pointed at Holly. "Your aunt, Milfred Lutes, signed a contract to sell the marina to the guy that owns the restaurant."

"Yes, to Syd Slade, he owns Three Jacks."

"Got it. Then you got divorced in Atlanta, came back, and your aunt had second thoughts about selling. She asks if you would run the marina if she can get out of the contract. You agree, and she calls Kit to take a look at the contract."

"That's right."

"Kit looks at the contract and it's iron clad, but your aunt produces a map showing where a pair of large diesel tanks are buried on the property. And then the four of you devise a scheme to unearth them just before closing, to kill the deal."

"Unfortunately, yes."

"But before *that* happens, Kit and…what was his name?"

"Hambone" I answered. "Me and Hambone get duped into boarding *The Job.*"

"And where is he right now?"

"He's probably out looking for the guy who killed Eight-Toe. You don't have to worry about Hambone, unless, of course, he's looking for *you.*"

"Good…OK, so you and Hambone get taken on what is supposed to be a one-way trip to Davy Jones' locker, but Tangles appears and saves the day. Gino kills Ratdog, you kill Gino, and Hambone takes care of Marco."

"They were trying to kill us. Make sure you highlight that in your report. That's kinda key."

"I will. But before *you* turned the tables, *they* revealed their boss had an interest in the marina deal, presumably a financial one."

"Is there any other kind?" cracked Tangles.

"None that pay interest."

"Touché."

Tangles nodded his head in respect and I had to admit I liked the guy's style too. After all, how many FBI agents drove a Porsche?

"So, you make it back to shore, and with the help of Eight-Toe and..."

"And Kodak. Eight-Toe and Kodak helped dig up the tanks."

"Where's Kodak?"

"Hambone talked him into visiting family out on Lake Okeechobee. He's pretty much off the grid, no worries there."

"Good. And you said neither of them knew anything about the Mob's involvement or the attempt on your life, right?"

"No, they didn't know anything about what happened on *The Job*."

"So, the bottom line is you guys dig up the tanks and the marina deal goes down the tubes. Holly ends up with the marina and the $400,000 deposit, and Donny Nutz ends up with two missing guys and a sunken boat."

"Half-sunk. If it sunk we wouldn't be here."

"You mean *I* wouldn't be here. But guess what? Donny Nutz still would, so you're lucky."

"Maybe I should play the lotto."

"I'm serious."

"So am I, it's a little hard for us to share your confidence after what happened to Eight-Toe."

"I'm sorry about that. That was unfortunate, and a little odd too, it's not really Nutz's style. We think he hired a freelancer who went overboard. What happened to Eight-Toe was completely unnecessary. It's the only thing that makes sense. But at least his death spurred you to finally wise up and call. You can thank him for that. That should give us an edge because Nutz wouldn't anticipate you doing so—you're incriminating yourself."

"Yeah, about that. The other FBI guys said they could provide immunity and protection if needed."

"They said *probably*, mister—uh…Kit. But don't worry, if you cooperate and help us nail Nutz, nobody's ever gonna know a thing about this. After all, you *were* acting in self-defense, right?"

"Yes, of course."

"And fortunately for you and your merry band of marina preservationists with bad nicknames, the real estate fraud you perpetrated pales in comparison to the crimes committed by Mr. Nutz."

"Great, so how do we go about nailing Nutz before he nails us?"

"The only thing that Donny Nutz enjoys more than having people killed is collecting on a debt beforehand. Make no mistake, in his mind you owe him for whatever he lost on the marina deal, his boat, and his guys. He's gonna want a lot and he's gonna shake down whoever's got the money. In this case that looks like you, Miss Lutes."

"Please, call me Holly, and I'll gladly pay what it takes to make him go away."

"I'm sure you would but guys like him have reputations to keep. Trust me, as soon as you paid him, he'd kill all of you. Unless he thinks he can get more money out of you, in which case he could haunt you forever."

"Oh, my God. This keeps getting worse."

"So what's the plan?" I asked.

"He's going to call Holly and try to extort money from her. I'm surprised he hasn't already, but trust me, it's coming. If we can nail him for extortion it would put him away long enough for us to finish building our arms trafficking case against him. That would put him away for good. From this point on we're going to be recording all your calls. Holly, hand me your phone; you too, Tangles, just in case."

"What about mine? You don't want mine?"

"Your calls are already being recorded."

"Thanks for the heads up."

"Don't mention it."

Holly and Tangles handed him their phones and he set them on the table. Then he pulled out his own phone and set it between them. He touched the display screen on his phone and all three phones rang once and then stopped.

"That's it, until I deactivate them, you can assume I'm listening in, and I will be."

"That's it? Nice. How do I get one of those phones?" His phone looked like a pimped out iPhone on steroids…like a jphone.

"Sorry, Kit, they're proprietary. But now that I think of it, hand me your phone too."

I handed mine over and he pulled what looked like a clear credit card out of his wallet. He punched out three little holes in the credit card the size of a standard hole punch. He picked one up, carefully peeled the back off, and stuck it to the corner of the display on my phone. It was nearly invisible. He did the same to the other phones.

"There you go, that little sticker will let me hear conversations you're having even when your phones are turned off. They're good for forty-eight hours. I figure this'll play out long before then."

"Wow!" gushed Tangles. "That's pretty slick, talk about 'big brother.'"

"Exactly. You can think of me as a big brother from another mother sent to save your ass."

"So let's start with the saving," I said. "What do you make of the bloody pipe and the potato soufflé we found on the side of the house?"

"I'm not gonna bullshit you. I'm not sure *what* to make of it. I can tell you I don't like it though. Is there anywhere else you three can stay tonight?"

"My apartment?"

"No chance. Nutz could be watching it by now. He might try to use you to get to Holly."

"What about the boat?" asked Tangles. "The *Lucky Dog*. Shit, that reminds me, I need to call my mom."

Tangles picked his phone off the table and called his mom. She answered right away and we heard his side of the conversation.

"Don't worry, everything's OK, I'm with Kit at Holly's. There's a problem though and we need to stay on the *Lucky Dog* tonight. We'll be over there in a little while...No, don't worry, there's enough room for all of us.... What?"

Tangles looked at us and held one of his hands open like he didn't know what his mom was doing. "You're gonna what? You don't have to—

I know, I know you can take care of yourself, Momma. OK...I said *OK*, I'll talk to you in the morning." Click. Tangles rolled his eyes before filling us in.

"She's gonna stay with Rudy tonight. We have the boat to ourselves."

"Is that it?" I asked

"No, she made me promise to have breakfast with her in the morning."

"It's already morning, it's two o'clock, guys." Holly was pointing at her wristwatch.

"You're right, it's late." said the FBI agent. "Why don't you grab what you need to and I'll follow you to the boat, just to be safe."

Five minutes later we piled into the Beemer and headed back to The Ole House. The FBI guy trailed us up A1A in his turbo something or other. Whatever it was, was *sweet* and it gave me newfound respect for FBI agents. When we got there the parking lot was pretty much deserted except for a cleaning service van parked by the chickee-hut. I parked the Beemer in front of the *Lucky Dog* and the Porsche parked next to us. FBI guy got out and followed us onto the boat.

"Nice lines…eighty-three Viking?" he commented.

"Pretty good guess; it's an eighty-two."

After I unlocked the cabin he had us wait in the cockpit while he checked to make sure the boat was empty. A minute later he reappeared, holstering an automatic weapon in the small of his back.

"OK, you guys should be fine…for tonight at least. Nobody knows you moved the boat here, right?"

"Nobody but the guy who owns the restaurant, Layne," I answered.

"Excellent. Try to get some sleep; I'm sure you could use some. And don't turn off your phones, especially you, Holly, for when Nutz calls."

"OK."

"That's it, then, I'll be monitoring your phones until Nutz makes his move. When he does, I'll be there, you can count it."

I thanked him and shook his hand before he got off the boat. Before he drove away he walked over to the cleaning van and shined a small flashlight in the window. He noticed the van too, and was being thorough, which I liked. I had planned on doing the same thing if he didn't— I don't like surprises. He turned to walk to his car and saw me watching from the cockpit. He gave me a thumbs-up, got in, and sped away. As I closed the cabin door behind me, I had the feeling he was being a bit overconfident. *That,* I didn't like. Overconfidence bred a lack of preparedness, which in this case, could be fatal. The stakes were high and we couldn't afford any slipups. We needed to have our game on. Holly was in the forward berth hanging up some clothes and Tangles was on the couch.

He must have noticed the look of concern on my face, and asked, "What is it? You look worried."

"I am, we got any beer?"

Chapter 47

Tangles opened the fridge and thankfully there was a handful of Bud Lights inside. While everybody may have been a little tired, there was *way* too much going on to be able to quickly doze off in a peaceful sleep. Tangles doled out three cold ones and plopped down in the club chair while Holly and I took the couch.

After taking a long pull, I looked at Holly. "So, do you feel any better now that I called the FBI?"

"I...thought I would, but...no, not really. I hate waiting around for something to happen."

"According to dapper Dan, the fancy-sports-car-driving FBI agent, we shouldn't have to wait long," commented Tangles.

"I sure hope not, I feel like everything's spiraling out of control. I'm not sure what to think anymore."

I took another pull and realized that Holly was still in the dark about Tangles' paternal situation.

"Well, get ready for another surprise. I just found out something that's gonna blow your mind. Tangles, you wanna tell her? Or can I have the honor?"

"It's all yours, bro, I'm still trying to get my head around it."

"Get your head around what?" asked Holly. "Wait, wait a second, don't tell me yet." She went in the forward berth and then walked back into the salon, holding something behind her back. "Whatever it is you're gonna tell me, I've got something even crazier to tell, guaranteed."

Tangles and I had to laugh. There was no way she was gonna top the Rudy being Tangles' father news, no way.

"I don't think so, honey, this is a real doozey."

"Well, mines a double-doozey, so it's a good thing you're sitting down…you first."

"You asked for it, lady, so here it is. Who's my favorite bartender?"

"C'mon, is this a quiz? I hate quizzes; just tell me."

"OK, Patty Patience, you want it, you got it. You know Rudy, right?"

"Of course I do, he's your favorite bartender. I like him too, he's a real sweetheart."

"Would it have *killed you* to say that when I asked who my favorite bartender was?"

"No, would it kill you to get to the point?"

I looked at Tangles.

"Go ahead, put her out of her misery."

Tangles finished off his beer and looked up at Holly. She was standing with her hands on her hips, holding some papers in one of them.

"Apparently…he's my dad."

Holly's neck suddenly looked like it couldn't hold the weight of her head as it sank with her shoulders.

"*What?*"

I had to admit, I loved it. It was time for rubbing it in a little.

"You heard right, only there's nothing 'apparent' about it. Tangles' mom broke the news at the track. Travis K. Rainbow, aka Rudy, bartender extraordinaire and honorary high chief of the Seminole Casino, is none other than Tangles' biological father. How you like them apples? I tried to tell you, it's a *doooooozey*."

"Oh-my-God. Are you *kidding* me? How did—"

"Trust me, it's no fairy tale. Rudy knew Marie in Biloxi, back in the day."

"Tangles, is he serious?"

"I know, it's hard to tell sometimes, but yes, it's true."

"Geez-Louise, how do you feel about it?"

"It probably hasn't sunk in yet, but I definitely could have done worse. My father—or who I *thought* was my father, was a world class alcoholic with a mean streak longer than Sarah Jessica Parker's face. Me and Momma are lucky to be alive. Who *knows*, if he hadn't had the accident, maybe we wouldn't be."

"Wow, that really is a doozey. For what it's worth, I think Rudy's great."

"Thanks."

"I told you it was gonna blow your mind. Can you believe it? You can't make this stuff up. Now, what was it you were going to tell us?"

"Nothing in this world could possibly give me more pleasure than to wipe that smug look off your face… which I'm about to do. Here, you're gonna need this." She opened the fridge, handed me another beer and grabbed a water for herself.

"Since you like quizzes so much, answer me this: who was Millie's favorite son?"

I looked at Tangles with a look that said, *is this broad nuts?*

"C'mon, no trick questions."

"It's not—answer, please." Holly was smiling, or was she grinning?

"Very funny, Millie didn't have a son, in fact—"

"Bzzzzzzzzz! Wrong answer."

"What are you talking about? She never had any kids at all, she was never married."

"Bzzzzzzzzz! Wrong again. Give that man a board game and send him packing, Charlie! You're lucky, if this was *The Gong Show*, you'd have got the hook." Holly held out the papers she had clutched in her hand. "Millie left me a letter, sort of a deathbed confession, if you will. Long story short; right after graduating high school, her father took her to St. Croix. They were checking out a marina for sale that a friend of her dad's told them about. His name was Kilroy. After a week, her dad went home, but she and Kilroy convinced him to let her stay awhile longer so she could learn more about the marina operation. She met a local boy, fell in love, got pregnant, got secretly married—"

"WHAT?"

"Wait, I'm not done. With the help of Kilroy, who also stayed on the island, they kept her parents in the dark. A couple of months before the baby was born, her husband was killed in a scuba diving accident. Kilroy convinced her to give the baby up for adoption so she could forever keep the entire thing a secret."

"Good God, that's incredible."

"Are you sure you're talking about your Aunt Millie?" asked Tangles.

"I know, I can hardly believe it myself. But there's more. Within a week after having the baby she left the island for good, never to return. She left behind a stash of gold buried on a plot of land that she and her husband bought. They planned on building a house and raising their family there. The gold was their 'baby fund,' which was started when they found out she was pregnant."

"*More* gold? And it's still there?" I asked.

"Yep, that's how she got started collecting gold in the first place."

"Holy mackerel!" exclaimed Tangles. "What happened to the baby?"

"She never found out who adopted him. She was given a sedative immediately after childbirth and when she woke up the next day, he was gone. She held him for only a minute before she was knocked out."

"Is that normal?"

Holly waved the letter in front of us.

"There's nothing normal about any of this. I need to read it again. I'd like you guys to read it too and tell me what you think. For now, at least, let's keep it among the three of us."

"What do you mean, 'what we think,' what's to think about?"

"I, I don't want to say anything, I want you to draw your own conclusions. There's some stuff I didn't go into in this letter. You need to read it for yourselves and then we'll talk about it."

"OK, but I can tell you right now I'm confused as to why she just didn't tell her parents from the git-go. She's not the first teenager to accidentally get pregnant, and if they were really in love, what's the big deal? Back then kids got married young anyways. Her parents might not have been thrilled but I'm sure they would have supported her. Wouldn't they?"

"She planned on telling them after she had the baby, but when her husband got killed, Kilroy pressed her to give the baby up for adoption and keep it all a secret. He told her that her parents would never understand and it would ruin her life if she kept the baby."

"That seems a little extreme...*doesn't it?*"

"Well, there is *one* thing I forgot to mention."

"What's that?"

"It was an interracial marriage; her husband, Joseph, was a young black man."

My mouth was hanging open and I couldn't speak, but Tangles could.

"Yeah, there is *that.* I could see it being a slight issue back in nineteen...."

"Forty-nine. It was 1949."

I finally caught my breath.

"Holy-cat-on-a-hot-tin-roof. Are you kidding me?"

"I told you it was a double-doozey."

"You lied, it's a triple."

"I don't think so," chimed in Tangles. "Girlfriend hit that clean out of the park, that's a round-tripper, in fact, it's a slam. Put her there, Miss Lutes, that's worthy of a stump bump."

Tangles reached out his little arm and fist-bumped Holly. I shook my head and had to laugh.

No sooner had one shoe dropped when another was on the way.

Chapter 48

DICK agent Thomas Cushing was on his way back to Delray to get a little shut-eye. As he headed south on Dixie Highway he reflected on his meeting with the unlikely conspirators. He had to admit their plan to queer the marina deal was a good one, born out by the fact that it worked. That Jansen and Hambone managed to escape death at the hands of a professional killer was impressive; even *with* help from the little guy Tangles. He had never seen anything like him. He was like a perfectly shrunk person with a full sized attitude. Cushing had his DICK phone attached to the visor above his head and was listening to their conversation after he left. It appeared to be stuff totally unrelated to the Donny Nutz case. Something about finding out who Tangles' father was and then Holly launching into a story about her recently deceased aunt.

The street was fairly empty at quarter to three in the morning and as he got south of Woolbright Road he noticed some flashing lights ahead on the right. As he slowed down in front of a place called the Homey Inn, the flashing lights suddenly went out and a couple of Homeland Security vehicles exited. *What?* What in the hell had Homeland Security there?

Since his primary priority as a DICK agent was the apprehension and elimination of terrorists, he turned around at the next block and circled back. He parked his Turbo Carrera out of sight of the main hotel entrance and walked into the small lobby. There was a greasy-looking guy of about forty behind the front desk. He looked like he smoked too much, drank too much, and looked at a mirror too little. Cushing knew exactly how to handle him; hell, he knew how to handle most anyone. He held out an FBI badge and took control.

"Dan Kramer, FBI."

The shaky-looking night clerk nodded. "You're a little late, Homeland Security just left."

"Maybe they were early."

"Huh?"

He glanced at the night clerk's name tag, which read "Walter."

"Listen Walter, it's late and this'll go quicker if you refrain from any time-consuming commentary. How 'bout I ask the questions and you answer them…fair enough?"

"Yeah, uh, sure."

"So why was Homeland here?"

"Because I called them."

"Why?"

"We had a suspicious guest but he must have slipped out the back before they got here."

"What made him suspicious?"

"He looked like a terrorist."

"And how would that be?"

The clerk punched a button under the desk and pointed at the TV monitor hanging in the corner of the lobby. "Like that." An image of a man handing a bill to the clerk was frozen on the screen. Cushing stepped closer to the TV and squinted a little.

"What's he doing?"

"Getting change for the vending machine."

"So how does being hungry make you a terrorist?"

"It doesn't, but look at this." The clerk lifted a binder from below the desk and sat it on the counter. He opened it up and stuck his finger on a passport sized photo inside. "If he ain't a dead ringer for *this* guy, I don't know who is. He's one of the nine-eleven terrorists; Diqueed al-Salaami. I should know, he stayed right here along with a couple of the other terrorist's. Management freaked when they found out and put together this binder. They said to call Homeland Security if anybody ever checks in looking like that again…so I did."

Cushing studied the photo of the known terrorist the clerk pointed to against the image of the guy on the screen. He was right, the resemblance was uncanny. They were both dark-skinned, mustached, and wiry, with very similar facial features.

"I'll be damned, it's Diqueed's doppelganger."

"His what?"

"His look-alike.

"Yeah, *exactly* alike, even so, what got me to call was the blood."

"What blood?"

"He had some blood on the back of his neck. On the video it looks like a shadow, but trust me, it was blood. I can't believe they missed him."

"Did he give a name? Use a credit card? Register a vehicle?

"Yes, no and no. He paid cash and signed the log as…let me see…"

Walter grabbed the sign-in log and spun it around. "Yeah, here it is, he signed in as…Artemis West; probably a fake name."

"You think?" Cushing laughed at the name. It was a cross between Artemis Gordon and James West of *The Wild Wild West.*

"Yeah, Homeland Security thought so too."

"So, they went to his room and he was gone?"

"Yep, they said the only thing he left behind was a toilet kit."

"That's all?"

"That's it, some toothpaste, a toothbrush, and some deodorant; the usual stuff."

Cushing smiled knowingly.

"Well you can rest easy, he wasn't a terrorist."

"How do you know?"

"They don't use deodorant."

"That's the same thing Homeland Security said… son of a bitch. Well, maybe he *wasn't* a terrorist, but he was damn sure *some* kind of criminal."

"And that would make him different from your normal clientele *how?*"

"Those Homeland fuckers said that too. Let me tell you something, mister, this is a nice clean place and we do the best we can, you can't have the Ritz-Carlton on *every* corner."

"No argument here, keep up the good work, if he happens to come back, call Homeland again."

'You don't want a call too?"

"Not tonight, Walter, have a good one."

As Cushing walked around the corner to his car, the hotel doors swung open behind him and the clerk warned him again.

"I'm telling you, Diqueed's double is up to no good. Mark my words!"

Chapter 49

It was after three in the morning before we decided to try to get some sleep. Holly and I took the forward berth and Tangles crashed on the couch. After fifteen minutes, Holly managed to doze off, but my mind was still racing and I couldn't sleep. I had a small reading light mounted to the bulkhead and flicked it on. Holly stirred, rolled over, and kept on lightly snoring. I picked up Millie's letter and started reading. Hearing the condensed version from Holly was one thing, but reading it in Millie's own words was another…and it was mesmerizing. I got tired about half way through but couldn't put it down. Sometime around four in the morning I finally finished it. I laid my head back on the pillow and remembered murmuring, "Jesus Christ," before dozing off.

It was a fitful sleep full of wild dreams involving a little brown baby, a psychopathic killer, a pregnant teenage Millie, and a sinister mystery man. I woke up startled with a hand on my shoulder and Holly's voice in my ear.

"Kit, wake up. Are you all right?"

I opened my eyes and she was looking down at me, concerned. It was just getting light outside and the cobwebs on my brain were still fluttering.

"Wha, what's…what's the matter?"

"You were tossing your head from side to side and making odd noises. Did you have a bad dream?"

I thought about all the weird images in my head and nodded. "Yeah, yeah, I guess so." I looked at my watch and it was a little before seven. Holly picked Millie's letter off my chest and held it up.

"Did you read this?"

"Yeah, I couldn't put it down."

'Well, what do you think?"

"I think I need a cup of coffee."

"Seriously, Kit, c'mon."

"I am serious, but I'll tell you this, something rubs me the wrong way about it. There are a few things she said that have me wondering what was really going on. Let me make some coffee and we'll talk about it."

"OK, I'm going to call Regina."

I rolled out of bed and slipped a pair of shorts on before making my way up to the galley. Tangles was still snoozing while I made coffee and I heard Holly talking in the forward berth. A few minutes later there was noise from the bathroom and then she appeared, looking great as always. She had on a pair of shorts and a *C-Love* tank top. Wow. She went to give me a kiss good morning but I declined until I brushed my teeth as well. With that out of the way, it was hello, smoochville. All hell may have been breaking loose around us, but a kiss is still a kiss; best to get one when you can.

The coffee maker beeped and I poured us a couple of cups as Tangles began stirring. He opened one eye and announced his presence.

"Can you pour me one too?"

"Sure thing, sport." I poured him one and Holly handed it to him. She turned back to me and started in about the letter.

"So, what do you mean about something rubbing you the wrong way?"

"I don't know, it just seems like she had some suspicions but never voiced them."

"Like what?"

"Like, why was this guy Kilroy so adamant she give the baby up for adoption and keep it all a secret? I mean, supposedly he was a *friend* of her father's. I can't believe it's because her father would blame *him* for her pregnancy and not invest in the marina. That's kinda crazy, isn't it?"

"Yeah, I had the same feeling. She said he was initially upset when she told him she planned on keeping it, but then he softened up."

"But he still convinced her to keep the pregnancy secret. And what about Kilroy's fiancée? Something weird was going on with her too…remember?"

"I know, it sounded like when Millie told her she was pregnant and keeping the baby, the fiancée got upset and left him. Right? She didn't even congratulate Millie or act surprised that she was pregnant. That means she already knew, but didn't tell her. Why?"

"But she was back to help the doctor deliver the baby."

"And the doctor was a friend of Kilroy's."

"That whole scenario is wacky too. She gives birth and gets to hold the baby for only a minute before they knock her out? Then when she wakes up, the baby's gone and she doesn't know who or where the adoptive parents are. It's crazy."

"That's exactly what I was thinking. There seems to be more to the story."

"The thing that really bothers me, though, is Joseph's so-called accident."

"What do you mean?"

"Think about it. Joseph planned on announcing to his family *that night* that they were secretly married and she was pregnant. Once that happened there'd be no adoption, secret or not."

Holly had a sick feeling in her stomach. She had a nagging suspicion about the accident too, but didn't want to face it.

"What are you saying, Kit?"

"Who was the one pushing for the adoption?"

"Kilroy."

"Yep, and there was only one person with Joseph when he had the accident. Only one person who knows what really happened."

Holly put her hand up to her mouth and mumbled, "Oh, my God."

"Right again…only God and Kilroy."

Chapter 50

Ricky had only one option when he got kicked out of Sarah's apartment—San Castle Storage. It was his "go-to" place whenever they had a big fight or when he stayed out too late partying and didn't dare return. The fact that he was wearing nothing but his underwear made the decision even easier. The gates to the storage center would be locked until about seven in the morning, so he would do what he always did; sleep in his truck until they were opened. The run-down storage center was on the edge of an industrial park on the west side of the train tracks, bordering an equally run-down residential area on the other side. The cops avoided patrolling the area almost as much as they did the Cherry Hill neighborhood; they came only when responding to a call. Ricky had slept in his truck outside the gates at least a half dozen times in the past two years and never had a problem with the police, or anybody else, for that matter.

Still, after what happened earlier in the night, he locked the doors to the truck and lay across the seat with a tire iron in hand's reach. He was hoping that Hanky somehow escaped the lunatic who surprised them and would head back to the storage center too.

He knew that if he did manage to escape, he probably needed a ride. Unfortunately, Sarah kicked him out before he remembered to grab his cell phone, so he had no way of knowing if Hanky was trying to reach him. That was too bad for Hanky, because he wasn't about to go cruising A1A in the middle of the night in his underwear. For what seemed like hours, he couldn't fall asleep. He kept imagining all the scenarios that might have played out between Hanky and the guy with the knife. The guy with the knife had the lead pipe in his hands when Ricky made his escape. Did Hanky manage to shoot him? Did the guy bash Hanky with the pipe first? Did he knock him out and then use the knife on him? Who *was* the crazy fucker who dared his buddy to shoot and what was he doing there?

Eventually, the rhythmic sounds of a passing train lulled him to sleep.

Chapter 51

Generally speaking, you never want to piss off an honest-to-God socio-psychopath, knowingly or not. Unfortunately for Walter, the night clerk at the Homey Inn, that's exactly what he did. Although Carlos managed to slip away before having a confrontation with Homeland Security, he couldn't easily fall asleep in his new room at the Barefoot Mailman. He tossed and turned, unable to figure out why Homeland Security was now in the picture. He was already trying to avoid the Boynton Beach police on the premise they wanted to question him as to Skeeter's whereabouts, and the last thing he needed was another law enforcement agency on his trail. When he finally *did* manage to doze off, it was for an hour or so at best. And his dreams were unusually disturbing, even for him. Unable to fall back asleep after being jolted awake by the Cannon-led cavity search dream, he decided to get up. He looked at his watch and it was only six in the morning. He had no doubt the night clerk had called Homeland Security on him. *Why?* There was only one way to find out. Figuring the clerk's shift probably ended at seven or eight, a return visit was in order. After a quick shower to try to wake him up some more, Carlos hopped back into his rented Chrysler and headed back to the Homey Inn.

It was just starting to get light out when he pulled into the parking lot, making sure not to pass in front of the main entrance. He didn't think the clerk knew what type of vehicle he was driving, but wasn't taking any chances. He drove behind the hotel and was trying to figure out his plan of attack, when he saw an old Buick LeSabre with dark tinted windows parked near the rear entrance. A sign in front of the car marked the parking spot as "Manager's Parking." Figuring the lowly night clerk was also the manager on duty, he was reasonably certain it was his car. He parked several spots away between two vehicles to further shield himself from view.

From his kill bag he removed his trusty switchblade and a nifty little tool that looked like a pry bar, for popping locks. He looked to make sure nobody was around and at quarter to seven on Sunday morning in the dead of a south Florida summer—nobody was. He walked up to the LeSabre and was about to pull out his lock-popping tool when he saw that the driver's door was unlocked. He tried the rear door on the driver's side and it opened. He slid into the backseat and there was a small pile of mail on the passenger side. The mail was all addressed to the same person; a Mr. Walter Sverdahl. *Bingo!* He remembered seeing "Walter" on the greasy clerk's name tag. He lay down across the floor and waited, reasonably sure the darkened windows would hide him from detection until it was too late.

Less than ten minutes later, Carlos awoke to the sound of the driver's door opening. He was so tired he managed to fall fast asleep even in the uncomfortable position he was in. He may have been a psychotic freelance killer, but he cherished a proper night's rest. The asshole who had him running on reserve power was about to find out how cranky that could make him. He heard the jangling of keys as Walter settled into the driver's seat and he made his move. In a flash he bolted upright, the switchblade snapping open. With one hand he grabbed Walter's chin and jerked it up and back, and with the other he pressed the ultra-sharp blade to his neck. Walter had one hand on the wheel and the other on the key in the ignition. He gasped in panic as he recognized the face of the suspected terrorist in the rearview mirror. He tried to scream and Carlos jerked his head back farther, cutting off the sound.

"You don't make a peep unless I ask you to, got it?"

Walter tried to nod and made a sound that was taken for a yes.

"Good, now take your hand off the ignition. I know it's hot and we'd both like some air-conditioning, but this won't take long."

Walter took his hand off the ignition as directed and stretched it out sideways across the back of the passenger seat. He was trying to gain a little leverage so he could breathe.

"Excellent, now I'm going to release a little pressure so you can answer a couple of questions. If you scream or do anything stupid I'll slice you from ear to fucking ear, understood?"

Again, Walter mumbled, "Yeah."

"OK, so why did you call Homeland Security on me?" Carlos released just enough pressure for him to answer.

"'Cause you look like, you look like, uh…"

Carlos was tired and impatient and pissed off to no end.

"*Who,* asshole? *Who* do I fuckin' look like would make you do that?"

He jerked Walter's head back just as he answered. Walter meant to say "a terrorist," but when his head got jerked back, he spit out the short answer: "Diqueed."

"*Who?*"

"Like Diqueed."

Carlos could not believe his ears. He had a knife to the guy's throat and he was saying he looked like dickweed?

"You think I look like a dickweed? You got big cojones, Walter, I'll give you that. Well, you may think I look like a dickweed, but you're gonna look like a guy with no fucking head in about two seconds."

Carlos yanked his head back and started digging the knife in when Walter managed to squeeze out,

"No! Like…terrorist."

Confused, Carlos released his grip again as he tried to process what he was saying.

"What the *fuck* are you talking about?"

"You look like one of the terrorists from the nine-one-one attacks."

"WHAT?" He released his grip further, wanting a better explanation.

"Please don't hurt me, I was just doing my job." Walter's eyes were darting from left to right, praying someone would walk by. He didn't know if he had the nerve to lay on the horn if someone did, but he was praying nonetheless.

"You're saying I look like a terrorist? Are you shittin' me?"

"No, you look *identical* to one of the terrorists who stayed here ten years ago…just prior to the World Trade Center attacks. His name, his name was Diqueed, Diqueed al Salaami. We have pictures for comparison in a binder under the desk. Plus, you had, you had blood on the back of your neck, and you, you paid cash."

Carlos was stunned, which took a lot.

"Some of those terrorist motherfuckers actually stayed right here?"

"Yeah, management f-freaked when they found out. Now it's company policy to call Homeland Security over any suspicious guests. They even sent a memo out reminding us 'cause of, 'cause of the tenth anniversary. Please, please don't hurt me; I swear, I swear I won't call again."

Carlos tightened his grip back up and had his mouth right next to Walter's ear.

"Let me tell you something, my friend, I'm from Brooklyn, and I knew some people who got killed that day. To think that some asshole like you could confuse me for one of those low-lifes really gets me going. And when I get going, sometimes I have a hard time stopping, especially when I don't get enough sleep. Thanks to you, that's precisely where I am right now. If you hadn't a been so fuckin' nosy, if you'd a just minded your own business, neither of us would be here. But don't worry; I've got a foolproof cure."

Carlos shifted so his left arm squeezed around Walter's neck and he slid the knife up to just below his nose; where the cartilage attaches to the upper lip. Walter's legs were pushing straight out and he clawed at Carlos's arm with both hands as he cut off his oxygen supply. His face turned red and he started lunging backward trying to free himself by pressing his feet against the floorboard. It didn't work. In one fluid motion Carlos yanked the knife straight up, severing off most of Walter's nose. As it fell to the seat between Walter's legs, Carlos swung the knife in a quarter circle arc and impaled the six inch blade deep into Walter's right ear canal. He yanked it back out while simultaneously releasing the stranglehold he had on his throat with his left arm. Walter's arms dropped to his side and his brain-dead head fell forward so that his chin was on his chest. Blood poured from his nose cavity and ear, and the gurgling sound of death filled the car's interior. Carlos calmly wiped the blade on the seat and quickly looked around the parking lot. He saw a couple loading suitcases into a car only sixty feet away but they were completely oblivious to him. He slipped the knife in his pocket and exited the backseat, then casually walked over to his rental car. As he drove past the slumped over body of Water Sverdahl in his twenty-year-old LeSabre, he couldn't help but laugh and make a comment.

"That oughta keep you from sticking your nose where it don't belong."

Heading north on Dixie Highway again, he plucked the business card from the overhead visor and noted the address of San Castle Storage, his next stop. Despite having next to no sleep he was feeling somewhat rejuvenated. A fresh kill nearly always had that effect on him. It also tended to make him hungry.

He spotted a McDonald's up ahead and set course for the drive-through. A little breakfast burrito with hot sauce and an Egg McSomething or other with extra ketchup was just what the doctor ordered.

Chapter 52

I looked at Holly in near total disbelief and shook my head. She had just finished explaining to me about the part in Millie's letter where she cryptically clued her in to where the gold was. It was early and I wanted to make sure I had it right.

"You're telling me that the place Millie took you to where she says to look for the gold is a storage center? She stashed five million in gold in a storage unit?"

"Maybe more. Regina just told me the name of the place where we keep all the extra marina stuff is called San Castle Storage. I can't remember where it is, do *you* know?"

Before I could answer, Tangles cut in.

"Yeah, it's a couple miles south of here, just a little west of Dixie on the other side of the tracks. It's a real crap-hole."

"I couldn't have said it better," I added. "Wow. Of all the places to keep a hoard of gold, that's about the last place I would look. They have more shady characters there than in a Carl Hiaasen novel."

"Maybe that's why she kept it there. Who'd a thunk it?"

"I guess we'll find out. What about the clue she gave as to *where* it's hidden in the storage unit?"

"I remember where the restaurant was, I just can't remember the name. Hopefully it hasn't changed. It's just west of I-95 on the north side of Hypoluxo Road."

"The Anchor Inn?"

"That's it! The Anchor Inn; it's on a lake, right?"

"Yeah, Lake Osborne."

"Well, what are we waiting for? Let's go to San Castle Storage."

"Sounds good. I'm starved though, why don't I have the Kona Café whip us up a few breakfast sandwiches for the ride?"

"The Kona Café?"

"Yeah, they're right there next to the bait shop." I pointed out one of the port-side windows at the building just east of the The Ole House. It housed an excellent sushi restaurant and clothing store as well. "It's a great place, way better than the last breakfast joint that was there."

"Sounds good to me."

"I better pass," said Tangles. "I told my mom I'd go to breakfast with her."

"Suit yourself, but don't be staring at my sandwich," I warned him.

"What are you talking about?"

"I'm talking about that thing you do when you lick your lips and raise an investigative eyebrow like a malnourished wolf eyeballing a crippled rabbit."

"Oh, I see, you mean like the way you get when there's three of us and only one beer left in the fridge?"

"What?"

"C'mon guys," pleaded Holly. "Let's get moving."

I phoned the Kona Café and ten minutes later we were heading toward the storage center in the Beemer. Holly and I were enjoying our bacon, egg, and cheese sandwiches while Tangles enjoyed the smell—or not. There was only one way to find out.

"Mmmmm, man is this good, don't you think?"

I looked at Holly who had a mouthful and she mumbled, "Uh-huh."

"Shagball?" commented Tangles from the backseat.

"Yeah?"

"You suck."

Chapter 53

Carlos finished breakfast and got done wiping the blood and burrito remnants off his arms just as he pulled into San Castle Storage. He realized he had made a serious mistake by killing the night clerk and wrote it off to sleep deprivation. If he had been thinking clearly, he would have remembered the hotel had his image on tape. Thanks to the Homeland Security visit, he would no doubt be a prime suspect once the body was discovered—and it probably already had been. It wouldn't be long before the police realized he was the same person they wanted to talk to about the missing dock rat Skeeter, who was one of the last people to see Eight-Toe alive. They would connect the dots and they would correctly all point to him. They might even plaster his face all over the news as a "person of interest."

Shit. He couldn't believe it. His cover was blown thanks to a dead terrorist named Diqueed, a nosy night clerk, and his own blood lust. He couldn't risk staying and making a play for the gold, he had to split town. He decided to have a quick look around the storage center, report to Donny Nutz, and then he was *gone.*

He slowed the car as he approached the open gates and saw a building on the left with a sign that read, "Office." A small placard was propped against the window facing the entrance and it read, "Closed Sundays." He looked at Hanky's business card again and it identified his unit as number twenty-three. He slowly pulled into the deserted center and proceeded straight up the middle aisle, looking at numbers as he went. The numbers on the units seemed to make little sense. Number one was followed by number six. He looked on the right side and there was a number two, three, and then nine. *What?* The aisle dead-ended into another building and he had to turn right or left. He turned right and followed the mix and match numbers. There were old boats parked in front of some units, empty boat trailers in front of others, an old RV, some broken-down golf carts; the place was a mess. He ran into another dead end and turned left this time. He saw a unit numbered nineteen and then twenty-one, then—he stopped. About thirty yards ahead on the left was an old pickup with a black, Zodiac-style raft sticking out of the bed. *Son of a bitch!*

He pulled to the side and parked behind what looked like an old milk truck. He pulled out the silenced Glock from his kill bag and tucked it in the small of his back when he exited the car. There was no time for subtlety. He gave a quick look around as he walked toward the pickup, keeping close to the building. The pickup was parked just short of unit number twenty-five, which had its overhead garage door half-open. The unit just past it was number twenty-three, the guy named Hanky's unit. He reasoned number twenty-five was probably his partner's unit; Johnny Jackoff. He sidled up to the open door and was able to peer under on an angle. There was a light on inside and he thought he could see a little smoke wafting out. He sniffed his nose and confirmed there was definitely some odd-smelling smoke in the air. *Good, his guard will be down.* It was time to get better acquainted. Carlos gave one more glance around the decrepit center, pulled the Glock out, and ducked under the door.

Chapter 54

Donny Nutz got to the boat early and something was bothering him. As much as he didn't like or trust "The Colombian" (as he referred to Carlos), he had given him permission to stay on the boat until he arrived. Yet Carlos had called him from a hotel. *Why?* If you were trying to keep a low profile, staying on a boat in a private marina was about as low-profile as you could get, especially if you compared it to a hotel. There were no maids or other guests to worry about, no checking in or out, and most importantly, there was usually no surveillance. Plus, he knew that contract killers were no different from the average businessman. They tried to keep their expenses to a minimum and staying on the boat was free. It didn't make sense unless he did something that might draw attention to himself. Then it made all the sense in the world. Then being on a boat could leave you dead on the water; like a sitting duck. *Hmmm.*

The first thing he did was a quick check of the boat from bow to stern. He was disturbed to find that the covers on the bed in the master stateroom were ruffled, but other than that everything appeared to be all right. OK, maybe he was more than disturbed at the thought of The Colombian sleeping in his bed, but he would deal with it in short order.

He plopped his substantial caboose onto the couch in the salon just as his bodyguard Eddie "The Ear," came through the cabin doors.

"Everything looks all right up on the bridge, boss. Find anything unusual inside?"

"No, except I think the greasy spic was sleeping in my bed."

"That's not too smart."

Donny's longtime driver, Johnny "Left Lane" Longo (or Lefty, as he was referred to), threw in his two cents.

"I think you hit it on the head before, Tooch."

"How's that?"

"The guy's suicidal."

The three of them laughed and Donny picked up the TV remote and clicked it on. The Ear walked over to the fridge and opened it.

"Shit, nothing in here but a few bottles of water and I'm fuckin' *starved.* Whadda you say, boss? Maybe Lefty can go pick us up something?"

Donny looked at his watch and nixed the idea.

"The Colombian's suppose' to call anytime and I wanna be ready to roll. Why don't you pull something outta the freezer? There should be something in there you can nuke."

"It's empty, boss, look." The Ear had the freezer compartment above the fridge open for all to see and it was indeed empty. Not even an ice cube tray.

"Not that one, Tooch, there's a full-size freezer behind the door across from the bathroom down the hall, on the left side. There's always something in there."

"Gotcha."

The Ear plodded down the hall and opened up a door across from the bathroom. It was filled with linens; strike one. He opened up the one next to it and was pleased to be staring at a full-size upright freezer. But why were all the freezer racks piled on top? And why was there a stack of thawed out packages of frozen food on top of them? He picked up one of the packages and it was a Stouffer's French Bread Pizza. *Shit.* He loved those things. He called back down the hall to Donny Nutz.

"Somebody forgot to put the food in the freezer, boss, I think's it's all spoiled."

"WHAT?"

"THE FOOD, IT'S SPOILED."

Donny Nutz hauled his big ass up out of the couch and started shuffling toward The Ear.

"Whadda you talking about? The freezer went out?"

The Ear turned to face him and reached for the handle on the freezer door.

"Must be, but I don't know why they took the food—AAAGGGH!"

As soon as The Ear opened the freezer door, the frozen body of Skeeter tumbled out and crashed into him. He screamed as he fell backward into the bathroom, hitting his head on the toilet. "Jesus Christ! Get him off me!"

Skeeter's body lay across The Ear's legs and he squirmed to get out from under him; a task made difficult by the close confines of the bathroom.

"What the fuck!" Donny Nutz cursed as he used a foot to try to lift the frozen body off The Ear but it was too heavy. "Lefty! Get down here!"

Lefty came hustling and was able to roll the dead body over and into the hall. Donny Nutz disappeared into a bedroom and came out holding a body bag. It wasn't the first time he needed to dispose of a body, but he was blindsided nonetheless.

"Holy shit! What's that in his mouth?" Asked The Ear. He got to his feet and was looking down at the dead body while rubbing his head. "What the—what *is* that, Lefty?"

Lefty knelt down and stuck his finger out toward Skeeter's mouth, stopping just short of the protruding object.

"Jesus…Jesus Christ," was all he could muster.

Donny Nutz looked down at the horrific scene in the companionway of his beloved Grand Banks Trawler. The dead guy's eyes were almost popped out of his face and his mouth was frozen open with something sticking out of it. The entire body was covered in a layer of frost except for the deep ligature wound on his neck.

"You heard him, Lefty, what is it?"

Lefty bent forward and exhaled directly over the thing sticking out of Skeeter's mouth. He did it twice, the way someone might when they're trying to clean a pair of eyeglasses. As the frost melted away, he shuddered and then stood up.

"It's a toe. Somebody shoved a big toe in the guy's mouth and it's not even his. Look, he's got flip-flops on and both his big toes are there, Jesus."

"Do you really think he'd feel better if it was *his toe?*"

"You know what I mean."

"Not really."

"You still feeling hungry?"

"Very funny."

"Enough, guys, get this stiff off my boat now! Put him in the bag and load him in the back of the car." Donny Nutz stepped over the body and handed the bag to Lefty. He went back to the galley and pulled a bottle of water out of the fridge, quickly gulping some down. A minute later, Lefty and The Ear lugged Skeeter into the salon and stopped by the cabin door.

"Shouldn't we wait till dark, boss?" asked The Ear.

"Quit worrying and do as your told; it's not even eight on Sunday morning, for Christ's sake. Somebody asks, tell 'em you caught a big striper."

"You sure?" added Lefty. "We could always put him back in the freezer till later."

"Lefty?"

"Yeah, boss."

"You drive for a reason. Now put that meatsickle in the trunk before I put *you* in the freezer!"

Lefty went out to the Escalade and backed it up as close to the dock as he could. Fortunately, there was little activity on the dock because the wind was blowing fifteen to twenty knots out of the east— It wasn't a good day for boating. It took only a few minutes for the men to put Skeeter in the back of the Escalade and return to the boat. Donny Nutz ordered Lefty to clean up the freezer area and was trying to figure out why The Colombian shoved a dead body inside it. The only thing that made sense was that he planned on using it to double cross him. Maybe he was gonna tip off the cops and try to frame him. *But why?* He'd been paid a large retainer and stood to make a lot more when the job was done. And it shoulda been easy; after all, it was amateurs they were dealing with. Why would he try to fuck him? There could be only one answer; the gold that he mentioned the girl inherited…and lots of it.

A breaking news story suddenly flashed across the TV screen. A reporter was standing in a hotel parking lot with emergency vehicles and police cars all over the place. The ticker on the bottom of the screen read… night manager found stabbed to death in parking lot…suspect sought…The picture cut away to a still frame of a man passing a bill to the clerk.

"Are you fuckin' kidding me?" Donny Nutz stared at the image in disbelief as he turned the volume up on the TV.

"What is it, boss?" asked The Ear.

"Shut up for a second."

The reporter was reporting; reporter style.

"Boynton police are searching for this man who is a person of interest in the brutal slaying of a hotel manager early this morning. Police have yet to confirm it, but a reliable source has told *this* reporter that homicide detectives believe the slaying may be the work of the same person responsible for the deadly home invasion of another Boynton man less than forty-eight hours ago. The same source reports in that case, the victim was discovered with most of his toes cut off and a bullet in his head. Another source inside the department who asked to remain anonymous, described the crime scene as the most gruesome he had seen in over forty years of service. If you have any information as to the whereabouts of the man shown on the screen, please contact detective Miller at 561-867-5309. If you see him, do not approach him, call nine-one-one. He's considered armed and extremely dangerous."

Donny Nutz muted the TV and shook his head, stunned.

"That donkey-humpin coffee farmer's even crazier than I thought. Holy fuckin' cannoli! I told him no carvin' anybody up until after I got paid. So what does he do? More slicin' and dicin' than a Ginsu infomercial."

"Who? What are you talking about, boss?"

He pointed at the screen with the image of Carlos still frozen on it.

"That's him! That's the fuckin' Colombian! I shoulda known better. I shoulda left the boat at home and brought somebody up from Miami to handle this. God dammit! " Donny Nutz slammed a fist down on the small table in front of the couch and his water fell over and spilled on the floor.

"What are we gonna do, boss?"

"First, you're gonna pick up that water. *Then* what are we gonna do? Well, I know what *I'm* gonna do. It's been a while, but as soon as I see that slice-happy spic, I'm gonna kill him myself. Then I'm gonna kill Tony Two-Teeth."

"Why Tony?"

"'Cause that asshole recommended him."

Chapter 55

The first thing that Ricky did after getting into his storage unit was to put on a dirty jumpsuit he had hanging on the wall. It was white at one time, back when he first started his pest control business a couple years earlier. It wasn't really necessary to wear one, or the respirator that he also used, but he thought it made him look more professional to the few customers he had. Maybe it did and maybe it didn't, but one thing was for sure, it made him sweat…a lot. So much so, that he even had it washed once.

The next thing he did was to smoke some crack that Hanky left in his truck prior to their ill-fated mission. Crack smoking is never a good idea, but it's an even worse one when the user is already jumpy and fearful. Like most addicts, he could find a reason for using anytime. This time, he half-heartedly convinced himself his brain needed a lift so he could figure out what the hell to do. He was right, of course, his brain did need a lift, but the crackavator only went one way; straight down.

He had just taken one mega-hit from the pipe and watched the little white rock glow red as he inhaled again. Then he leaned back in an old office chair and watched the smoke swirl toward the ceiling as he slowly exhaled. He tracked the wisps of smoke as they crept toward the half-open overhead door at the front of the unit; his mind quickly numbing from the effects of the concentrated cocaine. As he leaned forward to watch the smoke get sucked out the door, Carlos appeared in front of him with a gun pointed at his chest.

"Hey, Spanky, how's it going?"

Caught totally off guard, the rest of the smoke in Ricky's lungs forced itself out all at once and he had a coughing fit so bad his eyes started to water. He managed to set the crack pipe down and clutched his chest until the coughing finally stopped and he caught his breath.

"What, whadda you want? Where's Hanky? Where's, where's my buddy?"

"What do I want? Some answers. Where's your dipshit buddy with the Mr. Potatohead silencer? Don't worry about him, he's chillin'. So unless you want me to aerate that scrawny chest of yours with some high-velocity lead, you best be forthright, my friend."

"F-forthright?" Ricky's eyes were darting around, looking for something to defend himself with... *anything*.

"The truth, Spanky, I want the truth. And keep those beady little eyes focused on me, don't even think about making a move. My trigger finger's got Parkinson's."

"My, my names not Spanky, it's Rick-E."

"Ricky?"

"No, it's pronounced Rick-E."

"Say what? Who the *fuck* do you think you are? You think you're some fancy-ass celebrity like that black African bitch who calls herself Sharday when her name's spelled S-A-D-E? I got news for you, in my book, that's pronounced Sade, like 'made' with an 's.' So listen up, Spanky, or would you prefer Spank-A?"

Ricky could see in the guy's eyes that he was on edge, just like he was. He had no idea who in the hell Sharday, or Sade, or whoever it was he was talking about was. He only knew he was looking down the barrel of a gun—with a *real* silencer on it.

"Uh…Spanky's fine…I guess."

"Good, so tell me, Spanky, what were you and that rocket scientist planning on doing at the girl's house?"

Ricky's mind was racing and the crack had it in overdrive. *What should I tell him?*

"Uh, we were, uh, we were just, uh—"

"Don't lie to me!" Carlos lowered the gun and fired at Ricky's foot. It barely missed and ricocheted around the cluttered unit before imbedding in the tire of a stolen Schwinn. Ricky jumped as a concrete chip flew up in front of his face, and he put his hands out in front of him.

"Don't shoot! Please don't shoot me!"

"Last chance, Spanky, or the next one's pulverizing your lyin' face."

"OK, OK, we were…I was, I was gonna kill her."

"*What?* Why? Why kill her?"

"So my girlfriend, my fiancée…my ex-fiancée, would inherit all her stuff."

"Huh? How in the hell do you figure?"

"My girlfriend is her stepsister. Hanky said that if Holly got killed before she got married and didn't have a will, it would all go to her."

"Including the gold, of course."

"Yeah, the gold, the house, the marina...*everything*. Wait a sec, how'd you know about the gold?"

"I'm asking the questions here, my friend. So how much gold *is* there?"

"The lawyer at the will reading said at least five million bucks' worth."

Carlos let out a whistle and laughed as the bicycle tire hissed out its final breath.

"So it *is* true. And you really thought you could get away with it?"

"The plan was to knock her out and throw her in the water to try to make it look like an accident, like she fell off the dock or something."

"With a lead pipe?"

"Better safe than sorry."

Carlos shook his weary head.

"Do you have any idea how bad you fucked my night up? Because of you two clowns I didn't get any sleep and made a stupid mistake this morning. Now I gotta split town before getting my hands on that gold. Shit. I need to sit down for a minute. Keep your hands where I can see 'em, Spanky."

Carlos sat down on a cooler but kept the gun trained on Ricky's chest.

"Sorry, man, but you fucked up my night too. My fiancée broke up with me."

"Well boo-fuckin'-hoo to you. One more word and I'm gonna fuck up your day too." Carlos rubbed his temple with one hand and briefly closed his eyes. He needed some sleep badly.

Ricky picked up on it and had an idea. "Here, take a hit off this, I guarantee it will pick you up." He picked the pipe up and handed it toward Carlos. His thinking was that if he got him high enough, he might have a chance to escape.

Carlos stuck the gun out farther toward Ricky. "I said keep your hands where I can see 'em! I may be tired but I'm not stupid. You think I'm gonna smoke some weed and fall asleep? Please, I oughta shoot you right now."

"No, I swear, it's not pot, it's cocaine."

Carlos was a child of the seventies with Colombian roots and he had naturally experimented with cocaine as a younger man. He knew of its powerful effect as a stimulant.

"Bullshit. Even *I* know that you snort cocaine."

"Not this kind, this is the kind you smoke. It hits you even faster than when you snort it, I swear. Look at me, I've been up all night too, but I feel great after just a couple of hits."

Carlos scrutinized Ricky and he did indeed look wide-eyed and alert; maybe even a little *too* wide-eyed. But that was exactly what he needed. He thought about the call he needed to make to Donny Nutz and about ditching his rental car and finding a way out of town. Going to another hotel and trying to crash for a few hours was out of the question. Every hotel in the state would probably have his face plastered all over it. He squinted at Ricky and nodded his head in resignation.

"OK, get that thing going and then pass it to me. If you try something stupid, you're gonna smart like Einstein."

Ricky put another small white rock in the bowl and lit it. He inhaled just hard enough to get the rock glowing and then passed it to Carlos.

"Don't suck too hard or you might pull it through the chamber," he warned.

Carlos smoked the pipe with one hand while pointing the gun at Ricky with the other. He obeyed his instructions and took a modest hit before blowing it out.

"You gotta hit it harder than that, dude, or you're never gonna get off."

Annoyed, Carlos sucked on the pipe much harder and the little rock turned bright red. A huge volume of smoke filled his virgin lungs until he thought they would burst. He set the pipe down, then stood up and expelled the smoke in a painful fit of coughing. His head was spinning and he stepped backward toward the door to get some fresh air.

"Don't try to, don't try anything." He coughed some more and stuck his head under the door to gulp some fresh air. As he did so he saw a red convertible coming down the aisle between the buildings. He quickly ducked back inside and pressed himself against the wall. Crack-induced paranoia was already setting in.

"Somebody's coming. You know who it is? Shit."

Ricky leaned forward and rolled himself a couple of feet closer to the door so he could see under. His eyes got even wider as he watched a red Beemer roll by with its top down. It was Shagball with his girlfriend, Holly, and the midget Tangles in back.

"Holy shit, it's her."

"Who?"

"It's the girl, Holly, she's with Shagball and Tangles."

"What? Get back, move back." Carlos waved the gun at Ricky and he rolled his chair back to his original position. He was feeling a bit paranoid, for sure, but the crack definitely had him amped up. "What the hell are *they* doing here?"

"Hell if I know, I've never seen *any* of them here before."

"Could they be looking for you?"

"Me? Shit, they probably don't even know I have a unit in here. Besides, if they were, they just drove by. I don't know—wait! Shit, I forgot, the C-Love Marina has a unit in back where they keep all their marina crap. They must be going there."

Carlos looked at his watch.

"At eight o'clock on Sunday morning? What the *fuck's* going on here?"

Carlos was breathing hard as the crack cocaine coursed through his overloaded brain. It had been years since he had any coke in his system but he never remembered feeling anything like this. His pupils were little black peas and his eyes darted from side to side. His skin felt all tingly and his heart was racing. The thought of sleeping was a distant memory replaced by paranoia and doubt. "I gotta get outta here. I gotta make a call and then I gotta get outta here. Don't make a peep or I'll use you for target practice."

He pulled out his cell and dialed Donny Nutz.

Chapter 56

DICK agent Thomas Cushing was taking an early morning leak in his Delray townhouse when his DICK phone lit up and started playing the Paul McCartney and Wings classic, “Live and Let Die.”

“When you were young and your heart was an open book…” He hustled over to the nightstand by his bed and answered it.

“Yes, sir.”

“How y’all doin’ this morning, pardner?”

Per usual, the DICK head was using the Oralator. This morning he was talking in a southern drawl but Cushing couldn’t put his finger on whose voice it was.

“Could be better, I only managed a few hours sleep. What’s up?”

“Homeland Security got called to a hotel just a little ways yonder of yew last night.”

“I know, I happened to be driving by when they left and stopped in for a little chat with the night clerk.”

“Yew don’t say. How come yew didn’t give this ol’ dog a shout?”

“’Cause it was a false alarm, a case of mistaken identity....sort of. OK, I give, what’s with the country bumpkin voice? I can’t say I recognize it.”

"Shewt, yew kidding me? Yew don't recognize the voice of Dennis Weaver?"

"Dennis *who*? Never heard of him."

"Dang, I keep forgetting how young yew whippersnappers are. Does the name Deputy Marshall Sam McCloud from the great seventies detective show of the same name ring a bell?"

"You gotta be kidding me, my dad loved that show. You're really dating yourself, sir."

"Maybe, maybe not, I had a pappy too. So don't sell me short like those NYPD detectives yews to do with McCloud. There's some brains under that big ol' hat, don't yew forget it, boy."

"For once, *just once,* can you scratch the role-playing, sir?"

"Aw hell, so much for an old cowpoke having a little fun. Time to get serious, I suppose, let me find another voice…here we go, this one's always good for getting to the point."

"Switching to Peter Graves?"

"I'm getting too predictable, it's back to the archives after we finish."

Cushing shook his head and smiled as Stargazer's voice switched to the no bullshit voice of Peter Graves. Stargazer loved to role-play and Cushing loved to rain on his parade.

"So why are you asking about the Homeland Security call?"

"Because the night clerk was just found dead in the hotel parking lot."

"What?"

"That's right, Thomas. He was found slumped over in his car with his nose cut off and a fatal stab wound to the head. You still think it was a case of mistaken identity?"

"Jesus, I, uh, it doesn't make—"

"Sense? No. Not from a terroristic standpoint, but when I ran the image of the suspect through our database, we got a match. While it's true he's a dead ringer for a deceased terrorist named Diqueed al Salaami, he also looks like a known contract killer named Carlos Ramirez, aka The Colombian."

"Ramirez? Why does that name sound familiar?"

"Excellent recall, Thomas. It sounds familiar because one of his cousins was Richard Ramirez, otherwise known as the Night Stalker; the satanic serial killer who terrorized southern California in the late eighties."

"Jesus Christ."'

"Yeah, that's who got him all worked up. Anyways, it looks like The Colombian wasn't too happy about having Homeland Security called on him because he looked like a terrorist. Care to guess where he's based?"

"Miami?"

"No, but that would make sense. He's based out of New York and is suspect in over a dozen hits in the last three years along the East Coast."

"Right in Donny Nutz's backyard...shit."

"You got that right, in the plural."

"When Jansen and company filled me in yesterday they said they were leery of a dark-skinned guy who arrived on Nutz's boat, the *JC.*"

"With good reason too. I decided to have a look into the homicide investigation regarding the friend who got tortured and it seems there's also a missing person."

"What? Who?"

"Some kid that works on the docks who was one of the last people to see their friend alive."

"This just keeps getting better."

"Or worse, depending on how you look at it. I hope you left Mr. Jansen and his cohorts somewhere safe."

"They spent the night on his boat, which he just relocated to a different marina. He assured me nobody knows where he moved it, not yet at least."

"So what's your plan?"

"I'm monitoring their calls, waiting for Nutz to make his move."

"You shouldn't have to wait long. I just checked a satellite image of the C-Love Marina and ran the tags on a big black Escalade parked in front of the *JC*; he's there. Is Jansen still on his boat?"

"No, I've been listening in and they went to a storage center. His girlfriend inherited a bunch of gold and she thinks that's where her aunt left it."

"You think Nutz knows about the gold? If he tries to shake her down that sounds like a prime target."

"I don't know…I'm not sure—shit."

"What."

"There was something strange going on outside the girl's house last night. They found some potato chunks splattered on the side of it and a lead pipe on the ground, which looked like it had blood on it. Somebody was definitely up to something, maybe snooping, among other things, I don't know. That's why I had them move to Jansen's boat."

"I don't like it, Thomas; I want you shadowing them until this thing goes down."

"You don't have to tell me twice. I'll grab a quick shower and be there in twenty minutes."

"Good, we need to get Nutz off the street and start working this arms trafficking deal from the other end. We got word of a large shipment of surface-to-air missiles headed to Port Everglades from somewhere in South America; it's got to be tied to Nutz. And get this; the smugglers are using submarines."

"I heard the rumor."

"It's no rumor. The cartels have branched out into arms smuggling. I guess they figure why stop at cocaine if there's room for some boom."

"I'll say one thing, they know how to adapt."

"Like a chameleon at an ELO concert. But one thing at a time, focus on the situation at hand. Nutz and his henchmen are dangerous enough by themselves, throw in a wild card like a psychotic Colombian killer and it's a whole nuther ballgame."

"Don't worry; I plan on being there until the beer and hot dogs run out."

"I'm serious. The Colombian's gotten reckless, if he feels cornered there's no telling what he might do. Watch your back, Thomas."

"Understood, Jim."

"Jim?"

"Jim Phelps; *Mission Impossible?*"

"Hah. You got me there. Just remember what I said; keep your head down and your sights up." Click.

Chapter 57

San Castle storage had been neglected for years. The owner painted it orange at one point to try to make it look like one of the newer storage chains, but they used cheap paint and it started peeling within a year. The paint faded and cracked too, adding to its overall disheveled appearance. The center consisted of nine buildings that were arranged in no discernable pattern, like the way a child might spread out building blocks on a kindergarten floor. Storage units ranged in size from as small as a 5 x10 unit to as large as a 20 x 40 unit. The entire property was ringed with a rusted-out barbed-wire fence that included a one-acre parcel near the front gate that was for long-term boat and RV storage. It looked more like a boat and RV graveyard than storage center, and indeed, most were ancient and abandoned. If the center wasn't bad *enough* looking, there was even a rusted out old cell phone tower right in the middle. When the cellular company's lease with the center came up for renewal and they couldn't get permission to put in a taller tower, they opted out and left it behind.

As we pulled through the gates, Holly commented, "Wow, what happened to this place?"

"I heard the owner had a chance to sell it during the real estate boom to one of the big storage chains, but got greedy and lost out. The rumor is he borrowed heavily against it and is in serious financial trouble. It might even be in foreclosure as we speak."

"This place looks even worse up close than it does from the road," piped in Tangles from the backseat.

I looked over at Holly. "Which unit is it?"

"Regina said it's all the way in the back, in the northwest corner, number forty-nine."

I guided the Beemer toward the back corner like a rat working its way through a maze. The layout was incredibly poor and some of the lanes between the buildings were half-blocked by small boats on trailers and old pickup trucks. We saw one person at a unit in front and passed another that had its overhead door halfway open, but that was it. The place was otherwise deserted. Monday through Saturday it would be bustling with activity, but early on Sunday it was pretty much a ghost town.

"Here we are," I announced, as I parked alongside a building that had a "49" painted over a large overhead door. It also had a smaller, regular-sized door, at the corner of the building on the side. We piled out and followed Holly up to the overhead door. There was a big aluminum bar that slid across the center of it and it was secured by an old Master Lock, the combination kind. Holly started spinning the dials and nodded toward the small door.

"There's a key that works on the side door there, but it's in the office. Fortunately, there's a combo lock on this one and Regina gave me the combination."

I noticed she didn't have it written down and queried her.

"You memorized it?"

"It's Millie's birth date."

"Ah."

She finished spinning the dial and yanked the lock open. I helped her push the door up and we were greeted by a dank, musty smell. Holly found a light switch in the corner and flicked it on.

"This place is pretty big, man, look at all the stuff crammed in here." Tangles was right, the place was big and it was filled with all kinds of dock-related stuff. Rubber fenders, dock boxes, piling lights, a row boat, ropes, buoys, you name it.

"Regina said Millie's had this place for years. She started out with a smaller unit but ended up with this one. There's even a bathroom over by the side door if anybody needs to use one."

I stepped around some boxes marked C-*Love* on the side that had lifejackets in them and propped open the side door. It was hot and stuffy inside and I was hoping to get some airflow in the place.

Tangles suddenly pulled his phone out of his pocket and it was blaring a song by Kid Rock. I forget the name of the song, but he sings about "catching walleye from the dock."

Tangles answered his phone and said, "You're where? At the boat? Oh, yeah, yeah, I know I said I'd go to breakfast with you. What? I don't know, Momma, I'm kinda in the middle of something…All right, all right, let me see if it's OK with Holly."

Holly was working her way to the rear of the unit but heard him say her name and turned around.

“What is it?”

“I told my mom I’d go to breakfast with her this morning. She borrowed Rudy’s car and is over at the boat. She wants to come pick me up, do you mind?”

“Heck no.”

Tangles gave his mom explicit directions on how to get to the unit and hung up. “Thanks, Holly, I hope we find your aunt’s gold before she gets here. I don’t want to miss out on the excitement; this is like a treasure hunt.”

“I’m excited too, nervous, but excited.”

I think I knew what she meant, excited at the prospect of gold, but nervous about the looming presence of one Donny Nutz. And according to the FBI agent, Holly could be getting a call from him at any time.

Chapter 58

Four miles to the south in the salon of the *JC*, The Ear finished helping Donny Nutz strap a spring-activated, sawed-off, double-barrel shotgun, to his left forearm. It was a brutal weapon the inventor named "The Changer," which was short for "The Game Changer." It had no trigger; it fired when the arm was snapped straight out to the extended position. It was created by a Mob firearm expert named Frankie "The Nub" Barelli. He stressed to Donny that when firing you needed to make sure your fist was clenched and rotated with the palm of the hand facing down so as not to blow your thumb off. He also recommended not wearing lace-up shoes when armed with The Changer. To maximize its effectiveness at close range, Donny loaded it with twelve-gauge shells filled with buckshot. Once he was locked and loaded, he slipped on a seersucker jacket that had an enlarged interior sleeve opening so he didn't have to straighten his arm when putting it on.

No sooner had he donned his jacket when his phone rang. Donny flipped it open and waited for the other person to identify him or herself first, even though he was expecting The Colombian to call.

"You there? It's me, Carlos."

"Yeah, I'm here, where are you?"

Carlos thought he sensed tension in Donny's voice; he was right.

"I'm just a few miles up the road from the marina at an old storage center. Guess who else is here?"

"I got no time for games. I'm here to collect some money."

"Well you're in luck then, thanks to me. The girl who inherited the marina is here along with her boyfriend who dug up the tanks. The marina rents a storage locker at this place and that's where they are. I was following that lead I was telling you about last night and the next thing I know they come driving in."

Donny noticed he was talking abnormally fast and sounded edgy.

"I'm on my way, gimme directions."

"Just head north on US 1 about three or four miles and it's on the left, you can't miss it. The girl's unit is, uh, hang on a sec." Carlos put the phone to his chest and waved the gun at Ricky who was fiddling with what looked to be some kind of gas mask on his lap.

"Put that fuckin' thing down. Where's the girl's unit?"

Ricky set the mask down and answered, "It's, uh, it's in the back, in the north, northwest corner. Number forty-nine or fifty, I think." He was pointing at a spot on the wall trying to give him an idea of the direction.

Carlos put the phone back up to his ear and continued. "The girl's unit is in the back of the center in the northwest corner. Number forty-nine or fifty. Look for a red Beemer."

"Who you talking to?"

Carlos glanced at Ricky, who had the crack pipe back in his hand.

"A loose end."

"Figures. Hold the girl and the guy until I get there, it shouldn't take long."

Carlos turned his head toward the door to try to hide the sound of his voice but still kept the gun pointed at Ricky.

"No can do. I gotta tie up this loose end and then I'm outta here." Carlos didn't know if he had found Skeeter stuffed in the freezer *or* if there was any news out about the night clerk killing, but he wasn't about to take the chance.

"Why the rush? Don't you wanna get paid?" Donny Nutz wasn't about to let him know he found the body in the freezer and that his face was all over the news. If he did, Carlos would know he would order him killed because they both knew if Carlos got nabbed, he would rat him out to try and save his own skin. Donny Nutz wanted him dead. He *needed* him dead. Carlos turned back to face Ricky, who was smoking more crack.

"Yeah, I wanna get paid, it turned out to be more work than I thought; a lot more. I'll make arrangements later."

"OK, assuming I get my hands on some of that gold."

"Gold?" Carlos was so juiced up from the crack that he forgot all about the gold.

"Yeah, gold, as in the shiny stuff you told me the girl inherited. There is gold…*isn't* there?"

"Yeah, that's what I've been told; lots of it. In fact, I'd like to get paid in it, so save some for me. I gotta, I gotta go, we'll talk later." Click.

Donny Nutz folded up his cell phone and The Ear asked, "So?"

"So he knows I'm onto him, he's gonna run. Maybe we'll be lucky and get there before he leaves. Let's move it!"

Carlos put his phone away and looked at Ricky who had an expression on his face like a kid who just saw Santa Claus for the first time.

"What's with the face?"

"That's it! The gold!"

"What? What is?"

"That's gotta be what they're doing here, they came for the gold! It's gotta be in the storage locker, why else would they be here this early on a Sunday? Think about it, they've never been here before, but a couple of days after the will reading they're here at the crack of dawn. The old lady must have stashed some of that gold in the storage locker. Holy crap! It's probably been here all along!"

Carlos' mind was racing but it hadn't moved an inch. *Could it be?* He paced back and forth and looked at Ricky who was fidgeting with the gas mask contraption again.

"What the *fuck* is that thing?"

He held the mask up. "This? It's a respirator. I use it when I'm spraying for bugs. The center gives me a discount on my unit for spraying the outside of the buildings once a month. Actually, I should spray today, I got off schedule. But who cares? There's probably a pile of gold just around the corner. What are we waiting for?"

"We?"

"If it's there you're gonna need help. There could be a shit-pot full of gold."

Carlos continued to pace back and forth, wondering if the crackhead was right. One way or the other he needed to make a decision fast. The decision was made; *he had to know.* A big pile of gold would take care of him for life.

He trained the gun on the center of Ricky's chest.

"Get out of the suit."

"What?"

"You heard me, get out of the jumpsuit, now!"

Ricky was confused and not liking the tone of Carlos' voice. With great trepidation he unzipped the jumpsuit and set it on the chair. He was once again left standing in his Jeff Gordon underwear with bloody gauze wrapped around his throat.

"Why, why are you doing this?" Ricky was totally confused, *what was he doing making him strip?*

"Don't worry about it; you wanna go see your buddy?"

"Hanky? Sh-sure...I guess."

"That's what I thought."

Carlos took a step forward and shot him twice in the chest. Ricky crashed backward into the stolen Schwinn and the last thing he heard before his brain stopped functioning was Carlos' parting words, "Say hi for me when you see him."

Chapter 59

"Look for an anchor or any boxes marked 'anchor,'" instructed Holly. "That's what Millie's letter said. That's the clue to where the gold is. I'll start in the back and you two start in the front."

Tangles and I worked as a team; I went high and he went low. There were plastic bins and boxes stacked everywhere and stuff lying all over the place. An entire section of a side wall had spare fishing rods and gaffs for the *C-Love.* After ten minutes or so we were about halfway to the back of the large storage unit. It had to be twenty by forty or fifty feet long. Suddenly, Holly called out, "Here! Back here!"

She was about three-quarters of the way to the back wall and pointing to the side. We stopped what we were doing and joined her. Up against the side wall was a large dock box. On top of the box was a pair of anchors covered in chain with a blue tarp pushed to the side.

"The whole thing was covered by the tarp, it has to be it!" Holly was excited and I'm sure Tangles was feeling it too, just like I was. We fed the chain over the side of the dock box on to the floor and then pushed the anchors on top of it as they were too heavy to lift. There was a fine layer of dust coating the top of the dock box which was about six feet long, three feet wide, and two feet high. There was no lock on the latch. I looked at Holly and waved my hand in front of it like an usher offering a seat.

"The honor's all yours, it's the moment of truth."

She let out a deep breath and closed her eyes for a moment, then bent down and lifted the lid.

"No way," she muttered. "It's just more dock lines and life preservers, what the heck?"

"Wait a second." I saw something buried in the corner of the box and started pulling the dock lines and life preservers out. "There's something underneath this stuff…look." I pointed to a small canvas bag that was cinched at the top with heavy twine. "Check it out, Holly."

She reached a hand down to lift the sack out and groaned with effort.

"Good Lord, it's heavy!" With two hands she hoisted it out and set it on the floor. "Anybody have a knife?"

Tangles reached in his pocket and handed her a small pocketknife. She deftly sliced the twine and the bag opened just a tad. She went to one knee, peered inside, and gasped. With one hand she covered her mouth and with the other she reached into the bag and withdrew a fistful of something. Slowly she rotated her hand over and opened her fist to reveal a half dozen shiny gold coins about the size of a half dollar. Her hand was shaking so badly that one of the coins fell and clanged to the floor by Tangles' feet. He picked it up and inspected it.

"Holy crap, it's one ounce, just this coin is worth almost two grand!" He handed the coin to Holly and added, "Are there any other bags?"

Holly dropped the coins back in the open sack.

"Let's see."

Holly and I started tossing the rest of the ropes and other miscellaneous dock paraphernalia aside and bag after bag was exposed; five more in all.

I reached down and hoisted one of the bags up and then another, checking their weight.

"Jesus, I'd say they weigh forty to fifty pounds each! If it's all gold, you're looking at roughly..." I did a quick calculation based on eighteen-hundred dollars an ounce and came up with, "Seven to nine million dollars...Ho-Lee-Shit!"

***

Just inside the side door of the storage unit, shielded by the bathroom that jutted out from the wall, Carlos couldn't believe what he was hearing. A fortune in gold was within his grasp! His heart was beating wildly from the crack cocaine and the thought of that much gold. One major obstacle was in his way though; Donny Nutz would be there any minute and he was sure to have some muscle with him. The odds weren't in his favor, but he did have one thing on his side; the element of surprise. Not only did Nutz likely think he was long gone, but he had a trick up his sleeve.

Suddenly he heard a car door slam so he ducked out the side door. From the side mirror on the red Beemer parked in front of the unit, he could see a woman approaching. *Who in the hell?* He leaned back against the building and nodded to himself. His plan was audacious and would leave a pile of dead bodies behind, but it would also set him for life.

***

"What do you want to do with it?" I asked Holly.

"I- I don't know, where would I even put it?"

"I guess you could get a big safety deposit box or something. At least it would be secure."

"Yeah, but not today" said Tangles. "It's Sunday."

"Shit, that's right. I guess you could leave it here, but I don't know, I don't think I could sleep—"

"Helloooo, helloooo, is anybody—"

"Yeah, Momma, we're back here," replied Tangles to his mother. She was standing at the front of the unit and had her hand shielded over her eyes as she peered inside.

"Ask your friends if they want to join us for breakfast, honey, my treat."

Tangles already knew the answer and didn't bother asking as he walked toward her.

"They got their hands full right now, besides, they already ate."

"Are you ready, then? I'm starved."

"Yeah, but let me see if they need a hand with anything before we go. Just give me a second."

Marie pointed toward the walled off area by the side door. "That wouldn't happen to be a bathroom, would it?"

Holly responded, "Yes, but it's liable to be a little dirty. I don't know when it was cleaned last, sorry."

Marie started walking toward it and laughed.

"Nothing to be sorry about, dear, me and my bladder will be thanking you in a couple minutes." Marie disappeared into the bathroom and Tangles turned back to us.

"You need any help moving some of that before I go?"

I shrugged and looked at Holly.

"What do you think?"

She looked at the open sack of gold on the floor and the ones piled in the dock box.

"I think we can handle it, Kit, don't you? Why don't you grab one of the ones in the box and I'll take the one that's open. Can we put them in your trunk?"

"Sure, what do you want to do with the rest?"

"I don't know, we should probably bring them too; let me think about it while we load these."

"OK."

I lifted one of the bags out with one hand and supported it with the other as I led the way out to the car. Tangles was behind me and Holly was behind him. Just as I reached the overhead door I heard the sound of hundreds of coins hitting the floor. I turned around to see Holly sprawled out on a coil of heavy dock rope with the sack of gold lying in front of her. Gold coins were everywhere. Tangles helped her up and I asked if she was all right. Her face was red; she was more embarrassed than anything.

"Yes, I'm fine…stupid rope." She kicked at the rope that tripped her up and it tangled around her foot, almost causing her to fall again. I laughed and quickly opened the trunk of the Beemer to set my sack inside.

"I can't believe I just did that…look, they're everywhere!" Holly was exasperated and shook her head as Tangles and I crouched down to assist in picking them up.

Chapter 60

Donny Nutz sat in the back of the Escalade, silently cursing himself for hiring the crazy Colombian killer. They were lucky to get the dead body off the boat and get out of the marina before the place was swarming with cops. The Ear turned around in the passenger seat and asked, "Whadda you wanna do with the stiff?"

"There's probably a dumpster or something at this storage center where we can leave him. What a pain in the ass."

As they turned down the access road that dead-ended at San Castle Storage, he could see brake lights flash on a car about four hundred yards ahead. Lefty also slowed down as they got to the open gates and Donny was pleased to see a "Closed Sunday," sign on the building that was marked "Manager's Office."

Lefty caught his eye in the rearview mirror.

"Which way, boss?"

"He said it's number forty-nine or fifty, all the way in the back, in the northwest corner. Look for a red BMW. Keep your eyes peeled for The Colombian too. He's long gone if he knows what's good for him, but I ain't sure that he does."

As they meandered through the complex they saw a guy working on a trailer and a guy in some kind of hazmat suit spraying something at the base of a building. Other than that, the place appeared empty. Moments later they made another turn and saw a red Beemer about seventy yards ahead. It was parked in front of a unit that had its overhead door open. There was a small Toyota parked in front of it, which looked like the car that pulled in just ahead of them.

"Stop the car," ordered Donny Nutz. He pointed, and added, "Pull off to the side, behind that boat, but make sure Tooch has a view of the open unit."

Lefty did as he was told and parked the big Escalade behind a boat sitting on a trailer. It was on the same side as the unit in the corner with the Beemer parked in front of it. Lefty angled the Escalade so he thought The Ear would be able to see like Donny wanted.

"How's that, Tooch?" he asked.

Tooch angled his head a little to the side. "Yeah, I can see no problem. So what's the plan, boss?"

Donny thought about it for a moment. "You guys wait here. But if you see me looking your way, or hear or see anything funny, come and join the party. I don't expect it to play out like that, but they're not expecting me and you never know."

"You sure you don't want some company?"

"Are you forgetting? I got some right here." Donny Nutz tapped his left sleeve twice with a big ring on his pinky finger and it made a metallic sound. He stepped out of the car and warned them again, "Keep your eyes peeled."

As Donny Nutz lumbered the seventy or so yards toward the Beemer, the guy in the dirty white jumpsuit innocuously sprayed his way toward the Escalade. The Ear caught sight of him in the side view mirror and turned around to take a look.

"Whadda you suppose that guy in the suit's doing? Spraying for bugs?"

"Probably," answered Lefty. "I heard they got roaches down here make the ones in Jersey look anorexic."

Chapter 61

We were on our hands and knees picking up gold coins and putting them in the sack. I was facing the back of the storage unit and Tangles was next to me facing the side wall.

I heard Holly say, "Uh, uh—"

"What, what is it?" I swiveled my head around to see what she was doing and she was looking up at a blimp-sized man standing under the overhead door with his arms crossed. He was wearing a dark pinstriped seersucker suit and his face had more jowls on it than an episode of *The Biggest Loser.*

Wow. His hair was thin and pasty gray, like the color of his skin. What a nose he had too; it looked like Karl Malden's after running into a wall. He was one, big, fat, scary-looking dude.

Holly tentatively rose to her feet, as did Tangles and I. A couple dozen gold coins were still scattered around the floor. Holly shot a nervous glance at me and asked, "Who, uh, who are you?"

Instinctively, I knew who it was. She probably did too and was no doubt praying for a miracle. It was Donny Nutz, it had to be. But where in hell did he come from and how did he know where to find us?

"I ask the questions here, honey." He pulled a small sheet of paper out of his pocket and looked at it. "Are you Holly Lutes?"

"I, uh, I'm, uh—"

"Lie to me and this is gonna end worse than the last episode of *The Sopranos.*"

His voice was as menacing as his appearance. He sounded a little like a pissed-off Morgan Freeman impersonating Darth Vader.

Holly took a big gulp and confessed. "Yes, I'm, uh, I'm Holly."

He pointed a big, stubby, accusatory finger at her.

"You cost me a lot of money when you fucked me out of that marina."

Holly's face went white and I could tell she was petrified, so I waded in.

"We didn't know—"

"Shut up!" He glanced at the small piece of paper again. "So you're the asshole boyfriend, huh? The one named Shagball?"

"Last time I checked."

"Cute; a real live smart-ass, too. Well check this, Romeo, it's my unnerstanding that you and your little circus freak sidekick are responsible for—"

I knew his circus freak comment wouldn't set well with Tangles, Mob boss or not, and sure enough, he cut him off.

"Now wait just a sec—"

Donny Nutz stabbed his stubby finger at him.

"Shut up, you little munchkin or the next street you skip down won't be the yellow-brick road, it'll be the end of the road."

Suddenly the door to the bathroom opened and Tangles' mom came walking out. "What's all the—?"

"NO!" Tangles threw up his arms and leapt in front of her. She was to our left, which was on Donny Nutz's right. Caught by surprise, he instinctively pulled a handgun from inside his jacket and pointed it at the perceived threat.

"Don't shoot!" pleaded Tangles. "She had nothing to do with this. Please, please let her go." His raised arms were up in front of Marie's face and she leaned to the side to get a better look at who was pointing a gun at her.

Donny Nutz also leaned, but the wrong way. They were like two people trying to pass each other on the sidewalk who keep inadvertently stepping to the same side. Finally, Marie stuck her arm out and pushed Tangles a little to the side.

She finally had a clear look. "Who are…are…" Her tongue seemed to be tied as she took another step directly toward Donny Nutz and stared.

He took a step toward her and then stopped, but his head moved forward the way a snapping turtle's head does when it extends out before it snaps. A strange look came over his face. "Is that, is that *you?*"

She blinked, shook her head a little, and then took another step until they were only an arm's length apart.

"Oh, my…oh-my-God…*Donny?*"

Donny Nutz slowly shook his head and laughed as he lowered his weapon and slipped it inside his jacket.

"Son of a bitch, if it isn't the cutest little blackjack dealer in Biloxi; Marie Dupree. How the hell are you, Marie?"

I felt like I was in the *Twilight Zone*— totally stunned. I looked at Holly and her mouth was hanging open. We both looked at Tangles who had these Buckwheat eyes bulging out of his face. “Ma, *Momma?* You, you *know* him?”

Then, perhaps even more incredibly, they hugged. I couldn’t help but notice he kept his left arm bent and away from her body like it was hurting him or something. I was speechless; it was like watching King Kong cradle Jessica Lange. Shoe? This is face. Face? This is shoe. Thwack!

Chapter 62

DICK agent Thomas Cushing got dressed after taking a quick shower and was semi-listening to the audio feed coming from the storage locker. He couldn't hear anything from Holly's phone (because it was in her purse), but he had good reception from Tangles' phone because he had set it on a box while he picked coins off the floor. According to the feed, they found millions in gold that Holly's aunt left her. They were moving some of it to the car when she tripped and spilled some coins on the floor. Then, suddenly, another voice could be heard and the hair on Cushing's neck stood on end. He'd heard enough wiretaps to know exactly who it belonged to. It was Donny Nutz! Cushing had expected him to make contact by phone, but somehow he tracked them down at the storage center. He grabbed his gun and dashed down to the garage, quickly firing up the engine on his Turbo Carrera. He knew that the storage center was approximately eight miles north on US1 from his Delray townhouse. He calculated that, barring a collision, he would be there in roughly six minutes.

This was one of the reasons he drove a Porsche. Hopefully, he wouldn't be too late.

***

The Ear was momentarily distracted while changing the radio station and missed Donny Nutz pull a gun out. When he turned back and saw he was pointing a gun at someone he started to get out, but the next thing he knew, Donny had re-holstered his weapon and was hugging some broad. He let out a deep breath and closed the car door.

"False alarm, Lefty," he announced to the driver. Lefty also re-shut his door and leaned back in his seat. A Lady Gaga song started playing on the radio and The Ear said, "What is this shit? Don't they have any decent stations down here?"

"You kidding me, Tooch? You don't know who that is? That's Lady Gaga, the chick from New York who likes to wear a meat dress."

"A meat dress? No shit. She looking for any A1 sauce? Cause this guinea's got a pant-load."

They both busted out laughing, totally oblivious to the guy in the bug suit only fifteen feet behind the Escalade.

***

After giving Donny Nutz an affectionate hug, Marie stepped back and looked at all of us standing there slack-jawed. Then she turned back to Donny.

"What's with the gun, Donny? What on earth are you even doing here?"

"It looks like, uh, like we have a little misunderstanding." He pointed at Tangles. "The little guy, he's… he's your *son?*"

"My pride and joy," she beamed. "And his names T—his name's Tangles, he's a TV star." Then she pointed at me. "This young man's named Shagball, they have a fishing show together."

"You don't say. Did you remarry? You were a little young to be a widow."

"As a matter of fact I—wait a second, how'd you know my husband died?"

"I hear things, accidents happen, people die…it's just the way it is."

Marie looked skeptical.

"Donny? How did, how did you know it was an accident?"

"I think I read it in the paper. He was found dead on the dock, right? Something got dropped on his head, if I'm not mistaken." He shook his head. "Very unfortunate. Just like the situation we find ourselves in right now."

"What kind of situation is that?"

Donny pointed at the three of us.

Me and Tangles and Holly were standing near the side wall that had all the fishing gear on it and we were hanging on every word. It was surreal. It occurred to me that their names were Donny and Marie and I almost laughed out loud. Fortunately, I didn't.

"It seems these three, along with some others, successfully conspired to cheat me out of buying a marina. In the process, they sunk my boat and presumably killed a couple of my guys. The bottom line is they owe me a lot of money and I'm here to collect."

Marie looked over at us with disbelief written all over her face.

"This can't be right. Tell me this is some kind of mistake."

Everybody was looking at each other; no one was anxious to speak.

"He's mistaken, right? Please tell me he's mistaken."

Ultimately, the lion's share of the blame was on me, so I fessed up.

"Actually, he's sorta right. We did mess up the marina deal so Holly's aunt could retain ownership and keep it in the family. But we had no idea he was one of the investors trying to buy it. And yeah, we did sink his boat and kill those guys, but it was in self-defense, I swear."

Marie turned pale and put her hand to her mouth.

Tangles backed up my story. "It's true, Momma, I was there. Those guys kidnapped Shagball and Hambone and were about to kill them! They had just killed another guy from the dock, Ratdog, right in front of us. We had no choice, it was them or us!"

Apparently, Tangles' words did little to comfort Marie. She looked unsteady, and Donny Nutz put his hand on her shoulder as she muttered, "Oh, my God, oh, my God, oh, my—"

"Hold on a second." Everybody turned to Holly, who had her hands out in front of her like she was gonna do an air push-up. "Everybody just calm down for a second and I'm sure we can settle this equitably. Mr. Nutz, you said you were here to collect. How much money do you need to make this right by you? How much for you to walk away happy and leave us and our friends alone? *Forever.*"

Donny Nutz looked down at the gold coins scattered on the floor and squinted at Holly.

"It takes a lot to make me happy and forever's a longtime."

"I have a lot of money…how much?"

"I need at least three million bucks. You gimme three million and we'll call it square; let bygones be bygones."

"Three million dollars?" Marie was shocked at the figure, and frankly, so was I.

Donny looked at Marie and shrugged. "Hey, she asked and I told her. Three million's the magic number."

"That's a lot of money, Holly," I intoned.

"It's not up for discussion. Too many people have already died because of this mess and it has to stop. Kit, how much is each sack of gold worth?"

I decided to exaggerate a little. "Like I just said, they weigh around fifty-five pounds each. At eighteen-hundred dollars an ounce, that's about…one point six million dollars each."

She looked at me and Tangles and nodded toward the rear of the unit.

"Go grab a couple sacks."

"Are you—?"

"Sure? Yes, just do it, please…let's get this over with."

Chapter 63

Carlos momentarily panicked when the two guys started getting out of the Escalade. He thought maybe they made him somehow, but then they closed the doors and settled back into their seats. He didn't know what the heck was happening at the unit with all the gold in it, but time was getting short, so he made his move. He slipped between the building and the driver's side of the Escalade and knocked on the window. Both Lefty and The Ear noticed him spraying the buildings and didn't think too much about it when he knocked on the window. The Ear said, "If he wants us to move the car or something, tell him too fuckin' bad, he's gotta work around it."

Lefty powered the window down a little and looked up at the guy in the suit with the mask on. "Sorry pal, you're gonna have to work around the car."

The guy pulled the mask down so he could talk and smiled.

"No problem, my friend, I just thought you might want the inside of the car sprayed."

"What? What the fuck are you talking about?"

The Ear thought the same thing and turned to look at the guy.

"You know, I see a couple big cockroaches in the front seat and I think some extermination's called for."

A spark of recognition jolted The Ear's brain and he started reaching for his weapon as Lefty answered.

"Who the fuck—?"

In an instant a gun with a silencer on it appeared in the window opening and spat out two bullets. The first one went between Lefty's eyes at point blank range, killing him instantly. The second one smashed into the left corner of The Ear's temple. His head snapped back and cracked the passenger window before he slumped over in his seat, his right hand still clutching the weapon he didn't manage to pull out in time.

Carlos slipped the gun back inside the jumpsuit and made a beeline for the end unit—for the gold.

Chapter 64

Tangles and I were about to hoist two sacks of gold out of the dock box when he whispered, "I got a gun."

I forgot that Hambone slipped him a revolver, but this was no time for heroics. "Not now" I hissed back. "Don't do anything stupid."

***

Donny Nutz didn't get to be nearly sixty years old by being careless. While the dynamic duo worked their way to the back of the unit to retrieve the gold, he took a half step back and surveyed the surroundings. He was relieved to see that everything looked OK. He could see the edge of the Escalade nestled behind the boat and the silhouette of The Ear in the passenger seat. Nobody was around except for a guy in a jumpsuit spraying something along the edge of the building. He had no concerns about the guy, knowing that The Ear wouldn't let him pass without making sure he was on the up and up. He turned back toward the scene unfolding in the storage unit, not believing he was about to be handed over a hundred pounds of gold. He couldn't help but wonder how much *more* gold was in the back, and wished he asked for *five* million. If it weren't for the shocking appearance of Marie Dupree, he would have already mowed everybody down and made off with the entire hoard; however much it was. As the two guys slowly made their way forward with the gold, he had second thoughts; greedy ones—Marie Dupree or not.

***

Tangles and I set the gold down in front of Donny Nutz. I said, "There you go, that's about three point two million in gold."

"You can keep the change too," added Holly. "But that makes us all square, just like you said, right?"

"Open one up and let me see the gold."

As Holly bent down to cut off the twine that secured the top of the sack, I noticed a guy in a jumpsuit spraying something along the edge of the building. *Where the hell did he come from?*

Suddenly, the guy dropped the canister he was holding, flung off the mask, and pulled out a gun. He took three quick steps forward and yelled,

"Everybody get their hands in the air, that goes for you too, fat-ass." His eyes were wild and he swung the gun around in a threatening manner before training it on Donny Nutz. We all raised our arms in the air, some higher than others. That's when I recognized him as the guy who arrived on the *JC.* Robo said his name was Carlos, and he likely butchered our friend Eight-Toe. *Not good.* Donny Nutz turned his head sideways to look at him and shook his head.

"*You?* Figures, you're even dumber than I thought. I knew I shouldn't a hired a fuckin' spic." He appeared to lift his chin up slightly and look over the guy's shoulder toward a boat parked alongside the building next to us. The guy with the gun noticed it too.

"You can signal Tweedle-Dee and Tweedle-Dumber as long as you want, my friend, they ain't coming. They developed a fatal case of cerebral bulletitis. Now, what did you call me? A spic? Let me tell you something *fuckhead*: when I'm sittin' on a pile of gold in Rio, sipping pina coladas on the beach, you'll have maggots crawling through all the holes in your head that I'm about to put there." He took a step closer to Donny Nutz, who didn't appear to be too concerned that a crazed killer was about to pepper him with lead. "You got any last words, you fat, fuckin' piece of shit?"

The pissed off psycho with the gun was only five feet away from him on his left-hand side. Tangles, Holly and I had our backs up against the inside of the building. Marie stood only a few feet away from Donny Nutz on the right. Incredibly, Donny Nutz smiled. He had his arms held out parallel to the ground, with his hands sticking straight up; bent at the elbow. The air started to fill with the sounds of a passing train but there was no problem hearing Donny's reply.

"Yeah, as a matter of fact, I do. You should know I can eat a little fuckin' muchacho like you for breakfast, shit you out for lunch, and have your spic mother wipe my hairy ass clean before I bend her over and give her a 'Dirty Sanchez' for dinner."

Pure rage filled Carlos' face and he screamed something in Spanish as he extended the gun with the silencer on it toward Donny Nutz's head. With lightning speed, Donny Nutz snapped his left arm straight out and a monstrous explosion sent Carlos flying backward. His shredded body ended up sprawled on the pavement and blood spewed from the gaping hole in his torso. His jumpsuit turned from dirty white to dark crimson in a matter of seconds and Marie, who had the best view, screamed.

Holly buried her head in my chest and cried, "Oh, my God," as Tangles hurried over to comfort his mother.

Chapter 65

DICK agent Cushing came tearing into the storage center and swerved his Porsche between the old buildings making his way back to the northwest corner. As he was about to make what he hoped was a final turn around another building, he saw the tail end of a black Escalade parked next to the building in front of him. He pulled to the side and jumped out with his weapon drawn. He ran to the edge of the building and peered around the corner, surprised at what he saw. The unit in the corner had its overhead door open and a giant man in a suit stood with his arms in the air. It was Nutz! There was a woman to his right that also had her hands in the air, and Cushing saw why: a guy in a jumpsuit was pointing a gun in their direction. He looked straight ahead at the Escalade and noticed the passenger window was cracked and there was a head leaning against it. *What?*

Keeping low, he dashed across the exposed pavement to the rear of the Escalade. He held his gun out in front of him and quickly sidestepped along the building up to the driver's door. The window was partly down and he looked in to see two lifeless bodies with blood splattered all over the place. He was moving forward along the side of the boat parked in front of the car when a loud "boom" sounded over the roar of a passing train. It was quickly followed by a woman's scream. Throwing caution to the wind, he sprinted toward the end unit, keeping as close to the building as possible.

***

Holy Shit! Now I knew why Donny Nutz didn't seem too worried about the guy with the gun. He had some kind of shotgun contraption attached to his left arm and turned the guy into paella. Smoke was coming out the end of his left arm sleeve and he started waving it around and yelling. "God *damn,*that's hot! Shit, shit, shit!"

Out of nowhere, FBI agent Dan D. Kramer came running up with a gun pointed at him.

"Down on the ground, Nutz! NOW!" He was yelling extra loudly to make sure he was heard over the sound of a passing train.

Distracted by his singed flesh, Donny Nutz didn't see him coming and turned to face the FBI guy.

"Who the fuck are you?"

"FBI! Get down on the ground!"

Relieved at the "better late than never," appearance of the FBI agent, Holly and I walked over to Tangles and his mother on the opposite side of the unit.

***

One of the reasons Eddie "The Ear" Fanatucci had a semi-successful boxing career was his legendary ability to take a punch. Opponents eventually learned that the only way to bring him down was through a succession of well-placed body shots or maybe a crushing uppercut to the chin. Headshots were seemingly useless and only resulted in the mangling of one of his ears. His ability to take a punch wasn't the result of genetics though; it was because he had a metal plate attached to his skull. It wrapped all the way around his forehead and stopped just in front of his ears, courtesy of a near fatal grenade injury sustained in Vietnam. It was a minor detail that he failed to alert the boxing authorities of.

So when The Colombian surprised him and shot him in the temple, the metal plate stopped the bullet from penetrating into his brain. The force of the blow knocked him out cold and smashed his head into the window, but it didn't kill him, unlike his partner, Lefty. He was just regaining consciousness when he heard a loud "boom" that reverberated through the metal in his head. Being the ever loyal bodyguard and enforcer of Donny Nutz, he wiped the blood out of his eyes and opened the car door. His head was throbbing and he was seeing double, but he managed to stagger toward the end unit by using the building for support. With one hand he held his gun out in front of him and with the other he kept wiping blood out of his blurry eyes.

Chapter 66

The four of us—Me, Holly, Tangles, and his mom, were a few feet inside the entrance to the unit. Donny Nutz was standing in front of us, a few feet outside the unit, and the FBI guy was facing us, with Donny Nutz in-between. Because of the angle, I couldn't see along the building behind FBI agent Dan D. Kramer, who had his gun drawn on Donny Nutz. Suddenly, out from the side of the building staggered a bloody-faced guy pointing a gun at his back.

I pointed and yelled, "Look out!"

Agent Kramer ducked to the side just as the bloody-faced guy fired. The shot rang out and nailed Donny Nutz in the arm with the hidden shotgun up his sleeve. It made an odd, clanking sound, and spun him around. From a crouching position, Kramer pivoted and returned fire with three quick shots that hit the bloody-faced guy in the chest, sending him crashing to the ground. As he was returning fire, I saw Donny reaching for his other gun.

On the wall behind me was an eight-foot gaff that was used on drift-boats for hauling larger fish up over the side. I snatched it from its perch and swung it down on top of Donny Nutz's shoulder as hard as

I could. It caught him just right and he screamed as the sharp point of the gaff imbedded deep in his clavicle. Just as he was about to fire at agent Kramer, I yanked on the gaff and three shots rang out beside me; it was Tangles. He had pulled out the thirty-eight special Hambone gave him and shot Donny Nutz. One bullet missed, but one hit him high in the side of the chest and one in the stomach. His gun clattered to the ground and he fell backward, ripping the gaff from my hands. He ended up sprawled out in a sitting position with his head leaning against the left rear tire of the Beemer and the long gaff stuck in his shoulder.

Tangles' mom cried, "Donny!" and rushed to his side. His face was turning ashen and blood was trickling out of his mouth. He looked up at Marie with an amused look on his face.

"The little fucker…the little…fucker…shot me."

Agent Kramer hurried up to Tangles and issued an order: "Gimme the gun."

Tangles handed it to him and then he looked at me and Holly.

"Everybody needs to go. Lock this place up and get the hell out of here before the cops come—NOW!"

Holly looked confused, and said, "What?"

"You heard me, move it!"

I couldn't believe what I was hearing. It was loud because of the train and I was hoping I misunderstood him.

"What the hell are you talking about, 'Before the cops come?' You're with the FBI, you *are* the cops!"

"Not exactly."

"WHAT?"

"Just trust me and get out of here now. It'll be easier for me to handle the police without you here—I'll explain later."

I looked at his face to see if it was some kind of ill-timed joke, but he looked both anxious *and* serious. *Holy freaking shit!* Who *was* he and what the hell was going on? Shoes were dropping left and right; like in a Kardashian closet in an earthquake.

I looked at Holly who stood frozen with an incredulous look on her face, and I shook her by the shoulder. Another shoe was dropping, and it was time to run for cover.

"You heard him, let's go! Grab the open bag of gold and put it in the trunk. Tangles! Gimme a hand here!" Tangles was kneeling next to his mother and came hustling back. He looked shaken.

"What, what's going on?"

I pointed at the two sacks of gold that were for Donny Nutz. *Were*, being the past tense. "Put those in the Beemer. I'll grab the last two in the dock box. We gotta get outta here now! Ride with your mom and meet us at Holly's."

I ran to the back of the unit and grabbed a sack in each hand. With more than a little effort I trudged my way back through the unit and out to the Beemer. Holly had already put the open bag of gold in the trunk and I heard her behind me pulling the overhead door shut. Tangles heaved the other two sacks in the trunk which now held four bags. I noticed the rear end sagged a little because of the weight, so I put the two bags I was carrying in the backseat.

Holly appeared by my side, sounding anxious. "That's it, we're all locked up."

"You get the side door too?"

"Yeah, we're good to go."

Tangles was standing next to his mom, who was bent over Donny Nutz and trying to talk to him. The fake FBI agent put his hand on her shoulder.

"Ma'am, you have to go now, please!"

Tangles urged her too.

"C'mon, Momma, we gotta go!"

Holly and I walked around the Beemer and stood next to Tangles. We couldn't leave, because Marie had us blocked in. Donny Nutz looked like he was a goner, but his eyes flickered with life when Marie grabbed him by the lapels of his seersucker suit and shook him. The train finally passed and it grew eerily quiet.

"Donny!" she pleaded. "Please, I have to know, did you have anything to do with my husband's death?"

He had to have been in pain, but somehow he managed a crooked smile and spit out his final words along with some blood.

"What goes around…comes…comes…"

That was it. His eyes rolled back in his head and his head fell to the side.

Donatello DeNutzio, aka Double D, aka Donny Nutz, was dead.

The fake FBI agent pleaded one last time. "He's gone. Please, you have to go now."

Marie stood up on shaky legs, holding Rudy's car keys in her hand. Holly took the keys and nodded to me as she led her by the arm.

"I'll drive Marie, we'll meet you at the house."

Chapter 67

It was all over the news. Not just the local news, but the national news. We were expecting the police to show up at any time, but it didn't happen. Holly switched the station to CNN and we listened to the latest recap:

> Notorious East Coast Mafia boss Donatello DeNutzio, also known as Donny Nutz, was killed in a shootout early this morning at a storage center in the small seaside town of Hypoluxo, Florida. Also killed were his longtime bodyguard; Eddie "The Ear" Fanatucci, and driver, Johnny "Left Lane" Longo. A fourth body found at the scene has been identified as suspected contract killer Carlos Ramirez, a New Yorker of Colombian descent who is believed to be related to infamous satanic serial killer Richard Ramirez, also known as the Night Stalker. Ramirez was wanted for questioning by local police in regard to the gruesome killing of a Boynton Beach hotel clerk only hours earlier. A fifth, as yet unidentified body, was also found at the scene—in the trunk of a vehicle registered to a corporation controlled by DeNutzio. Police say evidence discovered with the body links the slaying to another case, the

> deadly home invasion of a local shark fisherman less than forty-eight hours earlier. *That* crime scene was described by seasoned investigators as one of the most horrific in the history of the Boynton Beach Police Department. Authorities were led to the storage center by an undercover operative from an unnamed federal agency who was involved in the shootings. How the crimes are connected and what the Mafia boss was doing in the area is unknown at this time. This is Rick Martinez, reporting for CNN.

The picture cut away to an aerial view of the storage center that showed police cars and ambulances everywhere.

"Oh, my God," said Holly. "That guy was related to the Night Stalker?"

I shook my head in disbelief.

"Wow, sounds like a nice family. I bet nobody was too slow to pass the gravy on Thanksgiving. This is unbelievable. Who do you suppose is in the trunk?"

"My bets on Skeeter," answered Tangles.

"Skeeter? You think?"

"Yeah, don't you remember? Hambone said the police were trying to locate him to back up his story that they drove Eight-Toe home from the bar. '*Trying*,' being the operative word."

"Jesus, you're right."

Suddenly my phone lit up and it started playing the ominous opening chords to the Weezer song, *Hash Pipe;* "Dun,dun,dun,dun,dun,dun,dun,dun,dun ,dun,dun,dun,dun,dun,dun,dun,

I can't help my feelings..."

I didn't know the number that was on the display but flipped open my Motorola and said, "Hey, hey."

"Kit? It's Hambone. I saw the news, hell, I heard the choppers. Are you guys OK? You weren't there, were you?"

"Yeah, we're fine, but, uh, what makes you think we were there?"

"I'm calling from the C-Love office 'cause the cops haven't given me my cell phone back and Best Buy doesn't open for another half hour. Regina said that Holly called earlier about the storage unit where they keep all the extra dock gear and it's at the same place where the shootout was."

"Shit. Ham, please, keep that under wraps and put Regina on the phone. I'll fill you in later."

"No problem, I'm just glad you guys are all right."

"I'm glad you are too, buddy."

I walked over to Holly who was talking to Marie and handed her the phone.

"You better tell Regina to keep quiet about the storage unit."

Holly took the phone, and after assuring her she was all right, instructed her to forget about the earlier phone call and to not mention to anybody that the C-Love even had a storage unit. Holly flipped the phone shut and handed it to me with a puzzled look on her face.

"I can't believe the police aren't here. With all that gunfire you would think somebody would have reported seeing us leave the scene."

"I thought about that too, but there were a few things working in our favor. Number one; being an early Sunday morning, the place was all but deserted. Number two; there was a train blowing by when the shooting was going on. It was loud and helped mask the sound of the gunshots. Number three, it's not like here in Ocean Ridge where hearing a gunshot is unusual and a person would probably go out and investigate. In the area surrounding the San Castle Storage Center, hearing gunshots is nothing new. Even *if* somebody heard one, their inclination would be more likely to shrug it off. But, putting those factors aside, we have to thank Mr. Pseudo-FBI agent who showed up in the nick of time. Without him we'd either be dead or at police headquarters getting grilled like day-old kingfish."

"Who the hell *is* he?" asked Tangles. "What did that CNN reporter call him?"

"An undercover operative from an unnamed federal agency…I believe," responded Holly.

"What the hell does *that* mean? He's with the DEA? Maybe the ATF?"

"Damned if I know," I answered. "If we can believe him, which is a little difficult at this point, he's not with the FBI. What else does that leave? The CIA? Why the hell would *they* be involved?"

"Maybe he's with JAG," guessed Holly.

I have to admit, that one through me for a loop.

"*JAG?* What the hell is JAG?"

"C'mon, Kit, you know, *JAG*; Judge-Advocate-General? It's an elite branch of military officers trained as lawyers who go after spies, murderers and terrorists. I can't believe you never saw the show, it was great."

"Whoa, whoa, whoa. You're talking about a *TV show? Really?* A friggin' *TV show?* C'mon, honey, we're talking about real life here and now."

"Don't you *honey* me, JAGs *are* real. Besides, he's cute enough to be a JAG and he drives a Porsche too."

Sometimes, hell, most of the time, arguing with women one-on-one puts the odds squarely in their favor. This was one of those times, so I called on Tangles for ground support; very low-to-the-ground support.

"Tangles? Can you help me out here, buddy?"

"Sorry, bro, she's right, they *are* real. And it *was* a good show. I loved that chick with the short hair, long legs, and big bazonkers. Do you remember her name, Holly?"

"That would be Lieutenant Colonel 'Mac' Mackenzie—my hero. The marine lawyer extraordinaire played by Catherine Bell. You're right, Tangles, she was a babe—smart as a whip too."

"Yeah, she was *hot*— hot and classy. She could prosecute the pants off me anytime."

"Tell me about it; it must be the uniforms." Holly fanned her face with her hand, like she was getting warm. "I feel the same way about Lieutenant Commander Harmon Rabb, played by—"

"Enough with the fantasy crushes. Christ, Tangles, I go to you for a little support and you turn into one of the girls. Well, guess what? Detectives are real too. Maybe he's the son of Mannix—but I don't think so. Let's just say that whoever he is, I'm glad he's on *our* side; at least so far."

"Who in the heck is Mannix?" asked Holly.

"Yeah," echoed Tangles. "Where the hell did you pull that one from?"

"Are you kidding me? You guys never heard of Joe Mannix? Mannix was my dad's favorite show; we watched reruns of it together when I was a kid. He was played by the late, great, Mike Connors; the coolest Armenian cat on the planet. Trust me, Mannix would kick JAG's ass."

"JAG's not a person, Kit. Like I said, it's—"

"Enough with the JAG! OK? I think we've established that we don't know who the hell Mr. Turbo Carerra is. He told me he'd be in touch though, so maybe we'll get some answers before too long."

Tangles' mom hadn't said a thing since we got back to Holly's, and when we got off track trying to guess the identity of the fake FBI agent, she walked out to the deck. Maybe she couldn't help with identifying who Peter Porsche was, but she could certainly fill in some blanks concerning her relationship with the recently deceased Donny Nutz.

"Tangles, you think your mom's ready to talk about Donny Nutz?"

"I was just thinking about that myself. I can't believe she *knew* him. And I can't believe she thinks he was involved in my father's—or who I thought was my father—I just can't believe she thinks he had something to do with his death. It was an accident; she even sent me the newspaper article. I don't care if she's ready or not. I need to know the truth about what was going on between those two, and you guys deserve to know too. C'mon, let's go find out."

Chapter 68

Marie was sitting on the sofa under the awning, looking pensively out at the water. Tangles sat next to her and put his hand on her shoulder.

"Momma? Please. We need to know how you knew Donny Nutz and why you think he had something to do with Dad's death."

She averted her gaze and looked at him.

"Rudy's your dad, honey, I told both of you last night."

"You know what I mean. How did you know him?"

"I, uh, I—does it really make a difference?"

"We won't know until you tell us. But seeing as how we almost got killed today by one of his associates, I think we have a right to know. Come to think of it, the way he was eyeing that gold, I'm not so sure he wasn't ready to kill us himself."

"He may have been a mobster, but I really don't think—"

"Momma? C'mon, it's time. Tell us what happened."

She took a deep breath and exhaled.

"All right, but just remember, this was a long time ago…almost twenty years."

Holly and I pulled up a couple of chairs and sat down to listen.

"I was working the blackjack table one night and the pit boss rolls out the red carpet for this East Coast VIP. We hit it off and at the end of my shift he asks me to have a late dinner with him. I accepted and we had a nice time. He was a real gentleman. Keep in mind he was also probably two hundred pounds lighter at the time and handsome—in a…James Gandolfini kind of way.

"Anyhow, the next night he comes back to the table and notices I have a black eye. I gave him my standard excuse; that I walked into a door. I joined him for dinner again and had a little too much to drink. When I went to the ladies' room I actually *did* yank the door open into my already black eye and it hurt like hell. He thought it was funny that I whacked my eye in the same spot, but still comforted me because I was in tears. I was embarrassed because he thought I was a klutz and blurted out that my black eye wasn't really from a door, but from a fist— my husband's. He got me talking and I admitted it wasn't the first time and that I was truly scared of my husband. I should have kept my mouth shut, but like I said, I had too much to drink. When I left his—when I left the hotel, he said something funny to me. He said, 'Don't worry, guys who beat on girls tend to get what's coming—things happen. What goes around comes around.' Two days later your fath—who you *thought* was your father, was found dead on the dock with his head caved in."

"Did you tell the police this?"

"No way. I wouldn't dare try to implicate a VIP in an accidental death just because of some passing words. It would have cost me my job. Besides, I liked him, he made me feel safe."

"Did you ask him if he had anything to do with it?"

"No, and I never saw him again, not until today. I probably wouldn't have gone to the police anyways, even *if* he admitted to killing him. It was a huge relief not living under a cloud of fear anymore; his death was a blessing, accident or not. Isn't it *awful* for me to think like that?"

"No, he beat the shit out of me too. But it still doesn't change the fact that it was an accident. He was off-loading his catch and a crate slipped from the crane and landed on him. Commercial fishing's dangerous, it can happen, it *did* happen. Besides, I doubt someone you just met and had dinner with would kill your husband because he gave you a black eye."

"We, uh, we had a little more than dinner."

"Huh?"

"He was nice to me, honey. He was nice to me when the world was a big bowl of digested gumbo and I was the toilet."

"Jesus, Mom."

I stole a glance at Holly and her eyes were wide. The story was getting crazier than even *I* could imagine.

"Don't you judge me, honey, you don't know what I was going through. I needed a shoulder to lean on and he gave it to me."

Now Tangles let out a deep breath. "OK, OK fine. It still doesn't prove it wasn't an accident though. Just let it go, Momma, it's time to let it go."

Tangles put his arm around her shoulder and gave her a squeeze.

"Thanks, honey, but there's a little more to it than that. About a month after he died I received his death certificate and a copy of the police report with some photos. He was found without his gloves on."

"What?"

"That's right. The problem is he was supposedly off-loading his catch when the accident happened. When he did that he *always* wore some gloves to keep his hands from getting nicked up. You know what I'm talking about, *you* always wore them too."

"Maybe, maybe he forgot to put them on."

"Did you ever forget?"

Tangles looked at me and Holly with a solemn expression on his face. Then he turned back to face his mother and slowly shook his head. "No, I, uh, can't say I ever did."

"I know what you're thinking. Even so, it still doesn't prove anything, right?"

Tangles looked a little less sure of himself.

"I, uh, I don't—"

"Well, you're right, if that's all there was, maybe I could let it go, but it's not. You remember what Donny said today when I asked him how he knew my husband's death was an accident? He said he read it in the paper. That he was found dead on the dock. Well, guess what? The paper had it wrong. The paper said he was found on the boat. The only way he could know that he actually *was* found dead on the dock, is if he read the police report, *or*—"

Tangles finished the sentence for her.

"If he had personal knowledge of it. Holy crap."

"And if that's not enough, you heard Donny's dying words, just like I did. 'What goes around…' Two days before the accident, that's what he told me, 'What goes around comes around.' Think about it, honey, you're the one that shot him. He killed my husband and you killed him. What goes around comes around."

Tangles looked shaken and let out another deep breath. Marie was staring out at the water again. I looked at Holly, she looked at Tangles, and Tangles looked at me and said, "Does anybody else need a drink?"

Chapter 69

Marie left to go see Rudy and we dove headfirst into a big batch of Bloody Marys. Some serious decompression was in order after the close call at the storage center and the bombshell news regarding Donny Nutz and Tangles' mom. Holly had just made a second pitcher full when we heard a car pull up. I knew by the distinctive purr of the engine who it was before I even looked: Peter Porsche. I walked over to the side of the deck and signaled for him to come around the house. By his appearance you would never guess he had been in a shootout less than two hours earlier. Apparently, it was just another day at the office for him. *What* office, I had no idea, none of us did, but I sure wanted to find out. As he stepped up on the deck I greeted him.

"Well, well, well…if it isn't mister 'I'm not *exactly* an FBI agent.' If you don't mind me asking, on behalf of my fellow Bloody Mary drinkers, exactly who in the hell *are* you?"

He looked at Holly and Tangles and nodded toward the kitchen door.

"Do you mind if we go inside?"

Holly said, "Sure, no problem." She picked up the pitcher and as she led us inside, added, "Would you like a Bloody?"

"Yes, thanks, after what we just went through, it seems like an appropriate drink to have. I'm sorry about what happened back there, I didn't expect it to go down like that."

We gathered around the kitchen island and Holly poured him a drink. After he took a big swig, he glanced into the living room. "Where's the other woman?"

"My mom?" answered Tangles. "She left; she had to return the car she borrowed from a friend. Why?"

"Please give her a call and tell her not to speak of what happened to anyone. Not her friend, not her priest, if she has one, not anybody. Will you do that for me?"

Tangles looked at me and I nodded. He pulled out his phone and quickly told his mom to keep a lid on it. As soon as he hung up I posed my unanswered question again.

"The CNN reporter said you were an undercover operative for an unnamed agency. Which one is it?"

"Mr. Jansen, I'm—"

"No more mister stuff, in light of the fact that we almost got killed together, I think we can dispense with the formalities. Kit will be fine."

"Sure. OK then…Kit, I'm not at liberty to discuss who I work for. Not with you, not with anybody. Suffice it to say that I *am,* however, employed by an agency of the federal government of the United States of America."

"That's it? That's all your gonna tell us?"

"No, I'm also going to tell you that the US government would like to thank you and your friends for helping bring down Donny Nutz and his associates. Inadvertently or not, it was your involvement that led to his downfall. He was not only a ruthless mobster, but he was an arms trafficker who helped supply suspected terrorist cells, whether he knew it or not. He was a really bad guy surrounded by some really bad people. I hope none of you feel any remorse because they ended up dead."

"I don't."

"Me neither," replied Tangles.

"No, none here," added Holly.

"Good." He looked at Tangles.

"Mr. Dupree? I hope you—"

"Please, you heard what Kit said, first names only. Mine's Tangles."

"Of course, sorry about that, uh…Tangles. As I was saying, please explain to your mother what I told you about Mr. Nutz. I sensed she had some feelings for him."

"Maybe not as much as you think. He killed her husband."

"What?"

"Yeah, she just put it all together and spelled it out for us. It's quite a story."

"She just told you about it now?"

"Yeah."

"Good, I've got it all on tape then. That reminds me, I can deactivate the bugs I planted on your phones if you have them handy."

We all pulled out our cell phones and laid them on the counter. He set his phone between them and pressed a couple of buttons.

"OK, that's it, no more eavesdropping." He took another swig of his drink and continued. "I'd also like to personally thank you for your actions today, Kit, and you too, Tangles. I thought that guy who snuck up behind me was *already* dead." He pointed at me. "If *you* wouldn't have warned me, I was toast."

"Don't forget, it was in my best interest too, we were next."

"Nevertheless, you saved my ass. And then you did it again by going after Nutz. Tangles, that was some mighty fine shooting. They say two out of three ain't bad, but in this case, it was clutch. Most people in that situation couldn't manage to pull the trigger, let alone hit what they were aiming for, even once."

"It was a big target."

"Maybe, but it was a target that could shoot back."

Then he looked at Holly. "I don't mean to diminish in any way what you did either. Once I gave the order to evacuate, you did what needed to be done. Thank you for that."

"No, uh, no thanks needed. I was more than happy to leave."

"All the same, thanks."

I was watching Holly and her face turned a little red. Was she blushing? *What the hell was that all about?*

My thoughts drifted back to the police and what we could expect going forward.

"What about the police?"

"Not to worry, they think I'm with the DEA." He pulled out a badge that said DEA and it looked real. "I told them the whole thing was drug related, that'll be the official version when it hits the news."

"But there *weren't* any drugs, *were there?*"

"There was by the time the police got there, I made sure of it."

"There...*what?* Let me see that thing." I snatched the DEA badge out of his hand and inspected it. "Is this thing real?"

"You bet, just like the FBI badge I showed you."

"But you're not with the FBI *or* the DEA?"

"Nope."

"How can you? — Who the hell *are* you?"

"Sorry, I explained as best I could." He took the badge back and added, "I need to be going now, but before I do, I have a little something for you. It's a token of appreciation from Uncle Sam for what you did today and for forgetting all about it— especially me."

He pulled a plain white business card out of his pocket and handed it to me. It seemed to have some sort of lamination on it and a semi-transparent holographic symbol on the back. There was nothing written on it except a phone number.

"If you're ever in trouble— deep trouble, of any kind, and you need help—big-time help, call this number. You'll be asked to identify yourself and give a password. Once you do it will activate the GPS transmitter embedded in the card and help will be there as fast as humanly possible."

"You mean like the cavalry will come charging to the rescue?"

"Yeah, something like that. But use your call wisely, you only get one, after that, the number will cease to exist."

Tangles said, "Let me see that thing," and I handed him the card. "Wow, this is pretty cool; a get out of jail free card."

“No, that’s not what it’s for. Like I said, use it wisely. It’s for helping you out if you ever get in way over your head like you did with Donny Nutz.”

I took the card back from Tangles and asked, “OK then, what’s the password?”

“Help.”

“What?”

“You heard right, the password is ‘help.’ Call the number, identify yourself, and when you’re asked for the password, say ‘help.’”

“That’s it?”

“That’s it.”

“Nice, I think I can remember that.”

“That’s the idea.”

Secret agent man thanked Holly for the Bloody Mary and we followed him to the door. After shaking hands, he said, “Thanks again for helping out today, but hopefully I won’t be seeing you anytime soon.”

Chapter 70

It was a week later and all was right in the world. At least in *my* little world it was. *Why?* Because it was an absolutely gorgeous day on the water and I was fishing, the way God intended. We were also doing some filming for *Fishing on the Edge with Shagball and Tangles,* the way my producer intended. The seas were flat, the skies were blue, and I had a full load of happy people on board the *Lucky Dog.* Namely, Holly, Tangles, Marie, Rudy, and my producer, Jamie. We were fishing in the annual Lantana Fishing Derby, which was normally held in May, but bad weather had forced its postponement until the end of July. Even though the fishing was so-so, Jamie was happy because we had enough footage to make a show thanks to a twenty-five pound wahoo we caught in two-hundred and forty feet of water off Sloan's curve. It wasn't huge by any stretch of the imagination, but it still might be big enough to finish in the money in the wahoo category. We wouldn't know until we got back to The Old Key Lime House for weigh-in.

I was up on the bridge, running the old Viking and loving every minute of it. I ran us about eight miles offshore and we hooked into a couple nice dolphin that Tangles helped his mother and Rudy reel in. Tangles' mom had never caught one before and she was ecstatic. Truth be told, so was I. I couldn't believe how my fortunes had so drastically changed for the better in such a short period of time. I actually felt like pinching myself when Holly surprised me from behind and did it for me. She pinched me right in the rear and then gave me a delicious kiss on the lips.

"Hey there, sailor, I saw you up here by your lonesome and thought you might like a little company."

"You thought right, beautiful." I pulled her in for a long kiss until Tangles yelled up from the cockpit.

"Keep an eye on the lines, lover boy, you're starting to crisscross 'em."

I straightened out our track and pointed us back toward the inlet.

"So what were you thinking about?" asked Holly.

"How'd you know I was thinking?"

"Lucky guess."

"Well, you're right…I was. I was thinking about how sure I was my fishing days were over once I called the FBI. Hell, I thought I might even end up in a witness protection program in some Godforsaken place. And if that's not bad enough, I thought I might lose, uh, I thought I might, uh—"

"What? What are you trying to say, Kit?"

She looked up at me with her big beautiful eyes and I realized how lucky I really was.

"I thought I might lose you. There, I said it."

She smiled her room-lighting smile and laughed.

"No way Jose, you couldn't lose me that easy. If you were going into a witness protection program, I was going with you."

"But, but the marina…and the house. What about—"

"But nothing, I'd sell them both."

"You'd sell them to be with me? But that's such a big part of your life. What about all the memories you have of Millie and growing up fishing on the *C-Love*? What about the house on Sabal Island and your grandfather teaching you how to snook fish? What about fishing for sheepshead and mangrove snapper with your dad off the seawall? You've got a lifetime of memories between the house and the marina. You'd give that up to be with *me?*"

"Kit, I'll *always* have those memories. Nobody can take them away from me. If Millie taught me anything, it's not the memories you have that are important, it's the ones you don't have. It's a cliché, but it's true, life's too damn short. We were almost killed in a seedy storage center last week, now look at us. Let's enjoy our time together while we can and make our *own* memories. I'd say we're already off to a good start. Besides, you're forgetting one important thing."

"What's that?"

"I've got four safety-deposit boxes at the bank stuffed full of gold. Even *if* we had to hide from the Mob we could live anywhere in the world in style and I could still afford to keep the house and the marina. But we don't have to, so let's not worry about it."

"Good point."

We laughed and kissed again. She was really something else. I glanced at my watch and saw it was time to head back. We had one more stop to make before going to the weigh-in back at The Old Key Lime House. I had Tangles pull in the lines and everybody got a fresh beverage for the ride. For the next twenty minutes Holly had her arm around me and her head against my shoulder as we ran back in silence. The smell of her hair mixed with the ocean breeze was as intoxicating as one of Rudy's rumrunners with a double Meyer's floater. It may have been the best twenty minutes of my life.

When we got to a hundred feet of water I turned us south of the inlet and ran a couple of miles to a favorite fishing spot of Millie's. It was a reef marked by the "champagne glass," which was actually the Boynton Beach water tower. It was referred to as the "champagne glass," because of its appearance.

Holly and I went down to the cockpit and she disappeared into the cabin. The rest of the crew was in the cabin having a good ol' time and came piling out when Holly went in. A minute later she reappeared, holding an urn full of Millie's ashes. We stood along the port side, facing the horizon. After some words by Holly, she opened the urn and dumped about half the contents into the crystal blue water. We stood silently and watched the ash cloud dissipate toward the reef. Holly wiped a tear from her eye and I hugged her close.

"What are you going to do with the rest?" I asked.

"They're going to St. Croix, to be with Joseph. She has a son down there too…somewhere. I'd like to find him and meet his family if he has any. The property she left should go to him. He needs to know who his parents were and the strange circumstances surrounding his adoption. That's another thing I'd like to get to the bottom of. Would you go down there with me and help me find out what really happened? Please?"

Before I could respond, Jamie, my beanpole of a producer, had a response of his own.

"Dude, I heard St. Croix has some *awesome* fishing! If you wanna go I'll spring for a charter or two and we can shoot a segment—if it's all right with Holly… that is."

Tangles was next to chime in.

"St. Croix is the one place I never made it to working the cruise ships, but I heard it's a cool place. I'm game if you are, Shagball."

There was really no question about it. I would have gone to the moon if she asked me to. I put my arm around her and gave her a tender kiss on the cheek.

"You know me better than that, baby, how could I possibly say no? St. Croix it is!"

After all, what could possibly go wrong?

The End